THE RUNAWAY ACTRESS

Victoria Connelly was brought up in Norfolk and studied English literature at Worcester University before becoming a teacher in North Yorkshire. After getting married in a medieval castle and living in London for eleven years, she moved to rural Suffolk with her artist husband and ever-increasing family of animals. She has had three novels published in Germany – the first of which was made into a film.

To find out more about Victoria Connelly please visit www.victoriaconnelly.com

By the same author

A Weekend with Mr Darcy
The Perfect Hero

VICTORIA CONNELLY

The Runaway Actress

AVON

AVON

A division of HarperCollins*Publishers*
77–85 Fulham Palace Road,
London W6 8JB

www.harpercollins.co.uk

A Paperback Original 2012

1

First published in Great Britain by
HarperCollins*Publishers* 2012

A catalogue record for this book is
available from the British Library

ISBN 978-1-84756-276-0

Set in Minion by Palimpsest Book Production Limited,
Falkirk, Stirlingshire

Printed and bound in Great Britain by
Clays Ltd, St Ives plc

MIX
Paper from
responsible sources
FSC
www.fsc.org **FSC™ C007454**

Acknowledgements

My sincerest thanks to Linda Gillard and Mags Wheeler who helped enormously with all my Scottish-related questions. And to Keith Lumsden at Scottish Tartans World Register. Any mistakes are of my own making!

Thanks to Sarah Jane Pearson for helping me to sort out Maggie's fleecy hair.

To Britta Horn and Sarah Duncan for acting expertise and to Elizabeth Law for introducing me to the wonderful book, *Act One* by Moss Hart – a must for anyone with an interest in the theatre.

To my husband, Roy, for the inspirational writing holidays that helped get this novel written, and to Clive and Sheila for their fabulous cottage in which I wrote so much of it.

To my lovely writer friends Deborah Wright and Ruth Saberton for constant encouragement and lovely days out away from the desk.

And special thanks to Annette Green, Ronit Zafran, Keshini Nadoo and Caroline Hogg and all the team at Avon.

Special thanks to all my lovely readers on Facebook and Twitter. It's always so good to hear from you. You make all those hours in isolation worthwhile.

And heartfelt thanks to my mum and Wyn who are always first in line for my new book.

I would also like to remember my two dear Scottish gentlemen – now departed and greatly missed: Alex Roan and my grandpa, Harold Forsyth. Both shared their great love of Scotland and their Scottish heritage with me. I haven't managed to buy that 'Ring of Bright Water' cottage yet but the dream is still there.

To my dear friends, Heather and Margaret.
Here's to our Scottish ancestry!

Chapter One

Maggie Hamill stared out of the window at the great green hills beyond the loch. The third bedroom really did have the best view from the house and she was glad she'd moved into it. There was only one problem: it was such a gorgeous distraction that it was sometimes hard to get on with her work and she had plenty to be getting on with. Only that morning, she'd received half a dozen letters – all with requests for signed photographs.

Dear Ms Gordon, the first one began. *I'm a huge fan of your films and think you're the most beautiful actress in the world. Would it be possible to send me a signed photograph of yourself? I enclose a cheque for £10 for your Theatre Charity and look forward to hearing from you soon and, if you ever happen to be in Portsmouth, give me a call on the above number, won't you? I know a fabulous restaurant where we can talk in private.*

I bet you do, Maggie said to herself. Still, it was quite tame as fan letters went and she pulled out a ten by eight glossy photograph from the top drawer of her desk. It was one of her personal favourites – a close-up shot of Connie Gordon with her long red hair cascading over her shoulders. Maggie sighed as she flicked her own dark mane away from her face, wishing she had fine silky, well-behaved sort of hair rather than a sheep's fleece straggling down her back.

Reaching for her silver pen, she paused, bit her lip and then signed across the bottom right-hand corner.

With love from Connie xx

'There you are, Mr Forbes from Portsmouth. You're going to love that!'

She was just about to stuff it into an envelope when the shop bell tinkled. Leaping to her feet, she left the room and ran down the stairs.

'Ah, good morning, Mrs Wallace,' Maggie said as Lochnabrae's biggest gossip entered the shop. She was wearing the yellow raincoat she never left home without and her tight perm had been squashed under a headscarf. 'You're bright and early this morning.'

'Not as early as Euan, though,' Mrs Wallace said, her formidable bosom rising with pleasure at being able to impart such news. 'I see he's been in already.'

Maggie nodded at Mrs Wallace's comprehensive knowledge of the goings on of Lochnabrae's inhabitants.

'Well now, I hope he's left some tobacco for my Wallace.'

'There's plenty left,' Maggie said, picking up a packet of what she knew to be Mr Wallace's chosen brand and handing it over the counter.

'And how's the fan club going?' Mrs Wallace asked. 'Any sign of Connie Gordon yet?' she asked with a little chuckle, knowing full well what the answer would be.

'No, Mrs Wallace, I'm afraid not. I don't think she'll be gracing our community for a while.'

'Och well, what would her sort do here, eh?'

Maggie shrugged. She'd often wondered herself. What,

indeed, would a Hollywood movie star do in a place like Lochnabrae?

'I've just written to her again,' Maggie said.

'Have you now?'

'Aye.' Maggie sighed, secretly wondering if Connie ever read the letters. She must have posted dozens over the years of running the fan club. Perhaps they were binned by some personal assistant who was put on stalker alert.

'And she's never written back?'

'No,' Maggie said. 'Too busy, I expect. All those films and premieres and things.'

'That'll be it,' Mrs Wallace said. 'No time for the likes of us,' she said, nodding towards her usual newspaper.

'Will that be all today?' Maggie asked, itching to get back to her correspondence upstairs.

'Aye. For the time being. Might be popping back this afternoon for some bits if we don't make it to the proper shops in Strathcorrie.'

'Right,' Maggie said. Mrs Wallace was, as ever, the complete embodiment of tact.

'Their prices are so much better,' she added.

'But they're not on your doorstep, Mrs Wallace, are they?'

Mrs Wallace chose to ignore this last remark.

'Bye, then,' Maggie said and, as soon as the shop door was shut, took the stairs two at a time and returned to her other, slightly more glamorous job.

Maggie had been running the Connie Gordon Fan Club for five years now. Set up by Lochnabrae resident, Euan Kennedy, it was to honour the screen presence of one of Hollywood's most beautiful actresses whose mother happened to be from their small Highland community.

3

'Ah, yes,' Maggie remembered Euan Kennedy telling everyone one evening in the pub, The Capercaillie Inn, 'her mother was a great beauty. Vanessa Gordon.' His eyes had lit up as he'd relived some long ago memory of Vanessa. 'But she had her sights set on bigger and better things. Hollywood, no less! Aye, she was an ambitious one.'

Vanessa Gordon had never made her mark in Tinsel Town, Maggie remembered Euan saying, but had passed on all her beauty and ambition to her daughter, Connie. There wasn't a resident in the whole of Lochnabrae who didn't know of the 'Connie connection' and there was always great excitement when a new Connie film was released, with carloads of residents making the short journey to the old cinema in Strathcorrie. It didn't matter if it was a thriller or a romantic comedy, a leading role or a voice-over in an animated movie, they were there to support their Connie.

'We really should have our own cinema here,' Euan had announced one evening.

'Where?' Maggie had asked, trying to imagine such a luxury in the main street of the village.

Euan shook his head. 'I don't know but we should do something – have some way of acknowledging our Hollywood lassie.'

And that's when he'd come up with the idea for a fan club.

'With websites and everything,' he'd said, waving a great hand in the air as if he knew what he was talking about.

'Oh, you have a computer now, do you?' Maggie had asked wryly.

'Well, no, but you do,' he'd said.

Maggie had leapt at the chance to run the fan club. She'd always adored movies and this was her chance to be a small part of that magical world, and so she'd got to work, creating a website, updating the pages with new pictures of Connie and all the latest movie news.

Then the fan mail had started to flood in with people asking for signed photos of their beloved actress.

'What shall I do?' Maggie had asked Euan. 'They all expect a reply!'

'Then send them what they want.'

'But surely we'll be done for fraud!'

'Och! Nobody will ever find out.'

'But it'll cost money if we start sending out signed photos and things,' Maggie said, thinking of the meagre income she had from the shop.

'Then charge them.'

Maggie had gasped and had taken the problem to the Connie Committee.

'We could make a *small* charge,' Hamish – Maggie's brother – had said. 'Just to cover costs, you understand.'

'That's not unreasonable, is it?' Euan had said. 'We can't have you out of pocket, can we?'

Maggie waited to hear what everyone else thought. 'Angus?' she probed.

Angus hurrumped from his corner in the pub. 'Waste of time. We should have a decent fan club. For westerns.'

Everyone groaned. They were all well aware of Angus's obsession with the western. He was even wearing cowboy boots just then.

'Westerns are the thing,' he said. 'I've got no time for anything else.'

'Rubbish!' Maggie said. 'I saw those tears in your eyes when we went to see Connie in *Waltz with Me*.'

Angus shifted uneasily in his seat. 'That was a fly,' he said. 'I had a fly in my eye that evening.'

'Right,' Maggie said with a grin. 'Alastair? What do you think we should do?' she asked, turning to Lochnabrae's resident playwright for a sensible answer.

'Well,' Alastair said, his dark eyebrows hovering over eyes the colour of the loch in summer, 'the village hall needs some money spent on it.'

'Aye, that it does,' Euan agreed.

Maggie frowned. 'What's that got to do with the signed photographs?'

'If we charge for them, any profit could go to the upkeep of the village hall.'

'But nobody would pay for that!' Maggie protested.

'They might if you call it the Theatre Charity. *Make a small donation to our Theatre Charity and we will be happy to send you a signed photograph of Ms Gordon*,' Alastair said.

'And where do I get all these signed photos from?' Maggie asked.

'There's the newsagents in Strathcorrie. They have one of them big printers now, don't they?' Hamish said.

'Okay,' Maggie said. 'But how do I get them signed?'

Everyone looked at Maggie.

'Use your imagination, lass,' Euan said.

And so Maggie had. She was really quite good at it too because, as a youngster, she used to daydream about what it would be like to be a film star or – at the very least – a character from a film like the ones Connie Gordon played. How wonderful it must be to be beautiful and adored like Connie Gordon and how very different from the little life that Maggie led working in the village shop in Lochnabrae. She would while away many a happy hour in the shop imagining that she was like a Connie Gordon heroine and that a happy ending of her own was just around the corner. For Maggie, running the fan club was like giving in to her inner film star for a few short hours a week and it didn't seem like she was doing anything wrong.

During those early days of the fan club, Maggie had found a copy of a signed photo of Connie Gordon online and had printed it out, studying the feminine flourish and practising it over and over again until she felt that the very spirit of Connie Gordon was with her and she'd got it just right. Which was just as well because demand was high even with the charge that they made.

Sitting back down at her desk, Maggie woke up her computer and stared at the image on the screen.

'Hello, Connie,' she said with a bright smile. 'How are you today?'

The beautiful face stared back at her. Soft white skin that was almost luminous, dark red hair like a silk curtain, bright hazel eyes and that gorgeous megawatt smile that regularly graced a million magazines.

'You'll be wearing that smile tonight, won't you?' Maggie said, checking the online Connie diary and noting that it was the 'Cream of the Screen' awards ceremony. Maggie gazed out of the window but, for once, she didn't notice the view. She was imagining the gowns and the jewels and the wonderful new photos of Connie that she would soon have for the website.

'How wonderful it would be to walk down that red carpet,' she said with a wistful sigh. 'Lucky, lucky Connie.'

Chapter Two

A big bright smile. That's what everyone wanted so why was it so hard to give? Connie walked down the red carpet, trying desperately not to trip over in the silver sequinned dress, which kept wrapping itself around her legs. It was most uncomfortable even if it did make her look like a million dollars. It was the last time she'd be wearing one of Tierney Mueller's designs, that was for sure. He'd practically submerged her with clothes for the last few months and she'd finally given in but she was regretting her decision now. She had to give an award tonight and that meant the long torturous walk out onto the stage with the whole of Hollywood watching.

It'll be fine, she told herself. Or at least it couldn't possibly be as bad as the time one of her spaghetti straps had fallen down, revealing far more of Connie Gordon than the press had ever seen.

'CONNIE!' they shouted now. 'Over here.'

'One more!'

'This way!'

Connie smiled. She felt like such a fraud. It was her third red carpet event that week and she knew she must be the envy of every woman in the world and yet what she wanted more than anything was to be sitting at home in her favourite jumper and jeans, eating a large tub of ice cream in front of the movie channel. It really was absurd. After all, she'd worked extremely hard to get to this moment, hadn't she? All the years of dance classes and auditions, drama classes and auditions, singing classes and auditions. This was what it was all about. This was the kind of event that said, *Hey world, I've arrived. Aren't you jealous? Don't you wish you were me?* Take that journalist over there, Connie thought, sidling over to a female reporter who was gesticulating at her so much her arms were in danger of spinning right off her body. What would the reporter give to change places with Connie – to wear the dress, to be photographed, to present the award? And what would Connie give to exchange places with her? The journalist would be going home in half an hour. For a moment, Connie imagined the scene. There'd be some cute guy cooking dinner for her and an adorable toddler would have just woken up to greet his mommy.

Connie sighed as she thought about the empty mansion that was waiting for her in Bel Air. She had a cook, a cleaner, a PA and a gardener. There was the boy who took care of the pool, the guy who took care of her cars. There was the hairdresser, the image consultant, the agent, the lawyer and the accountant. Then there was the orthodontist, the personal trainer . . . and on the list went. But there was nobody who'd be there to kiss her when she got home. Nobody to massage her feet and tell her she was gorgeous. Oh, she was told she was gorgeous often enough – by the fans, the journalists, the photographers. But they didn't count. When she went home, she left the adulation behind and life felt very empty indeed.

'Connie Gordon!' the journalist yelled as Connie joined

her at the barrier. 'I have Connie Gordon with me,' she said, turning to her cameraman. 'Who are you wearing tonight, Connie?'

'Oh, it's a Tierney Mueller.'

'And you look *gorgeous*. Absolutely *gorgeous*.'

'Thank you,' Connie said graciously.

'I hear you'll be presenting an award tonight.'

'Yes. Best supporting actor.'

'And which of the nominees do you favour?' the journalist asked.

'I think they're all incredibly talented. I couldn't possibly choose,' she said diplomatically. That was the game to play: be gracious, be diplomatic and keep bloody smiling.

The 'Cream of the Screen' ceremony was fairly new as award ceremonies went. Not quite as glitzy as the Oscars nor as prestigious as the Golden Globes, they were still an opportunity for the stars to come out and shine. As Connie entered the Art Deco theatre where it was being held, she caught sight of a few of the famous faces there. She had to stop and pinch herself sometimes. At events like this, she still felt like such a newbie even though she'd been in the business since she was six.

'Connie!' a voice called. She turned around and came face to face with Carter Maddox, the infamous journalist, and he had a camera crew with him. 'Over here, Connie!'

There was no getting away from him so Connie dug deep for her smile again and joined him.

'And you are looking very glam tonight. How are you?'

'I'm fine, thank you, Carter.'

'Who are you wearing?'

'Tierney Mueller,' Connie said, sighing inwardly at the originality of his questions.

'And who's accompanying you tonight?'

Connie's eyebrows rose. Now, that was a question she hadn't been expecting.

'Don't tell me the *gorgeous* Connie Gordon is alone tonight?'

'Yes, I am, Carter.'

'Well, men of America, you should be ashamed of yourselves,' Carter said, turning to the camera. 'I really think you should've made more of an effort.'

'No, really Carter – don't—'

'Isn't there anyone out there who'd kill to have this lovely lady on their arm?'

Connie rolled her eyes, imagining the crank letters from the men of America she'd be receiving over the coming months.

'Ladies and gentlemen,' a voice announced on the tannoy. 'Please take your seats. The ceremony is about to begin.'

Connie sighed with relief and made a hasty departure from Carter Maddox.

She was just entering the auditorium when she felt a hand on her bottom. Spinning around, she came face to face with Jeff Kline.

'Hello, gorgeous,' he said.

If anyone else called her gorgeous tonight, she would scream.

'What are you doing here, Jeff?'

'Nice to see you too! Not still sore, are you, honeybun?'

'Don't call me that. I'm not your *honeybun!* Not since you sold out to the *Hollywood Recorder.*'

'But sweetcakes! What did you expect me to do?'

'You're a piece of slime, Kline,' she said, rather liking the rhyme that made. 'Go to hell.'

She made her way to her seat and hoped that she wouldn't meet any more of her ex-boyfriends that evening.

But, alas, it wasn't to be.

They were half an hour into the ceremony when Connie was escorted backstage and given a scarlet envelope and statuette for the award for best supporting actor. It was the moment she'd been dreading.

Just take it slowly, she told herself, hoping she wouldn't trip over the ridiculously long dress. Nice and slowly.

Waiting for her cue backstage, she wondered how long it would be before she could sneak home. There was a party after the show – several parties – and she'd been invited to all of them but she could think of nothing worse.

'You're on!' a girl backstage suddenly yelled at her.

'Oh!' Connie yelled back, venturing forth onto the stage where she was greeted by wave after wave of applause. The host had stepped to one side and the microphone was left for Connie. Walking up to it, she dared to look out into the audience, which was a great mistake because her heart rate doubled almost instantly. It was one of the reasons that the theatre had never tempted her. A live audience – there was nothing scarier.

She cleared her throat and began. 'Being a supporting actor is no mean feat. It's often as strenuous and time-consuming as being a lead and yet these vital roles are often overlooked. Not so tonight. We are here to acknowledge and celebrate five fabulous actors in supporting roles.' She stepped to one side and looked to the screen, which had been set up on the stage to show clips from the five different films. As the lights dimmed, Connie sneaked a look out into the audience. There was Jeff, with a blonde to his right and a brunette to his left. In his element, as usual. And there was Harvey Andreas. She'd really fallen for him. What a mistake that had been, she thought, thinking of Harvey's inability to commit to just one woman at a time.

As the clips continued, Connie realised, with awful certainty, that she had probably dated about five per cent of the audience there tonight. What a depressing thought. And not one single Prince Charming amongst them. Not *one*.

As the clips finished and the house lights came on, Connie stepped up to the microphone and opened the envelope and saw the name she had been dreading.

Out of all the nominations . . .

'And the winner is—' she said.

A one in five chance and he had to go and win it!

'Forrest Greaves!'

There was a huge round of applause and she saw the dark-haired actor stand up from his seat and make his way to the stage. He was tall, fit and desperately handsome – your typical love rat – and he had double-timed Connie with some low-life extra on the set of her last film. She still couldn't believe it. Whilst he'd been sending enormous bunches of flowers to her trailer, he'd been sleeping with Candy in his. The press had had a field day with it and Connie was still coping with the fallout because Candy was about to have his baby and hadn't wasted any time parading her enormous naked body in front of the glossies.

And now the awards. It was unbearable.

'Hey, gorgeous!' Forrest said as he sidled up to her on the stage and leant forward for the obligatory kiss, his hand – unseen by the audience because they were standing behind the podium – copped a quick feel of her bottom.

She threw him a heated glare as he stepped back, thrusting the award at him and moving to one side as he gave his acceptance speech. She was *not* going to make it easy for the press to get a photo of the two of them together.

Once it was over, the two of them left the stage together and, as soon as they were away from the cameras, Connie felt Forrest's hand on her bottom again.

'HEY!' she yelled. What was it with men and her ass? She couldn't remember putting out an advert in the newspapers saying, *Men – please grab my ass whenever you pass.*

Forrest's hands leapt in the air. 'Only appreciating what was once mine.'

'You gave up all rights to that when I caught you with that sleaze in your trailer,' Connie said.

'That was a misunderstanding,' he said. 'I told you at the time. My zip was stuck. She was helping me fix it. I swear we weren't a couple until *after* you broke up with me! I swear, Connie!'

'God!' Connie said. 'Can you hear yourself? You might've fooled the judges on the panel tonight but you're the *worst* actor I've ever met.'

Connie didn't bother returning to her seat. She'd had more than enough for one evening. She found a nice member of staff who called a cab for her and showed her out of a quiet exit where she could make an escape without the clamour of fans and photographers.

Once home, Connie struggled with the dress fastenings. It was more difficult than she'd imagined and it took several minutes of yoga-like twists before she was free and could wriggle out of the skintight fabric. She shook her head upside down, ruffling her hair as she often did when she was stressed.

15

What a night, she thought. It was the end of a long and taxing week but next week would be just as bad and the week after that wouldn't prove any less demanding with parties, ceremonies, press junkets and rehearsals. She hadn't had a break for months – years. Her agent just kept on putting her up for role after role. It was what she'd asked for in the beginning but she'd made ten films in the last four years and she was exhausted.

Kicking off her impossibly high heels, she sighed and pulled on a cool linen dressing gown before making her way to the kitchen. She needed wine: a nice big glass of something very expensive to take the edge off the evening.

Opening her fridge, she was greeted by a positive jungle. Everything was green. It was the usual problem: a fridge full of food but absolutely nothing to eat. Connie groaned at the sight of it. It was all part of the latest LA diet but, however healthy it was, Connie couldn't help wishing she could just sit down with a hamburger and fries like a regular person. But hadn't her agent told her to watch her weight?

'You're piling it on again, Connie,' he'd told her last week. 'This industry doesn't tolerate fat.'

Fat! *FAT*? Connie had never been more than nine stone in her whole life and, at five foot eight, that was positively skeletal. Sometimes she wondered what it would be like to live a normal life. To get up and not have to worry about what the papers were saying about you, to choose your food because it was what you *wanted* to eat, and not to be constantly told what you were going to be doing for the next year – the next decade.

Grabbing the bottle of wine, Connie padded through to her living room, her feet sinking into the luxurious white carpet she'd chosen for the whole house. It was an enormous room that overlooked the vast swimming pool and gardens, and Connie had filled it with beautiful antiques, from the Regency mahogany sideboard to the satinwood table. A nineteenth-century chandelier hung from the centre of the room. It would have looked more at home in an English Georgian manor house rather than in her very modern Hollywood home but Connie had fallen in love with its sparkling teardrop crystals and insisted on having it.

Her bedroom was the same. Reached by a *Gone with the Wind* staircase, the room was stuffed with the very finest money could buy because what else did she have to spend it on? There was a vast French rococo bed in antique gold, an enormous gilt mirror that bounced the light back from the balcony doors and an exquisite brass-inlaid secretaire in that she locked away all her personal documents.

Finishing her wine and heading upstairs to her bedroom, she removed her dressing gown and realised that she was still wearing her diamond choker. She unfastened it and returned it to its blue velvet box. She'd bought it as a special gift to herself after she'd heard she'd been nominated for an Oscar. Most actresses hired their jewellery for Oscar night but Connie had wanted to wear something that was hers – something that she could keep. She remembered the gentlemen from the jewellers who had turned up at her house with a selection of necklaces for her to choose from. There had been an amazing egg-sized sapphire pendant, which had reminded Connie of the colour of the ocean. There was a square-cut emerald necklace, which had looked dazzlingly bright when she'd tried it on against her pale skin. Then there'd been the rubies – twelve blood-red stones nestling in a lace of sparkling diamonds. But, in the end, Connie had chosen the diamond choker. It was breathtaking in its simplicity and could be worn with so many of her gowns.

Brushing her fingers over the stones, she closed the box and took it to the vault in the corner of the room. There, it joined a family of jewels from Connie's favourite garnet earrings to platinum watches and rings set with every stone imaginable. There was even a diamond tiara in there. Connie had worn it just once.

Taking a quick shower and smearing her face with the latest skin-tightening cream that promised to keep her looking like a nineteen-year-old, Connie slipped between the silky sheets of her bed, her head crashing onto the pale pillows. She felt as if she could sleep for a fortnight. Or for ever.

Closing her eyes, she thought about her beautiful home filled with beautiful things. She had more than any young woman had a right to and she knew how lucky she was, she really did.

'So why am I not happy?' she whispered into the dark night.

Chapter Three

Connie woke up with a start. There was somebody in her house and that somebody was shouting. Really, really loudly. She groaned and turned over, hiding her head under her duvet. Why oh why had she given her personal trainer a key to her house?

'Up, up, *up!*' he cried as he took the stairs two at a time. 'Sleepyheads don't get fit!'

'I don't want to get fit. Not this morning,' she said to herself. 'I want to sleeeeeeep!'

'WAKE UP!' he shouted as he entered the room – all six foot five of him.

'I'm awake!' Connie said.

'I want twenty stomach crunches right now!'

Connie muttered something under her breath.

'What was that, sweetie? You want to do fifty?' he said with a naughty grin.

'Go away, Danny!' Connie said, sitting up in bed, her red hair tousled and tangled.

'You don't pay me to go away. You pay me to get your ass moving! Come on,' he said, clapping a pair of enormous hands together.

Connie sighed. She loved Danny dearly. He was loyal and

sweet and always made her laugh, but there were certain mornings when she wished he didn't exist.

Ten minutes later and they were in the basement gymnasium and Connie was being put through her paces. It was a rude awakening and she really should have been used to it by now because Danny had been turning up three times a week for the past four years.

'Your body is your business,' she would silently chant to herself whilst pounding on the running machine. 'You have to keep in shape,' she'd repeat with each stretch on the rowing machine.

But if only her body was *her* business. The trouble was, everyone seemed to have something to say about her body. Her trainer, her agent, her publicist – to say nothing of the press who regularly snapped her from all angles and then ran headlines such as 'Podgy Connie Piles on the Pounds'. The unhappy truth was that acting was about more than her ability to inhabit a role and convince an audience that her emotions were real. It was about how she looked both on screen and off and that pressure could sometimes be unbearable.

After ten minutes on the exercise bike, Connie hung her head.

'Can we go running, Danny? I want to get some fresh air.' She looked up and caught Danny's eye. He didn't look happy with the suggestion.

'You know what happened last time.'

'I know.'

'We weren't so much running as running *away!*'

Connie nodded, remembering the hoard of paps that had torn after them with their intrusively long lenses.

'I wish I *could* run away,' Connie said.

'Aw, don't say that!' Danny said, his face wrinkling in dismay.

'But I *do*. I want to go somewhere where I can just be me for a while without a telephoto lens poking at me or some journalist tearing me apart.'

'I don't think such a place exists,' Danny said.

'No,' Connie said. 'You're probably right. But can't we at least try to pretend?'

'You want to go to the park?'

Connie nodded.

'We'll have to go in my car, then. Everybody knows yours.'

Connie grinned and grabbed her towel.

Danny's black RV was parked in the driveway. 'Get in the back and duck down,' he said.

Connie climbed in the back of his car, buckled up and then laid her head down on the seat. She'd given Danny her remote control to open the wrought iron gates and, as usual, there was a group of paparazzi camping outside.

'Don't they have homes to go to?' Danny asked as he hit the gas.

'Apparently not,' Connie said. 'I thought about inviting them in for dinner one evening. I'd just come back from a charity gala and felt a bit lonely. It's always odd to be surrounded by hundreds of people one minute and then to come back here and be totally alone.'

'But you didn't invite them in, did you?' Danny asked, eyebrows raised.

'No, of course not!'

Danny breathed a sigh of relief. 'Okay, it's safe to surface.'

Connie got up from the back seat and it was then that she noticed the newspaper on the seat beside her. She picked it up.

21

'Oh, don't bother reading that,' Danny said a little too quickly. 'There's nothing in it.'

'Danny, you're a terrible liar,' she said, opening the paper and staring in horror at the headline that greeted her on page three.

Connie Alone!

Stunning actress, Connie Gordon, one of the world's most famous movie stars, attended last night's 'Cream of the Screen' awards ceremony on her own. The 29-year-old actress recently broke up with fellow actor, Forrest Greaves, and it would seem that she's not been lucky in love since . . .

Accompanying the story was a photograph of Connie from the red carpet but, instead of printing one of the hundreds of pictures they must have taken of Connie's famous megawatt smile, they'd published one of her frowning. It must have been the millisecond that she'd caught her heels on her dress. There was also a photograph of the heavily-pregnant Candy with the caption: 'Expecting great things – the woman Forrest Greaves left Connie for'.

'Goddamn it!' she cursed and then her eye caught something else. It was a quote from her mother.

'"Connie is devastated," Vanessa Gordon told us. "She'd already started planning the wedding with Forrest".'

'They've interviewed my mother!' she shouted.

'I told you not to read it!' Danny said from the front seat.

'Why do they do that? *Why?*'

'To sell more papers, that's all.'

Connie sighed. 'Take me home,' she said.

'What? You don't want to go running?'

She shook her head. 'I'm sorry. I just don't feel like it any more.'

'But it might do you some good. You know, pound it out of your system.' He looked at her through the rear-view mirror and noticed the tears sparkling in her eyes. 'I'll take you home,' he said.

Once Danny had dropped her off, Connie kicked off her trainers and wandered through to her office. Her personal assistant had left her diary open on the desk and there was a planner pinned to the wall too. Connie glanced at it. She was meant to be starting rehearsals next week for her next film – and the thought of it made her groan.

'It'll do your career no end of good,' Bob Braskett, her agent, had told her. 'This is a real up-and-coming director. Teenagers really go for him. You'll gain a whole new audience here.'

There was also a magazine interview penned in, and two charity events. She sighed. If only she could get away from it all. If only she could escape!

The telephone rang and made Connie jump. She didn't normally answer the phone but, as her PA wasn't in until later, she picked it up herself.

'Connie!' a voice drawled. It was Forrest Greaves.

'What do you want?' she snapped.

'Aw, don't be like that, sweetheart. You didn't give me a chance to talk to you last night.'

'Yeah? Well, *I* said all I wanted to say,' Connie said.

'Yeah, but I didn't.'

She sighed. 'What do you want, Forrest?'

'I want to say that I miss you,' he said, 'and I think we should give it another go.'

'*What?*' Connie couldn't believe what she was hearing.

'I miss you so much, honey.'

'Don't *honey* me! You're about to have a child with that Candy woman, for heaven's sake.'

'That could be anybody's child,' he said. 'Anyway, she means nothing to me. It's *you* I want to be with.'

Connie felt a shiver of disgust creep up her spine. 'Forrest—'

'Listen,' he interrupted. 'I know I messed up but I swear that won't happen again. You're my one and only, Connie. You know we're right for each other. I *know* you do.'

'But I don't want anything to do with you, Forrest. I—'

'I mean – come on – I'm an award-winning actor now. I'm right up there with you, baby. Just think about it – what a couple we'll make. We'll send Hollywood dizzy. They won't be able to get enough of us! "Forrest and Connie", "Greaves and Gordon"! Just imagine the headlines!'

Connie slammed the phone down and let out a scream. How dare he propose getting back together with her when he'd treated her so badly and when he was about to become a father. Why couldn't he just leave her alone? He really was the limit.

She closed her eyes and took some deep breaths. She needed to calm down before she began hyperventilating.

'Count to ten,' she told herself as she breathed in through her nose and out through her mouth for a few steadying moments. 'That's better,' she said. 'Don't let him get to you.'

It was then that something caught her eye. Sitting in a

neat stack on the desk was the latest fan mail left by her personal assistant. On the top was a curious pink and yellow checked envelope. Connie picked it up and looked at it. It was from overseas. Scotland!

'It's tartan!' Connie laughed, slipping the letter out and unfolding it.

Dear Ms Gordon

It seems rather a long time since I last wrote to you and I'm so sorry! We've been very busy here in Lochnabrae. As you know, the fan club is going from strength to strength. We get lots of hits on the website and we even had a Connie Gordon season last month showing a film of yours each night at our village hall. We then voted on our favourite film – it was Milly in the Morning, *by the way – and then Isla Stuart, who runs the bed and breakfast here, made a 'Milly' cake with pink and yellow icing. You'll notice we've got pink and yellow stationery now too – my brother, Hamish, designed a Connie tartan based on Milly's gorgeous dress in the film. I hope you like it.*

Connie took another look at the envelope and laughed. It really was very pretty.

So, as you can see, we've been keeping busy. But that doesn't excuse me forgetting to write to you and I just wanted to extend our invitation to you once again. You know you'll always be made welcome here in Lochnabrae. It's a beautiful part of the Highlands with mountains and rivers and our very own loch in which you can swim. (Well, about twice a year if it gets really hot!)

We have a small bed and breakfast and Isla says you'd be made very welcome if you wanted to stay. She has radiators in all the rooms and hot water bottles aplenty if you come in winter. Or summer. And I've got a spare room too. That's to say, most of the time – unless Hamish has too many at the pub and can't make it home which isn't often, thank goodness.

I know you're probably very busy in Hollywood with your films and stuff and we must seem like another planet to you but we're a very friendly planet and we'd love to see you.

All best wishes from
Maggie Hamill
(Administrator of the Connie Gordon Fan Club) xx

Connie read the letter through once more. Lochnabrae. She hadn't thought about that place for years. It had been the birthplace of her mother and she remembered being fascinated by stories of it when she was young. Stories about icy swims in the loch, thick mists that clouded the houses and snowdrifts that would cut the village off for weeks. It was a magical, almost mystical place on the other side of the world – so far away from the dirt and dazzle of Hollywood.

Connie's eyes widened as she thought about it. Hadn't she just been praying for an escape? For peace? For a place where she could lose herself and leave all her troubles behind her including lying, cheating ex-boyfriends and mothers that couldn't keep their mouths shut? And here was a letter from her fan club promising her all those things. It was fate. It was destiny. It was plain common sense.

Without losing a single moment, she picked up the phone and called her PA.

'Samantha? It's Connie. I'm sorry to ring you so early but I thought you should know that I'll be leaving town today. I'm going away. No, Bob doesn't know. Tell him it's family business. I don't know how long it'll be for. Yes, he'll have to deal with those film people himself, and the charity events too. Tell him I need a vacation. A really good vacation.'

Chapter Four

Maggie had got up extra early to search the web for photos of Connie at the 'Cream of the Screen' awards ceremony. It didn't take long to find some.

'Oh!' she cried, her eyes feasting on the sparkling silver dress she was wearing. 'That's *the* most beautiful dress in the world!' Maggie right-clicked on the image and saved it to her computer for use on the fan site. Copyright? Smopyright! This was fan business and fans needed up-to-date, drop-dead gorgeous photos of their idol.

She searched around some more and found two different angles, instantly recognising the diamond necklace Connie was wearing. Maggie could list the other three events her idol had worn it to and which dresses she'd been wearing it with. She prided herself on her knowledge; she was the keeper of all things Connie.

One of the photos she was now saving showed Connie in profile with her perfect nose. Maggie automatically wrinkled her own huge tuber of a nose, wondering if a lowly shopkeeper could justify plastic surgery. And then she found a photo of Connie handing the award to the actor, Forrest Greaves.

Maggie whistled. 'Now that must've been interesting,' she

said to herself, knowing how he'd double-crossed Connie on the set of one of her films. Still, he was devilishly handsome. Perhaps it had been worth having her heart broken. She saved the picture with a quick click and then got to work updating the website blog.

There was always so much to do. Connie was always in the news and Maggie loved unearthing the stories on the internet although she didn't publish everything because a lot of the stories were clearly fabricated. Like the time it had been reported that Connie had been abducted by aliens and given birth to ET's lovechild. Maggie shook her head as she remembered. Poor Connie. It must be so frustrating to have such rubbish printed about you. The UK press was bad enough but the US really did take some beating.

Maggie had often dreamed about visiting America and going to see the homes of the stars in the Hollywood Hills but she didn't suppose it was ever going to happen. People like her just didn't travel. She'd once been to Edinburgh on a school trip. They'd seen the castle and heard the canon fire, and had visited the dark narrow streets of the Old Town and the wide Georgian splendour of the New Town but all Maggie could remember about the trip was how sick she'd felt on the coach. It had taken hours to reach their capital city and hours back to the Highlands and Maggie had been completely done in by it all. So how on earth would she fare on a trip to America? She'd never survive the ordeal, would she?

'I'll never leave Lochnabrae,' she said to herself. But it wasn't so bad as fates went. She really did love the little Highland community with its tiny white houses and stunning views, and most of its residents were happy with their lot too. She couldn't think of anyone from the older generation who'd ever been over the border into England let alone left the UK. Mrs Wallace and her husband holidayed in Mull every single year and Isla had once had a trip to Oban but hadn't liked it. Sandy Macdonald had ventured further afield in his youth but he was a hearth and slippers type these days. He didn't even like going into Strathcorrie on market days any more.

'Too many damned people!' he'd say. 'You can't walk in a straight line without bumping into somebody or other.'

What would Connie Gordon think of them all, Maggie wondered? She'd travelled the whole world, hadn't she? The people of Lochnabrae would seem so very dull and unadventurous to her.

Maggie looked away from the computer screen, her eyes drifting to the view outside. What would Connie think of their little corner of the world, she wondered?

'I don't suppose we'll ever know,' she said to herself before returning her gaze to the computer in search of more images of her idol.

Chapter Five

Like most women, Connie had never been very good at travelling light and, as she waited for her luggage on the carousel along with everyone else at Glasgow Airport, she was beginning to wonder how she'd manage on her own. Of course, she could have travelled VIP and had everything done for her but she'd been determined that this trip would be different. She'd booked her own taxi to the airport and had even booked her own tickets, which was a new experience as she usually left such mundane jobs to her PA, but it had felt good doing something for herself for once in her life – even if she had got a bit lost walking into the airport and had nearly missed her flight when she couldn't find her passport.

To avoid the press and the fuss that usually went hand in hand with luxury travel, Connie had decided to fly to Scotland incognito. She'd scraped her trademark red hair into a ponytail and flattened a baseball cap onto her head. A face free from make-up and the obligatory enormous sunglasses completed the disguise. It was rather like playing a part, she thought – the part of an ordinary girl going on holiday – and she'd been enjoying the experience until it came to hauling her own luggage off the carousel and struggling with it.

'Can I help you?' a gentleman's voice suddenly asked with a soft Scottish accent.

Connie turned around. A tall athletic man in a nice suit stood looking at her. 'Oh, thank you,' she said and watched as he found a trolley for her and placed her three suitcases onto it.

'Are you wanting a taxi?' he asked.

'Yes, I am.'

'Allow me,' he said, leading the way to the taxi rank outside the airport.

'I can't thank you enough,' Connie said, removing her sunglasses and smiling. As soon as she did, she knew she'd made a mistake.

'Good God!' he said. 'Aren't you—' the man cocked his head a little and looked at her quizzically. 'Connie Gordon?'

'Oh, lord, no!' Connie laughed, exaggerating her English accent and pushing her sunglasses back on. For most of her childhood, Connie had had an English tutor which meant that she was often hired to play English roles in films and, although she occasionally had an American twang, she could easily get away with being English.

'I could've sworn!' the man said. 'You look just like her. Remarkable! You could be in the movies.'

'Well, I'm very flattered,' she said, looking up and down for a taxi and hoping for a quick escape to avoid further questioning. 'Ah! Here's one,' she said as the next available car pulled up and a man got out to load her suitcases. 'Thanks for your help,' she said to the suited gentleman.

'My pleasure,' he said, staring at her in wonder.

Connie hopped into the taxi and the driver was soon pulling out from the kerb.

Phew, she thought. She'd made it.

'Where to, lass?' the driver asked.

Connie leant forward in her seat. 'Lochnabrae, please.'

'Lochnabrae Road? Lochnabrae Street?'

'Just Lochnabrae.'

'In Glasgow?'

'No.'

'Outside Glasgow then?'

Connie nodded. 'It's near a town called Strathcorrie.'

'Strathcorrie?'

'You know it?'

'Aye, I know it. That's over a hundred miles. It won't be a cheap fare, lass. You got the money to pay for it?'

'Of course,' Connie said. 'I wouldn't get in a taxi if I didn't have the money for my ride.'

'Just checking. I don't want to be stranded in the back of beyond with a lass with no money.'

Connie held back a hollow laugh. Money was certainly no problem for her but that didn't necessarily mean she was happy. If she could buy some sort of happiness, she wouldn't be there now, tired and lonely.

The taxi left the airport and Connie felt her eyes closing. Transatlantic flights always took it out of her and she felt she'd been airborne for days rather than hours. A little sleep would do her the world of good.

When Connie woke up, she was surprised to see that the sky had darkened.

'You won't need them glasses now,' the taxi driver said.

Connie took them off but kept her cap on in case she was recognised, but the driver didn't seem to be interested in who she was.

'Had a nice sleep, have you?'

'Yes,' Connie said. 'Where are we?'

'Just approaching Strathcorrie now.'

'I must've been asleep for hours!' Connie looked out of the window. The road was narrow and straight and there wasn't a single house to be seen. The countryside had opened out into an elongated valley with a river silvering the land, and great mountains heaved up into the sky.

'Welcome to the Highlands.'

Connie smiled. She was here at last – the place that her mother had once called home.

'Can we stop?' Connie suddenly asked. 'Just for a moment?'

The taxi driver pulled up at a lay-by. 'You feeling all right?'

'Yes. Yes!' Connie said excitedly, opening the door and getting out. She stood absolutely still, looking left, right, up and down, and then she smiled. It was three hundred and sixty degrees of loveliness and she was smack bang in the middle of it. The mountains soared majestically up into the sky and there was a bright waterfall in the distance that cascaded down to the valley below.

The taxi driver switched the engine off and joined her.

'Not going to be sick, are you?' he asked.

'No,' Connie said. 'Although I think I might have been if I hadn't left LA in time.'

His eyes narrowed. 'American, are you? You sound English to me.'

'It's complicated,' she said, pulling her cap a little lower over her face. She shouldn't have said anything about LA; it was too much information. If he knew who she was, he'd most likely drag her off into the hills and demand a ransom for her.

'It's all so – so – big!'

'Aye.'

'Isn't it amazing?' she said, thinking how different it was from the manicured lawns and borders of hothouse flowers in Bel Air.

'Well, it is that,' he said.

Connie took a last look around before returning to the taxi. The light was almost violet now and the colours of the landscape were beginning to drain into the night and, for the first time in years, Connie felt a real sense of peace.

It was dark by the time they reached Lochnabrae and Connie peered out of the window. 'Is this it?'

'Aye,' the taxi driver said. 'That's the B&B,' he said, nodding towards a white house with a board swinging outside. Loch View. Connie gazed across the road. She couldn't see any loch. 'That is where you're staying, isn't it?'

Connie nodded. She'd managed to ring ahead before leaving LA and had booked a room for a week to begin with. 'What do I owe you?'

The taxi driver told her the total and Connie dug through her designer wallet until she found enough to pay him. She wasn't sure how much it came to in dollars – Connie hadn't had time even to try and understand the conversion rate as she'd grabbed her cash from the LAX bureau de change and run to catch her flight. But, if it meant not having to worry about driving on the wrong side of the road and navigating her way along dark single-track lanes after a long-haul flight, it was definitely a bargain.

'I'll get your bags,' he said, taking the wad of cash and stuffing it into his jeans pocket.

Connie got out of the car and breathed in deeply. It was

good to have finally arrived. She promised herself no more planes or taxis for at least a week. She'd walk – walk everywhere, that's what she'd do. Nobody ever walked in LA – it was too big – but she'd walk here: by lochs, by streams, through valleys and up hills.

The front door of Loch View suddenly opened, breaking into Connie's thoughts.

'Ms Gordon, is it?' the elderly lady greeted her. 'I'm Isla Stuart.' She had a sweet face completely caked in white face powder and her cheeks were two perfect circles of scarlet. 'I've been waiting up for you.'

'Oh, I'm not too late, am I?'

'Och, no! But I do tend to nod off in the evenings if there isn't someone to take care of. Now, I expect you'll be ready for a cup of hot chocolate and a wee slice of Dundee cake?'

'Thank you,' Connie smiled, wondering what Danny would say to that and wondering what on earth Dundee cake was anyway.

'And your driver too?'

'Not for me, thanks all the same,' he said, struggling with the cases. 'I've to get back and it's a fair drive.'

A few minutes later, Connie's cases were all lined up neatly in her room on the first floor at the front of the B&B.

Once back downstairs in the hallway, Connie gave her driver a big tip to thank him for all his patience.

'You know,' he said as she walked to the front door with him, 'there's something familiar about you.'

'Really?' Connie said, still wearing her baseball cap and exaggerating her English accent once again.

'You're not on the telly, are you?' he asked.

Connie laughed nervously. 'You know, I'm always being asked that. I guess I've just got one of those faces,' she said.

He continued to stare thoughtfully at her a moment longer. 'Well,' he said at last, 'best get back to the city. You have a nice time, lass.'

Connie watched as he left and then closed the door.

'Now then,' Isla said, 'how about that hot chocolate and cake?'

She led Connie through to a room at the back of the guest house. 'I don't often get to invite people here,' she said. Connie smiled as she saw that a fire had been lit and a small table set with cups and plates. 'I do like a real fire,' Isla said. 'It cheers the place up, doesn't it?'

'Smells wonderful,' Connie said, sitting down in an old armchair next to it. 'Really homely, isn't it? I've never had a real fire. Wouldn't dare in my house.'

'Why not?'

'White carpets!'

'Ah, well, that's why we all have these patterned ones,' Isla said. 'It's messy, a real fire, with ash and the like, but I can't imagine living without one. It's like a friend that keeps you company each evening.'

Connie watched as Isla bustled around cutting cake. She left the room briefly and came back with two cups of hot chocolate.

'The best hand warmer in the world,' Isla said, handing Connie a cup.

'Thank you,' Connie said, taking a sip.

'Why don't you take that cap off, eh?' Isla said. 'You'll warm through in no time in here.'

Connie was instantly on her guard. She was exhausted

and the last thing she wanted was to go through the whole, 'Yes, I'm really Connie Gordon' conversation. That would have to wait till the morning when she felt like herself again.

'Go on, now.'

'Oh, my hair's a real mess,' Connie said. 'I'd better keep it on.'

Isla shrugged her shoulders. 'Suit yourself.'

Connie ate her cake and took another sip of her chocolate, hoping she hadn't offended her landlady. They both watched the fire for a few minutes and Connie soon found that her vision was blurring as the orange flames danced wildly. Her body began to slump and it was soon a real effort to keep her eyes open.

'Why, you're practically nodding off there,' Isla said. 'And you're so pale too.' She leant forward in her chair. 'Och, and you've not been taking care of your skin. It's as dry as an autumn leaf.'

Connie flinched, a hand flying up to her face. 'Is it? But I've been using face cream every night.'

'Some cheap, nasty stuff, no doubt. You should try Benet's Balm. The monks make it. I swear by it, you know. I'll let you have some of mine.'

'Right,' Connie said.

'Now, get yourself to bed. A good night's rest will do you the power of good. Come down for breakfast when you're good and ready. We don't have a strict timetable here and you're my only guest so there's no rush.'

'Thank you,' Connie said, feeling mightily relieved that there was no pressure on her.

As she made her way to her room, she thought about all the people she should call. She should tell her PA, Samantha, that she'd arrived safely, and it would be courteous of her to ring her agent too but, when she saw the bed and the deep soft pillows, she thought better of being courteous. It could wait. Everything could wait.

Chapter Six

It wasn't until the next morning that Isla Stuart realised she had a movie star in her guest house. Connie had woken up just before eight o'clock and couldn't get back to sleep again. But neither did she want to. She couldn't remember the last time she'd had a free morning – a free *day*. If she wasn't up for an early morning make-up call on set, she was usually rudely awoken by Danny who would force sit-ups, squats and all manner of muscle-crunching tortures upon her.

'Not today,' she said, flinging back her duvet and padding across the carpet to the window. She drew the floral curtains back and gasped – really gasped – at the view that greeted her. So that was the loch of Loch View. She looked out in awe at the huge stretch of silver water and, on the distant shore, the mountains rose up into the sky, perfectly mirrored by the waters beneath them. It was the kind of morning that inspired great thoughts and Connie couldn't wait to rush out and be a part of it.

She flung herself under the hot shower in the tiny en suite, washed the travel-weary hours out of her hair, put on a dash of make-up and rooted around in one of her suitcases for jeans and a shirt. Was it cold outside? The sun was shining but Connie had a feeling that that was nothing to go by in Scotland. What was it her mother used to tell her? 'If the midges aren't biting you, Jack Frost is.'

Finally, she was ready to venture downstairs in search of breakfast.

'Morning, Isla,' Connie said cheerily.

'Oh, my dear, you're up already,' Isla said, turning around from the breakfast table in the front room. 'CONNIE GORDON!' Isla exclaimed, dropping the slice of toast she'd been buttering as realisation dawned on her.

Connie froze.

'Oh, my lordy! It's Connie Gordon, isn't it?'

Connie nodded, her face flushing with embarrassment.

'I didn't think. I mean, when you said you were Miss Gordon on the phone and last night – I didn't twig! Oh, how silly of me! How rude you must've thought me.'

'No, Isla! Not at all. You gave me such a warm welcome. I couldn't have asked for a warmer one.'

'But that's not the same thing at all. I didn't know who you were.'

Connie stepped forward and placed a hand on Isla's arm.

'Oh!' Isla exclaimed.

'You mustn't treat me any differently from your other guests.'

'What nonsense!' Isla said.

'I mean it,' Connie said, taking a seat at the table. 'It's one of the reasons I came here.'

Isla looked confused. 'How do you mean?'

'To escape all that. All that sycophancy!'

'I'm not sure I know what that means.'

Connie smiled. 'It means endless flattery. I read it in a script once.'

41

Isla's powdered forehead creased. 'You wanted to escape endless flattery so you came to the headquarters of your fan club? I think you might've made a mistake there.'

'You do?' she said and then sighed. 'Oh, dear.'

'Oh, aye! Everyone loves you here. Well, apart from Angry Angus – so he says – but I have my suspicions. I was walking by his house just last week and happened to see him watching *Just Jennifer*. He had three cans of lager on his coffee table. He was in it for the long haul,' Isla said with a smile and a nod.

Connie grinned. 'I'm sure everyone will be fine,' she said. 'Once they realise I'm just a normal person.'

'But you're *not* a normal person. You're a star – a famous movie star.'

Connie looked across the table at Isla. 'But I don't know if that's really *me*, all the parties and red carpets. I don't really know who I am and I've come here – away from it all – so I can find out.'

'Oh, my poor gal! Well, I'm not sure if I can help you finding out who you are but there's one thing I can do – and that's make you a big slap-up breakfast fit for a movie star!'

'Isla!' Connie protested but it was too late. She'd disappeared into the kitchen at the back of the guest house.

Connie bit her lip. Maybe she *had* made a big mistake coming here. It had been easy enough to get on a plane and leave Hollywood but it was going to be a lot harder to leave the movie star image behind her.

Maggie was teetering on top of a stool, stacking boxes of porridge on a high shelf when the shop phone rang. She clambered down to answer it.

'Maggie?' a voice squealed at the other end.

'Isla?'

'She's here,' Isla whispered.

'Who's here?'

'She! *Her!*' Isla said, her voice high and excitable.

'Isla, what are you talking about?'

'Connie. Connie Gordon.'

'What? On the telly? Am I missing something?'

'No. Not on the telly. Here. In Lochnabrae. She's in room number two right now.'

'No!' Maggie cried.

'Yes. I say, yes!'

'Why didn't you call me?'

'I am calling you!' Isla said, perplexed.

'I mean, when she arrived?'

'Well, I didn't recognise her last night.'

'What do you mean, you didn't recognise her? She's Connie Gordon – one of the world's most famous actresses.'

'But she was just a lass wanting a room for the night. And her hair was all scrunched up under a cap. Oh!' Isla suddenly yelled.

'What is it?'

'I told her that her skin was dry. I gave her my pot of Benet's Balm. She must think I'm so rude.'

'And she's with you now?'

'Aye.'

'And you're sure it's her? You're sure it's our Connie and not some lookalike pretending to be her?'

'No! It's her!'

'Oh my God!' Maggie exclaimed as the realisation dawned on her. 'It was my letter, wasn't it? She read my letter!'

'Maggie – you've got to come over here.'

43

'Yes,' Maggie gasped. 'I'll come over. MY HAIR!'

'What?'

'I've got to wash my hair. Oh, why couldn't you have rung me last night? My hair always goes frizzy when I wash it in the morning.'

'But I didn't know last night,' Isla said.

'Look, I'll come over as soon as I can.'

'Don't be long,' Isla said. 'I don't know what to say to her. Not after the Benet's Balm incident. She must think I'm mad.'

Maggie hung up the phone and stood perfectly still for a moment and then she did something she hadn't done since Jimmy Carstairs had dropped a house spider down the back of her blouse at primary school. She screamed.

There was a road that snaked its way out of Lochnabrae, winding up into the hills and affording anyone who walked that way the very best of views. The whole of the loch was visible from there and the cluster of houses along the main street looked like pearls on a string when viewed from above. In the autumn, the colours were spectacular, the rich reds and golds blazed like jewels, and the air was the purest in the Highlands. That's why Alastair McInnes had chosen it as his home. He'd spent so much of his life in noisy, dirty rented flats in London but, as soon as he was able, he'd left the city behind him and returned to his roots in the Highlands. It was what writers did, wasn't it? You found a quiet corner of the world to call your own and the words would flow out of you. Only they weren't flowing at the moment.

It was only half past nine but Alastair's eyes were already sore. Perhaps it had something to do with him glaring at his computer screen for half the night and not going to bed much before dawn. He looked at his computer in frustration. He just couldn't get the heroine right. She wasn't jumping off the page yet. She wasn't *real*.

'Come on, Bounce!' he said, and the black Labrador puppy that was snoozing by his feet under his desk leapt up immediately. 'Let's get out of here.'

A good hike in the hills was the remedy for many things: a hangover, a decision to be made or a broken relationship but, today, he was hoping it would be a cure for his constipated writing.

Throwing on a tatty wax jacket and shoving on a pair of ancient boots, he opened the front door of the old crofter's cottage. It was still a bit of a novelty to do such a thing. To open his front door and be able to see the hills and the sky – that was such a treat. For a moment, he remembered his last flat in London and the dark communal hallway that always smelt of rubbish and the litter-strewn street outside where it was impossible to park. No, this was the life for him, he thought. There was no going back and relief filled him at that realisation. Life in London had been difficult for him both professionally and personally and he didn't want to repeat those experiences ever again.

Shaking thoughts of his past away, he watched as Bounce leapt over the little stream that ran alongside the cottage. Alastair did the same thing only he didn't double back to drink from it like his dog. The grass was tussocky here and spongy after the rain in the night and made satisfying squelches as he walked.

'This way, Bounce,' Alastair called as he took the path down the hill. Bounce removed his head from a clump of bright bracken and then tore down the path, overtaking his master. Alastair laughed as he watched the sleek black streak of dog. That was another thing he'd always wanted but his previous landlords had always insisted on 'no pets'. He'd had Bounce just a few weeks now but already he couldn't imagine his life without him. It was good having a dog when you were a writer. They were silent companions. They didn't interrupt you with speech when your head was already full of words but they were there if you needed to reach out and touch something warm and, of course, Bounce got him away from the dreaded computer at least twice a day. Although Alastair was a great walker anyway and sometimes threw a bit of climbing in for good measure, he had no doubt that his physique wouldn't be quite as toned if it wasn't for Bounce. Whole days could fly by when his writing was going well and the world outside his walls was often forgotten.

Yes, he thought, it was good to get out, breathe in some fresh spring air and try to forget about plots, characters and speeches that sounded neither natural nor interesting.

The track led through a wood and then sloped steeply down towards the loch. The rain the night before had made the path slippery but the smell was wonderful. Alastair inhaled deeply, wondering why nobody had invented an aftershave half as good as that. Not that he needed it. He only managed a shave every couple of weeks, preferring a stubbly, low-maintenance complexion. He ran his hands through his dark hair. That could do with some attention too but it was such a hassle driving all the way to Strathcorrie and it wasn't as if there was a woman in his life to impress. His mother would go spare if she could see him but, luckily, she was in Edinburgh and he could sort himself out before his next visit. She liked the Alastair of a few years ago who'd had a nice wee office job in London with regular hours. The sort of job that required a suit, a tie, a briefcase and a nice neat haircut.

'And unrelenting boredom,' Alastair said, causing Bounce to look back at him.

No, his mother had not been impressed when he'd told her he was going to be a full-time writer, even though he'd had numerous plays published and even sold one to a film company.

'But the money, Alastair! What are you going to live on?'

'Fresh air and whisky,' Alastair had joked.

His mother had gasped in horror.

'I've bought a little crofter's cottage in the Highlands. It's as cheap as chips. Won't cost much to run. It's perfect.'

But it was no good. For his mother, there was no world outside of Edinburgh. The Highlands? That was a place for tourists. People didn't really live there, did they?

'Well, I do,' Alastair said out loud as he walked. 'I DO!' he shouted, his voice echoing beautifully as he neared the loch. He loved that about this place. It made him want to run and shout and be foolish. In short, it made him feel young again. Not that he was exactly over the hill but it was a long time since he'd shouted just for the fun of it.

Connie was walking around the loch when she heard a man shouting.

'I DO!'

She looked around, expecting to see someone, but there was nobody there. How strange, she thought. Was there some sort of wedding ceremony taking place? It would certainly be a stunning location for it but, as far as she could see, she was the only person there. There wasn't a single soul around – not in the mountains, by the loch nor even across the other side of the water in Lochnabrae. The whole world felt as if it were sleeping.

Connie took a deep breath, luxuriating in air that didn't smell of traffic. There was such a stillness here. LA was always in such a rush: people rushing to get to work, to lunch, to the gym, to the dentist's. There hadn't been any sign of rushing so far in Lochnabrae, Connie thought. It had been like stepping back in time, which was utterly delightful. Although she was slightly perturbed by the obvious lack of shops. There wasn't a single coffee bar or deli counter. Probably a small price to pay, she thought to herself, for such blissful calm and not a single long lens in sight. She was sure she could get used to it here.

Trying to put aside all thoughts of what she was going to do when she started to crave a skinny latte, Connie found a group of boulders by the sandy shore of the loch and chose one to sit on. She hoped it was clean because she had put aside her jeans and was wearing very expensive pale blue Chanel trousers and a matching jacket in celebration of the sunshine. Perhaps not the best choice for a walk in the Highlands, she admitted. She'd just have to take care.

She was just looking out across the sheeny water when her mobile beeped. Service! She took it out of her pocket. There hadn't been any service in the village but there seemed to be a signal at this side of the loch and it appeared that Connie had a heap of messages waiting for her. She sighed. She really should have left her mobile at home or at least in the B&B. For a moment, she deliberated throwing it in the loch but her curiosity got the better of her and she took it out of her jacket pocket. The first message was from her agent.

'Connie! Where the hell are you? Samantha told me some crap about you taking a vacation? Are you out of your mind? You can't do this to me. Don't you realise you have commitments here? I need you to come back—'

Connie deleted the message before getting to the end of it. The next one was from Samantha.

'I'm so sorry to disturb you, Connie, but Bob's been on the phone constantly. I told him you were away but he won't believe me. You've got to call him.'

Connie deleted it, and several more irate messages from Bob and anxious messages from Samantha.

The final message was from Forrest Greaves.

'Babe! Where are you? I can't stop thinking about you. You looked so *hot* in that dress at the awards. Give me a call. You know you want to.'

'Oooo! What a slime ball!' Connie said, switching her mobile off and stuffing it into her pocket. She still couldn't believe that she'd fallen for his smarmy charm.

Why couldn't everyone leave her alone? Couldn't she just have some time and space to call her own? She got up from the boulder and dusted down the bottom of her pristine trousers. She deserved a break, didn't she? She couldn't remember the last time she'd taken one. She stormed across the beach towards a nearby wood, feeling her stress level soaring. Why did there have to go and be a mobile signal?

Get rid of it, a little voice inside her said. *Go on!*

'Right,' she said, doing an about-turn and heading back to the loch, reaching in her pocket for the intrusive instrument. Taking a deep breath, she stretched her arm back and then flung it as far as she could into the silvery depths of the loch.

It was then that she heard a strange sound. Turning around, she saw a black dog hurtling towards her, its legs and belly covered in thick brown mud.

'WOOF! WOOF!' it barked, its great paws eating up the ground as it hurtled full on into the water.

'What the?' Connie stared, watching it as it swam out into the loch.

'BOUNCE!' a voice called and Connie turned, seeing a dark-haired man emerging from the woods and striding across the sandy shore towards her. 'Come here, Bounce!'

Connie watched, spellbound as the dog swam on towards the centre of the loch and, only after the man had called his name again, turned and headed back to the shore.

'*Here*, Bounce!' the man yelled but the dog didn't seem to be listening to him and, as soon as it emerged from the water, it took a few leaps towards Connie and only then did it shake the loch water from its coat.

Connie screamed as the icy, muddy water cascaded over her, splattering her pale outfit.

'Oh no!' she cried. 'No!' But the dog didn't seem to understand. In fact, her response only seemed to excite it more and it began leaping towards her, its puppy paws bouncing off the legs of her trousers until they were more black than blue.

Connie flailed her arms about as she tried to shoo the dog away. She'd only ever worked with well-trained animals on film sets and had no idea how to control such a furry ball of frantic energy.

'BOUNCE!' the man yelled, running towards the dog

and pulling him away, making the dog sit at a safe distance. 'I'm so sorry,' he said.

Connie looked up, her eyes full of embarrassed fury. Her cheeks were blazing with shock and humiliation. 'What . . . Who . . . Look at the state of my clothes! I'm a mess! That dog is . . . is out of control!'

The man's dark eyebrows drew together. 'I said I was sorry. I couldn't stop him in time. He's just a puppy.'

'He should be on a lead if you can't take charge of him,' Connie snapped.

'You can't keep a young dog on a lead.'

'Well, you should've stopped him!'

'He saw you throw something into the loch. He's a Labrador. They like to retrieve things. He didn't mean any harm. He was just doing what comes naturally to him.'

'I've heard that line from men before,' Connie said, 'and it's no excuse for bad behaviour! Just look at my trousers. They're ruined.'

'I'll pay for them to be dry-cleaned,' the man said.

'They're not just dirty. The material's snagged. They've been tugged and clawed—'

'Look!' the man said, sounding impatient now, 'I said I was sorry but if you're going to wear unsuitable clothes when you go hiking, you're asking for trouble.'

'Oh, so it's my fault now, is it?'

'I'm just saying, you should be wearing something a little more practical.'

'And when did I ask for your advice?' Connie asked, glaring at him and noticing a pair of blindingly blue eyes. She'd never been so embarrassed in her life and hated the thought of this stranger seeing her in such a state. 'I've got to get back,' she said. 'Don't let the dog come near me again!'

Connie pushed past the man and made her way – as dignified as was possible in the circumstances – towards the village in search of a pair of trousers with slightly fewer paw prints on them.

Chapter Seven

Alastair watched in amazement as the red-headed woman stomped off in the direction of Lochnabrae, her trouser legs splattered and stained.

'What were you thinking of, Bounce?' he asked, bending down and tickling him behind his sopping head. Bounce looked up at his master with big brown uncomprehending eyes. 'That is no way to introduce me to a lady! No way at all.' Bounce rolled onto his back presenting Alastair with a muddy wet belly. 'I'm not tickling that, mate,' he said. 'Come on.' As soon as Alastair stood back up to full height, Bounce sprang up too, running back into the shallows of the loch and splashing himself all over.

Alastair turned and watched the receding figure of the woman. There'd been something oddly familiar about her but he couldn't think what. He was quite sure he'd never met her before; he would've remembered somebody that rude. But there was a quality about her that he felt sure he recognised. And then it clicked.

'Connie Gordon!' he said, causing Bounce to turn and leg it towards him. 'That's it! She looks *just* like Connie Gordon.'

*

Maggie buzzed around the house like a bluebottle. Connie Gordon. Here in Lochnabrae! Was it because of her letters? Why hadn't she written to tell her she was coming?

She flung herself into the shower and washed as quickly as she could and then she started to attack her hair. It was far from ideal having to apply a hairdryer to her fleece-like hair but she couldn't meet Connie Gordon with unwashed hair, could she? And what was she going to wear? She thought of the sorry pairs of jeans in her wardrobe and the tired jumpers full of holes. There was the dress she'd worn to her cousin's wedding but wouldn't it be a bit odd to show up wearing that on a mid-week morning in Lochnabrae?

'It'll just have to be the cleanest and least holey things I can find,' she said to herself, hanging her head upside down in an attempt to dry it before Christmas.

It was half an hour later by the time she got to Isla's.

'Where is she?' Maggie said, breathless with excitement.

'She's gone,' Isla said.

'Gone! What do you mean, *gone?*' Maggie looked around in panic.

'She went out – a walk around the village,' she said.

Maggie's eyes widened in horror. 'And you let her go? You had Connie Gordon here and you let her go?'

'Well, what was I meant to do?'

'Keep her here!' Maggie cried. 'At least until I got here. Oh, my! She could be anywhere. She might've escaped!'

'Och! You're getting carried away. She just wanted a breath of fresh air. She wouldn't just leave. All her stuff's upstairs.'

'Stuff?'

'Suitcases. Three large ones. Goodness only knows what's in them.'

Maggie's mouth dropped open. 'Can I see?'

'Well, it's not usual for me to show people my guest's rooms,' Isla said.

'But it's not usual for you to have a Hollywood movie star staying here, is it?'

Isla and Maggie's eyes locked in mutual understanding. 'Oh, all right then. Just keep this between us, for goodness' sake,' she said, and the two of them hurried up the stairs together. 'Did I tell you she touched me?' Isla said. 'She actually touched me! I'll never wash this jumper again.'

'Come on,' Maggie said, anxious to get a look at the room before Connie returned.

Just as a formality, Isla knocked on the door. 'She's definitely out,' she said, unlocking the door with her landlady's key.

'Let us in then!' Maggie said excitedly and, once Isla unlocked the door, the two of them entered the room.

Maggie gazed in wonder at the sight that greeted her. The bed had been left unmade and the dressing table was cluttered with all sorts of things: two great bulging make-up bags spilled lipsticks, mascaras and tubes of pale foundation. There were hairbrushes and perfume bottles too. Maggie dared to pick one up. It was the most beautiful thing she'd ever seen. The bottle was an elegant teardrop shape in ridged glass that felt fabulous under her fingertips. Gently, she removed the golden stopper and sniffed.

'It's like heaven!' she said, spraying herself in a cloud of Wishes. 'So this is what a movie star smells like,' she said to herself, inhaling deeply.

'Maggie! Put that down! You shouldn't touch those things.'

But Maggie couldn't help herself. This was as close as she'd ever been to her idol and she was enjoying every single minute of it.

'Look at this mirror,' she said, picking up a silver hand mirror that gleamed in the bright light of the bedroom. 'Have you ever seen anything like it?' Maggie turned it over and saw a beautiful 'C' had been engraved on the back. 'Oh!'

'Maggie!' Isla suddenly yelled. 'Look at this!'

Isla had given into temptation and dared to peep inside one of the suitcases. Maggie gasped as she too saw the contents.

'They're evening dresses!' Maggie said.

'Where does she think she's going to wear all these around here?' Isla said, cooing as she touched the silky soft fabric of an ivory-white dress.

'Would you look at that?' Maggie said, pulling out a sapphire-blue gown trimmed with sparkling silver beads.

'Don't take it out,' Isla all but screamed.

But Maggie couldn't possibly leave it in the suitcase. It would be like showing a child a jar of sweets and telling it not to eat them.

The dark blue gown unravelled to the floor as Maggie held it up against her. 'I LOVE it!'

Isla giggled and pulled out a velvet gown in a sumptuous amethyst. 'Lordy lord!' she said.

'Oh, Isla!' Maggie said, placing the sapphire-blue gown on the bed and reaching out for the velvet. 'I remember her wearing this one. It was at a premiere for *Keep Me Close*. She looked so beautiful – like one of those Pre-Raphaelite women with her hair all loose and curly.'

Soon, the bed was strewn with gowns. Golds, silvers, greens and blues, satins, laces and velvets. Maggie was almost jumping up and down with excitement and both women lost themselves in the moment, surrounded by the kinds of couture they'd only ever glimpsed in magazines.

'Do you think I could try one on?' Maggie asked, fingering a lacy gown in emerald-green.

'Well, I don't think you should,' Isla said, trying to be stern.

Maggie's face fell. To be so close to so many beautiful dresses and not to be allowed to try them on . . .

'Oh, go on then!' Isla suddenly said. 'Just one!'

Maggie squealed and began disrobing quickly.

She'd just got down to her thermal undies when the front door slammed.

'She's back!' Isla gasped.

Maggie's eyes doubled in size. 'Quick!' she said. 'Put the dresses away!'

Isla began stuffing the gowns back in the suitcase as Maggie hurriedly put her clothes back on, falling onto the bed as she dragged her jeans up her legs and causing a zip-rip of static as she pulled on her jumper.

'We've got to get out of here,' Isla whispered and the two of them legged it onto the landing.

'Where is she?' Maggie said, relieved that they hadn't been caught.

'She must still be downstairs,' Isla said, locking Connie's bedroom door as quietly as she could.

The two of them crept down the stairs and, there by the door, stood Connie Gordon, examining her trousers with a defeated look on her face.

'Oh, hello,' she said, looking up.

Isla nodded. Maggie just stared.

'Are you all right?' Isla asked. 'Did you have a nice walk?'

'Yes,' Connie said. 'Well, apart from the complete madman I met by the loch.'

Maggie and Isla looked at each other.

'Angus?' Isla said.

'I didn't ask his name,' Connie said. 'And he didn't volunteer it. But he had a dog with him. A black one.'

Maggie's eyes widened. 'Bounce?'

'I beg your pardon?'

'The dog's name,' Maggie said. 'That'd be Alastair's. Alastair's your madman. Well, he's a writer actually but that's the same thing as a madman, isn't it?'

'You look like a Dalmatian,' Isla said, gazing at Connie's trousers.

'I've got to get out of them. They're sticking to my legs,' Connie said.

Isla and Maggie were still standing at the foot of the stairs.

'Can I get by?' Connie asked.

'Oh!' Maggie exclaimed. 'Sorry.' She moved out of the way.

'I'll be down again in a minute then we can meet properly,' Connie said with a smile, disappearing up the stairs.

'Oh my God!' Maggie whispered. 'It's really her, isn't it?' she said to Isla.

'Well, I told you it was,' Isla said. 'Isn't she beautiful? I mean, apart from those trousers.'

'Do you think she'll get them clean or just throw them away? Some stars do that, don't they? If they get a speck of dirt on something or a little snag, they put it in the bin.

Can I have them if she does?' Maggie asked. 'I wouldn't mind if the mud never came out.'

'Completely ruined!' Connie's voice suddenly called down the stairs. 'I'll have to chuck them.'

Maggie's eyes widened with joy as she immediately started planning what she could wear with them. However, looking at the svelte figure coming down the stairs, it dawned on her that she might actually be a couple of sizes out of the trousers' league. She gazed at the fabulously skinny pair of jeans Connie was now wearing and immediately promised herself that cream cakes were a thing of the past.

'At least I'm dry now,' Connie said, joining Maggie and Isla in the hallway. 'And now we can say hello properly.'

'I'm Maggie,' Maggie said, not wanting to wait a moment longer than she had to. 'Maggie Hamill.' She stepped forward, her right foot catching on the hallway rug, causing her to plummet towards Connie.

'Careful!' Connie gasped, getting a mouthful of dark hair.

'I'm so sorry,' Maggie said. 'I'm Maggie.'

'It's a pleasure to meet you. You write the letters, don't you?'

Maggie nodded. 'Astonishing!' she said.

'I beg your pardon?'

'You being here.'

'But you did invite me.'

'Yes! I just never thought you'd come,' Maggie said. 'I mean, I hoped you would.'

'I'm sorry I didn't ring to tell you first. It was a kind of spur of the moment thing but that's all right, isn't it?' Connie asked.

Maggie nodded, a huge smile plastered on her face.

Connie sniffed. 'You're wearing Wishes!' she said.

Maggie gulped. 'Yes.'

'I wear that too!'

'You do?'

'It's my favourite scent. I take it wherever I go.'

Maggie bit her lip, and quickly changed the subject. 'I wish you'd told us you were coming. I feel awful not meeting you last night.'

'Hey, don't worry about it. I don't need a welcoming committee,' Connie said.

'It's funny you should use that word,' Isla said.

'What word?' Connie asked.

'Committee. We have a *Connie Committee*, don't we, Maggie?'

'Oh! Yes, we do. It's really just the fan club organisers. You'll have to meet them. They'd all love to meet you. They won't believe you're here.'

'There's no rush for that, is there?' Connie said. 'I was kinda hoping to find my feet first – get to know the area a bit and relax.'

'Oh, right,' Maggie said, feeling a little deflated. 'But you'll come and see the Connie HQ, won't you?'

'What's that?' Connie asked with a frown.

'It's where we take care of the website and answer letters and things.'

'It's Maggie's bedroom,' Isla said.

'It's *not* my bedroom. I moved the HQ into the spare room at the front of the house,' Maggie said.

'Well,' Connie said, 'I don't suppose there's any harm in seeing the HQ, is there?'

'Great!' Maggie said, clapping her hands together and

only just stopping herself from jumping up and down on the spot in excitement. 'Will we go now?'

'Right now?'

Maggie nodded and grinned.

'I guess I didn't have any other pressing engagements,' Connie said.

'Brilliant! Oh, this is so much fun. You're going to love it, I know you will.'

'Will you be having lunch here, Ms Gordon?' Isla asked.

'It's Connie. Please call me Connie.'

Isla smiled and nodded. 'Of course.'

'I hadn't really thought about lunch. Or eating. I don't suppose there's a restaurant here?'

'In Lochnabrae?' Maggie laughed. 'You must be joking. There's The Capercaillie.'

'What's that?'

'The local pub but they only do baskets of chips and pies.'

'Right,' Connie said, wrinkling her nose.

'I don't suppose you eat that kind of thing,' Maggie said.

'I – well – I could give it a go, couldn't I? I mean, I'm on holiday, right?'

'Right!' Maggie said. 'We could get the fan club together in the pub. That would be fun, wouldn't it? It wouldn't be official or anything – just a gathering of friends, really.'

'Och, Maggie – will you let the gal settle in before you go parading her before the whole of Lochnabrae?'

'Oh,' Maggie said, looking somewhat crestfallen.

'I will meet them,' Connie said. 'I promise.'

'Okay,' Maggie said. 'I mean, we don't really need to rush. I can keep you all to myself for a while, can't I?'

Connie swallowed.

'Oh, dear,' Maggie said, 'that sounded a little bit like that film, *Misery*, didn't it – where the fan kidnaps that writer and ties him up and everything?'

'Well, just a little bit,' Connie admitted.

'But I'm nothing like that. Honestly. I promise I won't lock you up or prevent you from leaving or anything. You're free to come and go as you please,' Maggie laughed. 'As long as you tell me first.'

Connie looked at Maggie.

'I'm joking!'

'Right!' Connie said, giving a nervous laugh.

'Now, come and see the HQ,' Maggie said, opening the door and leading Connie outside.

When they were both in the street, Maggie couldn't help noticing that Connie was peering at her neckline.

'What's wrong?' Maggie asked.

Connie frowned. 'I think your jumper's on back to front.'

Chapter Eight

Maggie Hamill had never felt more important in her life than right there and right then – walking down the main street of Lochnabrae with Connie Gordon by her side. She could hardly believe it and kept taking little sideway glances at her companion just to make sure she wasn't imagining the whole thing.

They walked by a row of white cottages between the bed and breakfast and Maggie's shop and she couldn't help hoping that they wouldn't bump into anyone. Please don't make Mrs Wallace be twitching her curtains now, Maggie begged. Or old Mr Finlay. Not that he'd recognise Connie but that wouldn't stop him waylaying them. If there was one thing old Mr Finlay appreciated, it was a pretty young girl. Maggie shook her head as she thought of the time he'd managed to trap her as she was turning around from the chilled cabinet.

'My my,' he'd said, 'but you're a bonny lass, Maggie Hamill.'

Maggie had tried to move away from him but that would have meant sitting on the pork pies.

No, she thought, she couldn't subject Connie to old Mr Finlay.

Unfortunately, just as Maggie thought they were safe, she heard his front door open.

'Hello there, Maggie!' he called, shaking his walking stick in the air and making his way hastily down the path. He really could move at an alarming speed when he wanted to.

'Hello, Mr Finlay,' Maggie said, with a resolute smile on her face. 'Don't let him near you,' she whispered to Connie.

'What?'

But it was too late to explain because Mr Finlay was upon them.

'Why now,' he said, his thin face creasing into a slavering sort of smile, 'here's a bonny lass I've not had the pleasure of meeting.' And, before Maggie could even introduce them properly, he'd taken one of Connie's hands and had suckered his mouth to it.

'Oh!' Connie exclaimed, doing her best to pull it away but not succeeding. His grip was iron-fast.

'What a soft hand you have and what a lovely wee face. And what might you be doing here in Lochnabrae?'

'Connie's having a holiday,' Maggie explained, 'and we were just about to go out so if you'll excuse us, Mr Finlay.' Maggie grabbed Connie's other arm but Mr Finlay still had hold of her and, for a few seconds, there was a bit of a tug of war until Maggie won with one colossal tug.

'I'll see you again!' Mr Finlay said ominously.

'Quick!' Maggie said. 'Before he follows us into the shop. We'll never get rid of him if he makes it over the threshold.'

Connie allowed Maggie to drag her to safety.

'I'm so sorry about that!' Maggie said once they were

safely behind the locked door of the shop. 'He means well but he can be a wee bit – er – intense at times.'

'Is he always so attentive?' Connie asked, wiping her hand on her jeans.

'Yes. As long as you're female.'

Connie nodded. 'I wish I could say I've never met anyone like that before but the whole of LA is like that.'

Maggie grinned. 'Well, I promise you we're not all cut from the same cloth as Mr Finlay.'

'I'm glad to hear it,' Connie said. 'I don't think I could survive many of those encounters,' she said, rubbing her arms. 'So, this is one of the shops in Lochnabrae?' she said, looking around "Maggie's".

'Er, no,' Maggie said. 'This is the *only* shop in Lochnabrae.'

'No! *Really?*' Connie said.

'Yes, really!'

'How on earth do you survive without – without other shops?'

'What do you mean?'

Connie looked around. 'I mean, how can you live some-where without restaurants and coffee bars and – well, *every-thing* else?'

'Because this is Lochnabrae not Los Angeles,' Maggie said. 'We have to make do.'

'You must do a roaring trade, then.'

'We do when the weather's bad and people can't get to Strathcorrie. Other than that, it's a bit of a struggle. Folks love a bargain and local shops just can't compete with prices.'

'So, Strathcorrie has all the shops and restaurants?'

'I wouldn't say restaurants although the pub there does a nice Sunday lunch.'

'God! Where do you all eat? And what do you all *do* here?'

Maggie laughed. 'We mostly eat at home or in the pub. It's a quiet life, I'll give you that, but most of us are happy with it.'

'And you get by – with your shop, I mean?'

'Things could be worse,' Maggie said. 'Of course, they could be better. The shop was run by my parents and by their parents before that and I'd hate to think of it closing. It's so important to the community – especially for the old folks who can't get out much. We've already lost the post office and the school closed down years ago too. The shop's all we've got now.'

'And the pub?'

'Aye!' Maggie said. 'The pub will be here for ever. As long as there's men to do the drinking, the pub'll be safe. You'll get to see it later. It's a sight to behold,' Maggie said with a laugh.

'Is it near the HQ? You were going to show it to me.'

'Yes, yes!' Maggie said, suddenly wondering what sort of a state the HQ was in. It was fine when it was just herself but was it really fit for the arrival of its queen? 'Can I get you a cup of tea first?' she asked, thinking she could possibly nip into the room first whilst Connie watched the kettle.

'No, thank you,' Connie said.

'I might just make one for myself.'

Maggie led Connie through to the kitchen at the back of the house – a funny pokey room that was in a far worse state than the fan club HQ.

'You'll have to avert your eyes,' Maggie said as she realised that she hadn't done the dishes that morning. Or the ones from the night before. There'd been that really great movie on until late and she'd put off tidying up until the next day. Then there'd been the call from Isla. 'I'm usually very tidy,' she said.

'You don't have to explain,' Connie said. 'I live on my own too and it's easy to be a little sloppy.'

'Sloppy? You?'

'Well, I would be if I got a chance. The trouble is, if I drop something or leave something unwashed, somebody comes along and picks it up or washes it before I've even noticed.'

'Wow! It must be amazing having your own staff. Do you have a lot?'

'I have staff coming out of my ears,' Connie said. 'Drives me crazy. Sometimes, I'd just like the house to myself, you know? It's a bit like living in public at times.'

'Gosh,' Maggie said, trying to imagine what that must be like.

'That's one of the reasons why I've come here,' Connie said. 'I want to try and be – well – *normal* for a while. Find out who I really am without all the trappings of success, you know?'

'No,' Maggie said. 'I mean, I can't imagine what it must be like being you. And I have tried – many times! I read about you in all the papers and magazines and the online reports. I've always thought it must be wonderful. I can't imagine wanting to escape from that sort of life and come to a place like this.'

'Can't you?'

Maggie shook her head. 'It's so – ordinary here. Nothing exciting ever happens. Not unless you count my brother Hamish streaking down the main street once a year on Burns' Night after he's had one too many.'

Connie smiled. 'But you have something else here.'

'What's that?'

'Peace,' Connie said.

'Och, I don't know about that. You should hear the men coming out of The Capercaillie in the evenings. It's not very peaceful then.'

'No, not that kind of peace,' Connie said. 'I mean that sense of place. Of permanence, harmony, nature – that sort of thing. I felt it as soon as I arrived.'

'Aye, we've plenty of nature. You can't move around here for nature.'

'And the lake – I mean loch,' Connie said. 'It's so beautiful.'

Maggie nodded. 'Now, there's a place that's peaceful,' she said. 'You can hear whole conversations people are having on the other side. The sound travels right across the water.'

'Really?'

'Oh, aye,' Maggie said. 'There's no privacy here. My father used to tell a story about a young couple who were dating. It was rumoured that the man was going to propose to his sweetheart one night by the loch so the whole village turned out, watching from the other side and, after he popped the question, a huge cheer went up!'

Connie laughed and then looked out of Maggie's kitchen window. 'Just look at that view. There's something stunning wherever you turn.'

Maggie followed Connie's gaze towards the fells. 'It's not so bad.'

'Not so bad? It's the most beautiful place I've ever seen.'

'You should see the view from the HQ,' Maggie said,

completely forgetting her cup of tea and the mess she was going to try and tidy away before inviting Connie in. 'It's the best view in Lochnabrae. Apart from Alastair's, that is.'

'Alastair?'

'The man whose dog wrecked your trousers.'

'Oh, him.'

'He lives up the hill just outside the village. You can see the whole of the loch from there and the village too and all the mountains. It's amazing – especially when you get those great white clouds reflected in the loch. You'll have to go up there.'

'Will I?'

'Oh, yes! Only make sure you're wearing something dark and dog-proof.'

Maggie led the way upstairs and turned into a bedroom to the right of the landing. 'Here we are,' she said. 'The Connie Gordon Fan Club HQ.'

Connie stood looking dumbfounded and Maggie watched her eyes roving over everything from the magazine clippings on the noticeboard to the movie posters on the walls. There was a shelf filled with Connie's films on DVD and there were framed postcards of the films too. Everywhere she looked, her own face smiled right back at her.

'It must seem a bit strange,' Maggie said. 'It's not all mine, though. The whole fan club collects little bits and pieces. Hamish – that's my brother – he buys the posters from an online site. He just adores your films. He'd love to meet you.'

'You've got an Oscar!' Connie said.

Maggie giggled. 'Well, it's plastic,' she said, picking it up and showing it to Connie. 'We bought it when you were nominated for best actress for *Just Jennifer*. Which you should have won, by the way. You were completely robbed that evening.'

'Completely,' Connie agreed jokingly and then gave a little smile and handed back the plastic Oscar.

'What would you have said?' Maggie asked.

'What?'

'If you'd won the Oscar. What would your speech have been like?'

Connie took a deep breath. 'Well, I'm not sure.'

'You mean you didn't plan one? I thought everyone planned them in case they won and then forgot everything in the excitement of winning.'

Connie shook her head. 'Not me. I really didn't think I'd win so I just went along for an evening out.'

'Oh,' Maggie said, unable to hide her disappointment. 'But, if you had – what would you have said?'

Connie looked thoughtful. 'I'd probably have burst into tears like Gwyneth Paltrow and Halle Berry.'

'No,' Maggie said. 'I think you would've given a beautiful speech. Go on,' she added, handing her the plastic Oscar again, 'give your speech.'

'Maggie – I—'

'Go *on!* Maggie said, a pleading look on her face.

Connie didn't look too happy to be clutching the fake Oscar again and, for a moment, Maggie thought she was going to leg it out of the HQ altogether and never be seen again. Had she pushed things? Was it all a bit daunting for her to be trapped with a nutty fan and asked to give a speech? Maggie was just about to apologise when Connie suddenly started talking.

'I'm determined not to cry tonight because I don't have my waterproof mascara on but I would like to thank all the people who've helped me on my way. First, my mother, who has pushed and pulled me from the age of four, plastering my face with make-up and dragging me to endless classes and auditions even when I wasn't well. Remember when I'd cracked a rib from falling off a horse doing that remake of *Black Beauty*? You thought I was fooling and made me go tap dancing. Luckily, the teacher could see I was in pain and got me to the hospital in time. If it hadn't been for you, Mother, I might've had a slightly more normal upbringing and not be suffering from exhaustion after working tirelessly for so many years. I might also have made a few real friends too. Perhaps even gotten married and had kids. I wasn't really a person to you, was I? I was a commodity. Connie the commodity! To be sold to the highest bidder.

'But it's not just my mother I want to thank. I'd like to thank my agents past and present. The ones who have ripped me off, thinking I'm too thick or too busy to notice, and those who've put me forward for inferior jobs because they'll bring in the big bucks. I'd also like to thank the men in my life – all the slimeballs and the cheats I've had the misfortune of dating. I can safely say that they've behaved even worse than some of my stalkers. At least stalkers usually adhere to their injunctions. And, finally, I'd like to thank my fans. Some of the letters I receive are truly mind-blowing and I'd just like to settle some matters here and now if that's all right. No, I won't drop everything and marry you, Mr Complete Stranger, nor will I send you photographs of myself naked. So, please stop asking me and leave me alone.'

Connie stopped, her face red and her eyes looking slightly glazed. She blinked, as if suddenly remembering where she was.

'Right,' Maggie said, her eyes wide in surprise. 'Well, that was some speech.'

Connie handed back the Oscar. 'Sorry,' she said. 'I'm not sure where all that came from.'

'The very pit of your being, I imagine,' Maggie said. 'Would you like that cup of tea now?'

'I don't suppose you've got a skinny latte?'

Maggie shook her head. 'I'm afraid not. But I make a really good cup of tea.'

Connie nodded and slumped into the chair by the computer.

'Coming right up,' Maggie said, leaving the room and returning downstairs to the kitchen. Once there, she stood staring into space. What had just happened there? A famous Hollywood movie star had just let rip about the whole business, dispelling all the myth and magic. It had been the very last thing Maggie had been expecting. But then, what *had* she expected? She'd never really thought Connie Gordon would turn up in Lochnabrae at all and yet here she was.

'Poor Connie,' Maggie whispered, smiling at the irony of the words. She'd never thought those two words would ever be placed next to one another because not only was Connie one of the highest paid movie stars in Hollywood but she was incredibly lucky too. She was beautiful, intelligent, gifted, and she was happy, wasn't she? All those things made a person happy – that's what everyone believed. Yet there she was up in Connie HQ with a face as dark as December.

'But I can do something about it,' Maggie suddenly said, putting the kettle on and making two cups of tea. 'She came to me. She needs my help.'

Maggie stared into space, thinking about the enormity of her situation. The most beautiful actress in the world was upstairs and needed her help! It was a huge responsibility. Was she up to the challenge? She nodded. Yes, of course she was.

Stirring an extra large spoonful of sugar into her tea and leaving Connie's black and sugarless so she could add whatever she wanted, she returned to Connie HQ upstairs.

'Here we go,' Maggie said, entering the room. 'Two teas.'

Connie was sitting at Maggie's desk, her back to the door.

'You all right?' Maggie asked but Connie didn't answer. Maggie put the two mugs down on the adjacent coffee table and it was then that she saw what Connie was looking at. She'd found the folder.

'Maggie, what are you doing with all these photographs?'

'Oh, they're for the fans.'

'*My* fans?'

'Yes,' Maggie said, nodding. 'Well, I don't get quite as much fan mail as you do.'

Connie didn't laugh. 'My fans write to you here?'

'Yes. The address is on the website – look.' Maggie woke the computer up and found the relevant page. 'The fan site's going from strength to strength. We get so many visitors now and I do my best to keep them coming back with the journal updates.'

Connie began reading the contact page of the website, her face slowly turning to a menacing paleness.

'You charge for the photographs?'

'Yes,' Maggie said. 'Ten pounds. They're beautiful – real value for money – ten by eight glossies. Here,' she said, opening the folder.

'I've seen them.' Connie said, looking at the screen again. 'It says here that they're signed.'

Maggie nodded, biting her lip. She had a feeling she knew what was coming.

Connie turned to face Maggie. 'Would you mind telling me what's going on here?'

'It's the fan club,' Maggie said. 'We send out signed photographs of you to those who ask for them.'

'But who signs them?'

There was a pause before Maggie answered. 'Me,' she said.

Connie's mouth dropped open. 'You? *You* sign the photos – in my name?'

'Yes,' Maggie said. 'I'm very good. Look,' she said, pulling a piece of paper out from a drawer and signing across it with her big black pen before handing it to Connie, who studied it through narrowed eyes.

'Good?' Maggie asked.

Connie looked up. 'You forge my signature?'

'Well, I wouldn't call it forge—'

'And sell these photos – these copyrighted photos – for money?'

'Oh, the money isn't for me!' Maggie said quickly. 'It's for the LADS.'

'What lads?'

'The Lochnabrae Amateur Dramatics Society. We have

a hall – it's really run-down – and the profits from the signed photographs go towards its upkeep.'

Connie slowly shook her head. 'But this is all wrong, Maggie. You can't go on doing this. People think these photos have been signed by me.'

'Isn't my signature good enough? I thought I'd got it about right now.'

'But that isn't the issue here!' Connie said. 'People are paying because they think *I'm* signing the photos.'

'But you're too busy. We didn't want to bother you with them. And I've heard of movie stars' secretaries signing things for them or awful photocopied signatures being sent out too.'

'I'm not arguing with that. That happens a lot but – well – this just doesn't seem right. You've got to see that!'

Maggie looked down at the carpet and shuffled from foot to foot. 'Is your tea all right?'

'Maggie!'

'What?' She looked up. Connie's face had turned quite pink.

'What else has been going on here?'

'What do you mean?'

'Have you been selling other things?'

'Like what?'

'I don't know. Buying knickers and selling them as having been worn by Connie Gordon?'

Maggie looked as if she'd just been punched. 'No! I'd never do anything like that!'

'Are you sure?' Connie got up from the chair and started looking around the room. It was then that her eye caught something and her face instantly froze.

75

'Mortimer!'

'What?' Maggie said.

'What are you doing with Mortimer?'

Maggie turned and saw what Connie was looking at. 'The teddy?'

'Yes! What's it doing here?'

'I bought it online last year. The seller said you'd auctioned it for charity and they'd bought it.'

Connie's face now changed from pink to a frightening shade of red. 'That's a lie!' she said, crossing the room and grabbing the stuffed toy from the shelf. 'I never sold this bear. It's a childhood toy and it went missing two years ago along with other personal items. I was suspicious of my housemaid and fired her. Things stopped going missing after that.'

'Oh, Connie! I'm so sorry. I had no idea.'

'Really?'

'I'd never have bought it if I'd known. Or, rather, I'd have bought it to return to you.'

Connie nodded her head vigorously but she didn't look as if she believed Maggie. 'Sure you're not going to sell it on yourself?'

'What? No!'

'God almighty!' Connie exclaimed. 'I've flown all this way to try and escape this sort of thing.'

'But I didn't know he'd been stolen.'

Connie wasn't listening. She'd made up her mind.

'I can see now,' she said, 'that everyone's the same. Everyone's just out to get a piece of me.'

'Connie!' Maggie called in desperation as she left the room, teddy in hand, and thumped down the stairs. 'Don't go! *Please!*'

But it was too late. Connie left the shop, slamming the door behind her.

'Oh, dear!' Maggie said. 'That didn't go quite like I'd imagined it would.'

Chapter Nine

Connie marched back to the bed and breakfast, Mortimer clutched in her right hand. It had been the very last thing she'd expected to find in Lochnabrae – dear sweet Mortimer – the one remnant of a childhood that had lasted so brief a time.

For a moment, she thought about how lonely her childhood had been. She'd hardly ever met any other children because she'd been working most of the time. In fact, the only other children she'd met had been other child actors and, when they hadn't been acting, they'd been spending time with their tutors on the set, desperately trying to cram in schoolwork between takes. It had been a sad and strange time and Mortimer the bear had had more than his fair share of tears showered upon him.

She looked down at the yellow face of the bear and sighed at the scuffed black eyes and the fraying ears. He wasn't much of a bear, she thought, and she was bemused that anyone would seriously want to pay good money for him at an online auction but, then again, stranger things had happened. One of her actor friends had heard of a yoghurt pot that had been taken out of his trash can and sold. Fans were a bizarre breed.

Reaching the bed and breakfast, Connie did her best to pull herself together. The last thing she wanted was to attract the attention of Isla. She couldn't face that now so she opened and shut the front door as quietly as she could and was just about to make her way to her bedroom when a heavily-powdered face peered around the kitchen door.

'Is that you, Connie dear? Can I get you anything?'

'No, thank you. I'm just going up to my room. I have a bit of a headache.'

'Oh, dear! Let me get you—'

'No! Really. I don't need anything. I just need some space, okay?' Connie said, racing up the stairs and slamming her bedroom door. So much for sneaking in and acting normal, she thought, berating herself for her hot temper.

Connie sat down on the end of the bed, her hands holding onto Mortimer as if her life depended on it. 'What are we doing here, Morty? We don't belong here, do we?'

The worn glass eyes looked back up at her questioningly. And then she realised that *she'd* just stolen the poor bear. Whatever way she looked at it, Maggie had paid for Mortimer – whether it had been innocent or calculating – and Connie supposed it was only fair that she reimbursed her.

'What a mess!' she said, placing Mortimer on the bed. She walked across to the window and gazed out at the loch. She'd come here to escape and she couldn't help feeling frustrated and disappointed that things weren't panning out as she'd imagined. She tried to think back to what she'd expected when leaving LA for Lochnabrae. Peace. Well, it was certainly peaceful here. Solitude. Not as long as Isla Stuart and Maggie Hamill were on the scene. Escape.

Connie thought about that word. Was it ever possible to

truly escape? Maybe for some people. Perhaps just driving away from home without a mobile phone was enough for some people to escape; they could become who they wanted. They could leave their old identities behind them but it was different for Connie. No matter where she went, she'd always be Connie Gordon, movie star, and somebody would always expect something from her.

But you've come to your fan club! a little voice told her. *You couldn't expect them to treat you like a normal person.*

For a moment, she thought of Maggie's face when she'd first met her. Her eyes had had that peculiar dazed expression that Connie was quite used to seeing. She'd seen it on a thousand red carpets when fans jostled for attention.

'What's so special about me?' Connie asked her reflection. 'I'm not so different – not really. I want to be accepted for who I am, not the movies I make. That's not me. Well, not *all* of me.'

But there was a little niggling doubt in her mind that told her there might not be anything else. Who was Connie Gordon *really*? Once you stripped away the movie star hair-do, make-up and wardrobe, once you took her off the red carpets and film sets – what was left? That was the question that had taken Connie from Hollywood to the Highlands.

'But I'm so scared of what the answer might be.'

Taking a deep breath, she grabbed a coat from the wardrobe and went downstairs.

'You all right?' Isla called from the front room.

'I'm going out,' Connie shouted back.

'You know where you're going, do you?'

'There's only one goddamn road here, right?' she mumbled just out of earshot, slamming the front door and making a row of pottery Highland terriers jump on their little shelf.

Maggie couldn't quite believe what had happened. She thought about following Connie after she'd left the shop but saw that it would probably do more damage than anything else. So she'd returned upstairs to the HQ.

'I've blown it,' Maggie said to herself. 'And everyone's going to hate me when they find out.' Maggie had visions of Connie flying out on the first plane back to LA and then she'd have to explain to the fan club that they'd missed out on meeting their great idol because she'd screwed up big time. Unless . . .

Only she and Isla knew that Connie was in Lochnabrae. Oh, and old Mr Finlay. And Alastair. Maggie sighed. Mr Finlay hadn't even recognised her and he wasn't much of a gossip, and Alastair could be persuaded to keep quiet. He'd do anything for a quiet life. Isla too. Although she'd probably be tempted to rename the bed and breakfast, *Connie's Rest* at first.

Sitting down at her desk, Maggie sighed in frustration. She should have tidied things up before Connie had set foot in the HQ. But it was all very well being wise after the event. She hadn't known Connie would object so wholeheartedly to having those photographs signed in her name. It seemed an innocent enough thing to Maggie. She was proud of her ability to forge the signatures and they gave so much pleasure to the fans. Yet, in her heart of hearts, she knew it was wrong. She knew that she'd been more focussed on raising money for the Lochnabrae Amateur Dramatics Society than she had on any moral issues, and she'd also let her own vanity come before her better judgement. The truth was, she'd liked pretending to be Connie Gordon when she signed the pictures. It allowed the little film star that was buried deep inside plain old Maggie Hamill to have a life, and goodness only knew that she needed one even if it was fake.

It hadn't been easy growing up in Lochnabrae. There were only a handful of people her own age and most of them had left now. Even her brother was spending less and less time there and who could blame him? It was the back of beyond – the middle of nowhere. It was Lochnabrae.

Lochnabrae – you'd be mad to stay.

That's what she and Hamish used to chant as they'd plan their getaways as they'd been growing up.

'I'm going to be a footballer for Rangers,' Hamish would say.

'I'm going to be a film star in Hollywood,' Maggie would say.

But Hamish was working in the garage in Strathcorrie and Maggie had taken up the reins of the family store.

'I'm officially mad,' she said to herself, burying her head in her hands.

No, the Connie Fan Club was a bright beacon in her day-to-day existence. It was a beautiful escape from her world of tins and tobacco, it was a wondrous world away from her papers and postcards. Could anyone really blame her for being swept up in it all or looking forward to the latest news from Hollywood, for the buzz she got from discovering a new photograph of Connie on the internet, or the news that she had a new film in the pipeline? It was what got her through the daily grind. Life in the shop was bearable when she knew she could escape upstairs and bring out the glossy ten by eights of Connie. Mr Finlay's amorous attentions could be forgotten and Mrs Wallace's grumblings could be ignored.

It wasn't that Maggie really harboured any plans to leave Lochnabrae – it was just that she couldn't help wishing that some of the magic of the movies would find its way to her little village and make life a little bit more exciting.

When Maggie finally looked up, she saw Connie's untouched cup of tea on her desk. It was the saddest thing she'd ever seen: untouched, unwanted, left to go cold. It just reminded Maggie that she was unworthy. Connie not only didn't want to stay and get to know her but she hated her too. She'd never want to see her again, would she?

Maggie thought about the teddy bear.

'What on earth must Connie think of me?' she whispered. 'She'll probably have me arrested.'

Maggie could easily have spent the rest of the day moping in Connie HQ but the phone was ringing. Reluctantly, she got up to answer it. It was probably the police ringing with some kind of harassment charge.

'Maggie, it's Isla. What on earth did you do to Connie? She's just stormed out without so much as a by your leave.'

'I didn't do anything!' Maggie said.

'Are you sure? You were the last person she saw.'

Maggie sighed. It was time to confess. 'Well, she found out about the fan club – the photos I sign.'

'Ah!' Isla sighed down the phone. 'And she wasn't too pleased?'

'You could say that,' Maggie said. 'Oh, what are we going to do?'

'What do you mean? You think she might leave?'

'She wasn't happy – that's for certain,' Maggie said. 'I

can't bear the thought of having upset her. I'd never do anything to hurt her and yet I managed to do just that within a few minutes of meeting her.'

'I'm sure it's not as bad as you're making out,' Isla said.

'Are you? Are you really?'

'Well, no,' Isla said.

Maggie's shoulders slumped. 'She hates me. I know she does.'

'But can't you explain things to her?'

'I tried. I told her about the LADS but she didn't seem to want to listen.'

'Perhaps she should meet them, then,' Isla said.

'Meet who?'

'The LADS, of course! Get everyone together – down The Capercaillie – and I bet you anything she'll love them. Who wouldn't?'

'Oh, I don't know,' Maggie said. 'I think I might have put her off fans for life.'

'What have you got to lose? If she already hates you, what does it matter if she hates the rest of us too?'

Maggie frowned. She wasn't sure she was following Isla's logic.

'I suppose it might be worth a go,' Maggie said, 'if she hasn't left already, that is.'

'She's not left properly – just rushed off into the hills. All her stuff's still here. Once she's let off a bit of steam, I'm sure she'll be ready to talk to you again.'

'Really? You think so?' There was a pause. 'Isla?'

'Well,' Isla said, 'you can give it a go, anyway.'

Maggie hung up. She didn't feel reassured in the least.

Alastair was actually having a good morning. He'd written

five pages of – well, something – and his fingers didn't seem to want to stop. Okay, it wasn't perfect and it definitely wasn't a play and he knew he was going to have to go back and revise but, for the time being, he was happy with the way things were progressing and, whenever that rare moment dawned, it was almost always interrupted by the telephone.

'Damn!' Alastair yelled. He wished he was one of those writers who could ignore the demands of the world around him. He had a friend who could write through an earthquake but Alastair wasn't like that.

'Hello!' he barked into the phone.

'Alastair? It's Maggie. Did I disturb you?'

'Yes, Maggie. You did, as a matter of fact.'

'Oh,' she said, instantly making him feel guilty.

'What is it?' he said in a gentler voice. 'Everything okay?'

'Well, not everything. You haven't seen Connie, have you?'

'Connie?'

'Connie Gordon's here. Well, she was here but we've lost her.'

'What?'

'The actress. She's here in Lochnabrae.'

'The Hollywood actress?'

'Yes. Look, I'll explain later but I'm worried about her. She's gone missing. Isla said she saw her heading up the hill towards your place.'

'Why would she be coming up here?'

'I don't know – just out walking, I guess. Have you seen her?'

'No. I've been inside working.'

'Well, can you look out of your window?'

'Wait a moment,' Alastair said, annoyed that he'd been

interrupted but intrigued by the possibility that there was a Hollywood actress roaming around. He opened the front door and walked to the end of his garden, peering down the track that led through the woods to the loch but there was nobody there.

He ran back indoors. 'I can't see anyone. Do you want me to take a proper look around?'

'Oh, Alastair – would you? It would be a weight off my mind if I knew she was okay.'

'What's she doing here?'

'Trying to get away from it all but I'm afraid I've not been helping her do that.'

'Well, leave it with me and I'll give you a call if I find her.'

'Thanks, Alastair.'

Alastair put down the phone and sighed. Normally, he hated – *hated* – being interrupted when he was in full flow but he had to admit that this situation was a little out of the ordinary. After all, how often did a Hollywood star hang out at his croft?

And then it dawned on him. They'd already met. Of course! The girl by the loch he'd thought had looked like Connie Gordon *had been* Connie Gordon.

'Oh my God!' he said with a sigh, thinking of the appalling mess Bounce had made of her beautiful trousers – her beautiful movie star trousers. 'Best not tempt fate again,' he said. 'Sorry, Bounce. We'll have a walk later.'

Bounce's head tilted to one side as he watched his master put his coat and boots on but, as he hadn't been given the signal, he remained curled up in a black ball in his basket.

Alastair left his house, not bothering to lock the door – nobody really did in Lochnabrae and he was pretty sure he'd hear Bounce's bark if there were any intruders. He might appear a big softie but he was actually a pretty good guard dog.

He headed down the track towards the loch. The air was wonderfully still. It was the kind of morning that made you want to down tools and head for the hills – to climb right up into the clouds and breathe deep lungfuls of crisp clear air and bathe your skin in the brilliant light. But he couldn't do that today – he was a man on a mission and what a strange mission it was: to find an actress.

As a playwright, Alastair had worked with many actresses in his time and knew that they could be the most highly unpredictable of creatures although he had to admit to being drawn to them in the past. There was something about their passion and drive – their capability to focus so wholeheartedly on a performance and that uncanny ability to inhabit another persona and create magic on the stage. He had to admit that he found those qualities incredibly attractive but there was a downside, of course. At their very worst, actresses could be both egotistical and insecure – not the best of combinations.

Alastair wondered if Connie had these all too familiar traits. He'd seen many of her films. As a resident of Lochnabrae, he was, naturally, a member of the Connie Gordon fan club but, beyond her work, he knew very little about her unlike some of the members who liked to keep up-to-date with the latest Connie gossip.

She's been nominated for an Oscar, he thought to himself. She's best known for her romantic comedies. She once wore a white dress that went practically see-through at an awards ceremony due to some strange new lighting. Yes, Alastair remembered that.

Alastair cleared his throat. He shouldn't be thinking

about such things now. He had to *find* Connie not fantasise about her. She might have twisted her ankle or become lost.

But what exactly was he going to say to her if he did find her and would she want him to say anything at all after their last encounter? If she was all right maybe he could get away without saying anything at all but simply sneak away and tell Maggie that everything was okay. Yes, that would be the ideal, wouldn't it? But that wasn't to be because, as soon as he came out of the woods onto the shore of the loch, he saw her.

She was sitting on a solitary bench. Alastair knew the bench well. It had been placed there by the widow of Hector Campbell, 'Who loved this place above all else'. Alastair would often sit there with a sandwich, walking down from his croft and sitting quietly, his thoughts drifting from subject to subject as the gentle waves of the loch broke upon the sands. Had Connie come here seeking the comfort of Hector's bench too? He watched her for a moment. She sat perfectly still, her face turned away from him, eyes focussed on the silver-blue water before her. At first, he thought she looked peaceful but then her shoulders shook and he realised that she was crying.

He frowned and then took a deep breath, knowing he couldn't leave her crying there on her own.

'Hello, there,' he called softly once he was a few feet away. 'Connie, isn't it?'

Connie turned to face him and he could see that her eyes were red and her pale face was a little blotchy.

'Oh,' she said, wiping her face quickly with the back of her hand, 'it's you.'

'Yep,' Alastair said. 'That's a fact I have to live with every day.'

She stared at him for a minute and then the tiniest of smiles raised her lips. 'That's something we all have to face,' she said quietly.

Alastair dared to step closer. 'All right if I sit here?'

Connie shrugged. 'It's a free country.'

'Oh, no,' Alastair said, sitting down. 'Everything is paid for.'

'What do you mean?'

'Take this view – this seat. A man had to die to enable us to sit here.' Alastair nodded to the brass plaque and Connie turned to look at it, reading the words.

'You knew him?'

'No. Before my time here. But I've heard wonderful stories about him. He could be seen by the loch in all weathers. Didn't matter if it was icy cold or thick fog, you could guarantee that Hector would be pacing the shore.'

'Why? To get away from his wife?'

Alastair shook his head. 'To feel closer to his daughter. She drowned in the loch.'

'Oh!' Connie exclaimed. 'How awful.'

Alastair nodded. 'She was fifteen.'

'What happened?'

'Nobody's sure. She was out swimming on her own and she was a good swimmer too by all accounts. Perhaps she'd been racing and got cramp.'

The two of them looked out across the loch.

'Well, that's ruined the view for me now. I won't be able to enjoy it.'

'But you should,' Alastair said. 'Hector did. He loved this place – I guess he felt close to his daughter here and it's a very good place for being quiet in,' he said. 'A great place for being still and just – well – *being*. Not enough people give into that these days. Everyone's in such a rush. It's one of the reasons I moved here. It's great for a writer. You have time to breathe here. Time to think and turn the thoughts inward.' He paused. 'Sorry,' he added, 'I'm rambling, aren't I?'

'No,' Connie said, 'you're not. It's one of the reasons I came here too – to get away from everything and think.'

Alastair nodded. 'Yes. But you didn't tell me who you were when we met before.'

'Should I have?'

Alastair shrugged. 'Might've been nice.'

'Would you have behaved any differently?'

'No, I don't think so. I would probably still have thought you were incredibly rude.'

Connie's mouth dropped open. '*Me* rude?'

Alastair nodded and Connie continued to stare at him open-mouthed.

'And sad,' he added.

She looked down at the ground. 'I'm not sad.'

'No? Then you're doing a very good impression of a sad person. Oh,' he said, 'I just remembered you're an actress. You're just acting sad in practice for a future role, then?'

Connie stood up abruptly. 'Don't presume to know how I'm feeling,' she said, her eyes flashing. 'It's none of your business.'

'It is when you're being sad in my garden.'

She frowned. 'Oh,' she said. 'I didn't know I was in your garden.'

'Well, not officially, it has to be said,' Alastair said. 'But

I like to think of the whole side of this hill as an extension of my garden. I keep an eye on it, you see.'

'You're not one of these – what do you call them – lords?'

'Lairds?'

'You're not going to have me thrown off your land for trespassing, are you?' she teased.

'No,' he said.

Connie looked at him and then allowed her shoulders to slump.

'You look tired,' Alastair said.

'I am.'

'Why were you crying?'

'Why are you so nosy?'

'I'm not nosy. Well, perhaps I am. I'm a writer. It's kind of an occupational hazard.'

'You're not a journalist, are you?'

'God, no! Whatever gave you that idea?'

'Because I've had that before.'

'What?'

'Someone pretending to be all kind and caring. Asking me how I am and then printing it all in the paper the next day.'

'I'm a playwright,' Alastair said. 'So, are you going to tell me what's wrong?'

'If I do, you'll probably write a play about it.'

'I promise I won't.'

Connie stared at him. Her face had almost returned to its normal colour now, the blotchiness being vanquished by a beautiful paleness.

'I've been horrible to Maggie,' Connie suddenly said. 'You know Maggie?'

'Yes, I know Maggie.'

'Oh God! She's not your sister, is she?'

Alastair grinned. 'No, she's not my sister.'

'Because I know places like this – well – you're all related, aren't you?'

'That is one of the worst generalisations I've heard in a long time,' Alastair said. 'But go on. How were you horrible to her?'

'I found out some things about the fan club that I didn't like and I yelled at her. I made this big speech too. I think I might have shocked her.'

'Oh, dear.'

'Do you think she'll forgive me? She seems like a really sweet girl.'

'She is,' Alastair said. 'Maggie's as sweet as they come.'

'I feel just awful. I've only been here a few hours and already everybody hates me.'

'Not everybody.'

'What do you mean?' Connie asked.

'Well, you've not really met everybody, have you?'

'Who'll want to meet me now?'

'Are you kidding? You've come to the home of your fan club. *Everyone* will want to meet you.'

'Are you sure?'

'Sure I'm sure. And, as luck would have it, there's an official meeting in The Capercaillie tonight.'

'The Caper-what?'

'Capercaillie. It's a kind of Scottish bird. A bit like a turkey but black. It's the local pub and your fan club meets there once a fortnight and tonight's the night.'

Connie didn't respond.

'You'd be very welcome,' Alastair added.

'I don't know.'

'Don't know what?'

'That I should go. To the Caper-what'sit.'

'But you've got to!' Alastair said. 'You can't come all the way to Lochnabrae and not come to a fan club meeting. It would be like—' Alastair paused, 'like flying to the moon with your eyes closed.'

Connie smiled.

'Besides, I'd never hear the end of it if I let you get away. If everyone knew I'd been sitting next to Connie Gordon herself, talking about the fan club, and then not managed to persuade her to come, I'd be driven out of Lochnabrae quicker than you could say *Highland fling*. You wouldn't want that to happen now, would you? Wouldn't want me to be humiliated and embarrassed?'

'You mean like I was before when your dog covered me in muddy paw prints?'

'And he's unutterably sorry about that. He's in the doghouse as we speak. No more bones for a month, I've told him.'

Connie's mouth dropped open. 'You didn't?'

'Well, he certainly knows not to do it again,' Alastair said, 'Probably. You can never be quite sure with Labradors. Selective hearing, you see.'

'Like most men, then?'

Alastair grinned and they were silent for a moment. Alastair was the first to speak.

'You will come, won't you?'

Connie sighed but then a smile slowly spread across her face, lighting her eyes and making them sparkle. 'Okay,' she said. 'I'll come to the Caper-what'sit.'

'Great!' Alastair said. 'I'll see you there, then – eight o'clock?'

Connie nodded and Alastair got up to go. He couldn't wait to tell Maggie the good news and he couldn't help but acknowledge the feeling that he was looking forward to spending more time with Connie himself.

Chapter Ten

Maggie was just stepping out of the shower when she heard the front door of the shop open and close.

'Damn and blast!' she cursed.

It wasn't the first time she'd left it open. There'd been that terrible time when old Mr Finlay had wandered up the stairs and had caught Maggie in her nightdress.

'I just wanted a can of beans,' he'd said.

'Mr Finlay, the shop's been closed for four hours.'

'Och, you wouldna see an old man starve, would you?'

Maggie had had to endure his goggling eyes as she took his money from him and escorted him back down the stairs and out of the shop, locking the door securely behind him.

She hoped it wasn't him now.

'Hello?' she called anxiously, grabbing her dressing gown and wrapping it around her. She looked around the flat for some sort of protection. It wasn't likely to be a burglar, she told herself. They were as rare in Lochnabrae as tower blocks. Still, it was better to be safe than sorry and, grabbing a hardback novel from her bedroom, she inched her way down the stairs.

She could feel her heart thudding in her chest as she reached the squeaky stair that had once given away eight-year-old

Maggie who'd sneaked downstairs in the middle of the night to steal a gobstopper. She'd had her gob stopped all right – when her father had caught her and given her a hiding with his slipper.

Swallowing hard, she gripped her hardback with both hands and turned the corner into the shop, eyes wide, ready to strike.

'Hamish!' she yelled, spotting the scruffily-dressed chap standing in the middle of the shop flicking through a copy of the newspaper *Vive!*

'Hello, sis!'

'You gave me the shock of my life,' she said, lowering her hardback to a less threatening height.

'You really should lock that door, Mags. Any old oddball could be walking around.'

'So I see!'

'Haven't you got a kiss for me, then?'

'Aw, back off,' Maggie said, pushing her oil-stained brother away. 'I've just had a shower.'

'And I've just done a hard day's work. What do you expect me to look like?'

'Cleaner than you do! You've got a shower at the flat, haven't you?'

'That old thing! Have you been in that room lately? There's more mould than wall in there.'

'Then you should get your landlord to do something about it.'

Hamish scoffed and ran a hand over his hair. It was about as short as it could be and made his eyes look huge and cartoon-like.

Maggie shook her head. 'You really should give your hair a chance to grow. Girls don't like short hair like that.'

'Oh, I don't know,' Hamish said. 'I've had a fair few brushing their fingers against this crop.'

Maggie sighed. 'Well, you'd better get changed and spruce yourself up a bit. You've still got some clothes in your old room, haven't you?'

'Gawd, sis, you sound just like Ma. Why would I want to go to all that bother? It's just a night at The Bird.'

'You'll be sorry if you don't,' Maggie said in a sing-song voice.

'I just want to put me feet up for half an hour. Be a love and make us a cuppa.'

Maggie rolled her eyes.

They went through to the kitchen where Hamish read his paper whilst Maggie filled the kettle.

'All right if I stay the night?' Hamish asked over the top of the paper.

Maggie nodded absentmindedly. She was used to her brother's company when he wanted to sink a few pints and not worry about getting back to Strathcorrie. 'Sure.'

'Oh, guess who's back in town?' he said.

'Who?'

'Mikey.'

Maggie stopped stirring sugar into Hamish's mug. 'Michael Shire?'

'Well, of course Michael Shire. And he's crashing at mine. Snores like a pig. I'll be glad of a night's peace and quiet here.'

Maggie sighed, her eyes wide. She wouldn't have cared if Mikey snored like the Loch Ness monster if only he'd crash at her place instead of her brother's.

'He's back from his travels at long last,' Hamish added.

'Where's he been?' Maggie asked, trying not to

sound overly interested as she hung on her brother's every word.

'Everywhere,' Hamish said. 'Hitching and hiking in India, Nepal and China. Arizona. South America too.'

'Wow!' Maggie said.

'He's got the best tan in the world.'

'I bet he has,' Maggie said, thinking of what those strong biker arms would look like bronzed and toned from all that hiking in the sunshine.

Michael Shire.

Handing Hamish his cup of tea, Maggie wandered through to the bathroom to finish drying her hair before it set in a fleecy lump. Closing her eyes, she thought of Michael. *Mikey the Biker*, he was known as because of his obsession with motorbikes. He was always saving up for a new one or tinkering around with an old one until it roared and reared into life, and then you wouldn't see him for dust as he raced around the Highland roads, the wind blowing his hair back in a dark comet's tail. Maggie was always absolutely terrified for him and yet felt exhilarated by his passion too as she imagined him traversing the country on those two powerful wheels. She'd once climbed to the top of Ben Torran to watch him on the roads below. She'd sat down on a slab of granite, the wind turning her cheeks pink, watching the tiny motorbike and its rider below. She remembered feeling as if she were an angel peeping down from the heavens and – oh! – how she'd dreamed of flying down to land on the back of that bike, to wrap her arms around his thick leathered waist and press her face against his broad shoulders. But, even if she had, he wouldn't have noticed. She was just Hamish's little sister.

For Maggie, there had never been anyone else but Mikey.

She'd had her share of boyfriends, of course, from Alexander Brodie – the biggest cheat in Strathcorrie – to handsome Craig MacDonald who'd camped by the shores of the loch one summer, made Maggie fall in love with him and then left without so much as a goodbye.

No, there wasn't a man in the whole of the Highlands who could compare to Mikey. She'd been in love with him for as long as she could remember. It probably dated back to the time when she'd been seven years old. She'd followed Hamish and Mikey into Sandy Macdonald's garden and had watched as the two boys had climbed the old apple tree. It was a favourite hiding place and Maggie had been determined to follow them up there but she'd only made it to the first branch before falling, scraping her knees and hands on the way down. Hamish had shouted at her, knowing that he was going to get the blame from their parents but Mikey had been so sweet and attentive, cleaning up her grazes and drying her tears.

'Are you all right, our Maggie?' he'd said to her, and it was a greeting that he still used to this day.

Looking in the mirror now and catching sight of the tumbling mass of curls, she couldn't really blame him for never getting much beyond that greeting. He always asked after her but that was the beginning and the end of it.

'I look like a sheep. A wild woolly Highland sheep,' she said to herself. 'And he's a panther. A beautiful, sleek, muscular panther.'

She stared at her reflection. There was no way that a woman like her could ever hope of getting a man like Mikey. She'd seen the type of girl he hung out with. Like Miranda from her year at high school. Beautiful, svelte Miranda, with the shoulder-length blonde hair that hung straight and shiny. Or that woman she'd once seen him with at the

Strathcorrie shoe shop. She'd been trying on a pair of impractical red stilettos and Mikey had been helping her to balance as she placed her perfect petite feet into them.

Maggie just wasn't made the same. Her hair would never be straight and shiny and her feet were made for walking boots rather than anything with heels.

Unless . . .

Maggie opened the wardrobe door and her eyes fell upon a row of shoes that lay hidden from the world. They'd belonged to her mother and she had always been far more fashion-conscious than Maggie. There were three pairs of strappy sandals: one in cream, one in tan and one in black with a sweet diamanté clasp. Maggie's hands reached out to the black pair. She was the same shoe size as her mum had been and hadn't been able to bear to part with the shoes when her mum had died. She'd been much too young when she'd died from cancer but had always lived life to the full and the shoes seemed to hold the whole of her mother's personality in them – her frivolity, her joy, her laughter and her passion for living. She might have only ever been a shopkeeper's wife but life had never been dull for Cora Hamill. She'd bagged carrots whilst wearing cashmere, and stacked cans whilst wearing satin. So why shouldn't Maggie – just for one evening?

The next twenty minutes were a whirlwind of activity as Maggie blow-dried and spritzed her hair, sprayed herself with perfume and tried on everything in her wardrobe that was deemed half-decent.

Finally, she placed stockinged feet into the beautiful shoes and took a look at the results in the mirror. The simple black dress with the long sleeves and plunging neckline had the most startling effect on her figure. Normally a jeans and jumper girl, Maggie sometimes forgot that she was a woman in her efforts to keep warm in the Arctic conditions of the shop.

She took a deep breath. She didn't look half-bad, she thought, but then she did something that was pure Maggie. Reaching across to the bed, she pulled a jumper off the duvet and stuck her head into its cosy warmth. There, she thought, that was better. She'd never been one to flash her cleavage around and she couldn't be expected to freeze to death, could she?

Clacking her way back down to the kitchen in her heels, she saw Hamish. He was still reading the paper and was on his second cup of tea.

'I've been thinking,' she said. 'Why don't you give Mikey a ring – invite him to the pub?'

Hamish looked up at her. 'Why?'

'Why not?'

Hamish frowned at her and then his eyes roamed up and down the length of his sister, noticing the peep of dress from below the jumper, and the shoes. 'What're you up to? You don't fancy our Mikey, do you, Mags?'

Maggie could feel herself blushing. 'Of course not,' she said. 'But there's a special guest tonight. He might want to meet her.'

'Really?'

'Yes. Give him a call.'

'Okay,' Hamish said.

For one marvellous moment, Maggie felt elated; she was going to see Mikey – but then she remembered that the special guest was Connie. She'd been delighted when Alastair had called her with the news that Connie would be at the pub that evening but it was hard enough getting

Mikey's attention when she was the only girl in the room and Maggie knew that she didn't stand a chance when competing with Connie Gordon.

The Capercaillie was probably the noisiest pub in the Highlands. Small and imperfectly formed with its low, brow-bashing beams and sloping floor that were the bane of every Friday-night drinker, it was always packed to full capacity.

Connie could hear the noise almost as soon as she left the bed and breakfast, and wondered if it was too late to change her mind.

Don't be silly, she told herself. You've stood in front of vast audiences. You've had your image beamed all around the world and been interviewed by some of the toughest journalists in the business. What's so scary about a little pub?

But she knew what was scary – people. Not just any people either. These were her mother's people and she'd heard stories about them for years.

'They're your true family, Connie,' her mother had once told her. 'They're there for you. They might seem a million miles away but they're there all the same.'

Connie had always been intrigued by that. The family she never knew.

Family. She thought about that word. Her mother might have been born and bred in Lochnabrae but, as far as Connie knew, she didn't have any family there now. Connie's grandparents were long dead and there weren't any uncle or aunty Gordons that she knew of. Her mother had been an only child and yet she'd always thought of the whole of Lochnabrae as her family.

'They're the kind of people who treat you as one of their own,' she'd once explained. 'They look out for you. They care about you.'

'Why did you leave?' Connie once asked her. 'If they all cared about you?'

Connie's mother had looked uneasy at her daughter's question. 'I wanted a change,' she'd said.

Well, Hollywood was certainly a change from the Highlands, Connie thought, as she walked along the edge of the loch by the shores that met the main street. How on earth had she done it, Connie wondered? How could she have left such beauty and tranquillity? But Connie knew why. Vanessa Gordon had been ambitious beyond belief. She'd wanted to be a movie star. The trouble was, she'd left it a bit late. The Lochnabrae Amateur Dramatics Society hadn't been enough to prepare her for the demands of auditions, and six months of door pounding had soon put paid to her dreams. Then she'd become pregnant and never regained the figure that the industry demanded from its young actresses.

'So, I wasn't young any more. I wasn't skinny and I couldn't afford childcare,' she'd once told Connie. That's when she'd started to focus on her daughter, piling all her dreams onto the shoulders of her little girl.

Connie sighed. It hadn't been an easy childhood although she'd loved the acting, singing and dancing classes. They'd been a joy but her mother had always been pushing her. 'Shouldn't she be doing the next grade?' she'd ask her dance teacher or, 'Why doesn't she have more lines in the play?' Push, push, push, *push!*

But, if she hadn't pushed, would Connie have the fame and fortune that she had now? She doubted it. It was the toughest business to get into and you had to have talent oozing out of every pore as well as an enormous amount of luck. Connie doubted she would have got anywhere near her level of fame today if it hadn't been for her mother but the question was, did she want it any more?

She gazed out across the water to the mountains on the other side and thought about her mother. They hadn't spoken for years. After her mother had given what Connie had seen as an inappropriate interview, revealing details about her private life, Connie had erupted and had refused to take her mother's calls. It was just the final insult and, after years of unleashed resentment, Connie had had enough. Her mother had sent letter after letter but Connie had returned them all. It was still a source of constant pain and perhaps it was one of the reasons that had brought her to Lochnabrae. Perhaps this place could help her work out what was important in her life and give her a chance to sort out her problems and make things work.

The light was fading now and the mountains seemed to be cradling Lochnabrae as it prepared for night.

'What is it I think I'll find here?' she asked. There were so many questions to ask and so many answers to find, only there wasn't time just now.

Running her hands through her hair, she wondered if she should have tied it back. Did it look too glamorous loose? She'd washed it and run a comb through it, letting it dry naturally, and it was swinging about her shoulders in the red curtain she was famous for. She'd put the minimum of make-up on too – just enough to stop her frightening the fan club members.

It had taken her an age to choose an outfit. What exactly did one wear to a pub? Connie had never been to a pub before. There were award ceremonies, film premieres and charity lunches, which always demanded dresses and diamonds, but she'd never gone out to something as low-key as this. She looked down at her jeans and pumps. They were all right, weren't they? And her simple white shirt was surely acceptable? There was only one way to find out.

Taking a deep breath, she turned her eyes away from the darkening mountains and strode down the road to The Capercaillie.

Chapter Eleven

Maggie was beside herself with worry. Would Mikey really show up? Hamish had called him and, apparently, he'd said that he was going to join them later so there was no going back now. She tried to remember the last time she'd seen him. It'd been that night in The Capercaillie before Mikey had gone off on his travels over a year ago. The whole of Lochnabrae had turned out that night, all free with the drinks and the advice – even those who'd never travelled further than Strathcorrie High Street.

'Don't go carrying anyone's bag through security. We don't want to see you on one of those *Arrested Abroad* programmes, do we?' Isla told him.

'Don't go wandering off the beaten track,' Old Sandy McDonald had warned him.

'But the whole trip is off the beaten track,' Mikey had said. 'That's the whole point of it.'

'Well, keep your wits about you,' Sandy continued and then he waved Mikey's wallet in the air.

'Hey!' Mikey yelled. 'How'd you get that?'

'I told you – keep your wits about you!' The whole pub had roared with laughter.

He'd barely noticed her that night, Maggie thought, but

she'd been there, waving him off and wishing him well, and thinking about him when he'd gone, wondering where he was and worrying about his safety.

'It's no good!' she told herself as Hamish hollered from the shop for her to get a move on. 'He doesn't even know I'm alive.'

She took one last look at herself in the mirror, flicked back her hair and took a deep breath. Mikey was really the least of her worries tonight. What she should really be worrying about was Connie. Alastair had told her that he'd spoken with Connie and that she'd calmed down and promised to come but that didn't mean she was going to be friendly, did it?

Maggie felt just awful about what had happened at the Connie HQ and she so longed to make things right again. Hadn't they been getting on so well before the fan mail incident? And the website incident? And the teddy bear incident?

Maggie shook her head. It was certainly going to be an interesting night.

Alastair had been standing at the bar when almost the entire population of Lochnabrae descended. This was fatal because he was then obliged to get the drinks in.

'You're a rich writer, aren't you?' Angry Angus had said.

Alastair had spluttered into his pint. It was one of the commonest misconceptions about his job. It always sounded glamorous to say one was a writer. It created an image of style, sophistication and wealth. The truth of the matter was he had threadbare socks and a peephole in his jacket through which his elbow protruded. But he had just received the second part of an advance for a non-fiction title about the theatre and he thought he'd treat himself and his friends before he had to spend it on something sensible like tax.

Fraser behind the bar was just getting the orders in when the door opened and Connie walked inside.

At first, she went unnoticed. Angus was the first to spot her. 'Jaysus Christ Almighty!'

'What?' Alastair turned around and saw Connie standing there in a crisp white shirt and blue jeans, her hair as glossy as a sunlit fox. He swallowed. Hard. She looked beautiful. She wasn't mud-splattered like the first time he'd seen her or red-eyed like the second time. She was beautiful. Unequivocally, unmistakably beautiful.

'Connie?' he said softly, approaching her and leading her into the suffocating warmth of the pub.

'Hi,' she said, her mouth widening into a relieved smile. 'I'm not late, am I?'

'No, no,' Alastair said. 'Can I get you a drink? I think you'll need it.'

She nodded. 'Gin and tonic, thank you,' she said.

It was then that – quite suddenly – silence descended on The Capercaillie.

Alastair saw that everybody was looking at them. Angus had spread the word and they were all now staring at Connie.

'It's Connie!' someone shouted from the back of the pub.

'Connie Gordon!' somebody else shouted.

'She's come home. I always said she would!'

And then a heap of bodies engulfed her. Alastair was pushed out of the way and Connie was completely surrounded.

'I can't believe you're here!' someone said.

'How long're you staying?'

'Are you filming here? Can I be an extra?'

Alastair stood on tiptoe and tried to push his way through the circle of bodies. He could just see Connie. She was beginning to look flustered.

Alastair thought he'd better come to her rescue so he put his fingers in his mouth and whistled.

'Give the little lady some space, guys!' he yelled.

Nobody seemed to take any notice so he whistled again, louder and longer this time.

Everyone turned to face Alastair and Connie grabbed her chance to break free.

'Connie's come to visit us,' Alastair said, 'and she'd love to meet everybody but not all at once!'

There was some laughter.

'Now, I'm just getting her a drink and we'll find ourselves a seat and then I can introduce everyone, okay?'

'Aye, Alastair.'

'Good idea.'

'We'll give you a bit of space.'

'Good,' Alastair said, and got on with the business of getting the drinks in. 'Sorry about that,' he said as he joined Connie at the bar. 'They can be a bit enthusiastic.'

Connie pushed her hair out of her face. 'It's okay. I'm sort of used to that.'

Alastair looked at her. 'How on earth can you get used to that?'

'I don't know,' Connie said. 'It's just part of the territory. It comes with the job. You make movies, you get mobbed.'

'Thank goodness I never wanted to be an actor,'

Alastair said. 'Just look at them. They're all trying to work out where we're going to sit.'

They turned to watch as the people of Lochnabrae hovered between the bar and the tables. Where would Connie sit and who would get the honour of sitting next to her? They all wanted it to be them.

'We'll have to play musical chairs,' Alastair said.

'What's that?'

'It's when you all get up and swap seats. It's a kids' game. It means that everyone'll get their chance to sit by you.'

Connie looked a little uncomfortable at that. 'Right,' she said.

'You okay?' Alastair asked.

Connie took a sip of her drink. 'It's what everyone seems to want, isn't it? A little piece of me. I often wonder why.'

Before Alastair could respond, she'd left the safety of the bar and made her way towards the corner of the pub where nobody had thought to sit. Alastair followed and sat next to her and the table was soon swamped by everybody as they did their best to squash along the bench and pull chairs up. Alastair watched in amusement. He'd never seen anything like it before in his life. Well, apart from that time when old Wallace had won twelve hundred pounds on the lottery and was getting the pints in before his wife got wind of it. But Connie seemed to be coping admirably. Her hazel eyes were bright and her megawatt smile never left her face as she acknowledged everyone around her. If only they were as well-behaved, he thought.

'No need to push!' Alastair yelled above the hub. 'Angus! For pity's sake. Lay off with the elbow.'

'That was my seat. I was sitting there before,' Angus said, his face dour.

'You were not, Angus McCleod,' Mrs Wallace said. 'You were over by the bar when I came in.'

Angus glared at Mrs Wallace but knew better than to give her any cheek.

Sandy Macdonald – who was one of the longest-standing members of the LADS – had managed to squash himself next to Connie and was eyeing her up with enormous satisfaction.

'It's not every day we get a good-looking lass in The Bird,' he said.

'Thanks very much,' Catriona Kendrick said from the other side of the table. She was nineteen and was one of the most valued members of the LADS, as was her sister, Kirsty, who was sitting next to her, watching Connie with undisguised fascination. Both were attractive girls with long blonde hair but – as far as Sandy Macdonald was concerned that night – they were invisible.

There was one other person who'd managed to secure a seat at Connie's table. He had fading red hair, a ruddy complexion that looked as if it had taken the brunt of every winter for fifty years or more, and shoulders that looked capable of tossing any number of cabers. His name was Euan Kennedy and he was the founder of the Connie Gordon Fan Club. If anyone had a right to sit at Connie's table, it was him.

'Right,' Alastair said, clapping his hands together. 'Everyone here?'

'Maggie's not here,' Mrs Wallace said.

'We can't start without Maggie,' Euan said. 'She does all the work for the fan club. We can't start without her.'

'No,' Alastair said, 'quite right. Anyone any idea where she is?'

Everybody looked at each other as if someone else would have the answer.

'Angus,' Alastair said, 'why don't you go and find her?'

'Because I've just got comfy here,' Angus said, obviously not wanting to risk losing his place at the table.

But he needn't have worried because it was then that the pub door opened and in walked Maggie and Hamish.

'Maggie!' Alastair called. 'Over here. Come and see who's here.'

Maggie turned and looked at the figure sitting in the corner of the pub.

'Holy shit!' Hamish yelled. 'It's Connie Gordon.'

'It certainly is,' Euan said, 'and you mind your language around her.'

'Why didn't anyone tell me?' Hamish asked.

'Well, I did try,' Maggie said, a little twinkle in her eye, 'but you wouldn't listen.'

'Alastair,' Connie said, 'why don't you go and get Maggie a drink? Maggie, come and sit here.'

Maggie swallowed.

'Shove up, everyone,' Alastair said as he got up to go to the bar. 'Connie wants to sit next to Maggie and, no doubt, Hamish wants to sit next to her too.' Alastair gave Hamish a wink.

'Now, that's not fair,' Angus said. 'Why should Hamish sit next to Connie when he's late arriving and the rest of us were on time?'

There was a general murmuring of agreement from around the table.

'Perhaps because Connie wants to sit next to him,' Connie

said and, once again, the whole pub fell silent. Connie Gordon had spoken.

There was a sudden shuffling of chairs as everyone made room for Maggie and Hamish to come through.

Alastair grinned as he watched. Connie certainly knew how to get her own way, he thought.

Maggie wasn't quite sure what to say when she sat down next to Connie but, luckily, Connie was the one to speak first.

She leant forward slightly in a conspiratorial way. 'Maggie, I'm so embarrassed about the way I behaved before. Can you ever forgive me?'

Maggie looked at her. '*Me* forgive *you?*'

'Yes,' Connie said. 'I behaved badly. I overreacted and I'm really sorry.'

'But it's *me* who's sorry,' Maggie said. 'I really upset you.'

Connie shook her head. 'I was just a bit – well – surprised by some things. That's all but it's no big deal – really.'

'But the signed photos—'

'Don't worry.'

'And the website pictures.'

'It doesn't matter.'

'And Mortimer.'

Connie smiled. 'You can have him.'

Maggie's eyes widened. 'But he's yours. I've no right to him.'

'You have if I give him to you.'

Maggie didn't know what to say.

'It's my peace offering and I hope you'll accept him. With my love.'

They looked at each other and Maggie couldn't help smiling. 'I'm so sorry I upset you, Connie.'

'Not another word about it. We're friends, aren't we?'

Maggie gasped. 'Yes! Best friends!' And, before she could stop herself, she'd squashed Connie in a bear hug.

Chapter Twelve

When Alastair returned with a cider and a packet of crisps for Maggie and a pint for Hamish, he – predictably – found his seat was gone. Still, determined not to let Connie be swamped by her fans, he thought he'd better take control.

'All right, you lot,' he said, his voice rising above the others' with the ease of somebody who's had to fight their playwright's corner in a thousand theatres, 'let's get this meeting underway. This is a very special meeting of the fan club tonight because, as you can see, Connie Gordon is here in person.'

'Hurray!' Maggie shouted.

Hamish put his fingers in his mouth and whistled.

Euan clapped his great hands together and everybody else followed his example.

'Wait a minute,' Mrs Wallace said, 'I thought it was a LADS meeting tonight.'

'Och, Edna! We've got a Hollywood film star sitting in our midst!' Sandy said. 'And you want to talk about the boring old drama group.'

'I would've thought it was of particular interest to Miss Gordon,' Mrs Wallace said, pushing her great bank of a bosom forward. 'She's an actress, after all. Perhaps she'd be interested.'

Everybody turned to face Connie, who swallowed. 'Well, I – of course—' she began.

'Mrs Wallace has a point,' Alastair interrupted. 'A LADS discussion is long overdue. There's a lot to sort out and I've got a few issues I'd like to raise. Perhaps later in the evening. We don't want to scare Connie off now, do we?'

'That's exactly what I said,' Sandy said, nodding wisely and ignoring Mrs Wallace's bossy bosom that was pointing in his direction.

'Can we ask Connie some questions?' Kirsty piped from across the table.

'Oh, yes!' Catriona said.

'Connie?' Alastair said. 'Would you be up for some questions?'

Connie took a deep breath and Alastair watched as she surveyed the eager faces around her. 'I don't see why not,' she said.

'Good!' Alastair said. 'Who's got a question, then?'

Kirsty leapt in first. 'Why are you here, Connie? Are you filming something? Can I be an extra? I'm a really good actress!'

Connie smiled. 'I'm afraid I'm not filming although it's so beautiful in Lochnabrae, somebody really ought to make a film here.'

'Oh,' Kirsty said, disappointment flooding her face. 'Maybe I could be an extra in one of your films, though? I know! I could go back to Hollywood with you!'

'Kirsty,' Alastair said, 'I don't think the film industry works like that.'

'Oh,' Kirsty said.

'But, if I ever need such a beautiful, talented actress in one of my films, I'll let the director know where to find you,' Connie said.

Kirsty beamed.

'Any more questions?' Alastair asked.

Maggie nodded and raised her hand as if she were back at school. 'What made you want to visit us?'

Connie took a sip of her drink and then put the glass down carefully in front of her, her fingers stroking its smooth sides. 'I think I'm still trying to work that one out.'

'Why now?' Maggie persisted. 'I mean, we've written to you so often over the years – you know – inviting you to come.'

Connie nodded. 'I know,' she said, 'but it's only now that it's registered.'

'What do you mean?' Maggie asked.

Connie shrugged. 'I was looking for an escape. Everything suddenly seemed to be on top of me. I felt like I was suffocating and that was the moment I picked up your latest letter. It was just sitting there waiting for me to read it.'

'It was a sign!' Sandy said.

'Yes,' Connie said. 'I think perhaps it was.'

'Do you miss anything, Connie?' Alastair asked.

Connie looked into the middle distance. 'What, you mean like the LA smog and the early-morning calls and being chased by the paparazzi?'

Everyone laughed.

'I'm trying really hard to think of something I miss but, you know what? I can't. Not a single thing. Apart from a good skinny latte and my pool, maybe. I miss my early morning swim.'

'We've got the loch,' Hamish said and Alastair thought it was said rather too hopefully.

'I'm guessing it's not heated?' Connie said.

For a moment, nobody answered because they weren't sure whether it was a serious question or not but then Connie giggled and everyone followed suit.

'You know,' Connie said, 'you guys are so much nicer than the fans in the US. They're so pushy. I've lost count of the number of times I've had a photo taken with a so-called fan and then they crop it so it looks like we're an item and they sell some outrageous story to the press.'

'We wouldn't do anything like that, Connie!' Maggie said.

'But you did a pretty good job of suffocating her when you saw her a few minutes ago,' Alastair said, still anxious for Connie.

'But it was with the best of intentions,' Maggie said with a grin.

Alastair sighed. 'Any more questions, anyone?' he asked.

'I've got a question,' Angry Angus said, his voice low and monotonous and his eyebrows hovering darkly over his eyes. 'Why haven't you done a western?'

'Oh, Angus!' Maggie said. 'I *knew* you'd ask that!'

'And what's wrong with that? You got to ask your question,' Angus pointed out.

'It's all right,' Connie said. 'In fact, it's a very good question. It's true that I've stuck to genres which are familiar to me but that's not entirely my fault. The public soon builds up a perception about an actor and they come to expect certain things from you. If I did a western, I might disappoint some of those fans.'

'Not me,' Angus said.

'Well, no,' Connie agreed. 'And that's very kind of you. I

actually like variety in my roles. I really don't want to be typecast so perhaps a western would be a good idea.'

'Then you should tell them directors when you get back,' Angus said. 'I can be your agent if you like.'

The whole table laughed at this but Connie smiled politely. 'I'm sure you'd make a very good one.'

'He's certainly bossy enough,' Hamish said.

'You've got to know what you want in this world,' Angus said.

'That's very true,' Connie said.

'And westerns are the thing,' he continued in his monotonous voice. 'Mark my words. They're the future of film.'

Everybody tried to stifle their giggles. They were laughing just as much at his monotonous voice as the sentiment it expressed.

'Well, I think that's quite enough questions for the time being,' Alastair said. 'And you look like you could do with another drink, Connie. Our special guest of honour mustn't go without.' He got up from his chair.

'Oh, you mustn't treat me any differently from any of you guys. I want to be absolutely normal,' she said, her hand diving into Maggie's packet of salt and vinegar crisps as if to prove her point.

'Well,' Alastair said, 'if you want to be treated absolutely normally, you'd better get the next round in.'

'You mean more drinks? Sure!' Connie laughed and got up from her seat. 'You're on.'

Everybody had to get up for Connie to get out from behind the table and Sandy managed a quick squeeze of her arm as she passed.

Alastair accompanied her to the bar.

'How'm I doing?' she asked.

'You're doing fine,' he said.

'Good,' she said with a smile, her eyes sparkling with joy.

'You're not finding it all too much?'

'No, no. It's going okay, isn't it? I mean, I feel like I'm really socialising – with people who aren't journalists and – I don't want to jump the gun here – but I feel like I'm accepted – for who I am.'

'And who are you?'

She grinned. 'Tonight, I'm Connie Gordon – pint buyer and crisp eater.'

Alastair laughed. 'So you are.'

Maggie was watching as Alastair and Connie got the drinks in.

'They seem to be getting on rather well,' Hamish said.

Maggie raised her eyebrows. 'Why shouldn't they? She's an actress and he writes plays. They're bound to have things in common. Why? You jealous?'

Hamish didn't answer but continued looking towards the bar.

'You fancy her, don't you?' Maggie said, suddenly realising that her brother had gone completely doe-eyed. 'Look at me and tell me you don't fancy her!'

Hamish nudged his sister in the ribs. 'Mags, you'd have to be born backwards and blind not to fancy a woman like her. She's gorgeous.'

Maggie sighed and, looking around the table, realised that her brother wasn't the only man whose eyes were fixed on the beauty at the bar. Sandy was practically salivating, which wasn't a nice trait in a man in his seventies. Even Angry Angus's eyes were roving over her and he was famous for being incredibly hard to please when it came to the opposite sex. Maggie couldn't blame them all for staring.

'She is beautiful,' she said, watching the way Connie's glossy red hair moved as she talked animatedly to Alastair. Her face seemed to shine with life. Everything about her was beautiful and shiny: her skin, her eyes, her smile, and Maggie couldn't help but feel a little plain and dull in comparison.

'You all right, Sis?'

Maggie looked at Hamish. 'Yes. I'm fine.'

'Blimey, I'm a right bloody mess, aren't I?'

'Oh, stop fussing. Connie didn't even notice,' Maggie told him.

'No,' Hamish said. 'Someone like her wouldn't ever notice someone like me, would they?'

Maggie sighed and squeezed Hamish's arm. 'You mustn't fall in love with her,' she said. 'She's off limits.'

Hamish frowned at her. 'Why? She's not seeing anyone, is she?'

'Hamish! She's a movie star.'

'So?'

'And you're a – a—'

'What? Say it, Maggie! What am I? A lowly mechanic? You think she won't look at me because I fix cars? Because I don't own a mansion with a pool? Well, maybe she's not as shallow as that. Maybe she's come here to look for a real man – not one of them plastic models you get in Hollywood.'

Hamish got up and pushed his way around the table.

'Hamish!' Maggie called after him but he was out of the pub before she could stop him.

'What's the matter with him?' Angus barked.

'Nothing,' Maggie said but she couldn't help feeling

anxious for her brother because she knew how much unrequited love could hurt and she wouldn't wish that pain on anybody.

Alastair and Connie returned to their seats having distributed all the drinks, and Alastair thought that it was time for his announcement. He'd been thinking about it for the last couple of weeks and felt quite sure he was right. He was the unofficial director of the LADS and, as such, usually got to choose the plays that were performed. For many years now, his own had been chosen but Alastair was rather tired of his own work and wanted to do something different – something that would wake both him and the LADS up.

He thought of the ridicule that had been poured upon him when some of his theatre cronies had found out what he was doing.

'You're leaving the West End for where? Lochnabrae Village Hall?' Laurence Adams of The Countess Theatre had scorned. 'You're pulling my leg, right? I just can't understand why you're giving up directing in London.'

Yes, everyone had laughed. Alastair was obviously losing his grip even to contemplate such a thing but he didn't see it as that at all. As well as finding the peace he so desperately needed to create his work, he found working within a small community deeply rewarding and directing them in their annual play was always a pleasure. Okay, so they weren't professional actors but hadn't he had enough of them? The people of Lochnabrae were raw, they were deeply aggravating at times, especially when they put their favourite soap opera before rehearsals, but they were honest and true. They told him if his dialogue was crap. They let him know if his characters were wooden and unrealistic. You always got the truth out of them and that was rather refreshing. He'd even been inspired to write some really great new plays for them and had tried them out on his new friends before honing his material and sending it to his London agent.

'Right, everyone,' he said. 'I think it's time for some LADS business. Connie – you've heard about LADS? The Lochnabrae Amateur Dramatics Society?'

Connie nodded.

'Well, it's that time of year when we start to think about the Christmas play,' Alastair said, 'and I thought it might be a good idea if we had a change of direction this year.'

'What do you mean?' Sandy asked.

'I mean that I'm not going to write the play for this year.'

'Why not?' Maggie asked.

'Well,' Alastair said, scratching his jaw, 'I haven't got one for a start. And I think we need to branch out – challenge ourselves a bit. All actors need to do that, don't they, Connie?'

'Oh, well, yes,' Connie said.

'That's why you should do a western,' Angus said.

'Angus!' Maggie said in warning, raising a finger lest he should start up again.

'So,' Alastair continued, 'I was thinking about Shakespeare.'

'Shackspeare?' Sandy guffawed.

'Yes. Shakespeare. In the whole history of the LADS, not one Shakespeare play has been performed,' Alastair said.

'And with good reason,' Sandy said. 'They're boring.'

'We do Shakespeare all the time at school,' Kirsty complained.

'*All* the time,' Catriona agreed.

'Then you'll be experts,' Alastair said. 'We'll be needing your expertise.'

'You're pulling our legs,' Mrs Wallace said. 'Shakespeare's not for around these parts.'

'Why not?' Alastair asked.

'Well, it's the language,' Mrs Wallace said. 'It's all *thous* and *thees* and *thines*.'

'That's right,' Alastair said. 'I can see we've got another expert.'

Mrs Wallace's bosom quivered with pleasure at the compliment but the others around the table weren't looking convinced.

'Look,' Alastair said, 'it's nothing to worry about. Sure, it'll be a challenge but where's the joy in something if it's easy?'

'I like easy,' Angus said. 'Easy always works for me.'

'Maggie?' Alastair said. 'What do you think?'

'I don't know,' she said. 'I never really got on with Shakespeare at school.'

'But this isn't school. You won't be reading around the classroom in that god-awful way teachers force upon you. You won't have to write essays about it. You'll just be enjoying telling a story. So it'll be a four-hundred-year-old story – so what? It's stood the test of time – that's the thing with Shakespeare. He's special. He knew what was important: love, ambition, family, faith and he wrote about them with passion and great humour too, using the most beautiful language in the world. It's a language we should celebrate and we can't really call ourselves actors until we've done just that.'

When Alastair finished, a strange silence fell upon The Capercaillie.

'Well, when you put it like that!' Maggie said. 'It sounds rather tempting.'

'I'm glad you think so, Maggie. And Hamish will be taking part, won't he?' Alastair asked, looking for him.

'I'm not sure,' Angus said. 'I mean, most of us struggle enough to remember our lines when it's one of your plays, don't we?'

Alastair nodded. 'I know you think it'll be difficult but that's part of the challenge actors must face.'

'But we're not really actors, now, are we Alastair?' Sandy said.

'Humph! Speak for yourself,' Mrs Wallace said.

'But we're not!' Sandy insisted. 'I can't remember me own telephone number some days let alone a speech by Shackspeare.'

'Then we'll ease you in gradually,' Alastair said. 'I'm not going to give you Hamlet's soliloquies, for goodness' sake. I thought we could do *Twelfth Night*. It's a comedy.'

'Is it funny, then?' Angus asked.

'It's a comedy, Angus,' Alastair repeated.

'I know but some of that so-called comedy don't work now, does it? What them ancient folk thought was funny might not be funny today.'

'It's funny, Angus – believe me. It's got girls dressing up as boys and girls falling in love with the boys who are really girls. It's got mistaken identity and one of the best revenge plots ever.'

'It sounds perverted to me,' Mrs Wallace said. 'Can't we do a nice farce?'

'Oh, gawd blimey no!' Angus said, 'All them slamming doors and fainting women!'

'Or one of those nice Gilbert and Sullivan plays?' Mrs Wallace suggested.

'With singing?' Alastair said. 'Are you sure that's wise?' he said, looking around the table at the LADS present.

'Well, maybe you're right,' Mrs Wallace said. 'But *I've* got a very good voice, I'll have you know.'

'Aye,' Sandy said, 'a fine pair of lungs, I'll warrant ye.' His eyes, which were starting to blur with one Scotch too many, gaped at Mrs Wallace's impressive chest.

'So, what do you all think? Are we on for giving Shakespeare a go?' Alastair asked.

Nobody answered for a moment.

'I am,' Maggie said.

'Good gal, Maggie!' Alastair said. 'I knew I could count on you.'

'And me,' Kirsty said. 'Me and Catriona are in too.'

'Anyone else? I know this is a play where lasses dress as lads but it would be nice to have one or two *real* lads involved.'

'Well then,' Sandy said, 'I dare say I could give it a go.'

'Excellent! And Angus? What do you say?'

Angus cleared his throat. 'I say I'll do it as long as I'm not one of them cross-dressers.'

'You have my word for it,' Alastair said. 'Mrs Wallace, now you'll take a part, won't you? You know how I always value your work as an actress.'

Sandy spluttered into his tumbler but Mrs Wallace chose to ignore him. 'I will bring my own special magic to the Bard,' she said.

'I know you will,' Alastair said. 'And Euan?'

Everyone turned to face Euan Kennedy who'd barely said a word since the arrival of Connie Gordon.

'Aye,' he said softly and slowly. 'I'll play a part.'

Alastair rubbed his hands. 'And Hamish too and Isla. Where's Isla tonight?'

'Oh, she's over in Strathcorrie at Mrs Patterson's,' Maggie said. 'But I'm sure she'll want to be involved.'

'Great,' Alastair said. 'Well, if you can think of anyone else who'd like to be involved – on- or off-stage – let me know. We can always use more people.'

At that, Sandy cleared his throat.

'What?' Alastair asked.

Sandy nodded towards the head of the table and everyone turned to look at Connie who was sitting there, examining her beer mat as if she'd never seen one before in her life.

'Connie!' Angus all but shouted.

'What?' Connie shouted back, shocked into sudden alertness.

'Connie should have a part too!' Maggie said, following the train of thought. 'Oh, you will, won't you, Connie?'

Connie looked completely gobsmacked by the very idea. 'Oh, I couldn't possibly.'

'Why not?' Sandy asked.

'Oh, say yes!' Catriona said. 'It would be amazing. A real Hollywood actress in our play!'

'But I don't know how long I'm staying,' Connie said.

'That doesn't matter, does it? Tell her, Alastair! She *has* to have a part,' Maggie insisted.

'Now, don't go putting pressure on Connie. She's got her own roles to worry about,' Alastair said and there was an anxious expression on his face that hadn't been there a moment ago.

'Go on, Connie, lass!' Sandy said.

'Aye,' Angus said. 'If you're not going to make a western, the least you can do is be in our play.'

'Even if it's just for a wee while,' Maggie said.

'Go on!' Kirsty said. 'Please!'

'Yes, *please*,' Catriona echoed and, suddenly, the whole bar was full of 'go ons' and 'pleases'.

'ALL RIGHT!' Connie suddenly blurted. 'Enough already! I'll be in your play.'

A huge cheer went up in The Capercaillie followed by an ear-splitting whistle from Angus. Everybody was beaming. Connie Gordon – movie star – was going to be in their play. They couldn't have been happier.

Only Alastair and Connie didn't look happy with the arrangement. They both sat in stunned silence, a look of doom hovering over their faces as the rest of the pub went mad with elation.

Chapter Thirteen

Maggie wasn't as elated as she should have been by Connie's acceptance of a role in the forthcoming LADS play. Such news would normally have had her reeling for joy but she had something else on her mind that evening: Michael Shire. Where was he? Maggie looked at her watch. It was half past nine and there was no sign of him. Maybe he wasn't coming or maybe he'd met up with Hamish at the flat.

Everybody at the table was chatting away. Maggie looked at them. They all looked happy and contented. Even Connie was looking relaxed now and was leaning forward on her stool, nodding and smiling with Kirsty and Catriona. But Maggie didn't feel like smiling. At least, she didn't until the door of The Capercaillie opened and in walked Michael Shire.

Maggie gasped. He was just as she remembered him: tall, broad shoulders encased in his leather biker's jacket, and shoulder-length black hair that curled in such a way that made Maggie's fingers itch to twirl it.

Euan was the first – or rather second – to spot him. 'Michael!' he called. 'Get yerself a drink and join us.'

Mikey nodded, casting his eyes around the table.

Maggie caught them and smiled, her face heating up like a furnace.

'Are you all right, our Maggie?' he asked.

She nodded.

'I've got something I want to ask you later,' he said with a wink and then walked across to the bar.

Maggie's heart fluttered like a caged bird's. He wanted to talk to her. He had something to ask her. Perhaps he'd come to his senses at long last. He'd travelled the world and had come back to their little corner of Scotland because he had realised that Maggie was the only woman he wanted. He'd take her hand and lead her out of The Capercaillie into the velvet-soft night. 'Maggie, my Maggie!' he'd whisper, the stubble on his face brushing against her cheek. 'I've waited so long to tell you. I came as quickly as I could. My darling Maggie. How I've longed for this mo—'

'Maggie?' Sandy cried.

'What?' Maggie said, somewhat startled to be dragged out of so sweet a daydream.

'Alastair wants to know if you think Mikey will join the play.'

'I hope so,' Maggie said. 'I mean, I think so.'

'Good!' Alastair said. 'I'll let you ask him, okay?' Alastair said, raising his eyebrows.

'Aye, lass,' Sandy said. 'You ask him.' He gave a lascivious grin that Maggie tried to ignore, but then he did something that Maggie was secretly grateful for: he shuffled up on the seat and beckoned to Mikey who was walking towards the table with his pint. 'Here you are, lad. Park yerself here now.'

'Thanks, Sandy. You all right?'

'Ah, can't complain,' Sandy said. 'My memory's a little shorter and my nose hair's a little longer but I can't complain.'

Mikey laughed as he took the seat that had been Hamish's, his leg brushing Maggie's as he sat down.

At last, he turned to her, a huge smile on his face. 'So, then, Maggie!'

She took a deep breath. 'So, then, Mikey.'

'You're still running the shop, aren't you?'

'I certainly am,' Maggie said, wondering where this might be leading. Perhaps he wanted to move in? Perhaps he wanted Maggie to move out?

'Good, good,' Mikey said, shaking his long hair back over his shoulders. 'Cause there's something I've got to know. You don't still sell them packets of *Taste the Highlands* Shortbread Selection, do you? I've been dreaming about them all the way around the world.'

Maggie's mouth dropped open in befuddlement.

'Shortbread?'

'Aye! *Taste the Highlands*,' Mikey said. 'My favourite. They melt in the mouth. There's nothing comes close. Tell me you still sell them.'

'Aye,' Maggie said, her voice flat and emotionless. 'We still sell them.'

'Oh, Maggie! You're my queen! My empress of the world!' he said. 'Let me buy you a drink. Anything you like.'

'Scotch,' Maggie said. 'Double. Straight.'

Mikey nodded and leapt up from his seat, having no idea how furious Maggie was. He hadn't been thinking about her at all, had he? As he'd hiked through Nepal and trekked through Chile, he hadn't been thinking about her but of *Taste the Highlands* Shortbread Selection.

It was ridiculous. Maggie was now officially jealous of a packet of biscuits.

She didn't spend much longer in the pub after that. For most of the time, Mikey had his back to her as he and Sandy swapped tall stories about women from around the world that went something like this:

'I met this lass in Spain. She had armpits hairier than me but, man, could she kiss!'

'Reminds me of a holiday in Italy when I was seeing two sisters. And their mother.'

'No!'

'Yes. And the grandmother was a looker too.'

Maggie had had enough. She got up and left.

'I'll call around for that shortbread sometime, Mags,' Mikey called after her.

'Bloody shortbread,' Maggie said under her breath. 'Bloody men.' Honestly, why couldn't Mikey be more like a hero from a Connie Gordon film? They didn't go on about shortbread all the time. They were true romantics who knew how to treat a woman.

Maggie sighed in exasperation as she walked back up the main street in the dark. She never bothered with a torch even though there was no street lighting. She knew every step of the way, as did all the locals. Everything was still and silent and there was a cool breeze. She looked out into the great blackness where she knew the loch to be. It was strange to have its presence and that of the mountains even though she couldn't see them. It was like a kind of faith, she thought. *I can't see them but I know they're there and that's a comfort.*

'Far more reliable than any man!' she told the night.

When she got home, Maggie was surprised to discover

that Hamish was in bed. He'd helped himself to some beer from the shop, which, no doubt, Maggie would have to square with the till later.

'Bloody men,' she cursed as she went to her room and took off her jumper.

She looked at her reflection. What a waste of time it had been worrying about her appearance. Mikey wouldn't have noticed if she'd sported prosthetic elfin ears and a fake beard. He was only interested in her for her shortbread.

'Bloody shortbread. Bloody beer. And bloody men!'

Unlike Maggie, Alastair did take a torch out with him on his trips to the pub because his walk home was slightly longer and slightly more precarious. The road was steep and the drop to the right was sheer in some parts. It would take just one fatal footfall and – crash, bang, splash, he'd be 'deed in the loch' as Sandy often warned him. Which was a shame because it meant he had to watch his alcohol consumption. Still, there were compensations to walking, like the fresh night air and the enormous dark sky stuffed with stars and the whole magical peace of it all. He liked turning back to see the lights of the village getting smaller and smaller and to hear the sounds of the pub fading behind him. He felt like a king returning to his castle high up on the hill. Only it was a very small castle – a haggis-sized castle, perhaps – and he liked to whistle as he walked. Tonight, he was whistling 'Long Ago and Far Away' – a song he knew from childhood from the Gene Kelly film, *Cover Girl*, the rhythm in time to his footfall on the road. Why was he singing it? Because Connie Gordon had reminded him of Rita Hayworth – and not just for the obvious reason that her hair was red but she had that luminosity about her, and the way she held herself had reminded him of her too.

Alastair sighed. It was happening again – the pull of the actress. That flirtatious quality they held, that vulnerability. He shook his head. He mustn't think of Connie. He mustn't think of Connie.

'I mustn't think of Connie!' he cried out into the night, startling a nearby sheep. 'Sorry,' he said. But, even though he stopped whistling, the song kept playing in his head, and instead of Rita Hayworth and Gene Kelly dancing, it was Connie Gordon and himself.

Looking up at the Milky Way, he suddenly felt very small. The stars were so beautiful here and yet there was only one star he wanted to see and that was Connie. She'd been so nervous tonight. How could a world-famous actress be nervous about meeting a bunch of Lochnabrae locals, he wondered? But, in a wonderful way, it showed that she was human and everybody had loved her for it. She hadn't lorded her fame over them. She had answered their questions calmly and carefully and had even said she'd join in the play.

Alastair sighed. The play. That was going to be a problem, he just knew it.

Arriving home, he opened the door. 'Hello, Bounce!' he said as the turbo-charged animal crashed into his legs, a tail slapping into him painfully before Bounce rolled over onto his back for tummy-tickling pleasures. Alastair obliged, kneeling down and rubbing the furry belly. 'Why's life so complicated, Bounce?' he asked. 'I came here for uncomplicated things and now this woman – this *actress* turns up!'

Bounce looked up at him, his brown eyes un-comprehending.

'She bothers me,' he continued undeterred. 'She shouldn't be here. What's she doing here?'

Bounce didn't seem to have any ideas. His wasn't a world complicated by human emotions. For him, a walk – perhaps with the added bonus of a swim or at least a paddle – food and a belly rub were as complicated as things got.

Alastair, however, was very complicated. He didn't like to admit it but he had a thing about actresses. They got to him and, as a playwright and director, he'd met his fair share of them. They were a worrying species and part of coming to Lochnabrae had been to escape from all that – from the phone calls at two in the morning when an actress was panicking about her opening night, from tantrums when they thought they knew the character better than the playwright, from fits of jealousy if Alastair dared to praise anybody else on the stage. He had sworn off actresses. When he'd left London and headed north, he'd promised himself that actresses were a thing of the past and, if he was ever going to settle down, it would be with a nice normal girl who didn't scan the papers every day and get all insecure if she didn't rate a mention. No, he wasn't going to get involved with actresses again. Once had been more than enough.

He shook his head. He wasn't going to think about that now. The past was the past and it could jolly well stay there.

Getting up from the floor, Alastair took his coat and shoes off and walked through to the bathroom and turned the shower on. He got undressed, folding his trousers neatly over a chair and putting his laundry into the basket in a careful way that would raise a smile from any woman. Stepping into the shower, he thought about that evening. What would his old friends in London say if he told them he'd got Connie Gordon to star in his next production? He allowed himself a smile but it soon turned to a frown. The truth was, he didn't want her in the play at all. As beautiful and talented as she no doubt was, she was an actress and that meant one thing – trouble.

She'll be back in sunny LA before the first rehearsal, he told himself.

But what if she wasn't? What if she hung around? He'd really have to offer her a role – the LADS would demand it – and he couldn't very well offer her a small part, could he? Imagine how insulting that would be.

'Look, I know you're an Oscar-nominated Hollywood actress and everything but would you mind playing the role of Valentine? You have five lines in scene four.'

But then, if he gave her a main part, that would breed resentment in the others. He'd seen it before. Once a big name became involved, everyone else would feel insecure and tantrums would start.

As he got himself into a physical as well as a mental lather, Alastair couldn't help but realise that, whatever way he looked at it, trouble was just around the corner. He could only hope that Connie's visit to Lochnabrae wouldn't be a long one.

Having returned from her evening in Strathcorrie, Isla was waiting up for Connie when she returned to the B&B.

'You have a nice evening, dear?' she called.

Connie went through to the sitting room. Isla was sitting in front of the TV. There was some film on starring a male-model-turned-actor.

'I turned that role down,' Connie said, sitting down next to Isla.

'Alec Steven's?'

'No!' Connie said. 'The woman's role.'

'Oh,' Isla said. 'Well, I can't say I'm surprised you turned it down. It's the worst thing I've seen in ages.'

'That's what I thought when they sent me the script.'

There was a pause. 'So, did you enjoy your evening at our local?'

Connie nodded.

'And you were made welcome?'

'Oh, yes.'

'And you liked everyone? And everyone liked you?'

Connie took a great breath. 'I think so but it seems so strange that everyone's so friendly. I mean – are they genuinely friendly or are they after something?'

'After something? What do you mean?' Isla asked, looking puzzled.

'I mean, whenever people get close to me, I usually end up getting hurt. People pretend to be my friends and then – sooner or later – they sell me out.'

'You mean to the papers?'

Connie nodded. 'Yes.'

'And you think that's going to happen here? With the people of Lochnabrae?'

'I don't know. How would I know?'

Isla looked genuinely hurt by this. 'Because we all adore you!' she said. 'My goodness! We might not be the sharpest pins in the tin here but we know how to treat people and nobody – I swear *nobody* would ever even think to sell you out!'

Connie could feel herself blushing and felt ashamed for having doubted the people who had so far shown her nothing but kindness. 'I'm sorry, Isla. It's just – well – I'm so used to—'

'You don't have to explain, my dear. I read the papers. I see what goes on.'

They were silent for a moment and then Isla spoke.

'Something else is worrying you, isn't it?'

Connie sat looking down at the swirling carpet before speaking. 'They want me to be in their play.'

'The LADS?'

Connie nodded.

'Well, that's grand. That's really grand,' Isla said. 'Only, will you be around that long? The play's usually on at Christmas.'

'I know,' Connie said.

'But that's not what's bothering you, is it?' Isla said, with the perception of someone who'd seen all sorts of people – and their problems – come and go over the years.

'No,' Connie said, looking up from the carpet. 'It's a play,' she said.

'Aye. It usually is.'

'I mean, I've never done a play. I've only acted in films.'

'Then it'll be a new experience for you,' Isla said but, on seeing Connie's face, she added, 'Oh. Is that not what you want?'

'I don't know what to say to them all,' Connie said. 'They all seemed so *keen.*'

'Aye. The play's the thing,' Isla said. 'Och, listen to me – "the play's the thing", indeed.'

'What?'

'That's Shakespeare. From *Hamlet*, if I remember correctly.'

'And it's Shakespeare they're doing too.'

'Really? Not one of Alastair's plays?'

'No. *Tenth Night.*'

Isla looked puzzled. 'You mean *Twelfth Night*.'

Connie sighed. 'I don't care if it's Tenth or Twelfth, I've never read Shakespeare in my life.'

Isla's eyes widened a fraction. 'Never read—'

'Not a word of it.'

'But you're an actress,' Isla said.

'I know but I'm a *movie* actress. I've never been on a proper stage – only that make-believe one in that film I did when I was a kid.'

'I can't believe you've never done Shakespeare,' Isla said.

'It's never come up,' Connie said. 'My agent tends to steer me towards the popcorn movies. You know, he once told me that I'm not a thinking-man's actress.'

Isla's mouth dropped open. 'He said that?'

Connie nodded. 'I once asked him to look out for a more serious role for me. You know, something a little darker than the usual fluff that comes my way and he said, "Honey, that's real cute of you but stick to the fluff. That's your place".'

Isla looked at Connie. 'But that's – that's – so *rude!*'

Connie resumed staring at the carpet.

'You don't believe him, do you?' Isla suddenly said. 'Connie?'

Connie shrugged. 'I don't know.'

'Because that's not true. You're not just some fluffy actress who can only do the lighter roles. Just look at that thriller you did – *Keep Me Close. That* certainly wasn't light and fluffy. Gave me nightmares for a week after watching it, that one did.'

'Sorry,' Connie said.

'That's all right,' Isla said. 'Anyway, it proves that you're a dead serious actress. And what about *Just Jennifer* and your Oscar nomination? What did that agent of yours have to say about that, then?'

'He said, "Why didn't you win? You're a laughing stock. A complete laughing stock!"'

'He said that?'

Connie nodded. 'And more but I'm not going to repeat it.'

'Why the . . . if he ever crosses my path, I'll have a thing or two to say to him.'

Connie gave a little smile. 'I should leave him.'

'Yes, you should.'

'It's one of the reasons I came here. I was so fed up with the way things were. I mean, I love my work – don't get me wrong – but it's all the stuff that goes with it. Why can't I just be an actress? Why do I have to put up with all the shit that goes with it?' Connie cried. 'Oh, I'm sorry. I didn't mean to swear—'

'It's all right. *Shit* is the only way to describe it,' Isla said, which made Connie smile. 'But don't you see? This is your big opportunity.'

'What do you mean?'

'Didn't you just say you wanted to be an actress – without all the other shit – I mean business?'

'Yes.'

'And here's your chance – with the LADS,' Isla said, getting excited. 'This could be your chance to prove that agent of yours wrong. To prove *everybody* wrong. To do nothing but act.'

'The Shakespeare?'

'Aye! Shakespeare's the test of every good actress and you won't have anyone judging you here.'

'Are you sure?' Connie said. 'They all think I'm marvellous.'

140

'And you are.'

'But what if I let them down? What if I can't do it?'

'My dear, you're failing yerself before you've even begun!' Isla said, picking up Connie's hands and squeezing them tightly. 'Who says you won't be marvellous? Perhaps even the greatest Shakespearean actress there's ever been!'

Connie sighed. She couldn't help feeling swept along by Isla's enthusiasm but she still couldn't banish the terror that appearing on stage held for her. She'd never acted on stage in her life. She'd always managed to avoid it. It was, perhaps, her greatest fear.

Chapter Fourteen

When Maggie got up the next morning, she was half-relieved and yet half-disappointed to discover that Hamish had already left. She hated it when they fought and had hoped that they'd be able to talk things through over breakfast together but that wasn't to be.

'Silly boy,' she whispered. She was worried about him. He was always falling in love – not a bad thing in itself – but he would always pick the most impossible women with whom to do the falling. First, when he was just eight, there'd been the headmistress of their primary school, Miss Dalmeny. He'd written her little love notes and sneaked them into her handbag. The poor woman hadn't known what to do and had informed their father, who'd given poor Hamish a good talking to. School had been a torture for Hamish after that because word had soon got around that he was in love with 'Miss' and the teasing had been unbearable.

Then there'd been Miss Frobisher, the cute art teacher at Strathcorrie High who'd discovered that Hamish's first attempt at a nude sketch struck a frightening resemblance to her. The sketch in question went missing after that but Maggie had her suspicions that nasty Kevin Matthews had stolen it and sold it to the highest bidder.

Now, trouble was brewing with Connie Gordon. How silly could he be to fall in love with a movie star? How did he think that was going to pan out? Did he really think Connie could fall for a mechanic from the back of beyond? Why couldn't Hamish fall in love with someone normal – someone he stood a chance of being able to date – like sweet Kirsty Kendrick who'd had a crush on him for more years than Maggie could remember? But Hamish paid Kirsty about as much attention as Mikey paid Maggie. Wasn't that always the way with love? Love was a cosmic game of cruelty and Cupid's arrows were almost always fired in the wrong direction.

Washing and dressing quickly, Maggie went down to the shop to open up and couldn't help noticing the packets of *Taste the Highlands* shortbread. For a moment, she was tempted to scoop them all up and bin them but that would be wasteful and Maggie was anything but wasteful. So she just stuck her tongue out at them instead.

Connie woke up feeling peculiarly refreshed. She sat up in the double bed and yawned. Looking at the clock on her bedside table, she smiled. It was after eight in the morning. She flopped back down onto her pillow, safe in the knowledge that no personal trainer would be calling today and she didn't have any rehearsals to rush off to or charity events to attend. This, she thought, was bliss. She should have done this months ago – *years* ago. Normal people took holidays.

But you're not a normal person, a little voice told her.

'But I want to be,' she said.

Are you sure? Are you really sure you could step out of the limelight? It's not in your nature to be ignored, the little voice told her.

'I like being ignored fine,' Connie said. 'Besides, I'm hardly being ignored here.'

Connie could have sworn that the little voice sighed then.

And what would you do all day? it asked. *If you stepped out of the limelight, what exactly would you step into?*

'I haven't decided yet,' Connie said. 'Let me enjoy myself.'

You'd be bored rigid in a place like this in no time.

'No, I wouldn't. There's any number of things I could do.'

Like what? What do you think you could do in a dead-end place like Lochnabrae? There isn't even a gym, for goodness' sake. Or a shopping mall. Or – well – anything.

'Shut up!' Connie said, flinging the covers back and getting out of bed to escape the little voice.

It was true, she didn't know what she was going to do in Lochnabrae yet. She didn't know how long she was going to stay or what her plans were for the future. All she knew was that her life had to change. This was more than a little holiday – it was an opportunity to sort herself out and find some space. Decisions had to be made about her future because – right now – she wasn't happy with the way things were.

Connie groaned as she thought about her latest project. It was called *The Pirate's Wife* and was a big-budget piece of tat that her agent had signed her up for without even consulting her, and which she'd gone along with because she owed the producer a favour. She'd almost died when she'd got the script. Full of clichés, it was the worst thing she'd ever seen. An obvious *Pirates of the Caribbean* rip-off, it had stunk. It combined the very worst of several different genres: it was an adventure movie that didn't have any thrills, it was a love story without any romance, and it was a comedy without any laughs. In short, it was the worst movie Connie had ever been associated with and she'd wanted out before it did any long-term damage to her career. Trouble was, she was under contract and there were probably a lot of people chasing her now including her agent, Bob Braskett.

Stepping into the shower, she did her best to wash away all thoughts of Bob Braskett and *The Pirate's Wife*. They were far far away. She had a whole ocean separating her from them and she planned on them staying there.

Blow-drying her hair quickly and applying the lightest make-up, she stood before the wardrobe wondering what to wear. It didn't look so bright out today. The sky was the colour of stainless steel and there were some heavy clouds hovering with intent above the mountains. Connie wasn't used to such a depressing outlook and didn't really have the clothes for it. She'd only brought a collection of dresses, skirts and light jackets that wouldn't stand up to a shower let alone the full onslaught of the Scottish weather. Something would have to be done about that.

Choosing a pair of jeans and a pink and white checked shirt, Connie headed downstairs. Isla had set the table for breakfast and was on hand to make sure Connie had everything she needed.

'How are you, my dear?' she asked as Connie entered the dining room. 'Feeling better after a good night's sleep?'

Connie pulled a chair out at the table and sat down. 'You know, I rather think I am, thank you.'

'Good. And your complexion, if I may say, is looking bonnier than ever. Did you try the Benet's Balm I left for you?'

'Yes,' Connie said. 'Can you tell?'

'Aye. It's given you quite a glow.'

Connie smiled. She'd found a pot of the miraculous Benet's Balm on her dressing table and had smeared her face in its primrose creaminess.

It was then that she noticed the tiny television set on in the corner of the room. It was the news and she blanched as she saw her own image flash up behind the newsreader.

'Well, I never!' Isla declared. 'It's you on the news!' She moved with lightning speed to turn up the volume of the old set.

'Hollywood actress, Connie Gordon, is still missing after walking out on her latest film The Pirate's Wife. *It's been suggested that she had an argument with former lover, actor Forrest Greaves, who is now engaged to former model and actress, Candy Shore. Miss Gordon was last seen at an awards ceremony where she presented an award to Mr Greaves.'*

'Please turn it off, Isla!'

Isla did as she was bidden. 'At least they don't know where you are,' she said.

'Yet,' Connie said. 'They don't know *yet.*'

'Well, you mustn't fret about it. You must enjoy your time here. So, tell me, what might you be doing with yerself today?' Isla asked.

'I was just wondering about that myself,' Connie said. 'I thought I'd call in and see Maggie.' She took a sip of her fruit juice and looked up at Isla. 'I have a feeling that we can help each other.'

'Sounds interesting,' Isla said. 'Be sure to keep me informed with all the gossip now, won't you? We don't get much of it in these parts.'

Connie sighed inwardly. Gossip, she thought, was the very thing she'd come to Lochnabrae to escape.

It was twenty minutes later when Connie stepped outside, a carrier bag swinging by her side. The sky had darkened and now resembled a gigantic bruise. Its darkness was reflected perfectly in the loch and Connie shivered. The mountains no longer looked protective but menacing and there was a bone-chilling wind hurtling along the main street. She hoped it wasn't a bad omen – an omen that the world was closing in on her. The news report had shaken her and she couldn't help feeling fearful that her whereabouts would be discovered sooner rather than later.

She could only hope that Isla was right and that the people of Lochnabrae could be trusted. They'd all been so warm and so welcoming, which was a strange experience for Connie because she had become so used to the bitchiness and backstabbing that went hand in hand with the world she inhabited. People were only friendly when they wanted something from you and it was hard to imagine that anyone could offer friendship for friendship's sake.

Trying to put all thoughts of double-crossers and backstabbers out of her mind, Connie picked up her pace, reaching the shop and opening the door, the little bell announcing her arrival.

'Hello,' she said. 'Shop open?'

Maggie popped up from behind the counter.

'Connie! It's you!'

'Aye. I mean, *yes*. Jeez. If I stay here much longer I'm going to end up sounding like a local.'

Maggie grinned. 'That wouldn't be so bad, would it?'

'It's an occupational hazard. Actresses are pretty good at picking up accents.'

'And the Scottish one would suit you too.'

'You think?' Connie said.

'Aye. You have the look of a Scottish lass.'

'Not surprising really. I mean, my mom's from here. Did you know her?' Connie asked.

'No, I didn't, I'm afraid, she left before my time,' Maggie said, 'but I've heard lots about her. She was an ambitious one, wasn't she? Lochnabrae wasn't for her.'

Connie shook her head. 'She was drawn to the dazzle of Hollywood – as many are. But,' she said with a sigh, 'few make it.'

'*You* made it.'

'Yes,' Connie said. 'But there are many hundreds that didn't because of me.'

'What do you mean?' Maggie asked, putting down her duster.

'The roles I've had,' Connie said, 'I've got them because dozens of other actresses didn't.'

'But that's because you were the best for each role.'

'Was I?'

''Course you were,' Maggie said, moving out from behind the counter. 'You've been perfect in all your roles.'

They were quiet for a moment.

'What is it?' Maggie asked.

'Oh, nothing,' Connie said. 'I'm just having an insecure moment, that's all. Nothing to worry about. I'm just being silly. Anyway, I came to give you this.' She delved into the carrier bag she was holding and brought out a familiar-looking bear.

'Mortimer!' Maggie cried.

'He's yours,' Connie said.

'Really?'

'Truly. I want you to keep him,' Connie said. 'He belongs here – in the HQ.'

Maggie looked deeply touched. 'Are you sure?'

Connie nodded.

'Thank you, Connie! He'll be much loved.'

'I know,' she said. 'Now, that's not the only thing I came in for. I was worried about you last night. You didn't say bye.'

'Sorry,' Maggie said.

'Not anything I said, was it?'

'Oh, no.'

'Then it must have had something to do with the handsome man who arrived late,' Connie said.

Maggie took a deep breath. 'You mean Mikey.'

'You know, he didn't recognise me for the longest time,' Connie said. 'It was rather wonderful.'

'What happened when he did?' Maggie asked.

'Oh, the usual. His mouth dropped open and he asked for my autograph.'

'Did you give it to him?'

'He wanted me to sign his T-shirt.'

'Oh,' Maggie said.

'But I signed his beer mat instead. He's quite the charmer, isn't he?'

'Is he?'

Connie looked at Maggie. 'Oh, don't tell me you haven't noticed.'

Maggie started straightening the newspapers on the counter.

'Maggie?'

149

'What?'

'Is there something I should know?'

'You want a newspaper? The local one's out today.'

'No, I don't want a newspaper,' Connie said, folding her arms. 'Is there something you want to tell me?'

Maggie looked up and her eyes looked as large and as dark as the loch. She looked as if she was about to cry and Connie stepped forward.

'Maggie! What is it? You can tell me. You've read all about my love life, haven't you? I'm sure you know all the gory details.'

Maggie managed a little smile. 'But there's nothing to tell.'

Connie's eyebrows rose a fraction. 'You're not fooling me, Maggie Hamill.'

Maggie turned her head away a little and her fingers started fiddling with the buttons on her brown cardigan. 'What do you want to know?'

'Everything!'

'Everything?' Maggie said. 'That's a lot.'

Connie grinned. 'I never like to do things by halves.'

Maggie walked up to the shop window and looked up and down the road. 'Do you want a cup of tea?' she asked.

Connie nodded. She'd just had breakfast and had never drunk as many cups of tea in her life before but, if tea would pave the way for Maggie's confession, then Connie would drink yet another cup.

They went through to the tiny kitchen at the back of the shop and Maggie made the tea.

'Well, then. The History of Michael Shire,' Maggie said at last. 'Could be a film starring your good self.'

'Then I hope it's a beautiful love story,' Connie said.

'More like a terrible farce,' Maggie said. She sighed. 'He's a friend of my brother's so I've known him all my life. Him and Hamish were always mucking around together. You know – boy stuff. Getting into scraps and scrapes. He was always around here for tea during the holidays and we'd always go off and play together down by the loch.' Maggie paused, her dark eyes seeming to gaze deep into the past as if she were watching herself as a girl playing down by the blue waters. 'I was always just Hamish's kid sister. Scraggy Maggie.'

Connie frowned. 'He called you that?'

'Mikey didn't. Hamish did. But Mikey heard it and that's what I was.'

'I'm sure you were no such thing,' Connie said.

'I know what I am,' Maggie said and her voice sounded so small that it brought tears to Connie's eyes.

'But you're beautiful, Maggie. Just look at you. You have the prettiest hair I've ever seen.'

'You're joking, aren't you?'

'No!' Connie said aghast.

'But I look like a sheep!'

'You do *not* look like a sheep!' Connie said. 'It just needs a little—' she stepped forward and her hands reached out and touched Maggie's hair. It was thick and soft. And thick. Very thick. 'A little *control*,' she said. 'A good cut – a bit of styling and—' Connie ran her fingers through it, 'some special products to make it sleek and shiny.'

'Like yours?'

'If you like.'

'Oh, I do like yours. It's beautiful.'

'But not right for you.'

Maggie self-consciously pushed her hair away from her face.

'And is this the problem with Mikey?' Connie asked.

'What?'

'Low self-esteem?' Connie said. 'Because I know all about that.'

'You do?'

'Of course I do! I'm an actress – it's what we do best! I've already had an episode this morning – about my movie roles.'

'But you've got nothing to be insecure about,' Maggie said.

'And neither have you.'

For a moment, they both just looked at each other and then they burst out laughing.

'Of course we have!' Connie said. 'We're women. Insecurity is a given. It's part of us. In fact, I think insecurity's actually a gene.'

Maggie nodded. 'I wouldn't be surprised.'

'So what are we going to do?' Connie said. 'About Mikey.'

'Do? There's nothing to do,' Maggie said. 'I don't exist.'

'There's always something to be done,' Connie said. 'I know I haven't got a good track record with men and relationships but, if there's one thing I do know, it's how to get their attention in the first place.'

Maggie looked at her quizzically. 'But that's you. I just haven't got it in me.'

'But you could have,' Connie said.

'How?' Maggie asked.

Connie grinned. 'I have an idea. In fact, I've been thinking about it all this morning. How about, I help you get Mikey's attention and you help me with this play.'

152

'Alastair's play? How can I help you with that?'

'Well, you're English – you know Shakespeare,' Connie said.

'I'm Scottish,' Maggie corrected her, 'and I only read half a Shakespeare at school and I didn't understand half of that half.'

Connie waved her hand in the air dismissively. 'At least you're half of a half ahead of me. Now, Alastair said there's a read-through this Friday so we've got to get hold of the play before then. Does he usually give you scripts or what?'

'There are never any funds for that so we've been printing out the plays ourselves,' Maggie said. 'Well, not all of us. Sandy never seems to have one and Angus never remembers to bring his. Alastair usually ends up copying a few for us all.'

'I think we'd better buy the book. Let's get enough for everyone,' Connie said. 'Where's the nearest bookshop?'

'Glasgow,' Maggie said.

'Glasgow?' Connie said in horror. 'There isn't one in Strathcorrie?'

Maggie shook her head.

'Then we'll have to order it online,' Connie said and the two of them ran upstairs and Connie logged on to her favourite bookshop site. 'Mind if I put in your address here?'

'No,' Maggie said.

'I've got an account with them but my LA address won't be any use, will it?'

Maggie watched as Connie's fingers flew across the keyboard.

'Any particular edition?' Connie asked. 'There are hundreds.'

'The cheapest,' Maggie said without a moment's hesitation.

'Oh, come on – I'm buying. Why not this one?' she asked, pointing out a very pretty edition.

Maggie gasped. 'That's so expensive.'

'Nonsense,' Connie said. 'Now, how many copies?'

'There's usually about twelve of us.'

'So fifteen then – to be safe – or in case people lose or forget them one week. And we'd better have express delivery. That'll get them here tomorrow and give us a chance to get a head start.'

'It's very kind of you,' Maggie said.

'I'm just doing my bit to support the local actors. It's the least I can do really when you've all made me so welcome,' Connie said, getting up and stretching her arms. 'Now, how about some real shopping? Some really gorgeous clothes to get you ready for this dating business.'

'But I've got plenty of clothes already,' Maggie protested.

Connie looked at Maggie's attire and wondered how she could be diplomatic about things. 'But are they the *right* clothes?' she asked. 'Take mine, for instance. Hardly suitable for a hike in the hills, are they?'

'You're going hiking?'

'Well, not today, obviously, but after you left last night, Alastair mentioned something about a hike.'

'Oh!' Maggie said, the light dawning on her. 'The spring hike! It's something we do every year – a kind of bonding exercise before we all start rehearsals together.'

'Well, what if I choose you a new dating wardrobe and you help me pick out some hiking gear?'

'I'm afraid I haven't really got anything to spend on clothes.'

'Maggie!' Connie said. 'This'll be my treat.'

'I can't accept—'

'A kind of thank you for running my fan club for all these years.'

'But I thought you didn't like what I was doing.'

Connie sighed. 'I just didn't understand what you were doing, that's all. You've been doing an amazing job, Maggie, and I can't thank you enough.'

'But the fan club's been my pleasure – I love doing it. I can't accept payment for that.'

'Maggie, Maggie!' Connie said with a laugh. 'I have more money than I know what to do with and I never get to treat people. I'm so busy most of the time that I don't even get to treat myself, and designers are constantly giving me gifts for free so there's really no need to spend any money at all. So let me treat you. Let me spoil you just a little bit.'

Maggie stared at her with big wide eyes. 'You want to spoil me?'

'Yes! Yes, I do,' Connie said.

At last, Maggie grinned. 'Okay,' she said.

'Really?'

Maggie nodded. 'Yes, please.'

'Brilliant,' Connie said. 'Let's get going, then.'

Chapter Fifteen

Maggie was going shopping with a movie star. They were only going to make it as far as Strathcorrie but she couldn't name anyone else who'd been shopping in Strathcorrie with Connie Gordon.

'Aren't you worried about being recognised?' Maggie said as she grabbed her old handbag.

'Should I be?'

'Well, you never know who might be there. The local newspaper's based there and there's this horrible reporter – Colin Simpkins. He'd do anything for a story, that one. He went to the same school as me and he's a real creep. I'd hate to see him get hold of you,' Maggie said, feeling suddenly very protective of her ward.

'Oh,' Connie said. 'What do you suggest? Shall I get my sunglasses?'

'Och, no! That'll make you stand out even more,' Maggie said, looking around for inspiration. 'I know,' she said, running through to her bedroom and returning with an oversize cardigan and a woolly hat. 'Try these.'

'Are these yours?'

'Aye. They should fit you no problem. I'm miles bigger than you.'

Connie took the black cardigan and virtually disappeared when she put it on. It was like a big black hole.

'And the hat – tuck your hair up into it and nobody'll recognise you.'

Connie did as she was told and then stood to attention. 'Will I do?'

Maggie looked thoughtful. 'Well, *I* wouldn't stop you for an autograph.'

'Good, let's go then.'

After turning the shop sign to 'closed', they locked up.

'I hope you don't mind my old car,' Maggie said as they walked around the back of the shop. 'I keep meaning to replace it but you know how that story goes. It's a bit of an old banger but it usually makes it to Strathcorrie and back in one piece,' Maggie said.

They both got in and, after three unsuccessful attempts, the car started.

'I bet you've got a lovely car, have you?' Maggie said, pulling out onto the main street and following the loch out of the village.

'Yes,' Connie said.

'What kind?'

'What?'

'What kind of car have you got?'

Connie looked out of her window instead of answering.

'Connie? What is it?'

'It's just—'

'What?'

Connie grimaced. 'I've got five.'

'CARS? You've got FIVE CARS?'

Connie nodded and a faint blush coloured her cheeks. 'It's ridiculous, really. I never even use them. I get cabs everywhere.

To be honest, I don't even know what half of them are. I buy them when I'm bored. Isn't that a terrible confession?'

Maggie's mouth had dropped open. 'A rather *wonderful* confession,' she said. 'I usually buy half a pound of treacle toffees when I'm bored.'

As they headed up the hill out of Lochnabrae, Maggie nodded to the right. 'That's Alastair's,' she said.

Connie leant forward. 'It looks very small.'

'It is. It's an old croft. Barely room to swing a sporran inside but it's easy to keep warm and he only needs a desk and a chair and he's happy.'

'And he was living in London before that?' Connie asked.

'Yes, but he'd had enough. Wanted a bit of peace and quiet.' Maggie suddenly smiled. 'Like you!' she said. 'You've come here to get away from the world too – just like Alastair.'

'But I'm not going to live here,' Connie said, 'and certainly not in a croft.'

'Don't knock it till you try it,' Maggie said. 'They're very cosy. I can't really see why anyone would want anything more.'

'I must seem very spoilt to you, mustn't I?'

'Oh! I didn't mean to say that you were spoilt!' Maggie said in horror. 'I just meant that small is sometimes perfect – less complicated.'

Connie nodded. 'You're right. My life in LA is so complicated. I have everything a girl could want and yet I'm not happy. I thought, if I came here, where things were simple,' Connie said, 'I might be able to sort things out.'

'Is there a lot of sorting to do?' Maggie asked and could immediately feel Connie's eyes upon her. 'I didn't mean to pry. What I mean is, I care about you,' Maggie said, taking a bend in the road a little faster than Connie would have liked, 'and I don't mean to sound all weird and fanatical – because I'm not. Well, maybe I am a little bit but I'd really love to help you – if you need my help, that is.'

There were a few moments of silence.

'I've gone and embarrassed you now, haven't I?' Maggie said.

'No, no you haven't,' Connie assured her. 'It's really sweet of you, Maggie. I don't know what to say. I don't deserve it.'

'Don't deserve it? Are you kidding?' Maggie said. 'You're Connie Gordon. You're amazing! You're beautiful, talented, kind, wonderful – you're the best movie star around today, and you're here. You came to visit us and that means the world to me.'

Connie smiled but she didn't look too certain.

'What's wrong?' Maggie asked. 'You don't believe me? You don't believe you're the best thing to have happened to the silver screen since Marilyn Monroe?'

'Maggie! You heap praises on me that I don't deserve.'

'You *do* deserve them!' Maggie said. 'You're a great actress, Connie.'

'No. Judi Dench is a great actress. Meryl Streep is a great actress.'

'Yes,' Maggie said, 'they are but they're not Connie Gordon. You're a great comedienne, Connie. You should really do more comedies. You don't have an equal.'

'All right! Enough already!' Connie said with a laugh. 'What did I do to deserve you, Maggie?'

'You don't deserve me. You deserve *twenty* of me but I'll have to do for now.'

'Maggie, you mustn't be so – so giving. So trusting. I'll only let you down.'

'No, you won't. You couldn't possibly let me down.'

'But it's too much pressure to put on someone.'

'I see,' Maggie said. 'Well, I didn't mean to do that.'

'I know you didn't,' Connie said quickly. 'It's just – well – I don't want to be a movie star here. I want to be a friend. A normal, everyday friend. I want you to like me for *who* I am not for the films I've made.'

'But I *do* like you for who you are!' Maggie said. 'Truly! You're sweet and kind and—'

Connie raised a hand in protest. 'You don't have to compliment me all the time.'

Maggie looked disappointed for a moment but then she sighed. 'Okay,' she said. 'I get it. I'll treat you like anybody else, right?'

'Yes,' Connie said seriously.

They were silent for a few minutes. Maggie slowed the car down as they descended a steep hill and Connie peered up at the sky.

'Do you think it's going to rain?' she asked.

Maggie peered out of the car window. 'Och, no! Not for hours at least. We should be okay. But we'd better make sure you get a good quality waterproof whilst we're in town. Just in case. And some waterproof mascara whilst we're about it. I wouldn't dare use anything else in the Highlands. Not that *you* need make-up,' she quickly added, 'because you're perfect just the way you are.'

'Maggie!' Connie groaned.

'Sorry!' Maggie said. 'I'll stop flattering you. I promise. You have my *absolute* word!'

Chapter Sixteen

The road climbed higher before descending into Strathcorrie but the visibility was so bad that the views were obscured.

'On a clear day, it's marvellous,' Maggie enthused. 'What a shame we can't see much.'

Just then, a great hulk of a building loomed up at them from out of the rain.

'What's that?' Connie asked.

'Oh, that's Rossburn Castle. It's pretty old. Up for sale now but been empty for years.'

'Is it a ruin?'

'Part of it is,' Maggie said, pointing to the east tower, which was now home to rooks. It was grey, imposing and horribly dilapidated.

'I love it,' Connie said.

'Do you?' Maggie said in surprise. 'I've always found it really spooky.'

'It has a strange beauty about it, don't you think?'

'Strange is the right word for it,' Maggie said. 'When we were little, Hamish and I would cycle up here in the summer holidays and play in the grounds. We used to make up horrible ghost stories because we thought it was haunted. I used to have nightmares about it.'

'And is it?'

'What?'

'Haunted?'

'Oh, I don't think so. Just by a few bats and rooks,' Maggie said.

'It needs a lot of work doing to it, doesn't it?'

'Oh, aye. Whoever buys it will need a spare million.' Maggie suddenly turned around. 'Connie!'

'What?'

'*You* could buy it!'

'Me?'

'Yes! Oh, this is brilliant! It could be your Highland retreat.'

'But there's the B&B. What would I want with a draughty old castle?'

'But you said it was beautiful.'

'Yes, I did.'

'Do you want to look at it?' Maggie asked, her voice filled with excitement. 'I can pull over here. It won't take a minute.'

'Well,' Connie said, 'I suppose it would be interesting. You don't get many ancient castles in Hollywood. Well, not genuine ones anyway.'

Maggie turned down the track that led to the castle. 'Isn't this exciting? I haven't been here for years. I'd forgotten it was so beautiful up here although the weather can be pretty fierce sometimes.'

They'd reached the end of the short track and Maggie parked the car. Getting out, they both stared up at the great grey walls of the castle.

'It's amazing,' Connie said. 'Look at the size of it!' She

craned her neck back and gazed up at the monstrous walls that shot into the sky. 'Why are the windows so small?'

'You wouldn't want large ones with the winds up here,' Maggie told her.

Connie shivered, partly at the thought of the cold castle and partly because the wind was blowing strongly and coldly right now.

'Like it?' Maggie asked.

'I do,' Connie said. 'I really do.'

Maggie grinned. 'The estate agent's in Strathcorrie. We'll be walking right by it.'

'Oh, really?' Connie said.

'Aye,' Maggie replied with a twinkle in her eye.

'I'll bear that in mind, then,' Connie said.

Leaving the castle behind them, they followed the road over the brow of a hill and then descended into a wide valley and Connie got her first glimpse of Strathcorrie.

'That's it,' Maggie said.

'Strathcorrie?'

'The very same,' Maggie nodded. 'You were expecting something bigger, weren't you? Something more along the lines of Glasgow?'

'Well, I—' Connie wasn't sure what she was trying to say. 'It's lovely. Very quaint.'

'Oh, I hate that word – *quaint*. It's what people say when they mean *rubbish*.'

'But I didn't say that,' Connie protested. 'It's just a little smaller than I imagined.'

'You're used to big, aren't you?' Maggie said.

'I am,' Connie said, 'but you keep forgetting that I ran away from big.'

They drove down the hill and entered the town, and Connie got her first proper look at the place.

'Well,' Maggie said, pulling up in the car park outside the town hall, 'this is it.'

Connie looked around. There was only one street and a handful of shops. On one side of the road was a baker's, chemist and a greengrocer's. There was an ugly building that looked like some kind of bank and a prettier building next to it that looked like a newsagent's. On the other side of the road was a hairdresser's, a garage, a butcher's, a tiny shoe shop, a café, a florist's, a boutique, the old cinema, and an outdoor pursuits shop selling everything you needed for surviving the Scottish terrain. Then, there was the all-important pub.

'We're very lucky here,' Maggie said. 'To have all this within driving distance in the Highlands. Some people have to drive for half a day before they get anywhere. Strathcorrie's a godsend, it really is.'

'And where are we heading?'

Maggie nodded to the boutique. '*A Touch of Tartan.* Don't be put off by the name. That's just Enid's little obsession. Virtually every other item is made of tartan. It's for the tourists, really, but mind you don't get sucked in and come out looking like a bagpipe,' Maggie said, leading the way into the shop. 'Enid?' Maggie called as they entered, pushing the wooden door behind them and tinkling the little bell above.

A curly grey head bobbed up from behind the counter.

'Ah, Maggie, dear,' Enid said. 'And how are you?'

'I'm very well, Enid.'

'And you have a friend with you, I see,' Enid said, pushing her glasses up her nose and scrutinising Connie.

'Yes,' Maggie said. 'Con-Constance.'

Connie smiled and nodded. Would her disguise work or would she be discovered?

But Enid merely nodded.

'I have just the thing for you,' she said, bending down behind the counter and bringing out a large grey item.

Maggie took it from her and hugged it to her face. 'Lovely!' she said.

'What is it?' Connie asked, trying to make out if the shapeless item was for wearing or for placing on the floor in lieu of a carpet.

'It's a cardigan,' Maggie said, taking off her coat and brown cardigan and slipping on the grey creation.

'Just your size,' Enid said.

'Yes!' Maggie enthused.

Connie shook her head. 'It's enormous, Maggie!' But Maggie didn't seem to be listening. She was smothering her feminine form in endless folds of unrelenting grey. 'Maggie!' Connie shouted.

Maggie looked up from out of the depths of the woolly garment. 'What?'

'What would Mikey say?' Connie asked.

'What do you mean?'

'If he saw you wearing this?'

'He'd probably say what he usually says,' Maggie said.

'Which is?'

'Nothing at all. He usually just ignores me.'

'Exactly!' Connie said. 'You can't go around dressed like a bag lady if you want to get a man's attention.'

'But you have to keep warm, Connie, and these things last years and years.'

'More's the pity,' Connie said. 'Anyway, there are ways to keep warm in style.'

Both Maggie and Enid looked at her, seemingly stunned by this piece of information.

'Okay,' Connie said. 'Let's try again.'

Reluctantly, Maggie took off the cardigan and handed it back to Enid.

'Will you not be wanting this then, Maggie?'

'Well—' Maggie glanced at Connie.

'No,' Connie said.

'Not today,' Maggie added.

'Not ever,' Connie said. 'Now, let's get to work.'

Connie looked around the shop. There were certainly plenty of tartans from darkest blues, through vibrant greens to shocking scarlets but Connie thought them best avoided. Most of the rest of the stock looked tweedy and old-fashioned.

'Oh, dear,' Connie sighed, and then she spotted some real clothes at the back of the shop. They were the sort of clothes that middle-aged women wore to weddings and dinner parties: frumpy, mumsy and totally uninspiring but, as she rifled through them, she spotted one or two nicely cut pieces in materials that looked promising.

Holding up a dress in a pretty claret colour, Connie turned to Maggie.

'What do you think of this one?' she asked as she held up the dark red dress.

'Isn't it rather – well – boring?' Maggie asked.

'It certainly is but it's a good cut and it has potential and the colour will look good on you, I think.' She held it up to Maggie. 'I'm going to slash the front and show off that great cleavage of yours.'

Maggie gasped.

'And maybe shorten it so we can see your legs.'

166

'My legs?'

'Yes. Those two things that have been hibernating for so long.'

'I don't usually wear skirts or dresses,' Maggie said.

'I know,' Connie said, 'but it's about time you did.'

'They're not really practical in the shop.'

'But you're not always in the shop, are you?' Connie pointed out.

Maggie looked thoughtful. 'I guess not.'

Connie sighed. 'Don't you *want* to look like a woman?'

Maggie's eyebrows shot up into her hairline. 'Aye, I do.'

'Then find me some dresses and skirts that you like. They don't have to be perfect. Just pick the colours and materials you like. I'll do the rest.'

'What do you mean?' Maggie asked.

'Remember my film, *Guinevere*? Well, I spent hours bored out of my mind on that set. There was so much hanging around that I got friendly with one of the costume girls and she taught me a few tricks of the trade. I'm actually quite good with a needle and thread.'

'You mean you're going to cut up these dresses?'

'Cutting up is just the start. I'm going to turn these clothes into something really special. Have you got a sewing machine?'

'No, but Isla has.'

'Good.'

For a moment, Connie could have sworn that Maggie was about to burst into tears.

'You're doing all this for me?'

'Yes, of course.'

'But why?'

'Because I want to.'

Maggie's eyes shimmered with tears and then she launched herself at Connie, squeezing her in a hug the like of which Connie had never experienced before. 'You're the loveliest person I've ever met!'

It was a good half hour before they left the shop. Connie had bought four dresses and three skirts and Enid had been somewhat surprised and delighted at the sales.

'Och well, you two can come again,' she smiled, packing the garments into bags.

As they left the shop, Connie looked up and down the high street. 'Shoes,' she said. 'That's what we need next.'

'I don't really wear shoes,' Maggie said. 'I'm more of a boot kind of girl.'

Connie glanced down at her footwear. 'So you are,' she said, eyeing the manly hiking boots Maggie was sporting. 'But you can't wear those with these dresses, can you?'

They reached the car and dumped the bags they'd managed to gather so far and then headed to the shoe shop.

Like *A Touch of Tartan*, the stock was very limited but they managed to find three pairs of rather beautiful shoes in Maggie's size that would flatter rather than flatten her outfits.

'Now,' Connie said, 'what kind of accessories do you have?'

Maggie frowned. 'I've got a watch. It's got a compass and you can dunk it underwater and everything.'

Connie shook her head. 'A watch isn't an accessory. Well, not unless it's a Cartier or something.'

'I don't know what it is,' Maggie said. 'It was Hamish's.'

'Then I very much doubt it's elegant,' Connie said. 'We need proper accessories. Handbags, jewellery – that sort of thing.' She looked up and down the high street.

'Mrs Brodie at the chemist sells a few bits of jewellery,' Maggie said. 'But it's really for the bairns.'

Connie screwed up her nose. 'Maybe we could try online again. I know the most perfect site for jewellery.'

The sky had darkened since they'd been in the shop and the air had cooled dramatically.

'Come on,' Maggie said. 'My turn to help you shop now.'

Connie, who was still wearing her baggy Maggie disguise, pulled down her woolly hat and followed Maggie to the outdoor shop across the road. It was larger than the boutique and filled with all manner of strange things that Connie had never had reason to buy before – like ropes and rucksacks, boots and breathable jackets.

Like Enid in the boutique, the man behind the counter didn't pay very much attention to Connie. She was just another tourist who had been stupid enough to arrive in the Highlands without so much as a woolly hat.

'You have to respect the hills,' Maggie told her, 'and you can't do that in designer labels – not your kind of designer labels anyway. As beautiful as they are, they're not going to keep you warm.'

She soon had Connie fitted out with the very best of coats, jumpers, rucksacks and walking boots all in varying shades of grass, mud and rock. On top of that was a neat pair of walking trousers, a warm pair of gloves and a woolly hat of her very own.

'There!' Maggie said with great joy. 'You've dressed me and I've dressed you. You're gonna look great on that hike.'

As they left the shop, the first fat raindrops fell from the sky. They ran back towards the car, squealing as the rain became heavier.

'I should have put that jacket on straightaway!' Connie

yelled as they got into the car, squashing their bags on the back seat.

Maggie started the engine and had just pulled out onto the high street when she sounded her horn. Connie watched as she pulled over at the bus stop.

'Euan!' Maggie called as she wound her window down, and Connie recognised the gentleman from the pub. He'd been the least talkative one who had sat in the corner watching her all evening. Connie was used to being watched by men – the leers, the smirks and the smiles – they were all part of being who she was but this man had looked at her differently, as if he was trying to work her out. It had been strange and perplexing and Connie couldn't help but feel a little anxious in his presence.

Chapter Seventeen

'Would you like a lift?' Maggie called, wincing as the rain found its way in through the window.

'You're going to Lochnabrae?' Euan called back.

'Where else would I be going? Get in. Unless you prefer the bus,' Maggie teased.

Euan shook his head. 'That ole rattletrap! You must be joking. I only use it when I have to. My car's being serviced by your Hamish.' He opened the car door and got in. 'Connie!' he suddenly cried. 'I didn't see you there.'

'Hello,' she said.

He nodded and, as he settled, Maggie and Connie felt the car sink beneath the weight of their new passenger.

'Is there enough room there, Euan? Sorry about all the bags. We've been shopping,' Maggie said unnecessarily. 'Connie's a bad influence on me. She's trying to turn me into a shopaholic and I might be coming round to the idea.'

'Good,' Connie said, 'because we're going to do some more online when we get home.'

'*If* we get home,' Euan said from the back seat. 'I don't know how you put up with this car, Maggie,' he said as it started to stutter.

'Och, there's nothin' wrong with it.'

'Nothing that a crusher couldn't fix.'

Maggie glared at him through the rear-view mirror.

'Can you no' get a good deal from your brother's garage?'

'You're kiddin', aren't you? There's nothing I can afford there.'

But Euan's misgivings about Maggie's car weren't completely unfounded as they took the hill after Rossburn Castle and the car went into serious splutter mode.

'What's wrong?' Connie asked.

'I'm not sure,' Maggie said. 'Nothing probably.'

'You'd better pull over,' Euan advised.

'You want to get home, don't you?'

'I want to get home in one piece,' Euan said.

By now, the road to Lochnabrae had turned into a river and Maggie – although refusing to stop completely – slowed the car down.

'This is terrible,' Connie said.

'Och, it's just a wee shower,' Maggie said.

The sky had darkened to a slate-grey and seemed to be about to crush the earth at any moment.

'Maggie, stop the car!' Euan barked from the back seat.

A screech of brakes and a dramatic swerve and they were safely at the side of the road, the rain hammering down on the roof.

'We could've made it, you know,' Maggie said quietly.

'So, what do we do now?' Connie asked. 'Wait for the bus?'

'I think you two should stay here,' Maggie said. 'It's just a wee walk to Alastair's. He's got a Landy that'll see us safely home.'

'You'll get soaked to the skin, Maggie,' Connie said.

'I've got my boots and coat. It's no' so bad.'

Before Connie could protest further, Maggie had launched herself into the vile weather and disappeared into the white curtain of rain.

It was just Connie and Euan now and, for some inexplicable reason, Connie felt nervous. She sat looking down at her hands, which looked pale and felt colder than they'd ever felt in her life. She rubbed them together in an attempt to warm them up.

'You cold, lass?'

Connie nodded and turned a little to face Euan.

'Here,' he said, reaching into his pocket and passing her a pair of enormous gloves.

'Thanks,' she said. 'I've just bought a pair of my own but I'm not sure where they are.' She put on the gloves and they felt wonderfully soft and warm as she stuffed her hands into their voluminous depths. 'Won't you be cold?'

Euan shook his head. 'You get used to the weather up here. This is mild,' he said. 'You should stay for the winter.'

'What's it like?'

'A wee bit colder than it is now,' Euan said.

Connie smiled. She liked the way that everyone always understated everything. It was always a 'wee' this or a 'wee' that. It was the complete antithesis of LA where everything was always blown out of all proportion.

'So,' Euan said from the back seat, 'how are you finding life here?'

Connie turned around again, her gloved hands now warm in her lap. 'I'm liking it, very much.'

Euan nodded, as if he expected nothing less. 'It doesn't suit everyone,' he said. 'I've seen a fair few come and go in my time.'

'But you've stayed.'

'Oh, aye. Nowhere else for me to go.'

'What do you do? If you don't mind me asking.'

He shook his head. 'I'm head ranger over at the Craigross estate.'

'Oh,' Connie said. 'And that's an outdoor job, right?'

Euan nodded. 'I couldn't be sat behind a desk all day.'

'Me neither,' Connie said. 'I'd hate that.'

They were quiet for a moment with just the noise of the rain on the car roof.

'And you've always worked there?' Connie asked at last.

'Aye, and my father before me and his before him.'

'Wow,' Connie said. 'I like that. I like the continuity.'

'It's what places like this are all about.'

Connie nodded. 'I'm beginning to see that.' She unclipped her seat belt and turned to face him properly and that's when she saw it – the newspaper and one dreaded word in the headline: *Connie.*

Euan immediately saw where she was looking. 'Ah,' he said, 'I wasn't sure you'd want to see this. I bought it for the archives. I keep all the clippings, you see.'

Connie looked at him. 'Can I see it?'

Euan held her gaze and then took the paper out of the carrier bag and handed it to Connie.

It was *Vive!*, one of the more tacky tabloids. Even in the US, Connie was aware of it because she'd had run-ins with *Vive!* before. Like the time she had been filming *Guinevere* in Cornwall and had been snapped by one of their photographers when she'd walked out of the woods with her skirts hitched up around her waist.

'*Connie Caught Short*' the headline had read, which had been a load of nonsense. She'd actually twisted her ankle when she'd fallen due to the ridiculous length of her costume. So, she wasn't exactly looking forward to the latest headline. She took a deep breath and unfolded the newspaper.

Connie – Missing!

Well, she thought, that was pretty restrained stuff for *Vive!* but it was still infuriating.

She sighed. 'I thought I'd get more time before I became a missing person.'

'But at least they don't know where you are,' Euan said.

'Good,' Connie said, scanning the piece quickly and grimacing when she saw the photo they'd used. It had been taken by paparazzi whilst she'd been on a morning run with her trainer. Her hair was pulled back and she wasn't wearing a scrap of make-up. She was also wiping her brow after a particularly hard session involving squats. The caption underneath read: *Under pressure.*

'Bastards,' she said and then caught Euan's eye. 'Sorry.'

'No need to apologise, lass.'

'Those paps are like hyenas – they wait for you to be at your weakest and then they strike.'

There was a sudden roll of thunder that made Connie jump. She liked storms about as much as she liked the paparazzi.

'How long do you think Maggie will be?'

'Not long,' Euan said.

Connie returned to the article to try and take her mind off the storm.

Oscar-nominated Hollywood actress, Connie Gordon, has gone missing after she walked off the set of her latest film, The Pirate's Wife, *following a huge argument with its director.*

'Liars!' Connie said. 'Have you read this?'

'Well, I tried not to. It's all lies.'

'Yet still they print it. God! It makes me so mad! Look!' Connie said, reading on.

Gordon, who recently broke up with long-term boyfriend, Forrest Greaves, is thought to be mending a broken heart in her hideaway home in Malibu.

'It's rubbish! Why do they do that?'

'Ah, lass, you mustn't let it get to you.'

'It's hard not to sometimes,' Connie said, throwing the paper back at Euan. 'It's pretty much constant, you see. It's easy to ignore one or two stories from time to time but they come thick and fast and there's never any truth in them.'

'They're not interested in the truth. They're interested in sales.'

'But it's impossible to ignore when even your own mother sides with the press.'

'What do you mean?' Euan asked, concern in his voice.

'I mean, she talks to the journalists and tells them all sorts of things about my life.'

'How do you know?'

'Because it's in the papers!' Connie said in exasperation.

Euan frowned. 'And you're sure it's your mother's actual words?'

'Why wouldn't they be?'

'Because I thought you were just saying how the papers always manage to twist things and report things that aren't true.'

Connie bit her lip. 'No, I'm sure they're all her own words.'

'But you haven't talked to her about this? You don't know for sure?'

Connie could feel a blush colouring her cheeks.

'I think you need to talk to her about all this,' Euan continued from the back seat. 'You can't be thinking the worst of your own mother without any proof. She deserves better than that.'

Connie didn't say anything but his words resonated with her and she knew that things with her mother would have to be resolved at some point. It was eating away at her and she knew that the only way forward would be to talk things through. Connie sank back in her seat. 'Why is everything so complicated?' she asked. 'I hate it all sometimes. It's too much, you know? I just want to be left alone. Is that so much to ask?'

'In your line of work, I'm afraid it is.'

Connie sighed. 'Why did I ever become an actress? I should have just become a secretary. Or a lawyer or something. Why did I have to end up in a job that's so public?'

'Sometimes the jobs choose us,' Euan said.

Connie sat quietly, listening to the hammer of the rain on the car. 'It wasn't actually me who chose acting,' she said at last. 'It was my mother.'

Euan didn't say anything and the words hung in the air as if nobody wanted to claim them. Connie blinked. She hadn't meant to say such a thing. Why had she? And why to this stranger? Perhaps it was the situation they had found themselves in – trapped in a broken-down car by the rain. The car had turned into a confessional and Connie was making full use of it.

She cleared her throat. 'She was the one who always wanted to act. I thought I just inherited that urge although I often wonder if I really did. Was it inherited or enforced?' Connie asked. 'I really don't know.'

'Does it matter?' Euan said. 'If you love it, I mean.'

Connie shrugged. 'I suppose not. And I do love it – I truly do but I don't love all the other stuff that goes with it. That's more tiring than the job itself.'

Euan nodded and Connie felt safe to continue. She told him how much it meant to her to play the parts she chose for herself; how it was an honour, even. She loved the challenge of becoming somebody else. It was, she said, like mental and emotional gymnastics. You got into a different mindset. Becoming someone else meant that you thought how they thought and behaved as they would behave. It was incredibly liberating because it made you forget about yourself. Perhaps that's why people became actors, Connie reasoned, because they were unhappy with themselves. They didn't want to live in their own skins. But perhaps that was why she had been working so hard lately – because, when she stopped, she became just Connie Gordon again, and who was she? She had no idea who she was.

She stared out of the window, gazing at the drenched Scottish landscape. The road was still river-like with torrents of water flowing down it, and the sky was dark and marbled. A strong wind had picked up and was buffeting the car. Connie swallowed and her hands curled into fists inside the thick warm gloves Euan had given her.

'And I can't seem to find the right man,' she continued, her mind floating back to her life in Hollywood. 'Why is that? What's wrong with me? I keep thinking there's something wrong with them but what if it's *me* there's something wrong with? Well, that's what I've been thinking the last few days – or last few months really, if I'm honest. That's why I'm here. I had to get away and, I know it's a cliché,

178

but I needed some space – to find myself. I only hope there's something here to find.'

Connie stopped, realising that she'd just spilt the entire contents of her heart to a complete stranger. What was going on here? The same thing had happened with Maggie and the warped Oscar-winning speech. What was it about the people of Lochnabrae? Had they the secret to unlocking hearts? She was going to be in big trouble if they couldn't be trusted and were to sell her secrets to the tabloids.

She cleared her throat, not daring to catch Euan's eyes. She could feel her face flaming with embarrassment and stared out of the window. There was nowhere to go, of course. She couldn't exactly run out into the storm. This wasn't *Wuthering Heights* and she wasn't Catherine Earnshaw. She was just Connie Gordon, runaway film star, who'd made a mess of her life and now had to face the consequences.

She took a deep breath and turned to face Euan.

'I shouldn't have said all that, I'm sorry.'

'There's no need to apologise, lass,' Euan said in a voice that was low and soothing. 'We all need to talk now and again.'

'You won't say anything, will you? To anyone?'

Euan's eyes narrowed slightly. 'I wouldn't betray your trust.'

Connie nodded. 'I'm sorry to ask, it's just—'

'You don't need to explain,' Euan said. 'I know what's happened in the past. I know how many people have betrayed you.'

Connie gave a small smile. 'That seems strange. You know so much about me and I don't know anything about you.'

For a moment, they held each other's gaze and Connie felt quite sure that he was about to say something when they heard a car horn.

'Ah,' Euan said, 'Alastair to the rescue.'

Chapter Eighteen

Connie turned and saw Alastair's Land Rover pulling up alongside them with Maggie waving wildly from the passenger seat.

'Well,' Connie said, 'looks like we're out of here.'

Euan looked at her. 'Connie,' he said.

'Yes?'

Euan rubbed a hand over his face. 'Be happy, lass. That's all that counts in this world.'

Connie looked at him as if expecting more but was then startled by a mad knocking on her car window. It was Maggie and she was holding a huge umbrella that was threatening to take off – Mary Poppins-like – across the valley.

'Come on, you two, before you're drowned in all this rain!' Maggie shouted as she opened the door. Euan grabbed hold of the shopping bags and he and Connie ran towards Alastair's car.

'Hi!' Alastair called from the front.

'Alastair!' Euan said.

'Oh, Connie!' Maggie cried as she saw Connie's long red hair plastered to her face and neck. 'You're soaked to the skin. Let's get you back to the B&B.'

'What about your car?' Connie asked.

'Alastair will tow it home later,' Maggie told her. 'But we can't have you all wet like that.'

'I'm fine – don't fuss, Maggie.'

'You'd better let her fuss,' Alastair said from the front seat as he turned the Land Rover around. 'It's what Maggie does best.'

'Alastair, it might have slipped your notice but we have a drowned Hollywood star in the back of your Landy,' Maggie said.

'It certainly hadn't slipped my notice,' he said with a grin.

'Good. Then put your foot down and get her back to the B&B before she freezes to death. I don't want to have to announce on the fan site that I'm responsible for the demise of Connie Gordon.'

Alastair got them back to Lochnabrae before the cold and the wet got the better of them.

'I'll see you guys for the hike, right?' he called as they bundled out of the car.

'Right!' Maggie called back. There was then an almighty scrum to get into the B&B.

'You're a star, Euan,' Maggie said as he placed the innumerable shopping bags in the hallway and left with a brief wave. 'You two looked as if you were getting along,' Maggie said once the door had closed behind him. 'What were you talking about?'

Connie could feel her colour rising again. She'd never blushed so much in her life since she'd left America. 'Oh, you know – the usual.'

Maggie looked at her thoughtfully. 'I think he's rather taken with you.'

'Oh, don't be ridiculous!'

182

'No, really!' Maggie said. 'There was a look in his eyes.'

'Whose eyes?' said a voice from the sitting room and Isla appeared in the hallway. 'Och! Will you look at the state of yous twos!'

'My car broke down,' Maggie said. 'Alastair had to come and rescue us.'

'And is it *his* eyes you were talking about? Is he after our Connie?'

'No!' Maggie laughed. 'Not Alastair! *Euan!*'

'Euan Kennedy?' Isla said in disbelief. 'But he's way too old for Connie!'

'That doesn't usually stop men, does it?' Maggie said.

Connie took her coat off and put her hands on her hips. 'I don't know why you're both making such a fuss. We were just talking – that's all. He's a sweet guy.'

'Oh, aye. He's that all right. Sweet on *you!*' Maggie teased.

'Ah, leave the poor gal alone,' Isla said. 'And let her get out of those wet things. You too, our Maggie – before you catch your death.'

'You can change in my room,' Connie said. 'Give us the opportunity of trying on some of those new clothes.'

'Clothes?' Isla said. 'Maggie never buys new clothes.'

'I know,' Connie said. 'But all that's gonna change, right, Maggie?'

Maggie nodded, her hair glistening with rain.

'Come on, then,' Connie said, grabbing some of their bags. Maggie followed her up the stairs with the rest, placing them on the floor of Connie's bedroom. 'I'll take the bathroom,' Connie said. 'You have the bedroom. Here's a towel,' she said, throwing a fluffy white bath towel at Maggie.

'Thanks,' Maggie said.

The bathroom door was slightly ajar and Maggie could

see Connie dropping her clothes in a wet sodden heap at her feet. She didn't mean to stare but there, in the Lochnabrae B&B, was a Hollywood movie star and she was standing right before her in her underwear.

Connie looked up. 'Maggie!' she said. 'Get those things off. What's the matter with you?'

Maggie gasped at having been caught. 'Sorry,' she muttered.

'What is it?' Connie asked, walking out into the middle of the bedroom in her knickers and bra.

Maggie turned away and hid her head in her towel. 'It's just—'

'What?'

'You're in your undies,' Maggie said.

'You've seen me in my undies before,' Connie said. 'Blimey, if you've seen *City of Broken Hearts*, you've seen more than my undies!'

'Yes, but—'

'What?' Connie said. 'What's wrong?'

'You're – like – in the flesh now. I didn't mean to stare. It's just – you're Connie Gordon. I didn't think – I didn't imagine—'

Connie stepped forward and grabbed Maggie's shoulders, then slowly lifted the towel from her head. 'Maggie,' she said softly, 'you've got to stop doing this.'

'Doing what?'

'This! You keep treating me as if I'm some sort of goddess. Well, I'm not. I'm just a normal woman. Look!' Connie stepped backwards and pointed to her thighs. 'Cellulite.'

'Where?' Maggie said, not convinced.

'Right there.'

184

Maggie peered closer and saw a slight wrinkling of skin. 'That's not cellulite.'

Connie frowned. 'Well, whatever it is, it's damned well not perfection. And look at these,' she said, pointing to her eyes. 'Wrinkles!'

'You haven't got wrinkles!' Maggie said.

Connie's eyes widened and then she gave a broad smile whilst pointing to her eyes. 'See?'

Maggie took a step forward. 'Oh, aye. I can see them now.'

Connie laughed. 'I'm just like anyone else, right? A woman with wrinkles and cellulite. It's just I can afford to hide them under layers of designer make-up and clothes. That's all.'

'Okay,' Maggie said at last. 'I get it this time. You want to be treated normally, right?'

'Because I *am* normal!' Connie said.

Maggie nodded. 'Okay,' she said.

'Okay, what?' Connie asked.

'You're normal.'

Connie nodded. 'Good! I'm glad we've *finally* got that sorted out.' She grabbed a sweater from her suitcase, pulling it on and sitting down on the edge of the bed. Her legs were bare and looked snowy white.

'I'm *far* from wonderful, Maggie,' Connie said. 'I've done dreadful things.'

'No!' Maggie said. 'I don't believe you. You couldn't do anything dreadful.'

Connie shook her head. 'There you go again – believing the very best about me when I don't deserve it.'

'But—'

'No,' Connie interrupted, 'listen. Just listen.' Connie took

185

a deep breath and, for a few seconds, all that could be heard was the rain on the bedroom window.

'I've done some things in my time that I'm not proud of,' Connie began. 'I've discovered recently that I've been more ambitious – in my past that is – than I ever realised. When I first started acting, it was almost like a game. It was fun and I loved it and I did it because of that love. Then something changed and I can't really pinpoint exactly when that happened. I started reading my reviews. I became obsessed with them. Most of them were good but there were some dreadful ones too. *Gordon should be better than this. Her talent is wasted in this ridiculous vehicle.*

'I became competitive. I started looking around me and seeing what my peers were doing. Why did she get that role and not me? Wouldn't I have done a better job? Why haven't I worked with this director yet? I had so many questions all the time and it was driving me mad and it was affecting my performance too. Remember my reviews for *Autumn Serenade*?'

Maggie nodded.

'Well, I got pretty annoyed after that and really started pushing things. One of my friends at the time – you know the actress Jay Royale?'

Maggie nodded again. 'She was in *Milly in the Morning* with you. She was great.'

'I know,' Connie said. 'And I adored her. We got really close on that film. Well, as close as you can be in LA. She was my only real friend when I come to think of it. Isn't that sad? A place as huge as LA and I only really had one friend there. No wonder I used to get lonely. I was so busy working all the time that I never had time to make proper friends.' She shook her head at the realisation. 'Anyway, we used to share information about the business – you know, like different roles that were coming up, which directors to avoid and which actors tried to stick their tongues down your throat during love scenes.'

Maggie laughed.

'It's really unusual to make a friend on a film set – in my experience, anyway. Usually, you're close for the duration of the film. That's the nature of the business. A film set is like a family but then the director says, "that's a wrap" and the friendships are pretty much wrapped too but Jay and I kept in touch.'

Connie was silent, staring down at her hands and idly twisting a gold ring she was wearing.

'So, what happened?' Maggie asked in a soft voice.

'I betrayed her.' Connie said, her voice subdued. 'There was this film coming up, *Just Jennifer*. It was such a great role. I knew I had to have that part as soon as I saw the script and I didn't tell Jay about it. I'll never forget. She rang me the night after I'd auditioned and asked me what I'd been up to. I told her I'd been in bed all day with a migraine. I feel just awful about it now. I should've told her. She would have been amazing in that role.'

Maggie shook her head. 'But that was *your* role, Connie. You were amazing in it. It's one of my favourites of yours.'

'But Jay would've been better. I know she would have and that's one of the reasons I didn't tell her about it. I was jealous of her. I didn't want her to have that role.'

'No,' Maggie said. 'She wouldn't have been right for it. You were the right person for it. You, and only you, were Jennifer.'

Connie bit her lip. 'No. That's not true. And I've never been able to talk to Jay since. I've felt so guilty.'

187

'Did she ever find out?'

'No,' Connie said.

'Then it seems to me that you're worrying about nothing. It's all a business, isn't it? And I'm sure there are people who have done the same thing to you.'

'I know,' Connie said, 'but that doesn't make me feel any better.'

'That's because you're nice. You worry about people and care about them too. You've got a conscience,' Maggie said, 'and that's a rarity.'

'Then you don't think it was wrong of me?'

'No,' Maggie said. 'That film was so amazing and I can't imagine anyone else playing Jennifer. I mean, you did get that Oscar-nomination.'

'Oh God!' Connie said, running her hands through her hair and then standing up. 'I did! And I wanted that more than anything but was it all worth it? Was it worth losing a friend over?'

Maggie watched as she paced the room, her legs still bare.

'I just feel that was so wrong of me and that's not who I am now,' Connie said. 'I can't tell you how much I feel I've changed – I mean my whole attitude. I've been there and done it and the magic seems to have vanished for me. Does that make sense?'

Maggie nodded. 'You want a new magic, don't you?' she said. 'That's why you're here.'

'Yes!' Connie said and, suddenly, she was sitting beside Maggie and clasping her hands excitedly. 'I've heard so much about this place. It's always been in the back of my mind like a sort of dream world.'

'Like Disneyland?'

Connie laughed. 'Perhaps.'

Maggie squeezed Connie's hands. 'I'm so glad you're here.'

'Me too,' Connie said. 'I really need a friend right now and I feel as if I can trust you, Maggie.'

'You can. Of course you can.'

Connie smiled. 'Now,' she said, 'let's unpack those shopping bags. I can't wait to make a start on those clothes.'

Chapter Nineteen

Isla was sitting downstairs with a cup of tea and a copy of *People's Friend* when Maggie walked into the room.

'Well now, will you take a look at you!' she said, looking up from a recipe for coffee cake.

Maggie did a little twirl. She was wearing the burgundy dress from the boutique. 'It's a wee bit old-fashioned but Connie's going to fix it.'

'Fix it? How?'

'With your sewing machine. You do still have it, don't you?'

Isla looked confused. 'My sewing machine? I gave that away years ago, Maggie. Did you need it?'

Maggie flopped down into a chair opposite. 'You could say that. I don't suppose anyone else has one?'

Isla rested her magazine on her lap. 'The only person I can think of is—'

'Don't say it.'

'Mrs Wallace.'

Maggie groaned. 'You're sure you haven't got yours tucked away under a pile of *People's Friend*?'

Isla stared at Maggie. 'You're just going to have to try Mrs Wallace.'

It was then that Connie's head popped around the door. 'Everything all right?'

'Yes,' Isla said.

'No,' Maggie said. 'Isla hasn't got a sewing machine any more. We'll have to make the best of the clothes as they are,' Maggie said.

'You're kidding me, right?' Connie said.

'Aye, she is,' Isla said. 'There's a sewing machine right here in Lochnabrae.'

Connie looked confused. 'Then let's go and get it.'

'It's Mrs Wallace's,' Maggie said with a heavy sigh.

'So?'

'If we borrow it, we'll be beholden to her for the rest of our natural born lives,' Maggie said.

Connie grinned. 'I know casting directors like that in Hollywood. They think they're doing you a huge favour when they cast you in a role and expect you to fall over backwards for them forever more.'

'But Mrs Wallace is the *worst*,' Maggie said.

'But she didn't seem too bad the other night in the pub,' Connie said. 'Sure, she was a bit bossy—'

'A *bit*?' Maggie said.

'You just have to know how to handle these people,' Connie said. 'You mustn't let them get the better of you, that's all. Now, come on.'

'Where are we going?' Maggie asked.

'To butter up Mrs Wallace, of course.'

It was still raining when they left the B&B and the wind was hurtling down the main street and threatening to send anyone silly enough to be outside into the loch. Both Maggie and Connie had donned waterproof coats and hats and

191

made their first stop at Maggie's shop for wellies and briberies.

'What's her favourite tipple?' Connie asked, picking up a bottle of whisky. 'What about this?'

'That's a ten-year-old single cask!' Maggie shrieked.

'Does Mrs Wallace like it?'

'*Everyone* likes that!'

'Good. I'll get it, then.'

Maggie groaned, feeling sure they could *buy* a sewing machine for the same price as the bottle of whisky.

Then, with the whisky placed in a heavy-duty carrier bag and their feet tucked safely in heavy-duty wellies, they left the shop and headed for Mrs Wallace's.

Like most of the houses in Lochnabrae, Mrs Wallace's was a two-storey white home with deep windowsills and thick walls that kept the cold out and the heat in. The door was of solid wood and painted yellow, which was completely at odds with its very unsunny resident.

Sheltering under its simple porch, Maggie knocked.

'I don't think she'll be in,' Maggie said.

But suddenly, the door opened and the enormous bosom of Mrs Wallace appeared followed by her stern face.

'Mrs Wallace, you remember me?' Connie said modestly.

'Aye,' Mrs Wallace said. 'You'll be that film star from the pub. Of course I remember ye,' she said, her face breaking into a rare smile.

'Can we come in?' Connie persisted. 'We have a great favour to ask you.'

'Oh, well,' Mrs Wallace said, 'best come in then.'

'I've bought you a little something,' Connie said, unwrapping the boxed bottle of whisky.

Mrs Wallace gasped. 'Is that for me?'

Connie nodded. 'It's a sort of bribe,' she said. 'We believe you have a sewing machine at your disposal and we'd very much like to borrow it.'

'A sewing machine?'

'Yes. I have a bit of a project on the go and it would really help me out if I had a machine.'

'I see,' Mrs Wallace said. 'Well, I do have one, of course, and you're welcome to it.'

'Oh, Mrs Wallace, you're an angel.' Connie leant forward and dared to kiss the woman on one of her reddened cheeks.

The old matriarch looked quite shocked but pleasantly so.

'Well, I never!' she declared.

Maggie rolled her eyes. She could never have performed such a feat.

'Well, let's get this put away before Mr Wallace spies it and assumes it's for him,' Mrs Wallace said.

Maggie and Connie followed her through to the kitchen at the back of the house.

'Mr Wallace is sleeping in the front room,' Mrs Wallace explained. 'You'll not be wanting to hear him snore, I dare say. Can I get you a cup of tea?'

'Oh, I'm afraid we haven't got time, Mrs Wallace,' Connie said sweetly. 'Perhaps another time?'

'Then you'll be wanting the sewing machine straight away?'

'If it's no bother,' Connie said.

'Do you mind me asking what you're doing?'

'We've been in to Strathcorrie and bought some dresses and things but they're not quite right.'

'But weren't you recognised?' Mrs Wallace asked.

'Och, no!' Maggie said. 'Connie hid her hair under a woolly hat and wore one of my old cardigans.'

'I was incognito,' Connie said. 'It was such fun just shopping. I haven't done anything like that for years – *can't* do anything like that. Not in LA. I'd be mobbed by paparazzi. Although it really baffles me why anyone would want a photo of me shopping. That's why it's so wonderful here. I didn't get bothered at all.'

'But what if the press found out?' Mrs Wallace asked.

'Oh, but they won't. Nobody knows I'm here. Only my PA,' Connie said. 'But nobody else knows.'

'And nobody's going to find out either,' Maggie said. 'Just imagine if that slimy Colin Simpkins found out.'

'The local journalist?' Connie asked.

Maggie nodded. 'If he gets wind you're here, he'd probably sell it to the nationals.'

'Sell it?' Mrs Wallace said.

'Aye,' Maggie said.

'I'm afraid people are in the habit of selling stories about me. I've lost count of the number of so-called friends who'd rather make a buck or two out of me than remain loyal.'

'But that's why you've come here,' Maggie said. 'We're your fan club. We're as loyal as they come.'

Connie smiled. 'Right,' she said. 'Shall we take this sewing machine?'

Ten minutes later, the sewing machine was wrapped in two bin bags to protect it from the rain and handed over to Maggie.

'Are you sure you can manage?' Connie asked anxiously.

'You should see the number of newspapers I can shift. My arms are like a weightlifter's,' Maggie said.

'We won't keep it any longer than we have to, Mrs

Wallace,' Connie said. 'I can't thank you enough.' Again, she leant forward and kissed Mrs Wallace on the cheek.

'Come on,' Maggie said, 'before I collapse.'

The two of them left the house, Connie closing the door behind them.

'How could you be so *nice* to her?' Maggie asked in disgust once they were in the street. 'It was as if you were best friends or something. How did you do that?'

'I'm a good actress, that's how,' Connie said and the two of them walked back towards the B&B, laughing in the rain.

Chapter Twenty

Over the next few days, the little sewing machine whirred away on the dressing table of Connie's bedroom. The whole place had turned into a workshop with lengths of material, coloured threads, sequins, ribbons, zips and buttons all jostling for space.

'I didn't mean to cause so much trouble,' Maggie said.

'It's no trouble at all,' Connie assured her. 'I love it!'

'Really?' Maggie said, watching Connie working as she sat on the bed, hands guiltily empty. 'I always hated anything to do with needles and threads.'

'It's so soothing,' Connie said. 'I love the noise these old machines make and it's so amazing to have something in your hands that you've made. Look!' She held up the burgundy dress that she'd been working on. She'd cut away part of the front to make a sexy scooped neckline, had drawn in the waist and chopped a good six inches from the hem.

Maggie gasped. 'It's so beautiful.' She stood up and held the dress against her.

'Try it on,' Connie said.

Maggie hurriedly got out of her jumper, T-shirt and jeans.

'Oh, I'd forgotten,' Connie said.

'What is it?' Maggie asked.

'You need new underwear. You can't wear beautiful dresses over ugly underwear. It's a complete travesty!'

Maggie looked suitably shamefaced. 'I don't really need nice underwear,' she explained. 'Nobody gets to see it but me.'

Connie's eyebrows rose. 'That's not the attitude to take! Let me tell you something: beautiful underwear makes you *feel* beautiful. It's like a little secret between you and yourself.'

Maggie stepped into the dress and Connie zipped it up.

'That colour's just right on you. You look divine. Come and see,' Connie said, steering Maggie towards the mirror.

Once in front of it, Maggie's mouth dropped open. 'Oh!' she said. 'I've never looked like this before.'

'But we do have to get your underwear sorted. We can order some beautiful things online. You'll love what I have in mind and, if Mikey gets to see it in the near future, he'll love it too.'

Maggie blushed to the very roots of her hair.

It was shortly after the underwear conversation that Connie made a discovery at Maggie's place – her mother's amazing wardrobe.

'These clothes are beautiful, Maggie! Why didn't you tell me about them?'

'I didn't think to. I mean, I don't look in here very often. I've worn one or two items – it's like keeping them alive – but they're too lovely to be worn in the shop.'

'Maggie, you virtually spend your whole life in the shop and, if you're not going to look gorgeous there, then where are you?'

Maggie acknowledged that Connie had a point and

watched as she took out the assortment of velvet skirts, pretty jackets, dresses and scarves.

'These don't need altering at all,' Connie said. 'Not that I would – unless you wanted me to. Oh! Look at this one.' She held up a beautiful jacket in a dusky pink colour. It was lined with candy stripes, had large buttons down the front and was made from the softest wool.

'I remember her wearing this one,' Maggie said. 'It was one of her favourites.'

'It would be one of my favourites too,' Connie said. 'It's gorgeous. I'm so excited about all this.' Connie buzzed around the room like a mad thing. 'Let's have a sort out.'

Without a moment to lose, Connie found Maggie's wardrobe and began pulling out her clothes.

They soon got into their stride and developed a shorthand of funny faces to determine whether something was to be kept or discarded.

'Get rid of it!' Maggie would scream, wrinkling her nose in horror.

'You're not keeping *this!*' Connie would say, her mouth a straight line of disgust.

It really was great fun stuffing bin bags and Maggie could only wonder why she hadn't done it earlier.

'How on earth did I wear all these things?' she asked. 'I've never seen so much grey in my life. I mean, there's quite enough grey with the weather we have here.'

Connie smiled and nodded. 'Well,' she said, 'I'm glad we've got that sorted. Now, what shall we do about your hair?'

At the other end of Lochnabrae, Alastair was walking towards the village hall, a big bunch of keys in his hand

and Bounce capering by his side. It seemed an age since he'd been inside. It was mostly used by the youth club but that had dwindled to so few members now that the building was in danger of being abandoned completely. It was a shame but Alastair suspected if he'd grown up in Lochnabrae, he would have felt the same way and would have wanted to be somewhere more exciting.

Lochnabrae, he thought, was the sort of place one longed to get away from when young but longed to return to when older.

'Come here, Bounce,' Alastair said, trying to prevent his charge from leaving his calling card on the already rotting wooden steps that led up to the door. Slotting the great silver key in the lock, Alastair opened the door and stepped inside. The smell hit him at once. It was that old half-musky, half-damp smell that was quite usual for uncared for public buildings. Bounce seemed to like it, tipping his head back and taking in the air as if it were a delicacy. Alastair decided not to close the door behind him.

He made a slow survey of the space. The curtains were still as ugly and shabby as ever, made from some god-awful 1970s floral material. They were still waiting for a surplus from the Connie Gordon fan club to replace them. But there never was a surplus. There was only ever enough to pay for the lighting and heating. Everything else had to come out of their own pockets. Heaven only knew how much money Alastair had secretly thrown at the place over the years and it was still never enough.

He walked across the room towards the stage, noticing the cobwebs on the windowsills along the way. At least they were easily dealt with. He looked across at the stage and thought again how tiny it was.

'But adequate,' he said to himself. It wasn't The Palladium. It wasn't The Haymarket.

'It's Lochnabrae,' he said with a sigh. 'My choice.'

He walked up the steps on the left-hand side and listened to one of his favourite sounds in the world: feet on an empty stage. There was something rather exciting about it – it was a sound full of promise. He smiled as he thought of how many people must have trod these very boards in the name of entertainment – both their own and that of the audience. It didn't matter that it wasn't a West End stage; its objectives were just the same: to amuse, to provoke thought, and to pass the time. Wasn't that the real purpose of art, he thought? There was a lot of time to fill during this life and it was his role as a playwright to help people pass it in as pleasurable a way as possible.

For a moment, he stood in the middle of the stage, looking out into the empty village hall. He always thought that stages looked sad when there were no performers on them but auditoriums looked even sadder, making the room look like a face without a smile.

Turning around, Alastair looked at the space behind the stage. The moth-eaten curtain hung limply. It had needed replacing ten years ago but, like everything else, the meagre LADS budget didn't allow for such luxuries.

He walked towards the dressing rooms. Well, it was one room really, which had been divided by two curtains, which provided some sort of privacy when the cast were changing. Again, it smelt musty and mouldy. Flicking the light switch on, he caught his reflection in one of the mirrors. He hardly recognised himself. His hair was the longest it had ever been, tickling the neckline of his jumper, and the lower half of his face was covered in stubble. His mother would be appalled. His old London friends would be appalled. But he rather liked it. It represented him now: unstructured, unrestrained and – he laughed – unemployable.

So he hadn't written a play all year – so what? All writers had dry spells, didn't they? And he was sort of writing. Some sort of character was beginning to emerge only not with the same speed and technical brilliance that he was famous for.

What was happening to him? Had he been in the Highlands too long? Was he beginning to stagnate, just as his friends in the big city had told him he would? Perhaps he was just winding down and going at a more leisurely pace – a *normal* pace. He'd often been warned about his breakneck, workaholic attitude to life.

'You're heading for an early grave,' his agent had warned him. 'Or a cardiac arrest at the very least.'

Alastair had laughed. He was young and he loved his work. Until . . .

He shook his head. He didn't want to think about it. Instead, he walked around the rooms and corridors backstage, checking everything was in reasonable order. In just a few days, the place would be buzzing again with rehearsal mayhem. The costumes would be hauled out of the old wardrobes and Mrs Wallace would do her best to patch and repair them. There'd be a frantic scramble in the props chest to see if there was anything suitable at all, and then Hamish would be called upon to work his artistic brilliance on the scenery. Alastair felt sure that Hamish's true talents were wasted working as a car mechanic. When Alister had first seen his ability with a humble paint pot and a brush, he was completely taken aback. Hamish had seemed surprised too. It was as if a secret side of him had been unlocked.

It's what places like this needed: talented people to come together and give something back to the community. After the hassles and strains of life in London, Alastair had really appreciated being made to feel a part of such a community. It was a real privilege.

Now, as he walked the length of the corridor, he thought of the months that lay ahead with a sense of excitement. Okay, so it wasn't the buzz he got from putting on a show of his own in the West End but he'd given that up, hadn't he? He'd willingly walked away from that life and often wondered what his friends in Lochnabrae would think if they knew the real reason why he was there. They'd pretty much taken his arrival in their stride. It had helped that he was a Scot, of course, and, more importantly, he was always happy to get the rounds in at The Capercaillie. He'd been well and truly accepted. But what if they knew the truth?

No, he thought. He wasn't going to think about that. How could anyone possibly find out? As far as he knew, the story hadn't been widely reported outside of the London theatre scene and certainly wasn't talked about north of the border. He had been able to start again and for that he was eternally grateful.

He was just returning to the stage when something caught his eye. Half-hidden behind the curtain lay a copy of a book and, bending down to retrieve it, he discovered it was one of his very own plays, *Infinite Jest*.

Alastair let out a laugh that echoed in the emptiness because it had been that very play that had been the beginning of the end for him, or could have been if he hadn't left London.

He wondered who could have left it there and, picking

it up, flicked through the pages. On page seventeen, there was a ring mark – about the size of a whisky tumbler.

'Sandy,' he said and he frowned. He didn't know Sandy read his plays. He always seemed so reluctant to read anything other than the racing pages of the newspaper but maybe he hadn't made it beyond page seventeen, Alastair mused.

For a moment, he thought of his play. *Infinite Jest* was one of his most famous. 'A sparkling comedy' *The Times* had called it. 'A triumph of intelligent theatre' the *Guardian* had written, and yet it had led to one of the most miserable periods of his life.

He put the ragged copy in his jacket pocket and whistled to Bounce as he walked down the stage steps and made his way towards the door. His dark-eyed companion looked up at him, his face alert in anticipation of a walk.

'Yeah, yeah, all right!' Alastair said. A good long walk was just what he needed too.

Chapter Twenty-One

By the time the morning of the pre-play hike came round, Connie was feeling really settled with life in Lochnabrae. She'd been there for just over a week and her once hectic timetable had been abolished, leaving her with whole days to do exactly what she pleased. She was sleeping well, eating what she liked, and taking long walks around the loch each day. Her eyes looked brighter and she'd lost the shadows underneath them that would normally be hidden under thick slabs of make-up. Her skin had improved too. Isla's magical pot of Benet's Balm had restored her complexion and she had even been brave enough to go make-up free for a couple of days, luxuriating in the feel of the wind on her bare skin as she took her walks. She was almost completely relaxed but there was one thing nagging at her. There was something she knew she had to do and she couldn't put it off a moment longer.

Leaving her room, Connie went downstairs and found Isla dusting a sideboard in the dining room.

'Good morning, Connie,' Isla said. 'You look like a woman on a mission,' Isla observed.

'Yes, I am,' Connie said. 'I wonder if I may use your

phone. I've not replaced my mobile yet and – well – I really don't want to but I should make a call to the States. I'll pay, of course.'

'There's a phone in my room upstairs if you want a wee bit of privacy,' Isla said.

'Thanks,' Connie said.

Isla's room was small but beautiful. She'd given the three larger rooms of the house over to guest bedrooms and that had left her the tiny room at the back. Still, the view was lovely with fields rolling into the mountains beyond.

There was a small double bed, a wardrobe and a chest of drawers and that was it. An old-fashioned ragdoll sat on the bed looking woeful and there was a reading lamp under which was a stack of *People's Friend* and a couple of Rosamunde Pilcher novels.

And the phone.

Connie took a deep breath. 'Come on,' she told herself, closing the bedroom door. 'Just get it over and done with.'

She picked up the phone and dialled. There was no answer immediately and she was just about to hang up when a little voice answered.

'Hello?'

'Samantha?'

'Connie?'

'Did I wake you?'

There was a pause. 'Er – yes!' Samantha said. 'It's two in the morning.'

Connie gasped. 'Oh my God! I totally forgot! Listen, I'll call you later, okay?'

'No, no! Don't go, Connie. Just give me a minute,' Samantha said. 'There, that's better, I can see what I'm doing now.'

Connie smiled, imagining her PA finding the light switch and putting her neat little glasses on.

'I've been keeping a notepad by the phone in case you rang. Where have you been? I've left you messages. Did you lose your phone?'

'In a manner of speaking,' Connie said. 'Look, I'm so sorry I didn't ring earlier but I – well – I didn't really want to.'

'Are you okay?'

'Yeah, I'm fine. You all right?'

Samantha sighed, the weight of it travelling the Atlantic Ocean to assault Connie's ear.

'Oh, dear,' Connie said, 'you'd better fill me in.' She sat down on the edge of Isla's bed.

Samantha then began on the long list of messages that Connie's agent, Bob Braskett, had left her. On and on it went, unrelentingly nasty and totally unnecessary. Connie interrupted with the occasional, 'He didn't really say that, did he?' And Samantha had to assure Connie that he had.

'I hung up on him the last time,' she said. 'I warned him but he wasn't listening to me.'

Connie shook her head. 'It's about time I had a word with him. He has no right to speak to you like that and no right to talk about me in that way either.'

'He said he was coming over,' Samantha said.

'Well, don't let him in,' Connie said.

'No, not over here – over there.'

'There where?'

'Scotland. He's flying to Scotland, Connie.'

'No way!'

'That's what he said the last time I spoke to him.'

'And when was that?' Connie asked in panic.

'A couple of days ago. He sounded furious. I thought he was going to have a heart attack on the phone.'

'But how does he know where I am?'

Samantha was quiet.

'Sammy?'

'I'm sorry, Connie. I found the fan letter on your desk and you'd scribbled a flight number down on a pad. I just put two and two together.'

'And told Bob?'

'Oh, Connie! I wish I hadn't. I'm so sorry but he was really putting pressure on me.'

'It's okay. It's not your fault. I should've told you where I was. So, when did he leave?'

'I don't know. I've not heard from him since that call,' Samantha said.

'He's probably just bluffing, anyway, but let me know if you hear from him again, all right?'

'Sure, Connie.'

'Here's my number but don't pass it on to Bob, okay?'

Connie gave out the bed and breakfast's phone number and then hung up. She had a feeling that her face was now as woeful as that of the ragdoll on the bed. Bob wouldn't really come all the way to Scotland, would he? He'd never stepped foot out of LA, let alone the States. He probably couldn't even point to Scotland on a map. Still, Connie couldn't help worrying that, any moment now, he could turn up and spoil her perfect existence in Lochnabrae.

Maggie's bed was covered with clothes.

'It's a hike,' she told herself. 'Wear your hiking gear.' And she would. There were the trusty hiking trousers that were warm and waterproof and, if they got wet, would dry quickly.

What was causing her the problem was what she should wear on top. Normally, she had an old T-shirt with a faded Snoopy on the front. It was worn away to a whisper but was so wonderfully soft. However, it had gone in the bin bag when they'd had the sort out. Since then, they'd been shopping online together for replacements and there they all were on the bed. Five pretty T-shirts.

'One for each day of the week in case you insist on wearing nothing else,' Connie had told her.

They were lovely – really they were. It's just they were so *tight*. Maggie was used to big and baggy not small and tight. She took a deep breath and picked out a creamy pink one, pulling it over her head and her chest. It was certainly a tight fit, hugging her breasts before skimming down to her waist. She took a peep in the mirror and swallowed hard. Everything was on display. This was terrible – *terrible*.

Hunting around on the bed, Maggie saw one of the new jumpers Connie had chosen for her. Like the T-shirt, it was a pale pink and it might do something to hide her protruding chest. She pulled it over her head and stood in front of the mirror. She looked a little less obvious now, at least. For a moment, she stood looking at her reflection. Her hair was looking amazing. She ran her fingers through it, luxuriating in its silky softness. Not only had Connie bought her clothes online but hair products too. They'd arrived in a beautiful box, smelling heavenly and promising miraculous things for even the most wayward of curls. Maggie had spent last night wearing a conditioning treatment under a shower cap. It had felt funny crunching and sliding across her pillow but the results were pretty amazing. For the first time in her life, Maggie had a glorious head of shiny, manageable curls. She'd even applied a little serum for a bit of added shine and she couldn't stop looking at it now. The question was, would Mikey notice?

The meeting place for the pre-play hike was outside The Capercaillie and Connie and Isla walked there together from the bed and breakfast. It was a perfect spring morning; mild but with a crisp edge to it that would be just right for walking. The gently heaving hills glowed with their covering of bright bracken and the waters of the loch were the most perfect blue Connie had ever seen.

'The gang's all here,' Isla said, nodding at the little crowd.

Connie could see them all shuffling around in their walking boots and looking up into the hills beyond to check what sort of weather was waiting for them. There was Alastair, a huge rucksack on his back, his dark hair curling over his waterproof jacket and Bounce sitting beside him. He saw Connie approaching and nodded. Connie nodded back and he threw a smile at her and she couldn't help noticing – perhaps for the first time – how cute he was. Connie usually went for the clean-shaven type of guy – the sort to wear a sharp suit and tie but Alastair's slightly unkempt look was strangely appealing and she found herself gazing at his long hair and dark stubble. Why hadn't she noticed that before, she wondered? Maybe she'd been admiring the scenery too much to notice the very handsome man who lived smack bang in the middle of it.

It was just as she was pondering this that she felt a hand on her arm.

'Have you thought any more about a western?' a voice said.

'Angus!' Connie said.

'Because I think it would be a good move. I mean for your career,' Angus said, his long face solemn.

'I'm not thinking about my career today,' Connie said and quickly moved away from him as she caught sight of Maggie and Hamish.

'Connie!' Hamish said as she approached.

'You've got to save me,' Connie whispered. 'Angus is practically stalking me.'

Maggie linked arms with her. 'Stay with me,' she said. 'Hamish – get the other side of her.'

Hamish was happy to do as he was told and linked Connie's other arm.

'You look lovely,' he half-whispered, looking like a love-struck teenager. 'I like your hair like that.'

'Thanks, bro,' Maggie interrupted.

'Not *your* hair – *Connie's!*' Hamish said, admiring the way she'd tied it into a knot at the back of her head.

'But Maggie's hair's looking fantastic,' Connie said. 'Don't you think?'

'Oh, aye!' Hamish said, happy to agree with anything Connie said.

'It does, Maggie. It looks wonderful.' Maggie beamed at her and Connie looked around to see if the object of Maggie's affection was there to notice. There was Sandy, leaning on a sturdy walking stick, and Euan consulting a map. Young Kirsty Kendrick was there with her sister, Catriona. Both were sporting red hats and were giggling at something Connie couldn't quite make out but there was no Mikey.

'Anyone seen Mrs Wallace?' Alastair suddenly bellowed.

'Oh, she rang me this morning,' Isla said. 'Said she felt a cold coming on.'

'What a shame,' Maggie whispered to Connie. 'We'll all miss her friendly banter.'

Connie tried not to smile. She was so looking forward to this walk and getting to know everybody. In a funny way, she felt like she knew everybody already because they'd all made her so welcome but this was her time to start returning the favour and trusting them, *really* trusting them. She had to stop thinking that somebody was going to sell her out to the newspapers or that they only liked her for her fame. It was the only way forward and she had every intention of following it.

Just then, Mikey the Biker appeared around the corner, his sleek motorbike gleaming in the early morning light, its engine throbbing.

'Wow!' Maggie said before she could check herself.

Connie's mouth dropped open. Wow indeed, she thought. He was Lochnabrae's very own Marlon Brando.

He pulled over outside The Capercaillie in a cloud of dust and removed his helmet, shaking his dark hair free and nodding at the crowd. Kirsty and Catriona rushed forward, Catriona grabbing his helmet and pushing it on over her red hat.

'Let me!' Kirsty said, taking it off her sister.

Mikey laughed as he got off the bike, leaving the girls to fight over his helmet.

'Well, hello there, Connie,' he said, striding over to meet her. 'You've got your bodyguards, I see.'

'It's Angus!' Hamish whispered. 'He's been stalking Connie.'

'Has he now?' Mikey said, looking around to where Angry Angus was standing. He was watching them, a frown on his face as if he didn't approve of any of them.

'Well, I've just got to slip out of me leathers,' Mikey said, 'then I can join your little posse and make sure you're safe.' He sloped off to the porch of The Capercaillie.

Maggie did her best not to watch but she just couldn't help herself. It wasn't as if he was naked underneath – he'd managed to squash his hiking trousers on under his leathers – but she just loved looking at him: his long, strong legs, his tight bum as he bent over, and the way his jet black hair fell across his face. And she wasn't the only one to be captivated. Kirsty and Catriona were giggling and even Isla was happy to be getting an eyeful.

'Right!' Alastair called, breaking the spell. 'Ready to move on?'

Sandy waved his walking stick in the air and Mikey quickly folded his things away before joining Connie.

'All set?' he asked.

Connie nodded, taking in a great lungful of perfectly pure air and smiling. 'It's days like this when you truly believe that all is well with the world,' she said, 'and nothing – *nothing* – can ever go wrong again.'

Chapter Twenty-Two

Connie, Mikey, Maggie and Hamish walked in companionable silence, their feet setting a steady rhythm as they left Lochnabrae behind and headed up a steep track through the woods. It was so good to be out in the open, Connie thought. She didn't walk enough back in LA. All she managed was jogging with her trainer through the park followed by the paparazzi and that wasn't the same at all. This was real. There were pencil-thin firs and slender silver birches that looked so bright in the spring sunshine and, once they'd walked out of the wood and onto the open moorland, there was the sky. The enormous blue sky. Connie took a deep breath and tried to lock away everything she was seeing so that she'd remember it for ever.

On they walked, covering the miles with easy pleasure. They crossed a tiny stone bridge that straddled a burn they'd been following, the sound of tumbling water filling their ears. The sun was stronger now than when they'd left Lochnabrae and everyone had warmed up and started to shed layers. Bounce was also feeling the heat and charged right into the middle of the burn and drank until everyone felt sure he would burst. Then he bounded out and made sure he was standing in the middle of everyone before shaking, sending a cascade of water over the entire group.

Connie noticed how little groups kept forming as the walk continued. One minute, she'd be chatting to Isla, the next, Alastair would join in and then she'd find herself walking alongside Maggie and Hamish and a new conversation would spring up, but there was one man she never managed to talk to that morning and that was Euan. He seemed to be forever bringing up, the rear, walking at a pace that was somewhere between sedate and sleeping. Perhaps he was finding it tougher than everyone else, Connie thought, although he looked pretty fit. She'd glanced back to smile at him several times but he'd avoided eye contact with her each time. Odd, she thought. They seemed to have got on together so well when trapped in the car during the downpour.

Thinking nothing more of it, Connie marched on until it was time to stop for lunch. Alastair chose a slope of a mountain they'd been climbing. They were high enough up for a fabulous view down into the valley they had been walking through that morning, but sheltered enough so as not to feel the full force of the wind.

Everyone made themselves a little space on the ground, taking off their coats and laying them down to sit upon. For a moment, nobody spoke. There was just stillness here. A curlew cried as it took off from some secret hideaway. A distant sheep bleated and, just above the horizon, a buzzard soared.

Connie sighed as she took in the scene before her. It was all so huge. How many Hollywood mansions would be built on the same amount of space in LA, she wondered? How many swimming pools, liquor stores, malls and rehab centres? Here, it was just the hills, the forests and the clear bright sky.

She took off her coat and lay it on the ground, reclining on top of it with her head upon her arms. She closed her eyes against the warm sun and everything turned orange. Taking a deep breath, she could smell the unmistakable scent of pine trees on the breeze and thought how much lovelier it was than any perfume. She hadn't felt this calm or peaceful in months. Ever since she'd arrived in Lochnabrae, she had been slowly shedding the layers of stress that had accumulated over so many years.

'Hey, sleepyhead!' a voice said.

Connie sat up and shielded her eyes against the light.

'You should have something to eat before we move on again,' Maggie told her.

Connie nodded and was just undoing a small rucksack when Bounce bounded up to her and stuck his nose in.

'Bounce!' Alastair yelled and the dog backed off reluctantly.

'Haven't you got that dog trained yet, Alastair?' Sandy said with a chuckle.

'You might be able to direct a troupe of actors but you're no use with a puppy,' Angus said, his face dour.

'He's young,' Alastair said.

'Ah, the excuse of the desperate,' Sandy said and everyone laughed.

Connie blinked in the brightness and then she remembered something and delved into the depths of her rucksack once more.

'I've brought a few pairs of sunglasses,' she said, bringing out five beautiful cases. 'I thought we might need them.'

She handed them out: a pair to Maggie, Kirsty, Catriona and Isla, keeping a pair for herself.

'Oh, my goodness!' Kirsty said, opening her case and seeing a pair of enormous black Chanel glasses. 'These are GORGEOUS!'

'Look at mine!' Catriona said, revealing a pair of Armani's.

Maggie and Isla opened theirs and stared in wonder.

'You can keep them,' Connie said. 'I've got so many.'

Kirsty was on her feet in an instant and hugged Connie and, not to be outdone, Catriona, Maggie and Isla followed her lead.

Sandy shook his head and laughed. 'Will you look at that?' he said, staring at the five of them wearing their designer glasses on the side of a mountain.

A few minutes passed by with nothing heard but the happy munching of sandwiches, crisps and apples. Maggie, who was sitting between Connie and Mikey, had tied her hair back to stop it blowing into her mouth but was still wrapped up like an old woman.

'Maggie!' Connie hissed. 'Take your jumper off.'

'What?'

'Take your jumper off!' Connie mouthed, motioning to her own, which she'd removed and tied around her waist.

Maggie shook her head.

'You've got something on underneath, haven't you?'

'Aye. Of course!'

'Then take the jumper off,' Connie whispered. 'It's lovely and warm. Give your body a chance to breathe,' she said, eyes sparkling naughtily.

Maggie stuffed the end of her sandwich into her mouth, removed her sunglasses and reluctantly pulled her jumper off over her head. Sandy immediately did a wolf whistle

216

and everyone giggled and Maggie's face turned the colour of rowan berries, but Connie was encouraged to see that Mikey was watching and he had the kind of smile on his face that was most promising. So, she thought, he was finally beginning to notice Maggie.

The afternoon walk back to Lochnabrae was not quite as easy as the morning session and Connie soon found herself out of breath as Alastair led the way around the side of the boulder-strewn flank of Ben Torran. It was just as well that they weren't climbing to the top of it, she thought – she might well have disgraced herself. Then, whilst stumbling across a tussocky field, Connie suddenly found herself up to her shins in black mud.

'Connie!' Kirsty cried.

'Grab me!' Catriona yelled.

'No, grab me!' Kirsty said, both of them wading into the mud to rescue their idol.

'I'm okay!' Connie assured them as she squelched out onto dry ground.

'What's happened?' Alastair asked, doubling back.

'Connie's been swimming in the mud,' Sandy said with a laugh.

'You okay?' Maggie said as she hurried back.

'I'm fine. Stop fussing, everyone! There's nothing to worry about,' Connie said, looking down to inspect the damage. Her boots and trouser legs were completely black.

'What the heck is that stuff?'

'It's just mud,' Alastair said.

'Did you not see it, lass?' Euan asked, stopping alongside her and looking concerned.

'Well,' Connie said, 'I did but I thought it would be more solid than it was.' Her face flushed with embarrassment as everyone stood around laughing. Everyone except Euan and Maggie.

'It's not funny!' Maggie said. 'She could've been hurt!'

'I'm fine,' Connie said, a smile beginning to form on her own face now that she realised nothing was broken.

'I don't expect there's much mud in Hollywood,' Alastair teased.

'No,' Connie said, 'but there's a lot of bullshit.'

This set everyone off laughing again.

'At least the sun'll dry you off,' Maggie said, linking arms with her and leading her on. Catriona quickly skipped forward and linked the other arm and the strange linking trio walked on together as best as they could until they reached a stile. Connie assured them that she could cope on her own but Maggie and Kirsty insisted on helping and the air filled with hands for a mad moment as Connie hopped over. It wasn't a dissimilar experience to the hysterical fans she encountered outside premieres but, looking at their kind faces, Connie couldn't help but be moved. Their hands weren't clawing at her and smothering her like those of her fans in Hollywood. They didn't want to grab a piece of her – they wanted to help her and that was the wonderful difference about being there.

She spent the rest of the afternoon walking and talking with Maggie, Kirsty and Catriona and, after they'd exhausted everything connected with Hollywood, they turned their attention to more down-to-earth subjects like Mikey.

'I've always thought he was cute,' Kirsty said. 'He once kissed me under the mistletoe.'

'When?' Maggie asked.

'Five years ago,' Kirsty said.

'And you remember it?' Connie asked.

'You always remember a kiss from Michael Shire,' she said, her eyes wistful.

'He's the most gorgeous man for miles around,' Kirsty said. 'Not that your brother isn't cute,' she added. 'But Mikey's something different.'

'What do you think, Connie?' Kirsty asked.

Connie cleared her throat, not wanting to upset Maggie. 'I think he's very handsome,' she said.

Connie took a sideways glance at Maggie. She wasn't looking very happy.

'How about Alastair,' Connie suggested and then bit her lip. Why had she said that?

'Alastair?' Catriona said. 'Och, no! He's like a teacher.'

'Yeah,' Kirsty said, 'he's so bossy.'

'But he's good-looking,' Connie said, glad that she'd managed to steer the conversation away from Mikey but feeling uneasy in another way now.

'You like our Alastair, do you?' Kirsty suddenly said.

'I didn't say that,' Connie said quickly – perhaps a little too quickly.

'You've gone all red!' Catriona said.

'Shush!' Maggie hushed, motioning ahead to where both Mikey and Alastair were walking.

Luckily for Connie, it was time for their afternoon stop and rucksacks were downed and flasks produced for tea.

'Now, I wonder why we stopped here,' Sandy said with a chuckle.

'Because this is the Sprawling Rock,' Alastair said.

'Why's it called that?' Connie asked.

'Because I get to sprawl on it!' Alastair said, lying back on the great slab of sparkling granite that had been warmed by the sun.

'You can see yer belly!' Isla shouted and Connie couldn't help but stare at the few inches of bare flesh that were on display. His T-shirt had ridden up, exposing a good flat stomach.

'Not bad,' Kirsty whispered to Connie. 'For an old man.'

'He's not old,' Connie said.

'Och, he must be thirty-five at least,' Kirsty said. 'But not in bad shape for an oldie.'

Connie rolled her eyes and then realised that Maggie was looking at her.

'What?' she asked.

'Nothing,' Maggie said but there was a little smile growing on her face.

She was glad when they were all on the move again. It was just a short walk down through the valley. The great shadow of Ben Torran made it feel much cooler now and jumpers and jackets were quickly sought.

'You had a good day, then?' Alastair asked as he met Connie at a stile. She paused, him on one side and her on the other and, for a brief moment, their fingers touched.

Connie pulled her hand away.

'I mean, other than the muddy embrace,' Alastair said, as if he hadn't noticed the fact that they had touched.

'I've had a great time,' she told him, looking away. 'Mud and all. Nothing could spoil today. It's been brilliant,' she said.

'Good,' Alastair said, nodding lightly as he hopped over the stile and walked on ahead of her.

'What did he say?' Catriona asked as she caught up with Connie.

'Nothing,' Connie said.

'He likes you,' Kirsty said. 'He likes you a *lot!*'

Connie ignored them both but she couldn't help dwelling on their words. Did Alastair really like her?

She watched as he walked ahead of her, his stride so strong and sure, his dark hair blowing out in a dozen different directions at once. He wasn't like the men Connie was used to. But maybe that was the attraction. She'd left LA to get away from all that fakery. Here – right before her – was a *real* man. A man who was at home in the mountains, a man who didn't mind sitting amongst thistles and sheep dung. A man who apparently liked her. Connie smiled as she realised that she apparently liked him too.

They followed a stony track through the valley where the tallest thistles in the world grew, their huge purple heads swaying in the breeze. Everybody's pace had slowed down now. Legs and bodies were pleasantly tired after the day's hike and thoughts were turning towards home, supper and a chance to take one's boots off.

The final half-mile back to Lochnabrae seemed endless but, finally, they were in sight of the familiar white houses and everyone breathed a sigh of relief.

'We've made it!' Sandy said, waving his stick in the air. 'Pie and a pint for me.'

'A hot bath for me,' Kirsty said.

'Who's that?' Maggie suddenly said, removing her new sunglasses.

'Who?' Hamish asked.

'That strange man?'

Everyone looked towards the pub where a small, bald man stood holding a briefcase. He had a suitcase by his side and he didn't look at all happy to be there.

221

'Oh my God!' Connie cried.

'What is it?' Maggie asked.

'He's here. He's really here!'

'Who?' Maggie and Hamish said together.

'My agent,' Connie said, her mouth dropping open in horror.

Chapter Twenty-Three

Bob Braskett looked an odd sight standing outside The Capercaillie in a crisp navy business suit. His shiny bald head seemed to be glowing with anger and his eyes were narrowed behind his round spectacles.

'What the hell are you doing here, Bob?' Connie asked, taking her rucksack off as she approached him.

'I might ask you the same thing,' Bob said.

Everyone crowded around them, intent on finding out what was happening.

'What is this gawd-forsaken place, anyway?' Bob yelled. 'It's in the middle of nowhere. There's nobody here. Nothing's open.'

'We've all been on a hike,' Connie said.

'What – *every*one?'

'Most of the village,' Connie said.

'Where can a person get a drink around here?' Bob asked. 'This is a bar, ain't it?'

'We can get a drink later,' Connie said.

'Fine,' Bob said, clearing his throat noisily. 'Now how do I check into that damned awful hotel? There was nobody there when I knocked.'

'*I* run the bed and breakfast,' Isla said, stepping forward, her face clouded by a frown. 'And we're fully booked.'

Connie took hold of Bob's left arm and walked him away from the crowd.

'Bob,' she said, 'you can't talk to these people like that. You've insulted virtually the whole village and you've only just arrived.'

'Insulted? What about me? I've been stood here in the freezing cold for hours.'

'Then you should've told someone you were coming.'

Bob glared at her. 'I tried calling your cell phone.'

'Ah,' Connie said. 'I kinda lost it.'

'Look,' Bob said, 'just get me a goddamned room.'

'Okay,' Connie said, leaving him for a moment and rejoining Isla. 'Isla,' she said, 'are you *really* fully booked?'

Isla's cheeks coloured. 'Well,' she said, 'not exactly. But I didn't think he was very polite.'

'He isn't,' Connie said. 'He's a Hollywood agent. He's *my* agent.'

Isla gasped. '*He's* your agent? The man who was nasty to you?'

'He's flown all the way from America.'

'I don't care if he's flown all the way from Mars. He's been mean to you, Connie and I won't have him upsetting you again – not in my bed and breakfast.'

Connie sighed. It was nice, of course, to be defended like this but she had a real problem on her hands. This was the man who masterminded her career, as he was so keen to point out to her the whole time. So, she didn't like him very much. So, she didn't trust his judgement as much as she used to, but she still couldn't leave him standing there in the middle of the street, could she? He had too much power over her life to risk upsetting him.

'Please, Isla – you'd be doing me a huge favour,' she said.

Isla looked far from happy. 'I'd be doing it for you,' she said, 'and not for him.'

'Absolutely,' Connie said.

Isla's face was still clouded with disapproval. 'All right then,' she said. 'But I'm putting him in the smallest room.'

Connie breathed a sigh of relief and went to tell Bob the news.

'I've got you a room.'

'Where you're staying?'

'Yep. Come on,' she said.

'Connie,' Bob said. 'Why are all those people staring at us?'

'Because you're making a scene.'

'Who are they, anyway?'

Connie smiled. 'They're my fan club.'

'Yeah, well, they're creeping me out,' Bob said, taking one last look behind him before he hurried towards the bed and breakfast with his suitcase and briefcase in tow.

Connie had her own front door key and let him in before Isla had a chance to catch up with them.

'Jeez!' Bob said as he plonked his things in the hallway. 'This place is enough to bring on one of my migraines.'

'Oh, stop moaning, Bob. It's beautiful here.'

'It's like being inside one of those kaleidoscopes. Everywhere I turn, I see a different pattern.'

It was then that Isla entered. Connie swallowed hard, hoping that Isla hadn't heard but, from the look on her face, she had and she turned to face Bob, her eyes stony with loathing.

'This way,' she announced, her voice as spiky as a thistle. Connie and Bob followed her up the stairs and Isla opened the door into a small bedroom with a dizzying carpet. Bob's mouth dropped open.

'Is there nothing bigger?'

'No,' Isla snapped. 'Take it or leave it.'

'He'll take it,' Connie said.

As Connie disappeared into the bed and breakfast with Bob, Maggie and the rest of the fan club watched in wonder.

'Wasn't he just the rudest man?' Kirsty said.

'And his breath stank,' Catriona said.

'Who was he?' Euan asked.

'Connie's agent – from Hollywood,' Maggie said.

'I'll have to have a word with him,' Angus said.

'Yes,' Euan said, 'tell him to take better care of our Connie.'

'No,' Angus said. 'To tell him that Connie should be doing westerns instead of all them romantic comedies.'

'Angus!' Maggie shouted. 'Will you stop going on about bloody westerns for five minutes?'

For a moment, nobody said a word. Maggie never lost her temper, let alone swore.

'You okay?' Hamish asked, stepping forward and laying a hand on his sister's shoulder.

'I'm fine. I'm just worried about Connie,' Maggie said.

'She looked okay to me,' Angus said.

'Then you weren't looking closely enough,' Maggie said and, with that, she walked up the road towards the shop.

She was anxious and, if she was totally honest, she was

anxious not just for Connie but herself too. Connie had become such a wonderful fixture in Lochnabrae and Maggie wondered if the arrival of her agent marked the end of her stay.

'She said she'd do the play,' she told herself. 'She has to stay for that.'

She let herself into the shop and dumped her rucksack behind the till, leaning forward onto the counter and sighing. She knew she was being selfish wanting Connie to stay. Connie had her own life to lead – she had films to make, premieres to attend, and other, far more glamorous people than Maggie to meet. She wasn't going to stay in Lochnabrae for ever. Who was Maggie trying to kid by thinking that she would? It was an impossible dream – a Maggie dream – and it was nothing more than pure fantasy.

She wasn't surprised when she heard the bell at the door sound. She'd had a feeling Hamish would come after her so, when she looked up and saw Mikey standing there, she didn't know what to say.

'Are you all right, our Maggie?' he asked, his eyes dark and anxious.

Maggie nodded but didn't say anything.

'You think Connie's leaving?' he asked.

'Well, what's she got to stay here for?'

'Oh, I don't know,' Mikey said, 'there's plenty to keep a person happy here.'

'Really?' Maggie said. 'Then why did you leave?'

Mikey's brows narrowed over his eyes. 'I went travelling.'

'Why?'

'To see places. I needed to see what was out there.'

'Lochnabrae wasn't enough for you, was it?' Maggie said.

'I came back, didn't I?'

'But for how long?'

'What do you mean?' Mikey asked. 'What're you talking about, Maggie?'

Maggie turned away.

'Maggie?'

'Nothing!' she said. 'I mean nothing.'

'It didn't sound like nothing.'

Maggie blinked away the tears that were threatening to spill and then she turned to face Mikey again. 'What do you want?'

Mikey looked confused. 'What do I want?'

'You came in here. What did you want?'

'Oh!' Mikey said. 'I came in for that shortbread. You know, we were talking about it the other night?'

Maggie sighed. 'Middle shelf at the end,' she said quietly.

'Brilliant!' Mikey said, a fat enthusiastic smile on his face. 'How much is it?'

'Just take it,' Maggie said, waving a hand at him.

'Thanks, Mags,' he said. 'You're the best.'

And Maggie watched as he left the shop with the packet of shortbread clutched in his hand.

Chapter Twenty-Four

Connie's agent wasn't the type to calm down – the only thing that would ever calm him down would be a fatal heart attack and Connie was quite certain he was heading straight towards one.

'You were lucky to get this room at all,' Connie said.

'Lucky?' Bob said incredulously. 'It's a complete dump. I can't understand what you're doing here.'

'I told you – I needed a break.'

'Well, couldn't it wait, for pity's sake?'

'For when, Bob? Maybe you've not noticed but there's *never* a break. When I finish one film, I'm straight into another. You know my schedule – you've been orchestrating it for the past ten years.'

'And I haven't heard any complaints before.'

'That's because I didn't have any *time* to complain!' Connie shouted, sinking down on the single bed by the window.

Bob scratched his bald head and took his glasses off. He looked around the room and scowled. 'I need to eat,' he said. 'I haven't had anything decent since I left LA. You've got a car, right?'

Connie shook her head. 'I got a taxi from Glasgow airport.'

'You didn't hire a car? You mean you're stuck here?'

'I like it here. I don't need to go anywhere else.'

'But there's nothing here!' Bob shouted. 'No restaurants, no shops, *nothing*.'

'There's a small shop that sells everything you need – well, almost – and there's the pub. We can eat there,' Connie said, surprising herself at how strongly she defended the very village that she'd been unsure of just a few days ago.

Bob didn't look convinced.

'Look,' Connie said, 'take a shower, get changed and then we'll head out. You'll enjoy yourself – I promise.'

Connie waited for Bob in her own room. She took off her hiking clothes, had a hot shower and changed into a lilac cashmere jumper and a pair of jeans. Combing her hair, she wondered what the evening held in store for her. She was uneasy with Bob's presence in Lochnabrae. He was out here purely for business purposes and she wasn't sure she liked the implications of that. She'd come out here to find the time and space to make her own mind up about things. She didn't want her agent doing it for her and she knew he had every intention of doing just that. Why else had he flown out here? He wasn't anxious about her well-being – he was more concerned with his own. Connie knew that she was one of his biggest clients and he was protecting his own interests by following her to Scotland.

There was a light rap on her bedroom door.

'Connie?' a voice said. It was Isla.

'Come on in,' Connie said and Isla entered the room. Her face was pale and anxious.

'I've come to see if you're all right, my dear.'

Connie smiled. 'That's kind of you, Isla.'

'Is his lordship in his room?'

Connie nodded. 'We're heading out to the pub this evening. Would you like to join us?'

Isla looked startled. 'I don't think his lordship would thank you for inviting me, would he?'

'Probably not,' Connie said, 'but I'd like to have you with me.'

Isla walked across the room and took Connie's hand in hers. 'I think you might need to be alone with him, don't you?'

A huge sigh left Connie. 'Yes. You're right but I'm absolutely dreading it.'

'Are you going to leave him?'

'I don't know. I really don't know.'

'He's making you miserable,' Isla said.

'Yes, but he's been making me miserable for so many years that I'm kind of used to it and I'm not sure how I'd function with anyone else.'

'But there must be other agents you could try.'

'Oh, sure.'

'Then why don't you give a different one a go?' Isla asked.

Connie didn't answer for a moment. 'Because,' she said at last, 'I'm not at all sure what I'm going to be doing in the future.'

Isla stared at Connie, trying to discern what she meant. 'You mean you're thinking of giving up acting?' Isla suddenly blurted.

'Shush!' Connie hushed. 'He'll hear you.'

'But you can't give up acting!'

Connie looked up at Isla. 'Why not?'

'Because you're Connie Gordon!'

'People keep saying that! I wish I knew what it meant.'

'It means you're an actress,' Isla said. 'The best there is.'

'But I might be other things too,' Connie said.

'Like what?' Isla asked.

'Like – I don't know but that's what I'm trying to find out. Please don't say anything to anyone, will you?' Connie said.

Isla rested a hand on her shoulder. 'Of course I won't, my dear.'

'You see, Bob doesn't know yet although I think he has an inkling which is why he's here.'

'We could always lock him in his room until you've decided what to do,' Isla said with a wink.

Connie laughed. 'As much as I like the sound of that, I think I'd better try and sort things out as quickly as possible.'

'Do you think he'll stay long?'

'No,' Connie said. 'If I know Bob, he'll be out of here first thing tomorrow.'

'Good riddance,' Isla said.

'But I'm not looking forward to the time between now and then.'

'Maybe I should come with you tonight,' Isla said.

Connie shook her head. 'Thanks, Isla but I think I'd better face him alone.'

Twenty minutes later and Connie was standing in Bob's room as he was fastening a pair of flashy gold cufflinks.

'Are we going out for this meal or what?' he asked impatiently.

'I'm ready,' Connie said.

'You're going out like that?' Bob asked, turning around.

'Sure. Why not?'

Bob peered at her closely. 'You look different. Unwell.'

'I haven't got make-up on. That's all. It's no big deal, is it?'

'No make-up? You're going out and you're not wearing make-up?'

'I'm meant to be on holiday,' Connie said, shrugging.

'But you always wear make-up.'

'So I'm having a change. I'm letting my skin breathe!'

Bob looked startled. 'And what's that smell?'

'What smell?'

Bob sniffed, his sharp nose moving unnervingly close to Connie's face. 'Is that you?'

'It's my face cream. Benet's Balm. The monks make it. It's very nourishing.'

Bob shook his head in disgust. 'And you need a haircut.'

Connie tutted. 'I do not. It's just that I haven't blow-dried it this evening. I'm giving it a break. Skin, hair, me. *Everything* needs a break, Bob, so get used to it.'

He glared at her for a moment and she felt sure that he was on the verge of saying something quite horrible but he seemed to change his mind, grabbing his room key and leaving instead. What had happened to their relationship, she wondered? He hadn't always been so antagonistic. When she'd first signed with him, he'd been positively pleasant but maybe that was just to gain her business. One thing was for sure now – she didn't trust him.

They left the bed and breakfast just after eight. The sky was beginning to darken and there was a stillness that made Connie feel wonderfully serene.

'Wait till you see the stars, Bob. They're amazing. The sky's stuffed with them.'

Bob grunted. 'You're the only star I want to see,' he said.

'You and my other clients who I left to come and find you in this hell hole.'

Connie rolled her eyes. This, she thought, was going to be a dreadful evening.

The Capercaillie was packed with everyone who'd been on the hike and more besides. Pints were being downed at an alarming rate and everyone raised their glasses when Connie entered.

'Connie!' Maggie shouted across the room. 'I've kept you a seat,' she said, patting the bench beside her.

'I'll join you later,' Connie shouted back and then motioned to Bob who was making his way to the bar. Maggie nodded in acknowledgement. When Connie joined Bob, he was scrutinising the menu from behind his glasses. 'What's this meat pie like?'

'I don't know,' Connie said. 'Good, I expect. All the food's wonderful.'

'And loaded with cholesterol, no doubt.'

'God! Will you relax for one moment?' Connie snapped.

He looked up at her in alarm. 'What's the matter with you?' he asked.

'Me? Nothing! It's you who's uptight.'

Bob looked dumbfounded. He'd never been spoken to like that before by a client, Connie realised.

'This foreign air's affecting you,' he said, his eyes returning to the menu. 'Perhaps I should just have the salad.'

'Have the pie, Bob. Live dangerously.'

'No,' he said, snapping the menu shut. 'Salad for me. No dressing.'

'I'm having the pie,' Connie told Fraser. 'With chips, please.'

Fraser nodded and grinned.

'Chips?' Bob said.

'Fries.'

'I know what they are. I don't need a translation.'

'Then what's the problem?' Connie asked.

Bob removed his glasses and pinched his nose. 'That's what I'm trying to find out,' he said.

'Don't you think we should go and join her?' Maggie asked Hamish. 'She looks really stressed out.'

'He doesn't look as if he's in the mood for conversation,' Hamish said. 'Not with us, anyway.'

'Best leave them to it for a bit,' Alastair said, taking a swig from his pint.

'What do you think he wants?' Maggie asked.

'Probably come to take her back with him,' Alastair said, turning to look at Connie and Bob.

It was the answer Maggie had been dreading. She'd been hoping against hope that Bob might have some news for Connie that simply couldn't be imparted by phone and that he'd be gone the next day and Connie would stay for ever and ever.

'So she's really going, is she?' Sandy asked from the end of the table.

'Looks that way,' Alastair said.

'I thought she was going to be in our play,' Sandy said.

'Aye,' Alastair said. 'Just as well we didn't make a start then, isn't it?'

'I'm going to miss her,' Kirsty said from the other end of the table.

'Me too,' Catriona said and the two of them gazed over at Connie.

'It won't be the same without her,' Kirsty said.

'No,' Catriona said. 'Everything will just go back to being boring.'

Maggie sighed. It was absolutely no comfort that she wasn't the only one who was going to miss Connie.

Chapter Twenty-Five

Connie was halfway through her pie and chips, wondering why she'd never eaten proper food before in her life when it was so delicious. She could scream when she thought about the years that she had starved herself, the appalling diets she had been on and how listless and miserable they'd made her feel when, all the time, there was wonderful, home-cooked food out there just begging to be eaten and enjoyed.

She was just wondering if she could get the pie recipe from the pub landlord when Bob Braskett started in earnest.

'I've flown across the Atlantic to bring you home – back to where you belong, Connie.'

At first, Connie didn't say anything.

'I'm a busy man but I've made time for you because you're special to me.'

Connie almost choked on a chip. It was the closest Bob had ever got to saying anything remotely kind to her.

'Really?' she said, thinking it would be fun to milk this for all it was worth.

Bob looked suddenly bashful. 'Of course you are. You're my best client.'

'I bet you say that to all your clients,' Connie said.

'I do but, in this case, I mean it.'

'And I bet you say that to them all too.'

Bob put his knife and fork down and steepled his fingers together.

'It's time to come home with me, Connie. We can't afford to have you a missing person any longer.'

Connie sighed. That's what it all came down to, of course – money. She was a commodity and, when Bob said that she was his best client he meant that she was his best earner.

'There's a problem with that, I'm afraid,' Connie said, knowing that now was the time to be absolutely honest with him.

'Problem? What problem?'

Connie looked at him, her bright hazel eyes seeking his out. 'I'm not sure I know where home is any more.'

Bob paused for a minute before speaking. His high forehead was wearing a frown of Grand Canyon proportions. 'What? What did you say?'

'I said I'm not sure where home is any more,' Connie said again, slowly and clearly.

'I don't understand. What do you mean?'

'What do you mean, *what do I mean?* I don't know how else to put it,' Connie said.

'Wait a minute,' Bob said, raising a hand and closing his eyes. 'Let me get this straight. You're unsure about something.'

'Yes,' Connie said. 'To be honest – and I want to be honest with you – I'm unsure about a lot of things just now.'

'Okay,' Bob said calmly.

Connie pushed her plate to one side and started to twist her fingers in her lap. He was listening to her, wasn't he?

He was really trying to understand her. It was no less than she should have expected from her agent but, coming from Bob Braskett, this sort of understanding was nothing short of miraculous.

For a moment, neither spoke. Bob still had his eyes closed as if he was searching for the answer to some ancient mystery.

'Bob—' Connie began.

'I've got it!' he said, his eyes springing open.

'Got what?' Connie asked.

'What it is you want,' Bob declared smugly. 'More money, right? I can get you more money.'

'No,' Connie said, and she could feel herself deflating with disappointment. She'd sincerely believed that Bob was trying to understand her. 'I don't want more money. I've got more than I know what to do with in one lifetime.'

Bob looked a little crestfallen that he wasn't right. 'Well, why not enjoy it?' he said, determining to take control of things again. 'Buy yourself an island in the Caribbean – that's the latest craze. Or a fancy yacht or an airplane. Everyone deserves a treat.'

'I don't want a treat,' Connie said. Even to her own ears, she was beginning to sound like a petulant child. 'You don't understand. Even *I* don't understand what I want.'

'Oh, gawd!' Bob suddenly exclaimed. 'You don't want a baby, do you?'

Connie looked at him with bemusement. 'Who said anything about a baby?'

'Please don't tell me you're pregnant,' Bob said. 'Or – worse – going to adopt some little foreign kid with jaundice.'

'Bob! What a thing to say.'

'Because all the stars are doing it and it means their work suffers. I've seen it over and over again. The kid always comes first.'

'That's the most outrageous thing you've ever said,' Connie told him, 'and you've said some pretty appalling things in your time.'

'So you're not adopting a kid?'

'No, I'm not adopting a kid.'

'Thank Christ for that.'

'I'm getting a drink,' Connie said with a sigh, scraping her chair back. 'Do you want one?'

Bob shook his head and Connie made her way to the bar, her head throbbing. A drink was the last thing she needed when she was feeling the way she was but it was the only thing that was going to get her through this dire evening.

As the others chatted on their table, Alastair was surreptitiously watching Connie and Bob. Things weren't looking good between them. Connie looked pale and anxious and Bob looked red and angry. It was sad to witness. They were so obviously two people who wanted different things out of their business relationship.

Alastair thought about the Connie he'd seen up on the hills that day. She'd been laughing, smiling and chatting. Her face had glowed the most gorgeous pink and her eyes had been beautifully bright. Yet here she was looking like a doll whose stuffing had been ripped out of her. It was taking all his willpower not to get up and walk over there but what could he possibly say? He had no business over there. He wasn't a part of their world and, even if he did think of something to say, they wouldn't listen to him. This, he knew, was Connie's decision and he had to trust her to make the right one.

Still, he couldn't help thinking of that moment when their hands had touched at the stile and how easy it would be for him to cross the pub and take her hand in his now and run back up into the hills with her until she was laughing again.

I must not fall in love with this woman, he told himself. *She's an actress and I've sworn off actresses. They're bad news. Just remember what happened last time. And a Hollywood superstar would be far worse than any stage actress.*

'Alastair?' Maggie's voice suddenly broke into his thoughts.

'Yep?' he said, shaking the Cathy and Heathcliff image of himself and Connie from out of his mind.

'You okay?'

''Course,' he said, dragging his eyes away from Connie.

'What do you think's going on over there?' Maggie asked as Connie scraped her chair back and stalked over to the bar.

'Well, it doesn't look like a nice cosy chat, now, does it?'

'I'm going to go over there,' Maggie said.

'No,' Alastair told her, placing his hand on hers.

'But that man's going to take Connie away, I just know it.'

'That might be so but you've no business to interfere.'

'But I'm her friend,' Maggie said.

Alastair took a swig from his glass. 'Maggie,' he said quietly, 'we've got to let Connie go.'

Maggie's face crumpled. 'Don't say that.'

'She was only ever visiting – you must realise that,' Alastair said.

'She's happy here,' Maggie said. 'She told me so and I've

241

seen the change in her. You have too. And you like her, don't you? I know you do.'

'Aye,' Alastair said. 'I can't deny that but we can't keep her here. This isn't where she belongs.'

'How can you be so sure?' Maggie demanded.

'Because I know actresses,' Alastair said, 'and they don't live in places like Lochnabrae.'

'Why not?'

'They just don't. Oh, they might think that's what they want for a while. They might take a holiday or even buy a cottage in the middle of nowhere and play housekeeper for a while – I've seen it before – but it's a role that doesn't fit. Sooner or later – and it's usually sooner – they crave the bright lights and the adulation of an audience and head back.'

'But what about you?' Maggie said.

'What about me?'

'*You* made the break – *you're* here!'

'That's different,' Alastair said.

'How?'

'I'm not an actor. I'm just a playwright. I can settle anywhere.'

Maggie pouted. 'But you were as famous as any actor.'

'What do you mean?' Alastair asked, suddenly anxious that Maggie might know more about him than he'd ever let on.

'Don't you miss London?'

'No, I don't,' he said.

'Then Connie might not miss Hollywood,' Maggie said proudly, as if she'd just made the greatest discovery ever.

'Actors are different.'

'I don't believe that,' Maggie said. 'She's just a woman

underneath all the glamour. She wants the same things we do.'

Alastair looked closely at Maggie. 'You think?'

Maggie nodded. 'I'm sure of it.' She looked across the bar to where Connie was sitting with Bob, a new drink in her hand. 'She's lonely,' she said, 'and she's been let down. That's why she came here – to be with real people, not people like him. She wanted to be somewhere where people just treat her normally.'

'And you do that, do you?' Alastair asked her with a chuckle.

Maggie blushed. 'I might've been a bit star-struck at first.'

'A bit?' Alastair teased.

'What?' Maggie said.

'I thought you'd have Connie locked away in the fan club HQ by now, charging admission for the privilege of seeing her.'

'Och, you do talk some rubbish, Alastair McInnes.'

'What's that saying?'

'What saying?'

'About freeing something?' Alastair paused. '*If you love something, set it free.* That's it, isn't it?'

'I hate that saying,' Maggie said. 'If I love something, I want to keep it right by me. I want to cuddle it and hold it and never let it go.'

Alastair grinned at her. 'You can't do that, Maggie.'

Maggie sighed. 'I know.' And they both gazed over to where Connie was sitting, each of them knowing that she was slipping away from them.

'Look, kid,' Bob said with a grin that Connie found most disturbing, 'I know you need a break – we all do every now and again. But there comes a time when you have to come back. Think of it like *Roman Holiday*. You know what I'm talking about?'

'Of *course* I know,' Connie said. 'It's one of my favourite films.'

'Right. Well, Audrey Hepburn takes her break, don't she? She goes mad, has an affair, does a lotta crazy things but—' Bob held his hand up in the air, 'she goes home. She becomes the princess again and takes up her responsibilities.'

'And leaves the love of her life behind,' Connie whispered to herself.

'Look, you're a good actress – the best. You know the true meaning of work.'

'Do I?'

'You always do your best and that shows.'

'Not to me.'

'What do you mean?'

'There's got to be more to life, Bob.'

'More than work? You're kidding me, right?'

'And I want to try and find it.'

Bob's eyes narrowed. 'Here? You want to try and find it here – is that what you're saying?'

'It might be.'

'But you can't exist outside of LA.'

'No, Bob – *you* can't exist outside of LA. I'm existing very well.'

Bob glared at her in undisguised horror. 'Do you know who I've got clamouring for me to handle them? Do you?'

Connie sighed. She knew he'd turn nasty sooner or later. 'I'm sure you've got half of Hollywood clamouring for your services,' she said.

'You're damned right I have. So why do I waste my time on you?'

Connie didn't bother to try and answer him. It was best she let him get it all out of his system.

'Do you know the strings I pulled to get you that part in *The Pirate's Wife*? Do you know who they wanted for that role? You weren't even on their long list.'

It was on the tip of her tongue to say that she'd never asked for the role in the first place but it wouldn't do her any good.

'And what's going to happen now? What about your acting?'

'I'm going to be acting here,' Connie said quietly.

'What do you mean? The new Tod Fordham film? I thought that was shooting in London.'

'No, not the new Fordham film. I mean *here*, in Lochnabrae.'

'On location?'

'No. In the village hall. Shakespeare.'

Bob's face fell. 'You mean amateur dramatics?'

Connie nodded with glee. 'Why not?'

That was the last thing Bob wanted to hear and Connie watched as his face turned at least four shades darker than usual. 'You can't stay here, Connie! I'm telling you that right now,' he said, his voice mean and menacing.

For one dreadful moment, Connie thought he was going to physically attack her. 'Are you threatening me, Bob?' her voice rose an octave and the whole pub heard her words and, before either of them had a chance to say anything else, the great bulk of Euan Kennedy was shadowing their table.

'Is this man bothering you, lass?'

245

Connie looked up. So did Bob.

'Who the hell are you?' Bob demanded.

'I'm Euan,' Euan said, seeming puzzled that anyone wouldn't know who he was.

'Well, this is a private conversation,' Bob said.

'Not when the whole pub can hear it,' Euan said, which made Connie smile. 'We don't like shouting here. Especially where women are concerned.'

'God almighty!' Bob seethed through clenched teeth.

'Perhaps you should leave,' Euan suggested, looking at Bob rather than Connie.

Bob hesitated. He obviously didn't want to be seen to back down so easily. 'I'm not standing for this,' he said, immediately standing up, which also made Connie smile. 'Come on, Connie. Let's finish this somewhere else.'

Connie didn't move.

'Connie,' Bob shouted.

She took a deep breath. 'I think we've finished already,' she said.

The whole pub fell silent.

'Fine,' Bob said. 'If that's the way you want it. But this isn't it, Connie,' Bob said. 'You've not heard the last of this.' Bob looked at her a moment longer as if trying to work her out. 'You've let me down, Connie,' he said and then he stalked out of the pub.

Connie's head sank down onto her folded arms.

'Don't take it to heart, lass,' Euan said, sitting in the seat vacated by Bob. 'He's gone now.'

'I wish he'd never come,' Connie mumbled without looking up.

'At least you've said your piece now. You've made it clear what you want,' Euan said.

'Have I?' Connie said, looking up. 'Then why do I feel so nervous about it? Why do I feel like I've just made the biggest mistake of my life?'

Euan looked at her and his eyes were warm and understanding. 'Because change can be scary,' he said. 'What you've just done was a very brave thing.'

'It certainly was,' Sandy said, pulling up a chair and joining their table. 'He needed putting in his place.'

'You were amazing, Connie!' Maggie said a moment later. 'Really amazing. A real heroine!'

Connie smiled weakly, pleased to have their praise when she was feeling so low.

'If Euan hadn't broken things up, I was going to throw him out of The Bird myself,' Hamish said. 'Nobody should speak to our Connie like that.'

'Do you think he'll stay?' Alastair asked.

'I hope not,' Connie said. 'I expect he's packing.'

'Good riddance,' Angus said. 'Although I should've liked to have told him my idea for a new type of western.'

Everyone groaned, but Connie laughed. 'You're all so wonderful,' she said. 'What would I have done without you?'

'Probably caved in and gone back to Hollywood with that creep,' Maggie said with a wink.

'Oh, no,' Connie said. 'I'd never have done that.'

'So, you're staying?' Alastair asked, not bothering to disguise the smile that was so evident in his voice.

'If you'll have me,' she said.

'Aye, we'll have you!' Hamish said.

But Connie wasn't looking at Hamish. She was looking at Alastair and the look that passed between them made a very strong case for Connie staying in Lochnabrae just a little bit longer.

Chapter Twenty-Six

Connie was right about Bob Braskett. He'd left that very evening, throwing a wad of cash at Isla and waiting for his taxi further along the road to Strathcorrie in his attempt to avoid any more of Connie's bodyguards.

'I threw him out!' Isla said dramatically when Connie returned from the pub. 'I told him exactly what I thought of him. "You can't go around treating people like that", I said. "And certainly not someone like Connie".' Isla stood with her arms folded across her puffed-up chest.

They went upstairs together and Connie checked Bob's room as if she didn't quite believe he'd gone.

'Was he really here at all?' she asked.

'Oh, aye,' Isla said. 'There are towels all over the floor and the loo seat's up.'

When Maggie awoke the next morning, she felt like a prisoner just out of jail. Since the arrival of Connie's agent, she'd been holding her breath, terrified that she was going to lose her idol after such a short time, but that wasn't going to happen now and she wasn't going to listen to Alastair's warnings about her going at some point in the future. She was here now and that's all that mattered.

Opening the shop that day, Maggie was in such a good mood that she even welcomed Mrs Wallace with a smile.

'And how are you?' she asked. 'Is your cold any better?'

Mrs Wallace stared at her as if she'd lost her mind. 'Oh, my cold,' she suddenly said, 'it's just a light one.' And she gave a little sniff.

Maggie thought nothing of it. Until later that morning.

With the first read-through of *Twelfth Night* taking place that evening, Connie was becoming more and more nervous. Maggie had already told her the basic plot but it was the language of the play Connie was worrying about, and that's why she was going to do some more preparation with Maggie first.

When Connie entered the shop later that morning, Maggie flew across the room and flung her arms around her.

'What was that for?' Connie asked once Maggie had released her from her stranglehold.

'For staying,' Maggie said. 'I'm so glad you're here.'

'And I'm glad to be here,' Connie said.

'And you're not going, are you?' Maggie said.

'Well, not just yet,' Connie said.

Maggie nodded, knowing that that was the best answer she could hope for at the moment.

'How's about we get down to a bit of Shakespeare?' Connie said and Maggie nodded, producing their two copies from behind the counter.

'I'll make a cup of tea first,' Maggie said.

'Let me,' Connie said and went into the back room.

As soon as Connie disappeared, the shop bell tinkled and in walked Colin Simpkins.

'Good morning, Maggie,' he said.

'Oh, it's you,' Maggie said.

'A lovely welcome – as ever.'

Maggie tutted. Ever since Colin Simpkins had planted a slobbery kiss on her at one of the high school end of year dances, she'd done her best to avoid him.

'What do you want?'

Colin walked up to the counter and leant on it. 'I'm looking for someone, actually.'

'Oh, Desperate Dates dot com not work out for you, then?'

'Not that kind of someone,' Colin said, smoothing a hand through his oily hair. 'Someone famous, actually.'

Maggie was instantly on her guard. 'What do you mean?'

'You know what I mean, Maggie.'

'I've no idea what you're talking about,' Maggie said, busying herself with unpacking cigarette cartons and all too aware that Connie could surface from the kitchen at any moment.

'There's been a report that Connie Gordon's in town,' Colin said.

'A report?'

'From a reliable source,' Colin said. 'A *very* reliable source.'

Maggie gasped inwardly. She knew exactly who the report had come from: Mrs Wallace. She'd not had a cold at all, had she? She'd stayed at home yesterday so she could ring the local paper and tell them that Connie Gordon was in Lochnabrae. But why? Why would she do that when Connie had been so sweet to her? But Maggie knew why. Mrs Wallace wouldn't want to miss an opportunity to inflate her own self-importance. She could just imagine the story now.

'Connie knew she could come to me in her time of trouble and I was very happy to help her.'

There'd be no mention of sewing machines swapped for expensive bottles of whisky. Oh, no. Mrs Wallace would twist the truth and make it sound like she was the movie star's confidante, and scare Connie off in the process.

Maggie was seething but she couldn't let Colin see her like that.

'So, you're going to help me, Maggie?'

Maggie thought quickly and walked towards the doorway on the pretence of putting something in the bin.

'I don't know what you're talking about,' she said. 'Do you really think Connie Gordon,' she said, raising her voice as much as she could without being too obvious, 'would be here in Lochnabrae? The idea's ludicrous.'

'You think so?' Colin said, edging forward and looking in the same direction as Maggie. 'You wouldn't be hiding her here, then, Maggie? She wouldn't be staying at Isla's B&B, then?'

'Don't be ridiculous. Get out of my shop!' Maggie said, pushing him from behind the counter.

'All right then,' Colin said. 'Have it your own way, Maggie Hamill.'

'I will,' she said.

'But I'll find her – mark my words.'

Maggie slammed the door in his face and turned the sign around to 'closed'.

'Has he gone?' Connie asked, her head popping around from the kitchen.

'Get back!' Maggie hissed, hastening across the shop towards her. 'You heard, then?'

Connie nodded. 'How did he find out I was here?'

'I'm guessing Mrs Wallace,' Maggie said.

'Really? But what would she gain from it?'

'Are you kidding? She'd do anything for her name in the paper.'

'But why didn't she ring a national? She could've been paid for the story then.'

'I don't think it's about the money. The local paper's more her style. It's the one everyone reads.'

'But the reporter could then sell the story on,' Connie said. 'I've seen that happen before. We could be overrun with journalists before we know it.'

'I know,' Maggie said.

'What are we going to do?

'We'll have to come up with something to put Colin Simpkins off the trail,' Maggie said.

'But what?' Connie asked.

Maggie looked thoughtful for a moment. 'You're an actress, aren't you?'

'I think so,' Connie said. 'Why?'

'And Isla didn't recognise you when you arrived at the B&B, did she?'

'No,' Connie said. 'I wasn't wearing any make-up and I'd tied my hair under a cap. Should I do that again? Do you think that's enough not to be recognised?'

'No,' Maggie said. 'Colin's too sharp for that. We need a real disguise. Something that would even fool your own mother.'

'Like a wig and some false teeth?'

Maggie nodded excitedly. 'And I know just where to get them from.'

*

After Maggie had sent word around to everyone that Colin Simpkins was on the prowl looking for Connie, they sneaked around the back of the houses and made their way to the village hall.

'I've got a spare key,' Maggie said, opening the ancient door and entering the old building.

'What is this place?' Connie asked.

'The village hall. It's where we're doing the play.'

'Here?'

'Of course. Where else?' Maggie said and then grinned. 'I know what you're thinking. It looks like a shack, doesn't it? But we've got a stage and changing rooms and everything. It's a bit past its best but it's all we've got.' Maggie couldn't help noticing that Connie wasn't looking impressed. 'I know it needs a facelift but it's really very pretty when the lights are on and there's an audience.'

'So, this is what you were raising money for with those signed photos of me,' Connie said.

Maggie bit her lip. 'I'm so sorry—'

'No need to apologise again,' Connie said. 'I can see why you did it. I would've done the same thing in your shoes.'

'You would?'

'These places are important,' Connie said and then something caught her attention. 'Is that the stage?' she asked, looking at the ancient wooden floorboards.

'Yep!' Maggie said. 'Home sweet home for the next eight months.'

'Eight months? You're going to spend eight months here?'

'Well, it's a slow business getting it all sorted. You'd be surprised. Half of us don't turn up half the time and then something important always gets forgotten.'

'Like what?' Connie asked.

'The tea, mainly,' Maggie said, 'and nobody likes to rehearse unless tea's been laid on.'

'And who comes to see the play?'

'Oh, just the locals.'

'Just Lochnabrae?'

'Well, we advertise it in Strathcorrie but the weather's usually bad at that time of year and not many people show up.'

'I'm confused,' Connie said. 'I can't believe you go to so much trouble for so little reward.'

'But it keeps us all going especially in the winter months,' Maggie said. 'It's something to do and it's fun. You must have acted for fun. Some of your roles – didn't you choose them just for the fun of it?'

Connie looked puzzled for a moment. 'I'm not sure. Sometimes, the decision wasn't mine at all. My agent tends to steer me towards certain roles – you know, ones that'll be best for my career. Others are taken because the money's good even when I really don't like the script at all. Sometimes I have to do semi-nudity when I'd rather just not do that movie altogether. It's one of the reasons I walked out.' She strode up the steps onto the stage and took a deep breath. 'It's places like this where it all begins, isn't it? Where dreams begin.'

'Did your dreams start on a stage?'

Connie looked down at Maggie. 'No,' she said. 'But I think it's where my mother's dreams started – for her and then for me.'

Maggie nodded. 'You know, she probably acted on this very stage.'

Connie's eyes widened. 'You're probably right,' she said. 'How would we find out?'

'Euan would probably know. He knows everything about Lochnabrae. You know it was Euan who came up with the fan club idea?'

'Was it?' Connie said. 'He didn't tell me that.'

'He's a really big fan. Probably your biggest after me. And Hamish.'

Connie's face clouded over. 'You don't think he's some sort of pervert, do you?'

'Euan? You've got to be kidding! He was a friend of your mother's. He's just dead proud of you, that's all, and he might have a wee crush on you too,' Maggie said with a twinkle in her eyes.

Connie put her hands on her hips. 'Maggie!'

'Yeah, come on. Let's get down to business.'

The two of them headed down to the changing rooms behind the stage.

With a fairly decent eight hundred words written that morning, Alastair thought he'd walk down into Lochnabrae and give the village hall an airing before the read-through of the play that evening. Closing his door behind him, he called Bounce to heel and walked through the wood down to the loch. There was a stiff breeze about and the tops of the pines tossed against the blue sky. It was a stark reminder that summer was still a long way off.

Following the loch around to the village, Alastair thought of the play they'd be reading that evening. He'd spent some time thinking about the casting of the role of Viola. She was the character around whom the whole action of the play revolved. She was warm and witty, generous of heart and endearing to the audience and the actress who played her would have to be sensitive, moving and confident.

Catriona Kendrick was too young. Her sister Kirsty was about the right age but didn't have the experience needed for the role. Isla was too old. Mrs Wallace was – well – Mrs Wallace. And Maggie? She had the sensitivity to play the part but she wasn't the most confident of actresses. She'd do much better in the role of Olivia, which was a wonderful part but didn't demand quite so much stage time as that of Viola.

So that left Connie. Connie Gordon – Hollywood A-list movie star – to play Viola in the Lochnabrae Amateur Dramatics Society's production of *Twelfth Night*. At first, when everyone had persuaded her to take part, he'd been against it because he hadn't relished the idea of working with a real actress again. Indeed, the thought still made him nervous. But what else could he do? He'd chosen a play where the lead role was demanding and, unlike most of Shakespeare's plays, female. Connie was the only one who could do it, he was quite sure of that.

He groaned because he knew what that meant. They would be working closely together – there was no way around it. He would be directing her and the thought of that terrified him because the last time he'd directed an actress . . .

He shook his head.

I mustn't think about that, he told himself. *It's in the past. It's done.*

But was it? Didn't the past always have an unnerving ability to raise its head in the present, repeating itself like an ugly echo?

He took a deep breath. He couldn't allow himself to think like that. For the sake of the LADS, he had to be positive about the play. And Connie.

Arriving at the village hall, Alastair was surprised to find the door unlocked. He'd distinctly remembered locking it behind him when he'd left last time so that meant one thing.

'Maggie?' he called as he went inside. Maggie was the only other person with a set of keys. Perhaps she was tidying up the wardrobe. He knew she adored the costumes.

Bounce bounded up onto the stage ahead of his master.

'Maggie,' he called again but there was no answer.

Alastair saw there was a light coming from the changing rooms and walked down the stairs.

'Maggie – you in there?'

'Alastair?'

'Oh my God!' he exclaimed as he entered the changing room. 'Is that you, Connie? What the hell are you doing?'

Chapter Twenty-Seven

'Bugger!' Maggie exclaimed. 'Did you really recognise her?'

'Of course I did!' Alastair said. 'It's a good disguise but it's not that good.' He looked Connie up and down, taking in the old felt hat, the baggy dress and the oversized glasses. It was then that Bounce galloped into the room and started to lick Connie's hand.

'Even Bounce recognises you!' Maggie said, sinking down onto a bench. 'We'll have to try something else.'

'What's going on?' Alastair asked.

'Colin Simpkins has been snooping around looking for Connie.'

Alastair frowned. 'How did he find out she's here?'

'Said he had his sources,' Maggie said, 'and it's my guess his source stayed away from yesterday's hike in order to make a call to him.'

'Mrs Wallace?'

'I don't know who else it could be,' Maggie said.

'He muthn't find outh I'm here or lifthe won'th be worth living,' Connie lisped through the fake teeth before taking them out.

'If it makes it to the national papers, it'll be just awful for Connie,' Maggie said. 'You'll have to have a word with

Mrs Wallace, Alastair. She'll listen to you. She'd no business to report Connie here.'

Alastair nodded. 'I will.'

'She'll ruin it for all of us if she doesn't button that mouth of hers.'

'So, what are we going to do about Simpkins?' Connie asked.

'I thought we'd find the answer here,' Maggie said, 'but there aren't any decent costumes.'

'Maybe we could order something from the internet,' Connie suggested. 'The clothes and books we ordered before arrived pretty fast.'

'But not fast enough,' Maggie said. 'We need a disguise *now!*'

The three of them were silent as they wondered what could be done. Connie moved behind a screen and slowly began to take off her old lady disguise and Maggie sat slumped on the bench looking thoroughly despondent. Alastair began to rifle through the costume box but Maggie was right – there wasn't really anything suitable.

Unless . . .

'I've got an idea,' Alastair said.

'What?' Maggie asked, looking up excitedly.

'How's about Connie dressing as a man?'

'Ooooh!' Maggie said. 'That's good!'

'And it'll be in keeping with the play too. I mean, you're playing a girl pretending to be a boy, so it fits,' he told Connie as she emerged from behind the screen wearing her own clothes once more.

'A girl playing a boy?'

Alastair nodded. 'Viola,' he said. 'It's the best role in the play.'

'Is it the biggest?' Connie asked.

'I suppose so,' Alastair said.

Connie swallowed hard.

'What about this man's disguise, then?' Maggie asked.

'Well, we've got plenty of old shirts and trousers in here,' Alastair said. 'Start digging.'

They all got to work, holding out checked shirts, tartan trousers and all sorts of other horrors until they found a half-decent pair of jeans and a blue shirt that was passable.

'Try them on,' Maggie said.

'We'll have to do something with her hair,' Alastair said and Maggie nodded.

'I've got a baseball cap,' Connie said. 'I'm used to tucking it under that.'

'We could give it a go,' Maggie said. 'Isn't there a fake moustache somewhere too?'

'In that drawer over there,' Alastair said. 'There's a special adhesive to stick it on with. Get them both out.'

Connie emerged in her new attire. 'Will I do?' she asked.

Maggie grinned and nodded. 'Looks good.'

Alastair shook his head.

'What's wrong?' Connie asked.

'Nobody's going to believe you're a man.'

'Why not?' Connie asked.

'Well, I can see two very good reasons,' Alastair said, a naughty twinkle in his blue eyes.

Connie instantly blushed as she saw Alastair staring at her chest.

'This is just like *Twelfth Night*,' Alastair said with a laugh. 'Have either of you seen the Trevor Nunn film version? The opening shows Imogen Stubbs as Viola, strapping down her chest before she can hide it under her shirt.'

'Like Gwyneth Paltrow in *Shakespeare in Love*!' Maggie said.

'Oh! I've seen that,' Connie said. 'So, what do I use?'

'There's a roll of muslin somewhere. Hamish bought it a few years ago for one of our backdrops,' Alastair said.

'It's still backstage,' Maggie said. 'I'll go and get it.'

When Maggie came with the roll, she opened one of the drawers and produced a pair of scissors and cut a great length of muslin from the roll. Connie disappeared behind the screen again and did the honours.

'How're you doing?' Maggie asked a few minutes later.

'Okay,' Connie shouted back. 'Just a bit more to pad out my tummy, I think. Make everything equal, you know?'

Maggie got back to the roll and cut some more, passing it over the screen and then waiting with Alastair for the new-look Connie to emerge.

'Well, what do you think?' Connie asked a few minutes later.

'Very good,' Maggie said.

'A vast improvement,' Alastair said. 'I mean, on what it looked like before. If you're going to be a man, that is.'

Connie smiled and Maggie giggled.

'But I still look too much like me,' Connie said, looking in the mirror. 'I've got a pair of blue contact lenses with me. I could wear those but even with them and the cap and fake moustache, I'm sure people will recognise me.'

'It's your face shape,' Maggie said. 'It's too beautiful. We need to rough it up a bit or fill it out or something.'

'Can you do that with make-up?' Alastair asked.

'You know,' Connie said, 'I think you can.'

'Well, we've got plenty of make-up here,' Maggie said, opening another drawer.

'And I've watched enough make-up artists over the years,' Connie said. 'Remember *Keep Me Close*?'

Maggie frowned. 'But you were beautiful in that.'

'Not me!' Connie said. 'Curtis.'

'Oh!' Maggie said. 'You can do that?'

'What?' Alastair asked. 'I never saw that film, I'm afraid. I was away from home when the fan club saw it.'

'Just give me a few minutes,' Connie said.

'What's she going to do?' Alastair asked as he and Maggie left the room.

'Just wait and see,' Maggie said.

When Connie called them back in, she'd tied her hair back and shoved it under a hat she'd found on one of the shelves at the back of the dressing room. She'd used a foundation that had darkened her skin so that it now looked more weather-beaten than porcelain-delicate, and she was also sporting an ugly red scar down her left cheek.

'Wow!' Maggie said. 'That's amazing!'

'Blimey,' Alastair said. 'That's pretty impressive. It looks like the real thing too,' he said, stepping closer and examining it.

'Don't touch it!' Connie warned. 'I'm not sure how long it takes to dry and I don't want to smudge it.'

'You look like a real tough nut,' Maggie said. 'You know, I could almost fancy you like that.'

Connie laughed and then looked at herself in the mirror.

'That's it!' Alastair said.

'What?' Connie asked.

'That's your disguise. You'll be Maggie's boyfriend.'

Maggie gasped. 'Nobody will believe I've got a boyfriend.'

'They will when they see you holding hands in The Capercaillie this lunchtime,' Alastair said. 'It'll be the perfect opportunity to test-drive the disguise. You up for it, Connie?'

'I guess,' Connie said. 'Maggie?'

Maggie nodded. 'If you are, Connie.'

'You'll have to have a name,' Alastair said. 'We can't call you Connie any more, and you'll have to have some sort of story. Work it out between you – where you're from, Connie, and how you two met.'

'Okay,' Maggie said.

'So, what do you want to be called?' Alastair asked.

Connie looked at herself in the mirror. 'Ralph,' she said.

'Ralph?' Maggie said with a giggle.

'I had a dog called Ralph. I kind of remind myself of him with this funny little moustache.'

'Ralph it is, then,' Maggie said. 'Isn't this great, Alastair? It's like proper acting!'

'Aye, well, just make sure it's an Oscar-worthy performance,' Alastair said, 'or we'll all be in the newspapers by noon tomorrow.'

Chapter Twenty-Eight

It was a good job they'd moved fast with Connie's disguise because Colin Simpkins was still hanging around at lunchtime. Maggie had smuggled Connie out of the village hall and back to the B&B where Connie was able to complete her disguise with the blue contact lenses and baseball cap.

'I suppose we'll have to tell Isla when she gets back,' Connie said.

'She'll think she's got another guest,' Maggie said.

'Who else is going to know?' Connie asked.

'Hello?' a voice called from downstairs.

'It's Hamish,' Maggie said. 'Are we going to tell him?'

'We could try the disguise out on him, couldn't we?'

Maggie nodded. 'Okay,' she said and the two of them went downstairs to greet him.

'Hamish – you on your lunch break?' Maggie asked.

'Afternoon off,' he said. 'I tried the shop first then guessed you'd be here with Connie,' he said, nodding to Connie. 'Where is she?'

'I don't know,' Maggie said. 'Haven't you seen her?'

'Should I have?' Hamish said.

'Seems she's gone missing,' Maggie said.

'Really? She's not left, has she?' Hamish said. 'I didn't get a chance to talk to her properly. Tell her how much I love her – her films.'

Maggie grinned. 'I'm sure you'll get a chance yet but let me introduce you to my friend, Ralph. Ralph, this is my brother, Hamish.'

'Hello,' Hamish said with a brief nod.

'Hello,' Connie said, trying out her new Ralph voice. It was really rather good.

'You having lunch down the pub with everyone?' Hamish asked.

'Just on our way,' Maggie said. 'Ralph's coming too.'

'Great,' Hamish said and he was just about to open the door when Maggie grabbed his arm. 'I said, Ralph's coming too.'

'Aye, I heard you.'

Maggie grinned and wiggled her eyebrows.

'What?' Hamish said.

'Do you not recognise him?' Maggie asked.

'Ralph?' Hamish said. 'No. Should I?'

Maggie laughed and Connie joined in, causing Hamish to look confused because Ralph was laughing just like a girl.

'What's going on?' Hamish asked.

'It's Connie!' Maggie said.

'What is?'

'Ralph, you fool! It's Connie!'

'Connie?'

'Aye, you loon!'

Hamish took a step closer and Connie nodded.

'Hello, Hamish,' she said. 'Don't touch the moustache – it might fall off.'

'It's fake?'

'I hope so,' Connie said.

'But that scar!' Hamish said.

'It's good, isn't it?' Maggie said.

'It's amazing,' Hamish said with a laugh. 'But what are you up to?'

'Mrs Wallace has shopped Connie to the local paper and Colin Simpkins is sniffing around. We're trying to hide her,' Maggie said. 'Will you help us?'

'Aye, of course I will,' Hamish said. 'I've never liked him anyway.'

'Not since he stole your girlfriend from you,' Maggie said.

'Did he?' Connie said. 'That's awful.'

'Och, don't worry, it was in primary school,' Maggie explained.

Hamish looked hurt. 'I was still in love,' he said.

'Come on!' Maggie said. 'Let's try this disguise out in the pub.'

Alastair was already at the bar when Maggie, Hamish and Ralph walked in. Maggie caught his eyes and nodded her head towards Hamish and winked. Alastair nodded his understanding.

'Come on, Ralph. Let's get a drink,' Maggie said and a few heads rose from their meals as they approached the bar.

Maggie nodded and smiled at the regulars. 'Hello,' she said.

They nodded back, all of them staring at Ralph.

'Maggie's boyfriend,' Hamish said with a grin. 'Ralph.'

Fraser took their orders for lunch and they stood at the bar with their drinks.

'Shouldn't we be holding hands?' Connie whispered to Maggie.

'Yes, you should!' Hamish whispered back.

Maggie looked at her brother. He looked as if he was enjoying this a little more than was good for him.

'Maybe a little canoodle too,' he added.

'Hamish!'

'What?' he said. 'It wouldn't look amiss, would it?'

Maggie looked at Connie. 'What do you think?'

Connie leant her head towards Maggie and then did something that totally caught her unawares – she squeezed her bottom. Maggie leapt in the air and gave a little scream.

The whole of the pub turned and looked.

Maggie managed a giggle. 'Ralph! You're terrible!' she said and everyone returned to their meals and drinks.

Alastair sidled up next to them. 'Aren't you going to introduce me?'

'Oh, of course,' Maggie said. 'Alastair, this is Ralph.'

'Pleased to meet you, Ralph,' Alastair said in a voice that was loud enough to be heard.

And that's when Colin Simpkins walked in. 'Good afternoon, all!' he said. Fraser acknowledged him with a nod but he was the only one who did.

'Maggie,' Colin said. 'We meet again. Like I said.'

'Yeah,' Maggie said. 'Can't find anything better to do, then? Nobody else to bother?'

'Maggie,' Alastair said, 'you were telling me where you met Ralph.'

'Oh,' Maggie said, 'yes. We met at a concert in Glasgow. We bumped into each other – literally.'

'When was that?' Alastair asked.

Maggie was just about to answer when the pub door opened again and in walked Mikey. If there was one person she hadn't wanted to see at that moment, it was Mikey.

I have a boyfriend, Maggie thought. *I'm standing here having my bum squeezed by my boyfriend and Mikey's going to see!*

Mikey joined them at the bar, nodding to Maggie and Alastair and chatting to Hamish.

'So, how long have you been together?' Alastair continued.

Maggie wanted to die or, at the very least, to thump Alastair in the guts and run away but she had to keep the act up. If she didn't, Connie's stay might be in jeopardy.

'Oh, ages and ages,' Maggie said with a little laugh that sounded quite mad.

'How did you get that scar?' Hamish suddenly asked.

Maggie kicked him in the shins.

Ralph cleared his throat. 'Someone was asking me too many questions and we got into a fight.'

Maggie grinned. 'You should see the other guy, eh, Ralph?'

From the other end of the bar, Colin leant forward and peered closer at Ralph. Maggie saw and knew that, if he continued staring at Ralph the way he was, he'd soon twig. So Maggie did the only thing she could to make sure there was no doubt in Colin's mind that Ralph was a man. She kissed him. Her.

She'd intended it to be a quick kiss but once she'd pressed her lips to Connie's, she found that Connie soon entered the spirit of the thing and was kissing her right back.

'Well,' Hamish began but stopped, his cheeks red with embarrassment when the two of them finally came up for air.

Maggie looked around her. Alastair's eyes had doubled in size and his cheeks were as red as Hamish's. She turned to look at Colin who looked thoroughly disgusted and was now ordering today's special from the barman.

It had worked, Maggie thought, and she was just feeling a little bit pleased with herself when she caught Mikey's eye. He was staring at her, an expression on his face that she didn't quite recognise. She opened her mouth to say something but what, exactly, could she say in the circumstances?

'I don't know what you're talking about,' Mrs Wallace told Alastair before bustling into the kitchen.

'Nobody's blaming you, Mrs Wallace, but Connie came here because she wanted to escape the press. She thought she'd be safe here with her fan club. She loves it here and I think she'd like to stay a bit longer but that's going to be impossible if the press find her. You can see that, can't you?'

Mrs Wallace banged about with a few dishes in the sink. She wasn't going to admit to anything, was she?

'Look,' Alastair said, 'let's put all this in the past. I think we've got rid of Simpkins for the time being.'

He sighed. As much as he hated Mrs Wallace sometimes, it was better to have her as a friend than an enemy, and he decided that he'd better do as much of a repair job as he could and that meant flattering the old tartar.

'Of course you do,' he said. 'Look, we've got the read-through tonight.'

'Well, I don't know if I'll be in the play this year,' she said and then paused for a moment. 'Unless it's worth my while.'

Alastair knew exactly what she meant. 'Of course it'll be worth your while,' he said encouragingly. 'I thought you could play Maria. She's one of the main characters and has some of the very best scenes in the play. The audience always adores Maria.'

Mrs Wallace's chest seemed to heave upwards. 'Well,' she said, 'I'll have to think about it.'

'Okay,' Alastair said, knowing full well that she'd be one of the first through the door of the village hall later that evening.

'Do you really think Simpkins believes I'm a man?' Connie asked as she and Maggie left the pub – still hand in hand just in case anyone was watching.

'He must do,' Maggie said. 'He's not following us.'

'I think everyone bought it, didn't they?'

'Yes,' Maggie said, remembering the strange look on Mikey's face.

'Maggie?' Connie said as they stopped outside the B&B. 'Yes?'

'You okay? You've been real quiet.'

Maggie looked at Connie – or rather Ralph. 'I—' she stopped.

'What is it?'

'Mikey,' she said in a subdued voice.

'Oh!' Connie said, suddenly realising. 'He saw, didn't he?'

Maggie nodded. 'I'm afraid he was in the front row.'

'But you can explain, can't you?'

'I guess,' Maggie said. 'But when? I hardly see him.'

'But he'll be at rehearsals, won't he?'

Maggie shrugged. 'It's always pot luck with Mikey.'

'Well,' Connie said, 'it'll do him no end of good to be a bit jealous, won't it? Did he look jealous?'

'I don't know,' Maggie said. 'He looked more – disappointed to me.'

'Disappointed is good too,' Connie said. 'That could work in your favour.'

'Not if he's not interested in me in the first place,' Maggie said.

'Maggie!' Connie said, taking hold of her shoulders. 'You've got to be more positive about things. I've never known anyone with so little self-belief. You're a beautiful young woman and Mikey would be a fool not to be interested in you. Just look at you with your shiny dark hair and your gorgeous new outfit. *Any* man would love to have you as his girl.'

They entered the B&B together.

'You're so kind to me,' Maggie told Connie.

'But you've got to be kind to yourself,' Connie told her. 'Only then will things start to happen for you.'

'You think so?'

'I *know* so,' Connie said.

'Connie?' Isla's voice came from the living room. 'Is that you?' She appeared in the doorway and took one look at Ralph standing next to Maggie.

'Oh, I'm sorry,' she said, 'I thought I heard Connie's voice.'

Connie and Maggie burst into laughter.

Chapter Twenty-Nine

Alastair was right about Mrs Wallace. She was the first one to turn up at the village hall that evening.

'I'm not saying I'm taking part,' she said before Alastair had a chance to open his mouth, 'but I thought I'd at least take a look to see what's on offer.'

'And very good of you it is too,' Alastair said, turning his back to her as he wrestled with a stack of chairs and hoping she hadn't seen him rolling his eyes. He wished he could do without Mrs Wallace in the play, he really did, but they struggled with numbers as it was and she was a valuable – if disagreeable – asset to the group.

Sandy Macdonald was the next to arrive, which surprised Alastair as he wasn't one to leave the comfort of home easily unless a pint was on offer.

'Evening, Sandy,' Alastair said.

Sandy waved his greeting.

'Anyone else out there?' Alastair asked hopefully.

'Aye. I just saw Angus making his way here but he's taking his time,' Sandy said. 'So what's in store, our Alastair?' Sandy asked, hoping for a sneak preview.

'Oh, you know it's not right to divulge such information until everyone is here,' Alastair said, knowing full well that he'd earmarked the role of Sir Toby Belch for Sandy. It was a good meaty role and, although Sandy often gave the impression of being a bit vague at times, he was always the perfect student when it came to the LADS and every performance was near perfect.

Sure enough, the next figure through the door was Angus. As ever, he looked as if his day had been the worst that could be thrown at a man.

'I hope there's a cup of tea to be had,' he said.

'That's a very good idea,' Alastair said. 'Why don't you make a start?'

Angus sighed and made his way downstairs to fetch the ancient kettle and even more ancient cups.

'I'd better lend him a hand,' Mrs Wallace said, her bosom quivering at the thought of Angus being left alone with the catering.

'Hi, Alastair!' a cheery voice sounded and Alastair looked up to see Kirsty walking into the hall, closely followed by her sister, Catriona. 'Do you want a hand?'

By the time all the chairs had been arranged in something vaguely resembling a circle, Euan and Isla had arrived, and Mrs Wallace and Angus appeared with the tea things.

'Isn't Connie coming?' Catriona asked, her face already forming into folds of disappointment.

'Aye, she's coming,' Alastair said. 'Be sure not to miss her, mind.'

Catriona frowned. 'What do you mean?'

'You'll see,' he said. 'And we have Connie to thank for the books,' he said, handing around the new copies of *Twelfth Night*.

It was then that Hamish walked in, a great smile plastered on his face.

Alastair smiled back. 'Got anyone with you?'

'Aye,' Hamish said and he looked around as Maggie walked into the room with a young man.

'Ah!' Alastair said. 'I see we have a new member.'

Everyone looked up and saw Maggie hand in hand with a man in a cap with an alarming scar down his left cheek.

'This is Ralph, everyone,' Maggie said.

'Hello!' everyone echoed.

Maggie and Ralph sat themselves opposite the Kendrick sisters and Kirsty nudged Catriona.

'All right, girls?' Ralph said, winking at the two of them. They both giggled.

Alastair made sure everyone had a copy of the play and Mrs Wallace and Angus handed around the teas and coffees. It was then time to begin.

'You've all had a chance to read the note I sent?' Alastair asked the group.

'You mean the outline of the story?' Sandy asked.

'That's the one,' Alastair said. 'I thought it best you were familiar with the plot before the read-through.'

'Aye, well, about that,' Sandy began, stroking his chin, 'I mean, I don't like to think of meself as being dim but I didn't understand a word of it.'

'Ah,' Alastair said.

'I told you we should have done a nice Gilbert and Sullivan,' Mrs Wallace said.

'I'm not singing no poncy songs,' Angus said.

Alastair held his hand up. 'Okay,' he said. 'I'll run through the plot again.'

Five minutes later, the LADS all stared at Alastair with looks of varying bemusement.

'Well, it's a wee bit clearer now,' Sandy said.

'I still don't get it,' Mrs Wallace said, her chins wobbling in annoyance. 'Who are the twins?'

'Viola and Sebastian,' Alastair said.

'And Viola's in love with Orsino?' Angus said.

'Yes!' Alastair said.

'But he's in love with someone else?'

'Olivia,' Alastair prompted.

'Then who's Olivia in love with?' Maggie asked.

'Viola.'

'But she's a girl!' Mrs Wallace said.

'Disguised as a young man,' Alastair said.

'It's disgusting,' Mrs Wallace said.

'It's funny. Just think of it as a love triangle,' Alastair said. 'Tell you what. It'll help once we've sorted out the cast. I thought I'd better be Orsino.' Alastair placed his chair in the middle of the circle. 'Maggie – you'll be a great Olivia. Join me here, will you?'

Maggie moved her chair into the centre next to Alastair's.

'And Ralph – you'll be Viola.'

'But he's a man,' Mrs Wallace said.

'Och, now I'm really confused,' Sandy said. 'We're having a man playing a woman who's pretending to be a man?'

Alastair laughed. 'Not quite. Do none of you recognise Ralph?'

Isla and Hamish giggled.

'What's going on?' Catriona said.

'It's Connie,' Alastair said. 'Ralph's Connie!'

Everyone looked at Ralph.

'Hi, everyone,' Connie said, taking her cap off and unpinning her trademark red hair.

'Oh my God!' Kirsty screamed.

'You knew?' Catriona said.

'Just a few of us,' Alastair said. 'We had to disguise Connie before. Colin Simpkins got the idea she was staying in Lochnabrae and we can't have him finding her here.'

Mrs Wallace shifted uneasily in her chair.

'So you're going to be dressed up as a wee lad?' Sandy asked.

'For a wee while,' Connie said, smiling.

'It'll be a good way for you to get into character,' Alastair said.

'So let me see if I've got this right,' Sandy said. 'We've got Connie pretending to be Ralph who's playing Viola who's pretending to be Cesario.'

'That's it *exactly!*' Alastair said. 'Now we've got that cleared up, we can make a start.'

After two more tea breaks, the LADS finally limped to the end of *Twelfth Night* with Kirsty reading through Feste's final song.

A stunned silence fell over the village hall.

Mrs Wallace was the first to speak. 'It's not a very *happy* ending, is it?'

'Not for Malvolio,' Alastair said. 'But everyone else seems happy enough. They're all in love with the right people at last.'

'And Malvolio gets his just desserts. Annoying people usually do,' Maggie said, clearly aiming the remark at Mrs Wallace.

'Is everyone happy?' Alastair asked. 'Any questions, any concerns? Angus. You're looking worried.'

Angus's mouth twisted around in his long face. 'This Antonio character I'm playing.'

'Yes?'

'I see him as a sort of hero. He's willing to sacrifice a lot for his friend. A bit like a hero from a western.'

There was a collective groan.

'No, no,' Alastair said in defence. 'Angus has a point.'

'Don't encourage him,' Euan said. 'Else he'll play the part wearing a cowboy hat and boots and swagger across the stage like John Wayne.'

Everyone laughed. Except Connie.

'How about you, Connie?' Alastair asked. 'Or should I say Ralph?'

Connie nodded. 'Okay,' she said in a very small voice.

'Okay?' Alastair echoed. 'You're okay with the part, you mean?'

She nodded again.

'It's Connie's first Shakespeare,' Maggie said.

'And a very good one to start with,' Alastair said. 'Well, I think we can wrap things up tonight. We'll meet up again tomorrow night at seven thirty and start working on our parts in groups.'

Everyone got up, scraping their chairs back before stacking them against the wall. Mrs Wallace and Angus cleared away the tea things and the rest of the LADS made a slow exit to the door, Alastair holding it open and switching off the lights behind them. Bounce, who'd been present during the read-through, tore through the open door and legged it down to the loch, drinking thirstily from the icy evening waters.

'Night, Alastair,' Hamish said. 'I'll remind Mikey to actually turn up tomorrow.'

'Aye,' Alastair said. 'We missed him tonight.'

Alastair watched as everyone walked up the main street, turning off to their own homes and shouting their goodnights.

The read-through had gone well – better than expected if he was honest. He'd been anxious that the LADS might not be ready for Shakespeare but they'd coped brilliantly. Only one person didn't seem totally happy with everything and that was Connie.

Alastair watched as she walked up the road with Maggie and Isla flanking her like bodyguards. She'd been quiet that evening, reading through her part with a rare concentration as if it was a piece of homework she had to get through rather than something that might actually be fun. Her eyes had been wide and anxious and there'd been many a moment when he'd wanted to say something comforting to her to put her at ease. But she was a professional and Alastair was convinced that they were going to witness the best performance Lochnabrae had ever seen.

Walking up the hill to his home with Bounce walking nicely to heel, Alastair couldn't help wondering what the future held in store. Was Connie really going to stay in Lochnabrae long enough to perform with them at Christmas? He couldn't quite see it himself and yet she seemed to have made a commitment to them all that night.

Connie Gordon. He still couldn't believe she was here. Larger than life and far more beautiful than she'd ever appeared on the silver screen even when she was sporting a scar and fake moustache as Ralph.

He shook his head. *Stop thinking about Connie Gordon,* he told himself. *She's way out of your league. She's a superstar, and transplanting herself to Lochnabrae isn't going to change that.*

He'd just turned off the road and onto the little track that led to his cottage when Bounce started to pull on his lead.

'What is it, Bounce?' he asked, half-expecting to see a fox or a grouse breaking its cover.

Bounce started to bark and, as Alastair approached his front door, he saw that it wasn't a fox or a grouse that had caught Bounce's attention – it was a beautiful young woman.

'Hello, Alastair,' she said. 'Surprised to see me?'

Chapter Thirty

Connie sat down at her dressing-room table and stared at her reflection. Ralph stared back at her, scarred and scared.

'What am I doing?' she asked him. He didn't reply and Connie slowly began to take off her disguise, peeling off the fake moustache and cleansing off the heavy make-up.

The play had been a big mistake. She should never have allowed herself to be persuaded to do it but, when the whole of the village had been egging her on, how could she have said no? But the read-through that night had confirmed to her that she just couldn't do it. Reading through sections with Maggie explaining had been one thing but reading it with a group of people and then being expected to actually memorise it and perform it on a stage in front of a living breathing audience was just too much for Connie. But how was she going to tell them?

'Quickly,' she told herself. In fact, the sooner, the better.

It was after eleven o'clock but she knew she'd never sleep until she'd told Alastair and, as she thought the phone a cowardly way out, she decided to walk up to his house. The walk would do her good – burn off some of her nervous energy.

But her disguise? She'd just taken it off.

'Oh, no,' she said. Her hat would have to do. Besides, nobody was going to be hanging around the village in the middle of the night, were they? This wasn't exactly paparazzi country.

Putting on the new coat Maggie had chosen for her in Strathcorrie, Connie sneaked down the stairs and let herself out of the B&B as quietly as possible so as not to disturb Isla, grabbing the large torch on the table by the door and venturing outside. Connie had never known darkness like it. It was so all-consuming and it made her feel quite tiny, especially when she gazed up at the stars that spangled the sky. She took care to keep her eyes fixed on the ground, however. It would be all too easy to become distracted and end up in the loch. All she knew was that she had to get this over and done with as quickly as possible. Only then could she relax and she so wanted to enjoy her time in Lochnabrae. Since the arrival of Bob Braskett, she'd been feeling uneasy. He'd put doubt in her mind and she was determined that he wasn't going to succeed. Whatever her future held, it was a future that would be decided by her and her alone.

She hadn't gone far when she heard a rustling sound from behind her. She stopped, turning around with the torch at waist level.

'Hello?' she said into the night. She flashed the torchlight in an arc and gasped as it found a pale face in the darkness.

'Connie Gordon,' a voice said. 'I *knew* you were here.'

'I take it you're not going home tonight,' Maggie said to Hamish.

'Thought I'd crash in my own room, sis,' he said, taking another mouthful of the apple pie he'd found in the fridge. 'Wasn't Connie amazing tonight?'

'You think?'

'Of course,' he said.

'I thought she seemed nervous,' Maggie said. 'Like she wasn't really sure about anything. Even the scenes we'd talked through together.'

'Och, you're talking rubbish. She was brilliant.'

'And you're talking like a man with a crush,' Maggie said. 'I'm telling you, she wasn't happy.'

Hamish finished the last of the pie and looked at his sister. 'You think she'll pull out?'

'I don't know,' Maggie said, taking his plate from him and placing it in the sink. 'But I think we should keep an eye on her.'

Connie gasped out loud as the man stepped out of the shadows and into the full glare of the torch. It was Colin Simpkins.

'Nice disguise you were wearing before. Of course, I had my suspicions in the pub,' he said unconvincingly. 'Shame you didn't keep it on. I might've overlooked you.'

'What do you think you're doing, hanging around in the middle of the night?'

'My job, Miss Gordon. Just doing my job.'

'Oh, really? Scaring a woman half to death? You're lucky I didn't bash you over the head with this torch.'

'So, why are you here, Connie?' Colin asked, sounding all too familiar.

'You think I'm going to talk to you?' Connie said, and turned to walk away.

'What are you running away from?' Colin asked, jogging to keep up with her.

'I'm not speaking to you,' Connie said. 'You'll get no story out of me.'

'But you just being here's a story,' he said.

Connie tried to ignore him.

'And I won't be going away in a hurry, I can tell you, so you may as well talk to me – get your side of things out there before I make stuff up myself.'

Connie stopped in her tracks. 'Oh, please! Don't pollute my ears with such rubbish. I've had stuff made up about me all my life – whether I've given "my side" of the story or not. You journalists always manage to twist things. You write what you want to write, not what anyone tells you. You're not interested in the truth. You're only interested in yourself.'

'Ooooh! Biting words. The nasty side of Connie Gordon is coming out now.'

'I'm not being nasty. I'm being honest.'

'Aye, you might well be but I'm going to twist that, aren't I, because I'm a journalist and I'm the lowest of the low.'

'You said it,' Connie said. 'Now leave me alone.'

'Okay,' Simpkins said, reaching for his mobile phone and taking a quick snap of Connie. 'I've got what I came for, anyway.'

Connie listened as his footsteps retreated. She felt as if she'd been punched in the stomach by the man and just wanted to double back to the B&B and curl up in her bed.

'Connie? Is that you?' a voice suddenly said.

'Maggie?'

'Aye,' Maggie said. 'I heard voices. Are you okay?' Maggie took Connie by the arm and led her inside. 'What are you doing out here?'

They walked into the shop together, Connie blinking as Maggie put the lights on.

'I was—' she paused. What could she say? That she was going to see Alastair to tell him she was pulling out of the play? 'Just walking,' she finished. 'I felt a bit restless.'

'But I heard you talking to someone.'

Connie nodded. 'Simpkins was here.'

'Why, the low-level rat!' Maggie hissed.

'He was hanging around outside Isla's and followed me.'

'And you weren't wearing Ralph,' Maggie said. 'I suppose he recognised you?'

'He said he's got his story now too.'

'Oh, no! What can we do?'

'There's nothing we can do. We'll just have to ride it out,' Connie said. 'I'm sure it'll blow over soon enough. Once people know I'm here, the novelty will wear off. They'll soon get bored of me.'

'Isn't that what Princess Diana thought?' Maggie asked.

They were quiet for a moment.

'The thing is,' Connie said, 'if I run away, I'll just run into another story somewhere else. Anyway, I don't want to run away. I like it here.'

'And here likes you,' Maggie said with a smile.

'So, I have to stay and see it through,' Connie said. 'I want to stay. Only—'

'What?'

'If I stay, I'll have to be in the play, won't I?'

'I *knew* that was worrying you!' Maggie said.

'The play's so much a part of Lochnabrae and – if I stay – I want to be a part of that too,' Connie said.

'And you will,' Maggie said, resting a hand on her shoulder.

Connie sighed. 'But I don't think I can do it.'

''Course you can,' Hamish said, suddenly appearing in the middle of the shop in his pyjamas.

'Hamish!' Maggie scolded.

'I'm sorry,' Connie said, turning to go. 'It's late. I'm disturbing you.'

'No, don't go,' Maggie said. 'Come on through and have some hot chocolate.'

Connie relented and followed the two of them upstairs. There was a small lamp on in the tiny living room and the warm glow was comfortingly concealing, for Connie was feeling as if she might cry at any moment. She was tired and she'd been pushed, prodded and perturbed and wasn't quite sure which way was up and which was down any more. Maggie made sure she was comfortable on the saggy sofa before disappearing to make three cups of hot chocolate.

'You were great tonight,' Hamish said, sitting down in an ancient armchair opposite her.

'No, I wasn't. I was crap.'

Hamish frowned. 'How can you say that?'

'Because it's the truth,' Connie said with a shrug. 'I didn't understand the plot properly, I could hardly say any of my lines without stumbling and I'm terrified – physically terrified – of the idea of being on stage.'

Hamish chuckled. 'So's everyone,' he said. 'It's part of the fun of amateur dramatics. Who'll make an arse of themselves first?'

Connie looked confused. 'What?'

'It's true!' he said, leaning forward as he got into his stride. 'It's just a wee bit of fun to pass the time. We're not in it for artistic brilliance. Well, Alastair might be – he does

286

try and push us all to do our best. We're just out to have a laugh, really.'

'But you all looked so serious tonight,' Connie said.

'Aye. Well, that's nowt but a bit of healthy competition. We all try to outdo each other at the read-through – like we know what's going on,' Hamish said.

'But *you* knew what you were doing, didn't you?'

'Now and again,' Hamish said. 'But half those words are Greek to me. It takes time to learn a play. That's why we'll be having all them rehearsals. It'll come – gradually. You've just got to allow yourself to jump the hurdles and not shy away from them.'

Connie sniffed. 'Well, I'd never really looked at it like that before.'

'But you must have. What with all them films you've done.'

Connie shook her head. 'But they were easy. Films are never shot right through in one take. You do them in bite-size pieces. You only have to learn a few lines and perform for a few minutes at a time. I can do that.'

'Aye, I know you can,' Hamish said. 'And better than any actress I've ever seen.'

Connie smiled. 'You're sweet,' she said.

'But you can do this play too, Connie,' he said. 'I know you can.'

'You think?'

'Aye, I do.'

They locked eyes and Hamish smiled at her and nodded.

'Here we are,' Maggie said, entering the room with a tray loaded with three mugs and a plate of chocolate fingers. 'Now, let's discuss this problem.'

'Oh, there's no problem,' Connie said.

'It's all sorted,' Hamish said.

Maggie looked at her brother and then looked at Connie. 'Sorted?'

'Aye,' Hamish said.

'Aye,' Connie echoed, and they both leant forward to steal a chocolate finger.

Chapter Thirty-One

'Sara!' Alastair exclaimed. 'What are you doing here?'

'Oh, and it's lovely to see you too!' Sara replied. Bounce immediately leapt up at the unexpected visitor. 'Well, at least somebody's pleased to see me.' She bent down and patted the soft, ebony head.

'Of course I'm pleased to see you – it's just a bit of a surprise.'

'You know I've always liked surprises,' Sara said.

Alastair nodded, hoping that his expression of panic was hidden by the darkness. 'Yes,' he said. 'I remember.'

'Come on, then. Get this door open. I've been stood out here for ages. It's a wonder I've not frozen completely.'

'But it's open – didn't you try it? I never lock it.'

'You're kidding me?' She rolled her eyes in horror as Alastair opened the door for her without the aid of a key.

'Don't you have an outside light? It was really spooky standing out here all alone.'

'No, I don't,' he said. 'And it's not spooky. It's serene.'

'Trust me – it's spooky.'

'How did you get here?'

'Taxi from the airport.'

'You flew from London?'

'Well, I wasn't going to drive all the way to the back of beyond, was I?'

He switched a couple of lamps on in the front room and took his coat off before stabbing at the fire, which was now looking very sorry for itself. Bounce rolled in the middle of the floor, waving his fat paws in the air before hurtling across the room to his basket where he turned around precisely three times before settling down for a good night's sleep.

'This is all very quaint,' Sara said, stroking her short blonde hair, which had been hidden under a hat that was designed as a fashion statement rather than anything to keep a head remotely warm. 'It's all so small.'

'No smaller than the flat in London,' Alastair said, feeling as if he had to defend his little cottage against this interloper from the city.

'No, I suppose not.'

'And you didn't get a view like the one I now have in London.'

'I didn't see the view – it was dark when I arrived.'

'Did you see the stars?' Alastair asked.

She shook her head. 'No. I was texting you, trying to find out where the hell you were.'

'I was in the village.'

'Ah, yes. I drove through it on the way up here. There's not much to it, is there?'

'There's enough.'

'Enough for you and your new life, you mean?'

'I'm happy here, Sara,' he said. They stared at one another for a moment, both wondering what would come next. 'Listen,' Alastair said at last, 'take your coat off and I'll make us some tea.'

'Aren't you going to bring my suitcase in?'

Alastair's eyebrows rose. 'Right.' He opened the front door and saw the suitcase parked in the shadows. It wasn't exactly a modest overnight bag – more along the lines of a piece of luggage you might take on a fortnight's luxury cruise and that knowledge panicked Alastair. What exactly was Sara doing here and how long was she planning on staying? They hadn't been in touch with each other since . . .

He shook his head. He didn't want to think about it. *Couldn't* let himself think about it and yet her very presence brought all those memories crashing to the forefront of his mind, and he knew there was no getting away from them. He thought he'd done a pretty good job of running away from things when he'd found his modest little home in Lochnabrae but he was beginning to realise that you can never really run away from the past. It will hunt you down and make you face it sooner or later.

As he dragged the unwieldy case into the living room, he noticed that Sara had made herself comfortable on his sofa.

'How did you know where I was?' he asked and then realised how rude that had sounded.

'Jeff gave me your address.'

Alastair secretly seethed at the traitorous friend. Jeff was Sara's brother and, when they'd broken up, Alastair had kept in touch with Jeff just to make sure that Sara was okay but there'd been an unwritten subtext that his details wouldn't ever be passed on to Sara. But then he remembered what Sara had been through and guilt flooded him.

'How are you?' he asked, noticing that her skin was snowdrop-white, almost transparent.

She gave him a little smile that reminded him of how fragile she was. 'I'm well,' she said. 'Much better.'

He nodded. 'Good. I was worried about you.'

'I know you were and I'm so sorry for what I put you through. I can never forgive myself—'

Alastair's hand rose in the air. 'You don't need to say anything.'

'But I do.' She sat forward on the sofa. 'I wanted to try and explain—'

'Please. Not tonight, Sara.'

She swallowed and he saw the familiar look of uncertainty pass over her face and it made his heart plummet with fear.

'I'll make that tea,' he said. 'Okay?'

She nodded.

'Good.'

In the tiny sanctuary of the kitchen, he stared out of the window at the big black space beyond and wished that it would suck him out and split him into a million tiny pieces.

Don't be so crass, he told himself, switching the kettle on and trying to find two unchipped mugs in the cupboard. *You were in love with her once. Remember?* He nodded his head at his reflection in the window. *So stop thinking about yourself for five minutes and be kind to her – it's the least she deserves.*

He made the tea and returned to the living room, handing her a cup.

'Thanks,' she said, patting the seat next to her.

'I'll just get the fire going,' Alastair said, reaching into the log basket and chucking a couple of logs into place. He could feel Sara's eyes upon him as he stoked the fire into life and he delayed turning around to meet her gaze.

'Alastair,' she said at last, 'come and sit down. I want to talk to you.'

He did as he was told, an awful feeling of inevitability draining him of all energy.

'I know you don't want to talk about it but I never got a chance to thank you,' she said, her voice barely audible. He took a sip of his tea but didn't say anything. 'What I did – what I put you through – I can't begin to imagine what you suffered.'

'You don't need to do this, Sara.'

'Yes – yes, *I do!* Because you left before I could explain. You didn't give me a chance and that wasn't fair, Alastair!'

Alastair closed his eyes. 'Listen,' he said, 'It's not that I think we shouldn't talk about this – we probably should – but it's been a long day and I'm exhausted. I wasn't expecting this tonight.'

There was a moment of silence when the only sound audible was the crackle of kindling from the fireplace.

'You don't want me here, do you?' Sara asked, her voice suddenly becoming louder.

'I didn't say that.'

'You don't need to – it's written all over your face.'

He took a deep breath – the sort he remembered taking a lot of when he lived with Sara. 'Let's not fight. Please. I don't want to fight. Not again.'

There was an icy silence.

'Okay,' she said a moment later, 'we'll talk in the morning.' She stood up, placing her half-finished tea on the table in front of her. It was then that something caught her eye. 'You're writing again?' She picked up the notepad from the table.

'Trying to.'

'A play?'

'No,' he said abruptly, causing her to flinch. 'Sorry,' he added quickly. 'I'm not sure what it is. It's a bloody mess – that's all I know at the moment.'

'I'm sure it's brilliant,' Sara said and her voice was warm and gentle now, reminding Alastair of the early days when they had first met, before things had become so restless and strained. She waited a moment, looking as if she was hoping he'd say something but he remained resolutely silent. 'Look, I'd better go to bed,' she said at last.

Alastair nodded and then he realised what she was saying. 'You're staying here?'

'Well, of course I'm staying here!'

'I mean there's no room.'

'You've got a double bed, haven't you?'

'Yes, of course.'

'Well, then . . .'

For a moment, Alastair thought of suggesting Isla's bed and breakfast but Connie was staying there and he really didn't want Connie and Sara meeting. Sara represented his old life whilst Connie represented . . . what, exactly? He wasn't yet sure but he knew that he didn't want to jeopardise it; he didn't want the worlds of his past and possible future colliding.

'I'll sleep on the sofa,' he said at last.

'Oh, don't be silly, Alastair. We shared a bed for three years.'

'Yes, but not any more.' Their eyes met and Sara seemed to understand him at last.

'Look, we'll talk in the morning, okay?' he said. She nodded and he thought he could see tears in her eyes. *Please don't cry*, he thought. *Just let us get through tonight without incident.*

Chapter Thirty-Two

Connie silently cursed herself for having believed Hamish as Alastair ran his hands through his hair and paced up and down the stage. They'd been rehearsing for over a week now and the honeymoon period was well and truly over.

'Maggie, you've got just the right amount of coyness in this scene but, for goodness' sake, *keep still*,' Alastair told her. 'Don't keep roaming around the stage like a nervous animal. Olivia's more in control of herself than that.'

'Sorry, Alastair,' Maggie said.

'And Connie. You're meant to be having fun with this scene. The "Make me a willow cabin at your gate" speech is light-hearted. This is Viola imagining herself in love and, when she cries out Olivia's name, she really *is* crying out. Don't just whisper it. *Shout* it!' Alastair shouted.

Connie flinched. She wasn't used to being shouted at and she hadn't known that Alastair was a shouter either. Up until now, she'd only seen the sweet mountain-striding dog owner who took care of weeping women he found by the side of lochs but the Alastair she was witnessing now was a far cry from that incarnation.

She watched as he paced to the end of the hall, his teeth gridlocked as the rest of the cast looked on in astonishment.

Alastair's shouted at Connie, their faces seemed to say. This was better theatre than anything Shakespeare could have written.

'Again!' he bellowed from the back of the hall.

And Connie's torture began all over again. And again. And again.

'Right,' Alastair said at last after the sixth attempt to get the scene right. 'That'll have to do for tonight. We'll move on to scene three after a tea break,' he announced and Connie watched in relief as he disappeared below the stage.

'I have never *ever* met a ruder director,' Connie told Maggie. 'Well, I have, but I was being paid an obscene amount of money to work with him.'

'I guess that would make a bit of a difference,' Maggie said.

'We've only had a few rehearsals and he expects us to be perfect.'

'Aye,' Maggie said. 'He does.'

'I thought he liked me,' Connie said. 'I thought—' She stopped.

'Thought what?' Maggie said.

'Oh, nothing!'

'He *does* like you!'

'Then why's he treating me like this?'

'Because he's a sod,' Maggie said. 'Once a year, when he turns to his role as a director, Alastair McInnes becomes a sod.' Maggie sighed. 'But I've never seen him as bad as this before. I wonder what's wrong with him.'

'He's not talking to you like he talks to me,' Connie said. 'And the looks he's been giving me! I'm not going to take much more of this, Maggie. I'm warning you. And it's freezing in here,' she added with a theatrical shiver.

'Alastair doesn't allow us to put the heating on until the end of October but we really do need to take the chill off the place, don't we?' Maggie said. 'And there is that little heater over there. Hamish!'

Hamish looked up from where he was sitting reading his copy of the play at the back of the hall. Maggie nodded towards an ancient heater and Hamish wheeled it out and plugged it in.

'Is that thing safe?' Connie asked as it was switched on. Two bars glowed a pernicious orange and there was a terrible smell of burning.

'Probably not,' Maggie said, stretching her hands out to try and defrost them. 'Cheer up, Connie,' she said. 'It's just been a tough day. It'll get better.' But Connie didn't believe her. She sat down at the edge of the stage, her jean-clad legs dangling over. For a moment, she thought of the past week. Other than the rehearsals, it had been unnervingly quiet. There'd been nothing reported about her in the local paper although she was still worried about what the odious Colin Simpkins might be up too. Still, she'd felt safe enough to risk a trip to Strathcorrie with Maggie.

'I'll get the bus back,' she'd announced as they'd come out of the bakery loaded with goodies.

'The bus?'

'I'm going to do a bit more shopping,' Connie said.

'I can wait for you,' Maggie said.

'It's okay,' Connie said. 'I don't know how long I'm going to be.'

Maggie hesitated but then shrugged her shoulders. 'I'll see you later, then. You're sure you'll be okay on your own?'

Connie laughed. 'I'll be fine.' She watched Maggie go and then gave a sigh. What was she doing? But she knew what.

Ever since she'd first seen the castle with Maggie on their first outing together, she hadn't been able to get it out of her mind. She crossed the road towards the estate agents, Forsyth and Son, and opened the door and walked inside. Old Mr Forsyth was on the telephone, explaining that one of the farms on his books had just been sold and that there really was no use in trying to persuade him to unsell it.

Connie glanced around and saw a young man sitting at a desk.

'Mr Forsyth?' she hazarded a guess. The young man looked up and his mouth promptly fell open as he proceeded to fall over himself to stand up. 'M-m-miss Gordon?'

'Yes,' Connie said, wondering if she should have been wearing her disguise again.

'I love you,' the young Mr Forsyth said. 'I – er – I mean, I love your films.'

'Thank you,' Connie said, watching as the young man's Adam's apple bobbed up and down as he swallowed.

'Well, well,' old Mr Forsyth said as he came off the phone. 'And what can we do for you?'

'Father, it's Connie Gordon.'

'Pleased to meet you, Miss Gordon,' old Mr Forsyth said. His son stared at him. 'Father, *Connie Gordon!*'

'Aye?' he said.

'The actress!'

'So you're an actress,' old Mr Forsyth said. 'Not much call for work in these parts. You on holiday?'

'Kind of,' Connie said. 'Maybe looking to buy.'

'Then you've come to the right place. A small second home, is it? Quiet croft somewhere?'

'Not exactly,' Connie said. 'I'm interested in Rossburn Castle.'

Old Mr Forsyth's mouth dropped open. 'Well, I never,' he said. 'You can't be serious.'

'Why not?'

'You know the amount of work that needs doing to it? It's not the easiest option for a holiday home.'

'But I might not want it as a holiday home,' Connie said.

He nodded. 'Well, if you're interested, Miss Gordon, I'd be very happy to show you around.' And they'd left to see it straight away in Mr Forsyth's car, taking the winding road out of Strathcorrie, across the moors towards the rundown pile of ancient stones that had so piqued Connie's interest.

'Who's the owner?' Connie asked.

'Oh, Fletcher Gordon. An ancestor of the original Gordons who built the castle centuries ago.'

'A Gordon?'

'Aye.'

'Like me! I had no idea.'

'Perhaps that's why you're attracted to it. It's in your blood,' Mr Forsyth said.

'And where's he moving to?'

'California, I'm told.'

'Really? And I left there to come here. How strange the world is.'

'Aye,' Mr Forsyth said. 'I hope you've got a hat. It can be fair breezy up there.'

And so could Mr Forsyth's car, Connie thought. It was old and rattly and had several draughts that had caught Connie by surprise. Perhaps she should put her hat on now, she thought. She also couldn't help noticing the collection of sweet wrappers that lay on the floor and there was a pervading smell of mint.

'Humbugs!' Connie said.

'I beg your pardon?'

'I can smell humbugs. My mother used to eat them all the time.'

'Oh, aye – humbugs. That'll be Forsyth mark two. A devil for the sweets. Leaves this car littered, he does. No use telling him. He doesn't listen. Won't listen till the day his teeth fall out.'

Connie grinned. 'I've had mine filed and whitened and capped.'

'Your teeth?'

She nodded, flashing him a very white smile.

'Very nice,' Mr Forsyth said.

'And very painful and expensive. It's just another way I've given in to it all.'

'All what?'

'The business of being a movie star.'

'So it's not all glamour and sparkle?' Mr Forsyth said.

'I'm afraid not.'

'And that's why you're here?'

Connie nodded. 'I wanted to get as far away from it all as possible. I needed to learn how to breathe again. How to just live, you know?'

'Oh, aye,' Mr Forsyth said. 'And Lochnabrae is the right place for you to do this living?'

'I haven't decided yet,' Connie said. 'But it's looking like a very strong candidate.'

They made a turn in the road and that's when Connie saw Rossburn again with its sturdy walls and soaring turrets.

'I can't pretend that it won't be a lot of work for whoever takes it on,' Mr Forsyth said.

Connie nodded. 'I realise that,' she said.

301

'And a lot of expense,' he added.

Connie smiled. 'I've been looking for something to spend my money on.'

In fact, the castle wasn't half as bad as she'd been led to believe. Okay, so there were parts of the castle that were in ruins like the north tower and the old chapel. What else did you expect from a twelfth-century castle? But most of it had been habitable until fairly recently and, with the help of a few experts, Connie was sure it could be beautiful again.

'You'll have to spend three or four times the asking price on renovation,' Mr Forsyth warned her. 'All the electrics will need doing. You'll need to think about doing the roof straightaway and the plumbing will need updating.'

'I know. But it would be worth it, wouldn't it? Just look at it.'

Mr Forsyth looked around at the towering walls. 'I've always thought it was a mighty shame it'd been left to rot away.'

'It could be beautiful, couldn't it?'

Mr Forsyth nodded.

'Just think – my very own castle! It's every girl's dream.'

'Aye, well, as long as you're not afraid of a bit of hard work. Else it'll be a nightmare more than a dream. It's not simply a case of picking out your wallpaper and paint.'

'I know,' Connie said but she didn't really. She'd never even had to lift a finger when it came to the finer points of decorating in the past, but simply hired someone else to do it all, telling them what she liked and hoping for the best. It had usually worked out really well too. Although there had been one exception. After making the film, *The Pharaoh's Favourite*, Connie had gone all Egyptian and her designer had gone quite mad with the hieroglyphs, which appeared everywhere – Connie had even found them on the rim of the toilet bowl, and the bidet shaped like an inverted pyramid really was the limit.

'I'll take it,' Connie said at last, sounding as if she was buying a handbag rather than an ancient castle.

And that had been that. Mr Forsyth had dropped her off in Lochnabrae and had said he'd organise everything else.

Sitting on the edge of the stage now, Connie thought about the castle. What would everyone say when they found out, she wondered?

'Here's your coffee,' Maggie said, handing Connie an ancient mug and joining her at the edge of the stage. 'Better drink up fast. Alastair's gathering the troops and wants to get going again.'

Connie groaned. Alastair wasn't the only one who wanted to get going.

Chapter Thirty-Three

Alastair woke up on the sofa in the middle of the night sweating. Bounce, who was lying on the floor beside him looked up and whimpered and Alastair immediately knew that he'd been having nightmares.

'Did I disturb you, my boy?' he asked, swinging his legs out of bed and rubbing his eyes.

Bounce got up and stretched, nuzzling Alastair's left knee with a glossy wet nose. Alastair patted the warm familiar head before getting up. He threw on his dressing gown and walked into the kitchen where he poured himself a glass of water before moving through to the living room and sitting back down on the sofa.

He rubbed his eyes again and sighed. He wasn't happy. He hadn't had a nightmare for weeks – *months* now. He hadn't even so much as thought about it and yet it was still there – lurking and leering at him from some remote part of his brain. He knew what had caused it, of course – Sara's arrival. When she'd first turned up in Lochnabrae, he'd been so shocked that he hadn't known how to respond. He'd spent a sleepless night on the sofa trying to work out what to do and how he could send her on her way without seeming totally heartless.

They'd spent the next few days fighting, which wasn't surprising as Sara had insisted on staying at Alastair's. It had been like the bad old times all over again and Alastair wasn't sure which way to turn but Sara seemed quite intent on staying.

They'd gone for a walk in the hills together. Alastair had been quite sure that would do the trick. Sara was a city girl and liked clean concrete under her pretty shoes and he'd taken her up a particularly muddy track that was slick and sticky from a night's rain. It was mean of him but he'd thought she'd run back to the city in no time after that but she hadn't.

'It is beautiful here,' she kept saying. 'I can see why you left London.'

He didn't say anything.

'And I could get used to these hiking boot things.'

He looked down at the boots he'd lent her. They were far too big for her, of course, and were caked in mud but she was doing her best and his heart relented just a little bit.

Don't let her back in, he told himself. *If you let her see even the tiniest glimpse of kindness, she'll grasp on to it and never let go.*

For a while, they'd talked about inane things like the landscape and the sparse population, forever circling the real issue that hovered between them like a malevolent spirit. And then she'd said it.

'We can work things out. It's different now. I've changed.'

But he didn't believe her and he told her so. More or less. It was hard to be totally honest with someone like Sara because the truth wounded her, but he had to speak his mind because he knew that they were no good for each other and they couldn't risk being together again. He had to persuade her to leave and to get help. She needed help and he couldn't give it to her and it was killing him.

It was then that they'd fought – all the way up the mountain and down the other side. They'd argued for the whole length of two valleys and had shouted their way through a wood before returning to the cottage.

Alastair rubbed his sore eyes as he remembered. What a day it had been. The *Twelfth Night* rehearsals hadn't helped either. In fact, it was just as he'd dreaded. Connie was so deeply insecure about everything she was doing on stage and Alastair just couldn't seem to get through to her. Credit to her, she could remember her lines but it seemed as if it was like learning a foreign language to her – she could remember the words but there was none of the understanding that gave them meaning and life. Alastair had become more and more frustrated and had taken his bad mood out on Connie, which was wholly unfair. Maggie had thrown him some seriously dagger-like glances throughout the evening and had cornered him a couple of times too.

'What the hell do you think you're doing?' she'd hissed at him at the first available opportunity.

'I'm directing, Maggie,' he'd said, and stalked off to avoid further interrogation. He'd been an idiot. He knew that but there hadn't seemed to be much he could do about it with everything that was happening in his life at that moment.

He shook his head, trying to dispel the image of Connie. She'd looked so fragile – a look he associated with Sara and one he'd hoped never to see again yet, at the same time, he couldn't help being drawn towards Connie. Her vulnerability was compelling and he wanted to reach out and help her only he was going about it completely the wrong way.

He got up from the sofa and walked across to the table he wrote at. His laptop lay sleeping and his notebook lay closed. If only he could switch himself off so easily.

'What am I doing?' he asked himself, echoing Maggie's angry question. He flipped through the pages of his notebook. Everything was a mess. It usually was, of course – he was a writer who did little in the way of planning – but this mess was even messier than usual. It was a mess without method or merit and that wasn't any use to anyone.

He looked out into the dark of the landscape beyond his cottage. He had never bought a curtain for this window; there was nobody around to see what he was up to. Now, staring out into the darkness was like staring into his very soul. It was nothing more than a big blank: an empty nothingness that could easily be ignored as he filled his days with work but which would come back to haunt him at night.

You need to talk about it to someone – someone who isn't Sara, a little voice inside him said.

'No, I don't,' he said out loud, causing Bounce to question him with a tilt of his head.

All right, then. But you need to talk to Connie – tell her how you feel about her – explain why you've been acting the way you have. Tell her the truth!

The truth. That was a terrifying prospect and something he didn't relish at all especially when he thought he could get away with it. Sara was bound to leave after the furious rowing, wasn't she? As awful as that made him feel, she wouldn't want to stay after that. She'd have to see sense and realise that there was no going back for the two of them and then Connie wouldn't have to know about her, would she?

Alastair got up from his chair. This was no good – arguing in the middle of the night with himself. He drank another glass of water and returned to his bed on the sofa, hoping that, for tonight at least, the nightmares had ended.

Maggie had just opened the shop for the morning and had sneaked through to the kitchen to make a cup of tea when the doorbell went.

'Maggie?' a voice called.

'Mikey?' She dropped her teabag in the sink and went through to the shop.

'Is Alastair cross?'

'Yes,' Maggie said.

'Oh, bugger!' Mikey said, raking a hand through his unkempt hair. 'I couldn't get to rehearsals. Was he really furious?'

'Aye, he was but not with you. I don't think he even noticed you weren't there,' Maggie said cruelly.

'Didn't notice?'

'He's got other things on his mind like his new leading lady.'

'Connie? How is she?'

Maggie pursed her lips. 'Okay.'

Mikey nodded. 'And how's Ralph?'

Maggie flinched. So Hamish hadn't told Mikey about Connie's disguise then.

'Ralph's fine,' Maggie said, deciding to torment him for a while in an attempt to make him jealous.

Mikey frowned. 'He's a bit rough, isn't he, Mags?'

'Is he?'

'Yeah, he is,' Mikey said, looking concerned.

'What's it to you?'

Mikey shrugged. 'Just looking out for my pal's little sis.'

'Yeah, well, I'm not little any more in case you hadn't noticed,' Maggie snapped.

'Oh, I've noticed,' Mikey said in a slow, considered manner.

Maggie stared at him. 'Since when have you noticed anything about me?'

'What do you mean? I notice things,' Mikey said.

'Yeah, like I sell your favourite shortbread or I know where Hamish is at every hour of the day when you need to find him.'

'Maggie?'

'What?'

'You've turned all weird again like you were the other day.'

'Oh, really?'

'Yes, really,' Mikey said, taking a step closer. 'You're not normally like this.'

'Aren't I?'

'No,' Mikey said, 'you're not. You're usually sweet and kind and funny.'

'I don't like being funny.'

'But I mean that in a good way,' Mikey said. 'You always make me laugh.'

Maggie looked up at him, her eyes large and sad. 'I don't want to be laughed at.'

'I didn't mean that,' Mikey said. 'You're twisting my words, Mags. What is it with you lately?'

Maggie took a deep breath. She had his undivided attention and they were alone. She could tell him now. It was a good opportunity. But what could she say? How could she heave such words up from her heart into her mouth and what would he say when she did?

'What is it?' Mikey said. 'You've got something on your mind, I can tell.'

Maggie nodded.

'We're pals, aren't we, Mags? You can tell me anything, you know that?' He took a step towards her and placed a hand on her shoulder. She felt its warm weight and it was all she could do to stop herself from falling towards him then.

'Mikey, I—'

'What?'

'I – there's something I want to tell you,' Maggie said hesitantly. '*Need* to tell you—' She stopped. The doorbell tinkled and in walked Mrs Wallace.

'Is that your motorbike parked outside, young man?' she asked Mikey.

'Yes, it is, Mrs Wallace,' he said politely.

'You might have parked it straight. Had to walk right around it, I did,' she said with a heave of her enormous bosom.

'Oh,' Mikey said, 'sorry about that. I'm just going, anyway.' He looked at Maggie. 'What was it you wanted to tell me?' he asked.

Maggie had retreated behind the counter. 'Nothing,' she said with a flap of her hands. 'It'll keep.'

'You sure?' Mikey asked.

Maggie nodded. It had kept for so many long years already, hadn't it?

It was after eight o'clock in the evening and the LADS were rehearsing in the village hall. Well, they weren't so much rehearsing as fighting.

'What I can't understand is how *you* don't understand,' Alastair said, charging across the stage and grabbing Connie by the shoulders at that evening's rehearsals. She gasped and everybody else gasped too. 'This is one of the tenderest scenes in the whole play, Connie. Viola's desperately in love with Orsino but she can't tell him – not outright anyway. But she finds a way here. This is her saying, I love you. *I love you.*'

For a moment, silence hung over the village hall as Alastair stood with his hands clenching Connie's shoulders and she stood staring right back at him, her eyes wide and round like a cartoon character's.

Finally, he let go of her and she almost fell backwards, sure she was going to have ten perfect bruises to show where his fingers had been. Connie took a deep breath and counted to ten just as she did on-set back in Hollywood when dealing with a difficult director. She was never the sort to erupt unless it was absolutely necessary.

'And Connie – when you say, "She never told her love", you're hurting here because you're talking about *you!* Do you understand now?'

'I'm not sure I do,' Angus said from the back of the hall, 'and I was up reading it again all last night.'

Alastair scratched his head. His face was screwed up as if he was in pain. 'Connie!' he suddenly yelled.

'What?' she yelled back.

'Just act, okay? You're a professional. You know how to do it, right? You should be telling *us* how to do it, for pity's sake!'

Connie flinched at the anger in his voice. 'I'm doing my best!' she said. 'This isn't easy for me. I'm not Judi Dench or Maggie Smith! I'm just me!'

'Don't I know it!' Alastair said. 'Your trouble is, you're not used to *real* acting. Real acting isn't on some set somewhere where you get thirty takes to get four lines right. *Real* acting is in the theatre where you're standing naked in front of a live, unforgiving audience, hammering out eight performances week after week after week!'

There was a stunned silence.

'Jeez,' Alastair muttered. 'Miss Hollywood!'

Connie's eyes narrowed. 'What did you call me?'

Alastair looked up and suddenly looked shamefaced.

And that's when Connie retaliated. 'You think what I do is easy? You think my kind of acting is all glamour? Well, let me tell you – I work longer hours than any of you guys ever have. I bet you've never had to diet to within an inch of your life in order to get a job or have been so bone-tired that you fell asleep in the middle of a scene. You just see the finished product that's all nice and clean and shiny but you've got no idea what goes on behind the scenes! No idea at all!'

'And you've no idea how to handle a real piece of drama,' Alastair said.

'All right, guys,' Euan said, holding his hands in the air. 'That's quite enough.'

'Yeah, stop picking on Connie, Alastair,' Kirsty said.

'I'm not picking on her,' Alastair said.

'You bloody well are,' Catriona chipped in.

'Language, young lady!' Mrs Wallace said. 'I've never heard the like.'

'Never heard the like!' Catriona scoffed. 'You've used much worse to poor old Mr Wallace. I've heard you when I've walked by at night. Poor old fart. Can't you let him be and enjoy his retirement without getting on at him every five minutes?'

Kirsty giggled and Mrs Wallace glared at them. 'I'm not going to stay here and be insulted like this.'

'No?' Catriona said. 'Good!'

They watched as Mrs Wallace fled from the village hall, slamming the door behind her.

'Poor old Wallace is going to get it now,' Kirsty said.

'Girls!' Alastair yelled from the stage. 'What on earth's got into you tonight?'

'Probably the same thing that's got into you,' Euan said, standing up from the chair he'd been commandeering.

'I doubt that very much,' Alastair said, looking completely confused.

Connie took the opportunity to leave the stage.

'Where do you think you're going?' Alastair called after her. 'Connie? We've got a scene to do!'

But Connie had vanished.

'Let her go, son,' Euan said.

'What do you mean? She can't just walk off like that.'

'She didn't walk off,' Maggie said. 'You pushed her.'

'Aye,' Angus said, 'and you're lucky she didn't give you an earful first, the way you were speakin' to her.'

Alastair looked from one face to another. 'Bloody hell!' he said, jumping down off the stage and marching across the floor towards the door.

'Alastair, man, let her be,' Hamish said.

'Alastair!' Maggie cried after him but he wasn't listening. As he left the village hall, he spotted Connie tearing along the main street.

'Connie!' he shouted after her.

'Alastair!' Maggie shouted after him. The whole of the cast had left the hall and were following Alastair down the street. Nobody wanted to miss this scene.

'I wouldn't like to be Alastair now,' Hamish told Maggie. 'I mean, I *would*. She's obviously madly in love with him. Just look at the way they tear each other apart.'

'But it's Alastair tearing *her* apart,' Maggie said.

Hamish shook his head. 'They're crazy about each other. You mark my words.'

Chapter Thirty-Four

Alastair broke into a run in an attempt to catch up with Connie, cursing himself for his foolish behaviour and hoping he hadn't pushed her too far. She could really move when she wanted to and he didn't want her making it to the B&B and locking herself away in her room before he had a chance to talk to her. He had to try and explain things and tell her that it wasn't her fault.

'Connie!' he called but she didn't stop. 'Wait a minute. I just want to talk to you.' He'd nearly caught up with her. 'Will it help if I say I'm sorry?'

Alastair had drawn up alongside her now but he didn't stop, he kept on running, reaching the door of the B&B and blocking it.

'Get out of my way, Alastair,' Connie said, her hazel eyes narrowed.

'I'm staying here until you've heard me out.'

'You couldn't possibly have anything to say to me worth listening to,' Connie said, arms crossed over her chest.

'Oh, you think?'

'Yes, I do. And you couldn't possibly say it without raising your voice and completely humiliating me again.'

They stared at each other, eyes locked in stand-off mode.

'I shouldn't have spoken like that,' Alastair said at last.

'No, you shouldn't have,' Connie said, trying to sidestep Alastair who moved too quickly for her and blocked her way again.

'You're rude, impatient and patronising,' she said.

'I am, sadly, all those things.'

Connie nodded. 'Are you going to get out of my way?'

Alastair shook his head.

'Fine,' Connie said, turning and marching down the road again.

'Connie!' Alastair cried, leaving the door he'd been guarding and tearing after her. 'Where are you going?'

Connie didn't answer and Alastair had no option but to follow. She headed back down the main street but didn't make it as far as the village hall, taking a sharp right down the path that followed the loch.

'Connie, can't we just talk?' Alastair pleaded as he, too, took the path that edged the water. It was late now and the evening light had a strange purple glow. At any other time, he would have stood to admire it, the way the water looked almost violet and the deep indigo of the mountains beyond, but he didn't have time to be poetical now. He had a mission called Connie.

He quickened his pace as she did hers, watching her dark red hair fly out behind her like the flames of an angry fire. He stumbled and cursed at his clumsiness, glad that Bounce hadn't followed him for once to make matters worse.

Suddenly, just as he was catching up, Connie turned around.

'Stop following me!' she said in a voice that was barely above a whisper. Alastair was surprised. In fact, it had more impact on him than if she'd shouted and he almost felt bad enough to turn away and leave her in peace. Almost.

'Connie,' he said, 'give me a chance to explain myself.'

'You mean you can?'

'What?'

'Explain yourself!' she said. 'Are you really telling me that there's a good enough excuse out there to make it all right for you to treat people like dirt?'

Alastair sighed. 'No, I'm not,' he said. 'But there is some kind of explanation.'

Connie continued to glare at him and then said, 'Why are you so mean to me?'

Alastair frowned. 'I don't mean to be mean,' he said, 'and I'm truly sorry for the things I said to you. If it's any consolation, I'm like this with most actresses.'

'It *isn't* any consolation,' Connie said.

'It's why I moved here.'

'What do you mean?'

'It's why I moved away from London and stopped directing.'

'But you're directing here,' Connie pointed out.

'Yes, but that's not the same.'

'I don't understand,' Connie said.

Alastair took a deep breath. 'The LADS are amateurs. I'm okay with them. We rub along all right.'

'You're not making any sense,' she said.

'No,' Alastair said. 'I guess I'm not. It's just that – well, you're a professional.'

'What difference does that make?'

'All the difference in the world – to me, at least. You see, I wanted to get the best out of you. I mean, I do with all my actors whether professional or amateur, but it really matters to me when they're professional like you. I want to push. I want to reach those dizzying heights of perfection – to see a role come alive, you know?'

Connie nodded. 'And I'm sure your actors want that too, Alastair, but you can't treat them so badly.'

'I know, I know. It's why I gave up directing, I told you. I didn't like who I became.' He paused, wondering if he should tell her the truth. He wanted to, *desperately* wanted to. 'And I'm under a lot of pressure at the moment.'

'Oh, *really?*' Connie said.

'Yes, I—'

'You hurt me,' she interrupted.

'I never meant to,' he told her. 'I just wanted the best from you. Listen—'

'Well, I'm glad I never have to work with you again,' she said.

'Look,' Alastair said, trying to remain calm, 'I never encouraged you to join the LADS. I wasn't keen from the start if you remember.'

Connie frowned. 'And neither was I but how could I say no when I was staying here? Acting's what everyone knows me for!'

'But you knew you were going to struggle,' Alastair said.

'And I'm doing my best to learn.'

'But you're saying the lines like you don't care! Like they don't mean anything to you,' Alastair said, realising that his voice was rising again.

'That's because they *don't* mean anything to me!' Connie yelled, her eyes flashing with anger once again.

'I'm sorry!' Alastair quickly said. 'I didn't mean to say that.'

'Yes, you did. You meant to say it,' Connie said. 'All you can think of is what a bad actress I am.'

'I didn't say that.'

'No? Well, that's what I heard!'

'Connie!'

But she was on the move again. She'd reached the sandy shore of the loch and was walking as fast as she could over its sugary surface.

'I can't believe it!' she shouted into the night.

'Believe what?' Alastair said, almost crashing into her as she suddenly stopped.

'That I was actually beginning to fall for you!' she said.

There was a pause. Alastair looked completely thunderstruck and Connie's face had flamed.

'What a *fool* I've been!' she cried. 'I can't believe I almost let it happen again. What is it with me that I always fall for the wrong guys? I don't want to be treated badly and yet – time after time – I make the same mistake and fall for the guy who treats me like dirt. And you know what?' she continued, 'I even believed you were beginning to fall for me.'

Alastair was silent for a moment. It was the opening he'd been dreaming of but now that it was here, he didn't know what to do. He'd been thinking about Connie, dreaming about her since the day he'd first seen her by the loch but he hadn't dared to hope that she'd ever look at him.

'But I was mistaken,' Connie continued, looking up at him as if willing him to prove her wrong, but Alastair didn't say a word and so she turned to go.

'No!' Alastair reached out and grabbed her arm, spinning her back to face him. 'You weren't wrong.'

Connie frowned.

'I am falling for you,' he said. 'I've fallen already.'

Connie looked at Alastair, her eyes full of incomprehension. 'But you never said anything. You—'

'I didn't know what to say,' he told her. 'I didn't want it to be true. You're an actress and I swore it would never happen again.'

'Swore *what* would never happen again?'

He shoved his hands in his jacket pocket and looked down at his boots.

'Alastair,' Connie said, 'you're not making any sense.'

'Okay, okay,' he said quietly, biting his lip and taking a deep breath. It was time to explain himself. 'You deserve to know the truth.'

Connie waited a moment before he began.

'You know I used to write and direct in London?'

Connie nodded. 'It's about all I do know about you.'

'It's about all anyone here knows,' he said.

'What happened?' Connie asked, calming down a little.

Alastair began walking and Connie joined him. The violet sky was slipping into darkness but a bright moon silvered the shore.

'I'd just had a big hit in the West End. A play called *Infinite Jest*. The critics loved it. Audiences loved it. And actors were clamouring for parts in my next one. I'd never felt under such pressure in my life.'

They walked on, their feet silent in the sand and only the lapping of the loch's waters breaking the silence.

'There was an actress in *Infinite Jest* – Sara Constantine. She wasn't very well known before the play but things really took off for her in a big way with that role and we – we became involved with each other. It was great at first. We were both so heady with our achievements but once you've achieved that level of success, you want to hit those heights again, you know? Once wasn't enough. Once could be a fluke but twice – that would prove you were made of the right stuff. So I began to write the next play.'

'What happened then?' Connie asked gently.

'I couldn't do it,' Alastair said. 'I was writing but it was awful. It just wasn't working. I still can't explain it today. It was as if I'd written the very best thing I was capable of and I knew it was all going to be downhill from there but nobody else saw it. Sara thought her part was the best yet and she threw herself into it. She even turned down a film role that was offered to her. I didn't direct this next play of mine. I made excuses when asked. I just wanted to walk away from it but it's not that easy, is it? And, when it came out, there was nowhere to hide.' Alastair fell quiet.

'I'm guessing it didn't do well,' Connie said.

Alastair gave a pained laugh. 'That's the understatement of the century. It flopped like I've never seen a play flop before. The papers tore it to shreds and it was closed almost immediately. It was a total disaster. But that's the theatre – if you're not spinning with the dizzying highs, you're consumed by the dreadful lows.'

'And what happened to Sara?'

'She was heartbroken. She was already totally insecure about herself but *Infinite Jest* had really built up her confidence and to see that taken away from her was appalling.'

'Were you still writing?'

'I was trying. Sara was on at me to write another play. It was like she was holding me responsible for her professional demise as well as my own. It became impossible. The more unable I was to deliver, the more hysterical she became. I've never seen anything like it. I was terrified and the scary thing was, she wasn't drinking and she certainly didn't do drugs. It was pure hysteria,' Alastair said, his eyes wide and wild as if he was witnessing that very hysteria all over again.

'I didn't know what to do. I couldn't handle her and it wasn't any comfort when friends told me that nobody could handle her – that she needed professional help. But, like most people who desperately need it, she didn't think she did.'

Again, Alastair paused and the two of them stopped walking.

Connie was the first to speak. 'Alastair? You okay?'

He nodded and sighed. 'She tried to kill herself,' he said in a quiet voice.

The LADS were standing on the other side of the loch listening intently. It was common knowledge that sound carried across the stretch of water and many an indiscretion had come back to haunt locals over the years.

'God, she sounds furious,' Kirsty said.

'Wouldn't you be if Alastair had spoken to you like that?' Catriona said.

'It's like having our very own Elizabeth Taylor and Richard Burton, isn't it?' Maggie said, with just a hint of glee in her voice.

'He had it coming,' Euan said. 'I warned him but he wouldn't let the lass be.'

'He's been an absolute sod to her,' Maggie said.

'But he fancies her, doesn't he?' Catriona asked.

'Of course he does!' Kirsty said. 'You've seen the way he looks at her.'

'Aye,' Catriona said. 'Like he wants to bed her one minute then murder her the next.'

'True love, then,' Hamish said.

'Shush!' Maggie said. 'I can't hear anything.'

They all stood silently for a moment.

'It's gone very quiet,' Sandy said. 'I'm not sure we should really be listening to this.'

'Nobody's stopping you from going home, Sandy,' Hamish said.

Sandy shook his head. 'Well, I wouldn't want to miss anything.'

'What *are* they doing?' Maggie asked.

'What are they doing? What do you *think* they're doing?' Hamish said.

'Oh my God! You think they're kissing?' Kirsty squeaked in excitement.

'And the rest,' Hamish said.

'I wish I could see,' Angus said.

'You pervert!' Maggie said, punching him in the ribs.

'Pipe down,' Hamish said, and they all strained to hear what was happening down on the southern shore of the loch.

Chapter Thirty-Five

Connie looked at Alastair in horror at what he'd just told her.

'I came home one day to find her on the bed. There was an empty bottle of pills in her hand. I felt so guilty because I hadn't seen that coming. I knew she wasn't happy but she hadn't said anything to indicate she was so low. I still remember making that call for the ambulance. I felt so cold, so numb – as if it wasn't really me. My hands were like ice and they didn't warm up the whole evening. It was as if I'd died or something. God!' Alastair yelled into the night as he remembered. 'And I stayed with her until she came round from having her stomach pumped.'

'Poor Sara,' Connie said. 'Was there any lasting damage?'

Alastair shook his head. 'They got her in time, thank God, but I should have been there. I should have known what was going on with her.'

'It wasn't your fault,' Connie said. 'You couldn't have known what she was thinking or feeling. You had your own worries.'

'No, it wasn't my fault,' he said, 'but it still *feels* as if it was.'

'But is she okay now?'

'She's living with her sister,' Alastair said, carefully navigating his way around the fact that she was actually in Lochnabrae right now and very likely in his bedroom, which wouldn't look good if it was discovered. 'We couldn't stay together. We just seemed to bring out the very worst in each other.'

Connie bit her lip. 'And that's why you came here?'

'I had to get away from it all. You know what it's like to have the press on your back? I couldn't stand it when they kept on and on with the stories about Sara's overdose.'

'But you're still writing, aren't you?'

'I don't know if you can call it writing,' he said, 'but I've got to come up with something soon. You can't live on fine air and scenery.'

'But don't you miss it?' Connie asked.

'What?'

'The theatre – the noise and the buzz?'

'Do you?'

Connie sighed. 'I'm still trying to figure that out.'

'I miss it, sure I do, but I didn't like the person it turned me into. When I started writing for the theatre, I got a real buzz, you know, but then it became a job that was no longer just about the words and then the directing began and – well – you've seen what happens to me when I direct.'

'Yes,' Connie said and then she was quiet for a moment.

'What is it, Connie?'

She looked up at him. 'I just wish you'd told me about Sara – about *everything*. I'd have understood, then. I do understand about pressure, you know. We could have talked about things and maybe you would have told me about—' she paused.

'About what?'

Connie bit her lip. 'About how you feel about me.'

They stared at each other, neither speaking.

'God, I'm sorry,' Alastair said at last, taking a step towards her. 'I so wanted to talk to you and I never meant to hurt you. I've been so stupid and I've treated you so badly, Connie. I just wanted to get the best from you because I know you're brilliant.'

Connie shook her head. 'It's too late for flattery now,' she said with a tiny smile. 'It won't get you anywhere.'

'Are you sure?' Alastair asked and he crossed the space that parted them. 'Listen,' he said, 'I should have told you how I felt ages ago. I've been such an idiot. But you know how I feel, don't you?'

Connie looked up at him, her face bright in the moonlight. 'I'm not sure,' she said but there was a tiny smile playing around her lips and Alastair bent his head down to meet those lips with his.

It was a sweet, tender kiss that seemed full of moonbeams and starlight but it soon deepened. Connie closed her eyes, the warm rush of desire flooding her body. She couldn't remember the last time she'd felt like that and the feeling excited her beyond belief.

They kissed until they could no longer tell whose lips were whose and then there was a mad rush of limbs as they undressed each other, their skins gleaming white in the moonlight as they made love on the sand by the loch.

Everything else was forgotten. Hollywood agents, film contracts, dreadful exes, stressful rehearsals – all were banished and the world focussed simply on the purity of a shared moment. A warm, wondrous, wicked moment, Connie thought, as she closed her eyes and listened to the waters of the loch lapping against the shore in the inky distance.

Maggie and Euan were looking around for Bounce but he'd disappeared.

'I hope he's all right,' Maggie said.

'Probably after some rabbit,' Euan said. 'He'll turn up sooner or later.'

The rest of the LADS had decamped to the pub after finally growing bored of having a very suggestive soundtrack and no picture to go with it.

'Do you think it's a good idea?' Maggie said. 'Alastair and Connie?'

'I'm not sure what kind of an idea it is but they're both adults. They both know what they're doing.'

'Do they?' Maggie asked. 'I'm not sure they do. I think we should wait and make sure they're both okay.'

Euan frowned at her. 'Why would you be wanting to do that?'

Maggie shrugged. 'I just want to make sure.'

'Maggie, lass—'

'I'm worried. I'm worried for Connie,' she said.

'You can't be worrying yourself for somebody else,' he said. 'Connie's a worldly enough sort of lass. She'll not come to any harm by her own hands.'

'But it's Alastair's hands she's fallen into,' Maggie pointed out.

'Aye,' Euan said, 'and we know him to be a decent sort of fellow.' He ushered Maggie towards her home.

'Do you think Connie will stay here?'

'In Lochnabrae? I don't think she'll stay just because she's had a fling with a local boy.'

'I want her to stay,' Maggie said.

'Aye, I know you do but we can't always have what we want.'

'Connie?'

Down by the loch a voice came out of the darkness.

Connie opened her eyes and sat up in the sand. 'It's suddenly turned cold.'

'Here,' Alastair said, reaching for his coat and draping it around her shoulders.

'I should get going,' Connie said, getting dressed.

Alastair grabbed her arm. 'What's the rush?'

'Isla will probably be wondering where I am.'

'No, she won't. She'll know where you are by now.'

Connie looked at Alastair and cringed. 'She will?'

'The whole of Lochnabrae will know by now.'

'Oh God!' Connie said, hiding her face in her hands as she suddenly remembered the story Maggie had told her about the young sweethearts whose proposal had been overheard by the entire village because the sound of their voices had carried right across the loch. 'I'll never be able to look anyone in the eye again.'

'Don't be daft!' Alastair told her. 'Everyone knows everybody's business around here. Nobody will think anything of it.'

'You're sure about that?'

'Well, they'll tease you mercilessly for a couple of years but it'll pass.' Alastair laughed. 'You can't belch in a place like this without it being noticed.'

'And reported in the local paper?'

'Ah, well, I hadn't thought about that.'

'Simpkins is still lurking out there somewhere,' Connie

said, standing up and brushing the sand from her clothes. 'But he hasn't actually put anything in print. If he gets wind of this, though—'

'He won't,' Alastair said, standing up too. 'Anyway, he wouldn't dare write about it even if he did find out.'

Connie frowned. 'Why do you say that?'

'Something Euan said.'

'What did he say?'

'Only that he had a word with young Colin. Told him to steer clear of you or he'd ram a haggis down his throat and throw him in the loch,' Alastair said.

'*Really?*'

Alastair nodded. 'Euan said he'd known Colin since he was a wee lad and that Colin was still scared of him boxing his ears if he stepped out of line.'

'Wow,' Connie said. 'He did that for me?'

'Of course. We look out for each other here. So you don't need to worry about Colin any more. We can get up to whatever we want,' he said with a wink.

Connie giggled. 'You seem very light-hearted about all this.'

'What other way is there to be? We just had a very nice time. Why spoil it with worrying?'

'A very nice time?' Connie said. 'Was that all it was?'

Alastair moved towards her and stroked the back of her neck. His hand was warm and strong and had an almost mesmeric effect on her.

'It was wonderful,' he whispered. 'We must do this more often.'

Connie smiled. 'But maybe not in the sand.'

'Aye, maybe not,' he said, leaning forward and kissing her.

For one blissful moment, the whole of the world was in that kiss and nothing else existed.

'We should go,' Alastair said at last and the spell was broken.

'I'll see you tomorrow?' Connie said.

'Aye, no doubt,' Alastair said.

They walked together along the shore, the moonlight casting everything silver. Connie looked out into the centre of the loch where the reflection of the moon floated.

'It's so beautiful,' she said. 'I don't know how my mother could ever have left.'

'She's in LA with you?'

'Not with me as such,' Connie said. 'I'm afraid we had a falling out some time ago. But she wouldn't live anywhere outside of LA now.'

'Never talks about coming here?'

'No,' Connie said. 'But then, we never really talk much now.'

'Ah,' Alastair said. 'Families.'

'Yes,' Connie said. 'But I love it here. Isn't that strange?'

'Not really,' Alastair said. 'You're probably just rebelling.'

'You think?'

'Aye,' Alastair said. 'Your mother couldn't get away from this place fast enough and you, on some level, probably just want to wind her up by coming here.'

'But she doesn't know I'm here,' Connie said.

They walked in silence for a moment.

'And you won't be here for ever, anyway,' Alastair said at length.

Connie stopped. 'What makes you say that?'

'Because you won't,' Alastair said. 'You're an actress and you've seen what's on offer here in Lochnabrae.'

'But I'm more than an actress,' Connie said. 'Nobody seems to realise that!'

'Then you're staying?' Alastair asked in surprise.

Connie paused before answering. 'Would that make a difference – to us?'

Alastair didn't answer.

'Is that why you made love to me?' Connie asked. 'Because you thought I was getting the next plane home?'

'*No*,' Alastair cried.

'Because it's sounding like that to me.'

'Connie,' Alastair said, 'you're reading far too much into everything.'

'Am I?'

'Yes, you are,' Alastair said, pushing a strand of long red hair away from her face. 'You're on the defensive all the time.'

'And you aren't?'

Alastair chuckled. 'I guess we're very much alike in that respect.'

'We've both had our hearts broken, you mean?'

Alastair stroked the side of her face but didn't answer. 'What say you to taking things nice and slowly?'

Connie's eyebrows rose. 'After what just happened here? I think we might need to go into reverse to even things up a bit.'

'Then let's do that,' Alastair said. 'I'd like to get to know you – properly.'

Connie smiled. 'Me too. I mean *you*. I want to get to know *you*. Oh, you know what I mean.'

They laughed and, hand in hand, walked back to the main street together.

'I'll see you back to the B&B,' Alastair said.

'No need,' Connie told him. 'I can see it from here in this moonlight.'

'And I can see a dozen pairs of curtains twitching.'

Connie looked around. 'Where?'

'Only joking,' he said. 'Night, Connie.'

'Night,' she said, moving forward for his kiss goodnight.

'I don't suppose Isla would allow me to sneak upstairs with you for a repeat performance?' Alastair whispered.

'She'd more likely force a mug of hot chocolate upon you and ask you to unblock the sink in the spare bathroom.'

Alastair nodded. 'I'll see you tomorrow,' he said.

'Bet on it,' Connie said, watching as he walked down the main street away from her.

Turning around, Connie walked to the B&B. She felt light of heart and floaty-footed and it had been a very long time since she'd felt like that. The only problem was, whenever she felt like that, she was usually just around the corner from having her heart broken.

When Alastair reached his cottage, it was late. He'd taken the long route around the loch, Bounce returning from having made a dignified exit whilst his master had been with Connie.

Alastair's mind flitted from Connie to Sara and back again. He couldn't believe what had just happened and he smiled as he remembered it.

'Connie Gordon!' he whispered to Bounce. 'I said I was never going to fall for another actress and then I fall for the most famous one in the world!'

Connie had been so warm and giving and he knew that he was irreversibly in love but there was still Sara and, when he opened the front door, he saw the warm glow of lamp-light from his bedroom. Hoping she was asleep, he tiptoed through to switch the light off. Her eyes were closed and her normally pale skin was flushed a rosy-pink. The Highland air was doing her some good, at least, he thought.

He was just making his exit when he heard her voice.

'Alastair?'

'Go to sleep,' he said, trying not to make it sound like an order.

'Where have you been?'

'Just for a walk,' he said.

'How's the play coming?'

'Good,' he said. There was a pause.

'Come to bed,' Sara said.

Alastair sighed. 'I'm going to.'

Sara sat up in bed, pushing her blonde hair out of her eyes and smiling at him in the way that used to make his heart melt. 'You know what I mean,' she said.

He looked at her for a moment. 'Goodnight, Sara,' he said at last, and he left the room, closing the door firmly behind him.

Chapter Thirty-Six

Connie awoke with some of the moon glow from the night before still upon her. She sat up in bed and sighed. There'd been a moment last night when she'd thought things might go horribly wrong but why should they? Why should the events of the past keep repeating themselves? She wasn't in Hollywood now. Alastair wasn't likely to run off and sleep with an extra on a film set, was he? Or sell her story to a newspaper. That wasn't his style.

She scrambled out of bed and showered before dressing in a pair of jeans and a khaki jumper Maggie had chosen for her, which wasn't designer but would keep the spring chill away from places it shouldn't venture.

Skipping down the stairs, she greeted Isla.

'Morning, Connie dear. You were late last night. I hope Alastair saw you back okay?' she said and there was a little twinkle in her eyes.

'Alastair took good care of me, thank you, Isla.'

'Aye,' she said, 'I thought he might.'

They smiled knowingly at each other.

'I'm just popping to Maggie's.'

'Before your breakfast?'

'I'll be back soon,' Connie said and made her way out of the B&B towards Maggie's shop.

'Connie!' Maggie gasped when she walked through the door. 'Are you okay?'

'Of course I'm okay!' Connie said. 'What, did you think I'd been kidnapped or something?'

'I didn't know what to think!' Maggie said, her dark eyes wide.

Connie laughed.

'What's so funny?'

'Your face!' Connie said. 'You look like an outraged parent.'

'But I was worried about you.'

'I was with Alastair. You must've known that.'

'That's why I was worried,' Maggie said, coming around from behind the counter. 'Was he mean to you?'

'No!'

'Because the last we heard was the pair of you shouting at each other.'

'Oh, right,' Connie said. 'That was before.'

'Before what?' Maggie asked.

Connie put her hands on her hips. 'Oh, come on, Maggie. You know before what.'

'Oh,' Maggie said. 'Well, I'd kind of guessed but I was hoping you might just be talking.'

'We talked too,' Connie said.

Maggie nodded. 'Talking's good.'

'Maggie – you're acting awful strange. What's the matter?'

Maggie's mouth twisted up and down, left and right before she answered. 'I just want to make sure you're happy.'

'Happy?' Connie said. 'Maggie, I'm *so* happy here. I never thought I'd feel like this ever again.'

'Because of Alastair?'

Connie grinned. 'Well, partly,' she said. 'He is wonderful.'

'You mean apart from all the yelling and shouting?'

'Yes,' Connie said. 'He has his faults but who hasn't?'

Maggie smiled and Connie looked out of the shop window towards the loch. 'It's a magical place, this.' As she stared at the blue waters, she could feel Maggie's eyes upon her.

'You should stay,' Maggie said. 'We all want you to.'

Connie smiled.

'What is it?' Maggie asked.

'Nothing,' Connie said.

'You're plotting something, aren't you?'

Connie shrugged. 'I might be.'

Maggie grinned, her smile stretching from ear to ear.

'I think I'm finally beginning to find something of myself here,' Connie said. 'And the thought of LA gives me the shivers. You know, I felt like such a fake there. I was making all these romantic comedies yet there was no romance or humour in my own life. How phoney is that? How am I meant to be this great actress, portraying all these emotions, when I've rarely experienced them myself?'

'So you still want to act?'

'Maybe,' Connie said, 'but not like I was. That was more like an endurance sport. I feel I've acted away half my life. I've been living through fictional characters instead of living my own life and I want things to be different now. I want to choose my projects more carefully – have more control, you know? I want to enjoy things more.'

Maggie nodded. 'That's great, Connie. Although I'm sure your fans will be sorry you'll be making fewer films but they're bound to be glad that you're happier.'

'Thanks, Maggie. You've been a really good friend to me.' Connie moved forward and wrapped Maggie up in a hug. 'Well, that's me happy but what about you?' Connie asked. 'What about Mikey? How are things going there? He has noticed you, hasn't he?'

'Yes. He noticed I was hanging out with "Ralph".'

'Oh, Maggie! Why haven't you said anything? You should have sorted that out by now. You can't have him going around thinking that you're seeing somebody.'

Maggie looked woebegone. 'I keep hoping against hope that he'll say something first. I thought Ralph might make him jealous.'

'And it hasn't?'

'It doesn't seem to have bothered him at all.'

'Then you'll have to try something else,' Connie told her.

'Like what?'

'Oh, Maggie!' Connie said. 'This isn't a Jane Austen novel. You're allowed to tell a man how you feel and not wait for him to call upon you first. Goodness, if all of us did that, nobody would *ever* get together.'

'I nearly said something last time he was here,' Maggie said, 'only we got interrupted.'

Connie groaned. 'Can't you meet up somewhere where you won't be interrupted?'

'I don't know.'

'Well, where does he work?'

'At the garage in Strathcorrie with Hamish.'

'And can you talk to him there?'

'Well, I—'

'Maggie!' Connie said. 'Do you want to move forward with this or don't you?'

'Yes, of course I do.'

It was just then that the doorbell went and Angry Angus walked in. Immediately, he clocked Connie.

'All right, Connie?' he said with a lascivious wink. 'Still finding sand in your hair?'

'Oh God!' Connie exclaimed, turning away and blushing.

'Shut it, Angus!' Maggie said. 'She doesn't need your smutty remarks first thing in the morning.'

They watched as Angus disappeared behind the shelves before continuing their conversation.

'I'm worried, Connie,' Maggie whispered. 'What if Mikey doesn't feel the same way?'

Connie gave her a smile. 'But what if he does?'

As Connie returned to the B&B, Isla's head popped around the door of the kitchen.

'You've had a visitor,' she said.

'Alastair?' Connie asked hopefully.

'No, Euan.'

'Euan?'

'Aye. He wanted to speak to you.'

'What about?' Connie asked.

'He wouldn't say. Said you're to call on him before rehearsals tonight. You know where he lives?'

'Number twelve?' Connie said, knowing all the residents' addresses by now.

'Aye. Have yourself some breakfast first, mind.'

Connie did as she was told and, as she sat down, couldn't help noticing that the waistband of her jeans was feeling decidedly snug. Too much of Isla's buttered toast, she thought, promising to resume her early morning jog. At some point.

'You off?' Isla asked ten minutes later after Connie had finished.

'Thought I'd see Euan now. It's probably about the play. He might have some tips for me.'

'Aye, well, make sure you don't let him shout at you like Alastair does.'

'I will,' Connie said, walking out into the street but, as she closed the door behind her, she began to wonder. Euan was a very well-respected member of the community. He was almost a village elder, in fact. What if he was going to put Connie in her place after her behaviour last night?

'Connie lass,' he might say, 'this sort of thing might pass for normal behaviour in Hollywood but you're in Lochnabrae now.'

Oh God! How embarrassing would that be? She shook her head, trying to free herself of the stern face of Euan Kennedy. She was just being silly. He probably just wanted to talk about her films and have her autograph a DVD or something. Or maybe tell her about his conversation with Colin Simpkins just to keep her in the picture.

The bright sky of the morning was beginning to darken now and it looked as if it might rain. Connie looked up at the clouds and thought how beautiful they were. She'd place a bet that her mother would have hated the sight of clouds. She'd always told Connie about the dreadful Scottish weather.

'Rain, rain and more rain,' she'd say.

But that's what keeps it so lush, Connie thought, looking at the glorious tapestry of green mountains. Sure, it was a lot cooler than California but Connie was getting used to that. It was nice to snuggle into warm clothes and she loved her new hiking boots; they were far more comfortable than high heels.

With thoughts of woolly jumpers filling her head, Connie found Euan's cottage. It was pretty much like the others in Lochnabrae – a two-storey whitewashed house looking out over the loch. Dark red curtains hung in the downstairs windows and there was something wilting in a terracotta pot by the doorstep.

It was then that Connie realised how little she knew about Euan. Had he ever been married? Perhaps he was a widower? Maybe she'd find out, she thought, as she knocked on the door.

When it was opened, she noticed that his frame completely filled the space.

'Ah, Connie,' he said. 'Come in, lass.'

'Hi, Euan,' she said, smiling in an attempt to win him over just in case he was about to scold her for the night before.

They walked through to the sitting room at the front of the house. It was small and sparsely furnished but comfortable. One wall was almost completely lined with books and Connie gravitated towards it.

'Wow,' she said. 'That's quite a collection.' Her head tilted as she read the spines.

'They're mostly wildlife books,' Euan said.

'For your job as a ranger?' Connie asked.

'Mostly,' he said.

'I'd like to know more about wildlife. About everything really. All I know about is my job. Isn't that boring?'

'No more than most people. We all do what we can to survive.'

Connie smiled. 'But there's so much more to know,' she

said, her eyes scanning the rows of books. 'Like—' she paused, 'grouse. I don't know anything about grouse.'

'You want to learn about grouse?'

Connie nodded. 'Why not? They sound – fun!'

Euan gave a little smile. 'Connie,' he said.

'Uh-huh?'

'Do you want a cup of tea?'

'Sure,' she said. 'Better make it black, no sugar. I've been overdosing on this rich Highland cream and it's gone straight to my waist.'

Euan disappeared and Connie looked around the rest of the room. There was a row of photo frames on the mantelpiece above the fire and Connie went to look at them. There were several of Euan with a young boy. One of them fishing. One of them halfway up a mountain. Another of them coming out of a cave.

'Who's this?' she asked as Euan came back into the room with two cups of tea that he placed on a small table.

'That's Jamie,' he said. 'My sister's boy.'

'You spend a lot of time together?'

'Aye,' he said. 'His father died when he was small. He comes here from time to time.'

'That's nice,' Connie said. 'And what's this?' she asked, her eyes attracted by a small wooden shield hanging on the wall with the name 'Kennedy' emblazoned across the top.

'Oh, that's the clan crest badge,' Euan said.

Connie looked closely at the shield decorated with a round metal crest containing what looked like a mythical dolphin. It was set against a fabulous tartan that was predominantly green with stripes of vivid blue, red and yellow crisscrossing it.

'Wow!' she said as the colours danced before her eyes. 'That's really beautiful.'

'Aye,' Euan said.

'*Avise La Fin*,' Connie said, reading the inscription on the crest. 'What's that mean?'

'Consider the end,' Euan said. 'That's the clan motto.'

'Consider the end,' Connie repeated. 'I like it. And not many of us do, do we? We just bulldoze our way through life, not really thinking about the consequences.'

Euan cleared his throat and Connie looked at him.

'You okay?' she asked. He nodded and Connie looked back at the crest. 'What exactly is a clan?' Connie asked.

'A clan? Well, it's a family, united by a common ancestor. There's a tradition that clan members take care of each other – defend their heritage – that sort of thing.'

'That's nice,' Connie said with a smile. 'I should like to have a clan.'

'You do,' Euan said.

'You mean the Gordons?'

'Connie,' he said, 'will you no' sit down?'

Connie looked at him and saw that there was something urgent behind his eyes.

'What is it?' she asked. 'Is everything okay?' She suddenly became nervous. What if he was going to tell her something awful? Maybe it was something about Alastair. Maybe Alastair was dying. Or worse – *married*.

Connie sat down and Euan took the chair opposite her. 'I haven't been completely honest with you, Connie,' he said.

'About what?'

'About Vanessa,' he said.

'My mother?'

342

'Aye.'

'You knew her?'

'Well, everybody knows everybody in a place like this.'

'Of course,' she said. 'I wondered if you'd known her. I mean, you're about the same age, aren't you?'

Euan nodded. 'We were at school together. Grew up together.'

Connie smiled. 'She's never mentioned you. Mind you, she hardly ever talked about the people of Lochnabrae. There's so much I want to know.'

'Aye, well, maybe I can help you there,' Euan said.

'Really?' Connie said. 'That's great! So, tell me more about my mother. What was she like when she was at school? And why did she want to leave Lochnabrae so badly?'

Euan shifted in his chair and cleared his throat. 'Well,' he said, 'I think I might've been the reason she left Lochnabrae.'

'Really?' Connie said, frowning, and then something dawned on her. '*Oh!*' She gave a little laugh as her mother's past suddenly became a little clearer. 'You mean – you two were—'

'Connie, lass,' Euan interrupted, 'I'm your father.'

Chapter Thirty-Seven

Alastair was watching Sara from the kitchen door as she turned a few meagre ingredients from his cupboards into something appetising for lunch. She was wearing her nightie having taken a walk and showered late and her blonde hair clung damply to her face.

'You never used to cook before,' he said.

She turned around and smiled at him. 'I told you – there've been a lot of changes since—' She didn't finish her sentence.

Alastair nodded. 'That's good.'

'I feel like a brand new person,' she said, 'and I want to make the most of life, I really do. Natalie's been brilliant. She enrolled me on this cookery course and I'm thinking of doing it professionally.'

'Really?'

'Yes,' she said. 'Don't laugh!'

'I'm not laughing. I think it's brilliant. Your sister always did know what was best for you.' There was a pause. 'So, you're not acting any more?'

Sara turned to face him. 'You're not writing plays any more?'

'Right,' he said.

'I think that time is over, don't you?'

He nodded. 'Listen, Sara – I'm sorry I didn't do more to help you. I really wanted to but I didn't know what to do.'

Sara put down the frying pan and turned to face him. 'You did everything you could,' she said. 'You were the one who found me, remember? You saved my life! And you stayed with me too – far longer than anyone should have expected you to – but I had to do the rest by myself. You've got nothing to blame yourself for. You know that, don't you?'

Alastair looked down at the kitchen floor.

'Alastair?' She moved towards him and planted a kiss on his cheek. 'I'm so sorry for what I put you through. I can't seem to say it enough.'

He looked down at her and then took her in his arms and hugged her. The emotion took him so completely by surprise and it felt good but not like when he'd held Connie on the beach by the loch. It was different between him and Sara now. He would always love her in a special kind of way – rather like a brother might love a sister. He would always care desperately about her and want to know that she was okay no matter how many miles separated them.

'I never meant to come up here and fight with you,' Sara added, 'but I did want to talk and try to explain things.'

'I know.'

'And—' she paused.

'What?'

'I was kind of hoping I could win you back.' She looked up at him, her eyes wide and appealing but then she sighed. 'But I can see that's not going to happen, is it?'

'I'm sorry,' he said.

'I'm too late, aren't I? I think you've already lost your

heart to somebody else? Who is it? Some cute little Scottish lass?'

Alastair smiled. 'Something like that.'

'Well, that's good,' Sara said with a smile but her face was edged with sadness. 'Then, you don't mind?'

'Mind what?'

'Me coming here.'

'I don't mind,' he said. 'It's been good to see you again.'

They looked at one another and smiled.

'I'm so glad I came.'

'Me too.'

She took a deep breath. 'Come on, let's have this food before it gets cold.'

Chapter Thirty-Eight

After Connie had left the shop and Maggie had dealt with Angus – telling him bluntly that she was not about to divulge what happened on the beach between Connie and Alastair and that he should mind his own business – she returned upstairs and stood in front of the mirror. What she saw was a vast improvement on how she'd looked before Connie's intervention. Her hair was in better condition and no longer looked like a woolly jumper, her figure looked womanly in the new clothes they'd chosen together and her face had certainly benefited from the tinted moisturiser, which had helped to tame her wind-blasted complexion. So why did she still feel so shy about approaching Mikey? Why hadn't the make-over given her the confidence she so desperately needed? But she knew the answer to that. You couldn't buy confidence from a catalogue or order it online; it had to come from *you*.

She looked at herself and tried to see her as Mikey might. Had he noticed the new-look Maggie and would it make any difference to him if he had? Or would he just see the old Maggie? Hamish's little sister who sold shortbread?

Maggie took a deep breath and let it out slowly. There was only one way to find out and that was to confront him.

'Right now,' she said, running downstairs and shutting up the shop before she lost her nerve.

Just as she was leaving, she spotted Mrs Wallace heading up the road.

'Margaret Hamill!' she called. 'Surely you're not closing at this time of the morning, are you? I need a pint of milk.'

'Come back this afternoon!' Maggie called, laughing to herself as she saw the expression on the old bat's face. 'There are more important things than a pint of milk,' she added, making a quick getaway before she could hear her reply.

As Maggie drove into Strathcorrie, she swore she could feel her heart knocking against her ribs. Her whole system seemed to be flooded with adrenalin as if she was about to give a speech before hundreds of people rather than talking to an old friend, but that was because he was more than an old friend. Michael Shire was a god. The sexiest thing ever to have been seen in a kilt, Maggie thought, remembering the outfit he'd worn at his older brother's wedding and how her own knees had weakened at the sight of his.

Parking her car in the main square, Maggie walked towards Dougie's Autos where Mikey and Hamish worked. She could hear someone banging from underneath a car but couldn't make out who it was so stood waiting until the person emerged.

It was then that the phone from the garage office began to ring.

'Bugger!' a voice said. It was Mikey and Maggie watched as he crawled out and stood up to full height. He hadn't spotted her and she watched as he wiped his grimy hands on his jeans before answering the phone. She'd never known anyone who could make grease look so sexy. His dark hair hung in waves around his tanned face and his bright eyes were narrowed in concentration. He was wearing a dark green T-shirt that was edging towards black and the cut of the sleeves showed his arms off to perfection. Maggie had always had a thing about men's arms. There were some women who went on about a man's bum being the thing but, for Maggie, it was always the arms – good, strong, lean arms that could wrap around you and pull you into a warm embrace.

Just as she felt her face heating up like a furnace, Mikey came off the phone and spotted her.

'Are you all right, our Maggie?' he said. 'What a nice surprise. You shopping?'

'No,' she said.

'You okay? You look a bit red,' he said, examining her face.

'I'm fine,' she said.

'Come to see Hamish? He's just scooted off to the shop to get us some supplies. He'll be back in a mo.'

Maggie took a deep breath. 'I didn't come to see Hamish,' she said. 'I came to see you.'

Connie marched up the hill towards Alastair's, her mind a whirlwind. She hadn't stopped to give herself time to think. She'd just upped and left without saying very much at all to poor Euan after his revelation.

'Oh God!' she cried into the sky, thinking of how she'd

just sat there on his sofa as Euan had tried to explain what had happened that summer before her mother had left Lochnabrae.

'Vanessa was never happy here,' Euan said. 'Some people get like that. Most are content with their way of life here – can't think of any other way – but your mother wasn't one of them. Always dreaming, she was. Always talking of going to Hollywood and becoming an actress.'

Connie had listened, wondering – dreading – where this story was going to end.

'That last summer was crazy,' Euan told her. 'All she went on about was getting away. She drove me mad. I kept telling her she couldn't go – that I didn't want her to go and she'd just laugh. *I have to go*, she told me. *You can't keep me here.*

'I began to notice she was acting strangely. She'd lost a little of that mad sparkle of hers. So, I confronted her one day,' he said, stopping to rub his chin thoughtfully. 'She didn't tell me, of course, but I had my suspicions.

'And then, one day, she wasn't here any more. She'd left without even saying goodbye. The first I knew about it was a postcard from LA.'

Euan got up and opened a chest drawer, handing Connie a bright card featuring the famous Hollywood sign. She turned it over and read the message, acknowledging that it was, indeed, her mother's writing.

I told you I'd make it! Found a place to stay and have auditions next week! You wouldn't believe the weather out here. Beats Lochnabrae! V x

That was it. Four brief sentences that gave very little away.

'There was a second card,' Euan said, pulling it out of the drawer. 'Seven months later.'

He handed it to Connie.

You have a daughter. I've named her Constance after my grandma. Please don't try and find us. Making a new life here. V x

'I did try to find her, of course,' Euan said, 'but people get swallowed up in a place like Hollywood and she changed her name for a while so, when I asked around agencies, nobody had heard of Vanessa Gordon.'

'But my father?' Connie said, thinking of the man she'd thought was her true father all these years.

'She met him shortly after moving out there. They got married pretty quickly and I guess he must have known he wasn't your real father. I know this is a lot to take in, lass,' Euan said. 'I still can't believe it myself. But, seeing you here – getting to know you – I *can* believe it.'

Connie had stood up at that point.

'Connie?' he'd said. 'Will you no' stay a wee while?'

She hadn't said anything. She'd simply fled and the only place she could think to flee to was Alastair's.

Reaching his cottage, she knocked on the door with an impatient fist, causing Bounce to bark from inside.

'Alastair?' she called, opening his door after remembering that he'd said that he never locked it. 'Are you there?'

'Connie?'

His voice was coming from the kitchen and Connie went through but she stopped dead when she saw he had company. It wasn't just any company either. It was a pretty blonde woman in a nightdress – her hair damp from a recent shower.

'Hello,' the woman said, turning around to address Connie. 'I'm Sara. Who are you?'

Chapter Thirty-Nine

Mikey wiped his hands on an old rag and faced Maggie. 'Do you want a cup of tea?'

'No,' Maggie said.

'So, how can I be of service?'

A thousand wicked thoughts raced through her mind of just how Mikey could be of service to her but she tried to shake them.

'Well, there's something I've been meaning to say to you.'

'Oh, aye?'

Maggie nodded. 'Only I didn't know how.'

Just then, Hamish appeared with a jar of coffee in one hand and a packet of ginger snaps in the other.

'Mags!' he said.

Maggie turned and glared at him. Hamish stared at her as if weighing up the situation and then his eyes suddenly widened in understanding.

'I'll go and call Mr Benton,' he said, 'and tell him his car's ready.'

Mikey's eyes followed Hamish but quickly returned to Maggie. 'What's going on?' he asked.

Maggie's heart was racing wildly and, because she couldn't think of a single thing to say, she did the next best thing and launched herself at Mikey, kissing him passionately until she felt like there wasn't a breath left in her body.

'Oh, my!' she said, once they'd parted.

'Maggie!'

'I'm sorry!' Maggie blurted, looking everywhere but at Mikey.

'Don't be sorry,' he said. 'It was very nice.'

A laugh suddenly exploded from Maggie and she looked up at him. 'Was it?'

'Very nice indeed,' Mikey said, 'but what on earth have I done to deserve it?'

Maggie looked at him, her eyes wide and bright with love. 'You're you,' she said simply.

Mikey frowned. 'What about Ralph?'

Maggie looked at him in disbelief. 'Mikey – Ralph's not real!'

'What do you mean, not real? I saw him with my own two eyes and you were kissing.'

'Aye, I know but it was Connie.'

'What was Connie?'

'*Ralph!* Ralph was Connie. She was in disguise to get away from Colin Simpkins. It worked too – for a while.'

'I don't believe it.'

'Well, you'd better.'

'You snogged Connie?'

'Aye.'

'Oh my God!' Mikey said, wiping his hand over his jaw. 'I wish I'd known at the time. That's really hot.'

'Mikey!'

'What was it like?'

'Oh, stop it!'

'Go on – tell me,' Mikey said. 'I'm heating up just thinking about it.'

'You great pervert, you!'

He moved towards her and bent his head a little. 'Kiss me again,' he said.

Maggie could feel herself blushing. 'I have to know how you feel about me first.'

Mikey cupped her face in his huge hands. 'You're the one for me, Maggie Hamill, and, if you hadn't come here today to tell me then I would have come to tell you.'

Maggie felt tears welling up in her eyes. 'Really?'

'Aye,' he said. 'It's been coming on a while now only I've been too stupid to say anything. That day I came into the shop to buy shortbread?'

'What about it?'

'I meant to tell you then but I was too tongue-tied.'

Maggie gave a little smile. 'I wish you *had* told me,' she said. 'I was cursing you that day, Michael Shire.'

'Why didn't you tell me?'

'I'm telling you now!' Maggie said.

Mikey smiled. 'How much time we've lost,' he said.

'But I thought you only saw me as Hamish's little sister,' Maggie said.

'Aye, well, I did for a while,' he said. 'But then you blossomed, Mags, and I couldn't stop thinking about you.'

'But you went away,' she said. 'You left. For months!'

'I know. And that's when I couldn't get you out of my head,' he said, his long fingers combing through her hair. 'That gorgeous little smile of yours followed me right around the world.'

'Liar!'

'It *did!* Swear to God.'

'And what about all those exotic beauties you met?'

'Och!' Mikey declared. 'Mere distractions from the good stuff at home.'

Maggie didn't look too convinced. Until he bent forward and kissed her.

'I came back, didn't I?' he said.

'For how long?' Maggie asked.

'What do you mean?'

'How long will it be before you get itchy feet again and want to leave?'

'Has Hamish not told you?'

'Told me what?'

'We're taking over the garage. Dougie's retiring at the end of the year. Hamish is going to do most of the mechanic work and I'm setting up a motorbike hire company on the side.'

'What?'

'Aye. It's a done deal. It's one of the reasons I came back,' he said, pulling Maggie close to him. 'Why on earth didn't he tell you?' Mikey asked. 'Hamish?'

'HAMISH!' Maggie yelled.

Hamish stuck his head around the office door. 'You two got things sorted out, then?'

Connie had walked away from Alastair's cottage at the kind of pace Bounce would have had difficulty keeping up with. She wondered if Alastair would run after her and hoped he wouldn't because she didn't think there was any explaining to do.

Blinking away stinging tears, Connie cursed herself.

'Stupid, *stupid* girl!'

What had she thought she was doing? But that was it

– she hadn't been thinking, had she? She'd let go of all that and simply fallen – deeply and hopelessly in love – and, all this time, he'd been living with Sara in his cosy little love nest at the top of the hill. How hadn't she known? How hadn't the village known? Surely Maggie would have said something. But maybe Alastair was cleverer than they all thought. Maybe he enjoyed the subterfuge, sitting in his snug little cottage, laughing at the inhabitants of Lochnabrae.

'STUPID!' she cursed again.

They'd made love and she'd thought he was in love with her. She'd trusted him, *believed* him, when he'd told her the story about Sara. She'd assumed that Sara was part of his old life and the reason why he'd come to Lochnabrae. She hadn't realised that he'd brought Sara with him. He hadn't told her that.

He lied to you.

Connie thought back to that moment in LA when she'd read Maggie's letter, remembering how she'd envisaged Lochnabrae as some sort of retreat. In her mind, it had been a perfect place where the mountains shielded you from the miseries of the world and you could drown your sorrows in the beautiful blue depths of the loch. But Lochnabrae was just like anywhere else with its problems and its secrets. It wasn't a perfect place where she could hide from the world and she wasn't going to meet the perfect man there – far from it. It was just as Bob Braskett had told her. She couldn't stay there. She didn't belong.

Connie stopped and took a deep breath and let it out slowly. The castle, the new home and friends, it was all just a dream but, like Audrey Hepburn in *Roman Holiday*, Connie had to wake up to reality and, for her, reality was LA.

Tears filled her eyes, obliterating the view of the village before her, the loch becoming just a long blue smudge. She didn't want to go. There was so much that was good in Lochnabrae: dear sweet Maggie and Hamish, Isla with her motherly ways, funny old Angus and the rest of the LADS. She'd even miss grumpy old Mrs Wallace.

And Alastair? And Euan?

Of course she was going to miss them – more than she wanted to admit. But it would be impossible to stay now.

'CONNIE!' a voice cried behind her as she entered the village. She kept on walking, picking up speed once again. 'Connie – wait!' She felt a hand grab her shoulder but, still, she didn't stop.

'Keep away from me!' she shouted.

'Listen to me – Sara's just visiting.'

'Right.'

'You've *got* to believe me. She turned up the other night *completely* unexpectedly. I had no idea she even knew where I lived.'

'I saw her – in your kitchen – in her *nightdress!* How can I trust you? Why didn't you tell me she was staying with you the other night?'

'I was scared you wouldn't believe me.'

'Scared I wouldn't sleep with you, more like!'

'No – Connie – I didn't want to hurt you. I didn't want you getting embroiled in all this. Sara's my past and I'm doing my best to sort things out and she's leaving today – we were just talking about that when you arrived.'

They'd almost reached the bed and breakfast and it was only once they were outside the door that she slowed down and looked at him.

'Have you *any* idea how many times I've been deceived?

Have you? I've spent my life giving my heart to men who think nothing of breaking it! I thought you were different. I *trusted* you!'

'You can *still* trust me!'

'But you didn't tell me the truth.'

'I know and I'm *so* sorry.'

Connie opened the front door.

'Don't go like this – *Connie!*'

She slammed the door behind her.

Her head was spinning with what she'd just heard – from Alastair as well as from Euan. *I have a new father*, she thought to herself, because there was no doubt in her mind that Euan – at least – had been telling her the truth. She'd seen it in his eyes and she'd also held the proof in her hands in the postcards from her mother. So why hadn't her mother told her? Why had she made Connie believe that Steve Lassiter was her father?

Connie had a feeling she knew why. It was because her mother had left Lochnabrae behind her. It represented her past and, even though the father of her child lived there, it meant nothing to her.

Please don't try and find us. Making a new life here.

That's what she'd written and it had been her last words to Euan. Poor man, Connie thought. What had he suffered all this time?

Connie marched up the stairs to her room thankful that Isla was nowhere to be seen.

Euan was a good man, she thought; she'd known that almost from the moment she'd met him. There was a strength of character about him. You knew you could trust somebody like Euan.

And he's my father, Connie thought. *Euan Kennedy.*

Connie Kennedy. My name is Connie Kennedy! I even have my own clan!

Now she thought about it, it was rather strange that she'd taken her mother's name rather than Steve Lassiter's. Considering her mother had married him shortly after her birth, it would have been perfectly normal for them to take his name but she hadn't. Did that have anything to do with her mother's feelings for Euan? Was she reluctant to name another man's child after Steve? And did Steve even know that Connie wasn't his child? It was all so confusing.

Then there was Alastair who had lied to her. Connie was so angry at him and she knew she couldn't stay in Lochnabrae for a moment longer. She had to leave, and the sooner the better.

Maggie was floating on air as she went to rehearsals that night. Mikey said he was going to make a special effort to join everyone and Maggie couldn't wait to see him again. They were a couple! He didn't love her just for her short-bread – he loved her because she was Maggie and she was bursting to tell the whole world.

Nothing – absolutely nothing – was going to dampen her mood that evening. Or so she thought. She was just pulling herself out of a very pleasant daydream involving herself, Mikey and a midsummer swim in the loch when she heard Alastair and, as usual, he didn't sound in a good mood.

'Catriona,' he said. 'I want you to take over the role of Viola.'

'But I'm Sebastian,' Catriona said. 'I can't play both twins.'

'You won't have to,' Alastair said. 'I'll take over Sebastian for now. We'll sort it out properly later.'

'Hang on a minute,' Maggie said. 'Where's Connie?'

Alastair scratched his head. 'Connie won't be coming back,' he said.

'What do you mean, she's not coming back?' Maggie asked.

'Och, she's not given it up, has she?' Sandy asked.

'Alastair?' Maggie said. 'What's happened?'

'Nothing's happened.'

'Well, something must've happened because the last time I saw her, everything was hunky dory,' Maggie said. 'What have you said to her?'

'What's going on?' Angus asked.

'That's what we're trying to find out,' Maggie said.

Alastair looked from left to right as if assessing whether he could make it to an exit before having to explain.

'Alastair!'

'All right, all right!' he shouted. 'We had a misunderstanding.'

'Oh God!' Sandy groaned. 'You've scared her off, haven't you, lad?'

Maggie's mouth dropped open. 'Oh, Alastair! What have you done?'

Alastair shrugged hopelessly. 'I had a visitor – an old girlfriend – staying at my house and Connie got the wrong idea.'

A terrible silence fell as everyone stared, open-mouthed, at Alastair.

'The wrong idea? You're sure it was the wrong idea?' Maggie said sternly.

'Of course I'm sure! There's nothing between me and

Sara but – well – Connie wouldn't listen to me and we had a big fight.' Alastair looked completely defeated and everyone watched as his shoulders sank heavily.

'He might not be the only one to have scared her off,' Euan suddenly said from his seat at the back of the room.

'What do you mean, Euan?' Maggie said. 'What on earth could you have done to upset Connie?'

Euan blew out a huge sigh. 'You'll find out sooner or later, I guess,' he said.

'Find out what?'

'That I'm Connie's father.'

For a moment, nobody spoke. They simply stared at Euan in disbelief.

'What?' Alastair said at last.

'You can't be serious,' Sandy said. 'I mean, she's a good-looking lass. You can't have spawned a movie star.'

'Sandy!' Maggie shouted. 'Is it true?' she asked, looking at Euan.

'Aye, lass, it's true.'

'How long have you known?' she asked.

'Shortly after Connie was born. Vanessa sent me a post-card from LA telling me the news.'

'Jeez!' Sandy said. 'A postcard! I've never heard the like.'

'That's why you set up the fan club, isn't it?' Maggie said.

'Why didn't you tell us?' Hamish asked.

'Because you wouldn't have believed me,' Euan said.

'We don't believe you now,' Angus said.

'Shut up, Angus!' Maggie said. 'I'm trying to sort things out here.'

They were all quiet for a moment.

'And you've told her?' Maggie said.

'Aye. This morning.'

'After you called at the B&B?' Isla said.

Euan nodded. 'I thought it was time,' he said.

'So, that's why she's left?' Isla said.

'Connie's left?' Maggie screamed.

'Well, she wasn't at the B&B when I came out,' Isla said.

'Did you check her room?' Maggie asked. 'Have her things gone?'

'I don't know,' Isla said.

Suddenly, there was a stampede towards the door of the village hall as everyone left for the B&B.

Chapter Forty

'If she's left Lochnabrae,' Maggie yelled as they all ran down the street, 'I'm knocking your two heads together then drowning you in the loch.'

'Aye,' Angus said, 'and I will too.'

'Maybe she just went for a wee walk,' Hamish said hopefully.

'I should've known something was wrong,' Isla said.

'It's not your fault, Isla,' Maggie said.

'It's nobody's fault,' Euan said.

'Oh, really?' Maggie said, glaring at him. 'You've probably scared her half to death!'

'She had a right to know, Maggie,' Euan said. 'I did nothing wrong.'

The gang – Bounce included – arrived at the B&B and Isla opened the door.

'Connie?' Maggie shouted, taking the stairs two at a time and banging on her bedroom door. 'Connie? You in there?'

'Is the door locked?' Isla asked.

'No,' Maggie called back as she dared to open it. 'Oh, Isla! She's gone.'

Everyone ran up the stairs and stared into the empty

bedroom. Every single possession of Connie's had vanished, along with their owner.

'We've lost her,' Sandy said, shaking his head. 'Well, it was nice while it lasted.'

Maggie felt anger bubbling up inside her. 'How can you be so calm? She's left, Sandy! Gone for good!'

'But she was never going to stay, was she?' Sandy said. 'Not here. Not with the likes of us. You didn't really think she would, did you?'

Tears rose in Maggie's eyes. She did her best to blink them away but one escaped, splashing onto the highly-patterned carpet.

'She was happy here,' Maggie said.

'Aye,' Hamish said, 'until Euan dropped his bomb.'

'And I messed things up good and proper,' Alastair said.

Maggie walked into the room and sank down onto the bed and Kirsty and Catriona joined her, all three of them the picture of sorrow.

'I know it's stupid of me but I really thought she might stay here,' Maggie said in a little voice.

'She didn't even say goodbye,' Kirsty said.

'I've just remembered something,' Isla said. 'Mr Forsyth popped around this afternoon and left a package for Connie.'

'What sort of package?' Maggie asked.

'I left it in the sitting room,' Isla said.

Maggie got up off the bed. 'Can we see it?'

Everyone left the room and returned downstairs.

'Mikey!' Maggie screamed as she saw him standing in the hallway.

'What's going on?' he said. 'I went to the village hall and nobody was there.'

'Connie's gone,' Maggie cried, and they all entered the tiny sitting room together.

Isla put a lamp on and picked up the small padded envelope Mr Forsyth had left.

'I shouldn't really open it,' Isla said.

'Och, get it open, woman! We forged her autograph so we can open her post,' Angus said.

'What is it?' Mikey asked Maggie, a hand on her shoulder.

'Mr Forysth left it for Connie,' Maggie said. 'It might be some sort of clue to tell us where she is.'

Isla sighed and opened the envelope, her hand diving inside and retrieving a fat silver key.

'What's that?' Sandy asked.

'A key, you dope!' Angus said.

'Well, I can see that but where's it a key to?'

Maggie took the envelope from Isla and peered inside. 'There's a note,' she said, pulling out a small compliment slip headed 'Forsyth and Son'.

'Drawing up the papers now for Rossburn. Owners have given permission for you to have the key early so you can make arrangements re: builders. Good luck! A.S.T Forsyth.

'Rossburn?' Euan said.

Maggie looked up from the note. 'Connie's bought Rossburn Castle?'

'No!' Hamish said. 'That place is a ruin.'

'It needs a hell of a lot of money thrown at it,' Mikey said.

'Aye, but she has that, hasn't she?' Catriona said.

'Didn't I tell you?' Maggie said. 'Connie was going to live here and you two great oafs went and chased her away!'

'Now, let's not jump to conclusions,' Euan said.

'But it's all here!' Maggie said. 'The key to the castle. Why else would she buy it?'

'Maybe it's a business acquisition,' Euan said.

Maggie glared at him. 'She was going to *live* here, Euan. Your daughter was going to stay right here in Lochnabrae.'

'His daughter?' Mikey cried.

'Aye, his daughter!' Maggie said. 'She was happy enough here in Lochnabrae to buy a home.'

'And not just any home,' Hamish said. 'She was going to invest in a medieval wreck!'

'Oh, my!' Maggie said. 'We can't let her leave now. We've got to get her back!'

'But where's she gone?' Isla said.

'She's taken her bags,' Alastair said. 'She must be going back to LA.'

Maggie looked up at him. His face was ashen. He was feeling as desperate as she was, wasn't he?

'Come on,' Alastair said. 'We'll take the Landy.'

'Shouldn't some of us stay here?' Isla asked. 'In case she changes her mind and calls or something?'

'We won't all fit in the Landy, anyway,' Hamish said.

'Right,' Alastair said. 'Who's coming to the airport with me? Maggie?'

Maggie nodded.

'Euan, I guess?' Alastair said.

'And Mikey,' Maggie said. 'I can't go without Mikey.'

'Can I come too?' Hamish said.

Alastair nodded. 'That'll about do it,' he said. 'So Angus, Sandy and the girls will stay here with Isla?'

Everyone nodded.

'You too, Bounce,' Alastair said, and Bounce cocked his head to one side as if wondering if he was going to miss out on some fun. 'Okay then,' Alastair said, 'we'd better get to the airport before she makes the first plane out of here.'

Chapter Forty-One

The taxi ride to the airport had been torturous. Connie had wanted to take one last look at Rossburn Castle but the taxi driver had told her that would add ten miles to the journey and she might miss her plane. What am I to do with the old place? Connie wondered as they approached the outskirts of Glasgow. It was too late to back out of the sale now and, besides, she wouldn't want to mess dear Mr Forsyth around. Besides, there was a part of her that still wanted to own the old place if only for a brief time.

Of course, the easiest option would be to buy it, do it up and sell it on but the thought of that pained Connie. As long as the castle was hers then a little bit of her would remain in Lochnabrae and, even though things hadn't worked out quite as she'd expected there, she couldn't bear to cut all her ties just yet.

How horrible it had been to sneak away like that, she thought. Her sense of guilt was overwhelming. She'd owed so many goodbyes – to Isla for being like a mother to her, and to Maggie for being such a good friend and confidante. For a moment, she thought about how she'd dressed up as Ralph, and laughed out loud at the memory of the naughty kiss in the pub.

'You okay?' the taxi driver asked.

'Yes,' Connie said, 'I'm okay.' Only she wasn't because her heart was breaking as she remembered the fun she'd had and the people she'd left behind. She thought of Angry Angus and his obsession with westerns. She thought of cheeky Sandy and the sweet Kendrick sisters. She remembered Hamish and Mikey. Could anyone ask for better friends? And then she remembered Euan and Alastair. The two men in her life.

If only things could have been different, she thought. If only . . .

'Why's everything always so complicated?' she asked.

'It's not so bad,' the taxi driver replied. 'I'm dropping you right outside departures and you'll find your way no bother.'

Maggie leant forward from the back seat where she was sandwiched in between Hamish and Mikey. Mikey had hold of her hand and kept squeezing it, which Maggie was finding more unsettling than comforting.

'Listen,' she told Alastair and Euan in the front, 'we've got to have a plan. We can't just turn up and expect her to want to come back.'

'Well, what are we going to say?' Euan asked, turning to look at Maggie.

'What do you *want* to say?' Maggie asked.

'We might not get to say anything if we don't make it,' Hamish said.

Maggie elbowed him. 'We'll make it.'

Euan cleared his throat. 'I've said all I can to the lass,' he said.

'Then that's not enough,' Maggie said.

They were silent as they drove through the hills. It was getting dark and the landscape took on a menacing quality that quite spooked Maggie.

'Aye, Maggie, I reckon you're right,' Euan said. 'I've told her nothing but the facts.'

Maggie nodded. 'So, you've something else you'd like to tell her, then?'

Euan nodded. 'Aye, and I've been wanting to tell her for years.'

'Good,' Maggie said. 'Alastair? What are you going to say?'

'I don't know,' he said in a strange half-whisper.

'Well, you'd better think. This is one time you shouldn't leave it to improvisation.'

Hamish laughed at his sister.

'What?' she snapped.

'You'd make a good director, Mags.'

Maggie sat back in her seat and frowned. 'This has got to work,' she said quietly. 'We've got to tell her how we all feel about her.'

Everyone fell silent for a few moments.

'So, Alastair?' Maggie said a few minutes later. 'You're going to tell her you love her, aren't you?'

Alastair shifted uneasily in the driver's seat.

'Euan?'

Euan wiped a large hand over his face.

'*Guys?*' Maggie pushed. 'She needs to know. We've all got to tell her because we *all* love her, don't we? It doesn't matter about gender or age or if we only like westerns: *everyone* loves Connie and love's the one thing that will keep her here.'

Alastair shook his head. 'Not in my experience. Love's the thing that makes you leave.'

'You're talking rubbish, Alastair!' Maggie said. 'Tell him, Mikey.'

'Aye, Alastair. You're talking out of your backside, mate. Love's the thing that brought me back,' he said, giving Maggie's hand another squeeze. She squeezed his right back.

'You've got to put your past behind you, Alastair,' Maggie said.

'What do you know about my past?' he asked, turning around from the front seat for a brief moment.

'Oh, everyone knows about your past!' Maggie said. 'You can't move to a place like Lochnabrae from London and not expect people to find out.'

Alastair's forehead furrowed in consternation. 'Do you know about it?' he asked Euan.

'About Sara Constantine? Aye.' Euan nodded.

'Hamish?'

'Aye,' Hamish said. 'Everybody knows.'

'And we're really sorry,' Maggie said. 'It was a terrible thing to happen but you can't let it follow you around forever.'

Maggie watched as Alastair stared straight ahead at the road. He had a strange expression on his face that seemed to blend anger, insecurity and tenderness all at once. What was he thinking of? Maggie so desperately wanted to know and be able to reach out to him and assure him that everything would be all right. The only problem was, she wasn't at all sure that it would be.

Chapter Forty-Two

After Alastair had left Connie at the B&B, he'd returned to his cottage and told Sara what had happened. He told her about the night by the loch and how he'd fallen in love with Connie and had been unutterably grateful that Sara hadn't made a scene.

'Do you want me to talk to her?' she'd asked, her eyes full of compassion.

He'd shaken his head. 'I don't think she'd listen to anyone.'

'Well, I think it best if I go – right now,' she'd said. 'I don't want to be the cause of any more trouble.'

She'd called for a taxi and they'd said their goodbyes and Alastair had spent the rest of the day in a stupor, wondering what on earth he could do to make Connie believe him.

Now, sitting in the car surrounded by his friends, he prayed he wasn't too late to make things work with Connie. He cringed to his very soul when he thought of the way he'd treated her – treated *all* the LADS during rehearsals. He'd just been so afraid of working with a professional actress again. After his experience with Sara, he was terrified of the past repeating itself.

But Connie isn't Sara. Even Sara isn't Sara any more, he

told himself. The past was well and truly wrapped up and Sara was gone.

Aye, he thought, *but that doesn't mean Connie wants any part of the present with me.*

His mind wandered for a moment.

Perhaps if I gave up directing, he thought. If he was absolutely honest with himself, it was a feeling that he'd been slowly acknowledging for a long time now. He could still write for the LADS and the theatre although he realised that he'd been slowly moving away from that too. What was happening to him? Was this a new Alastair? Just like Connie had been trying to find a new person by coming to Lochnabrae, so too had he. Perhaps they could find themselves together, he thought wistfully.

'Turn here, Alastair!' Mikey suddenly bellowed from the back seat.

Alastair blinked in surprise. They'd arrived at the airport.

'Here! Park here!' Maggie shouted a moment later.

Euan fished in his pocket for some coins and the five of them were soon running towards departures.

'How often do planes leave for LA?' Hamish asked.

'I have no idea,' Maggie said. 'Too often, in my opinion. Gosh, I hope she's still here.'

They reached a huge board listing departures and five pairs of eyes urgently scanned it.

'I don't see anything,' Maggie said. 'There's no LA here.'

'Maybe she's changing somewhere,' Hamish suggested.

'I'll go and ask someone,' Euan said.

'I'll go,' Alastair said, and they all watched as he walked over to an information desk.

'What's taking so long?' Maggie asked a moment later.

'Calm down, Maggie,' Mikey said. 'Panicking won't help.'

'Everything's taking so long. *Too* long!'

Mikey sighed. 'I don't like it any more than you but we've got to be patient,' he said and then nodded and smiled. 'There, you see.'

Maggie watched as Alastair walked back towards them.

'Is she here?' Maggie blurted.

'Are we in time?' Hamish added.

Alastair's face was grim and he shook his head. 'The last plane to LA left ten minutes ago. We're too late.'

It took at least twenty minutes for the men to get Maggie to leave the airport. She just wouldn't believe that they'd failed.

'Ask again, Alastair!' she kept saying. 'You must've got it wrong.'

Finally, Mikey took her hand in his and pulled her into his body in a warm embrace and Maggie cried. It was what she needed to do and he knew that. Alastair felt terrible because he knew it was all his fault but what could he do now? He couldn't stop a plane in mid-flight, and following Connie to LA wasn't likely to work. He had to face facts: he'd let her go. More than that – he'd chased her away.

'You can write to her, Mags,' Hamish said, placing a hand on his sister's shoulder. 'We could *all* write to her.'

Maggie looked up, her head emerging from Mikey's chest. 'You could tell her how much you want to see her again,' she told Euan. 'And you could tell her how much you love her,' she told Alastair.

Alastair nodded. Although his profession was writing, he was lousy when it came to letters but he thought it best not to tell Maggie that right now.

'Do you think she'll come back?' Maggie asked.

'She came once, didn't she?' Mikey said. 'She could come again.'

Maggie mopped her eyes and gave an almighty sniff and the five of them left the airport.

They drove in silence all the way back, each lost in their own thoughts. Alastair tried to think of something cheerful to say, knowing how upset Maggie was and only guessing at the pain that Euan was in, but nothing came to mind and so they drove on, the Land Rover devouring the miles until they reached the familiar hills of home at last.

'Alastair?' Maggie asked from the back seat. 'Can we go via Rossburn Castle?'

He glanced at Maggie quickly through the rear-view mirror. 'What do you want to see that old place for, Maggie?'

'Can we?'

'She won't be there,' Euan said softly from the front of the car. It was the first time he'd spoken in hours.

'I know,' Maggie said. 'I just want to see it.'

Alastair sighed. 'Okay then,' he said, and he made the turn that would lead to Lochnabrae via the old castle.

Alastair knew what was going through Maggie's brain. She was hoping Connie would be there – that, somehow, she wasn't crossing the Atlantic in a plane for America and that she'd chosen to stay in Lochnabrae. He sometimes envied her that optimism. When the whole world seemed bleak and black, Maggie would invariably spy a ray of light. But there was no ray of light for Alastair; he felt awful. He didn't even dare think about tomorrow or the day after that. How was he going to be able to go on with the knowledge that he'd probably ruined his one good chance at happiness and broken the heart of someone who'd finally put their precious trust in him?

He thought of Connie's beautiful pale face and those enormous bright eyes that were so full of life, and knew he was going to punish himself for the rest of his life for having lied to her. What had he been thinking of? Did he really think he could have sorted things out quietly with Sara and that Connie would never find out about it?

As the road steepened, the car slowed, taking the bends in its stride. Alastair noticed that Maggie had moved forward and was staring out of the window so that, when they made it over the brow of the hill, she was the first to see it.

'There's a light on,' Maggie said.

'Don't be daft,' Alastair said.

'There is – look!'

Everybody looked out into the night and, sure enough, a solitary arch-shaped window in Rossburn Castle was lit up.

'Now, don't go getting your hopes up, Maggie,' Euan said. 'There's probably a perfectly good explanation for it.'

'Like what?' Maggie asked.

'It could be Mr Forsyth keeping an eye on the place,' Euan said.

'It's the middle of the night!' Maggie said.

'Or Isla – tidying it up a bit,' Euan added.

'Euan!'

'I'm only saying – don't get your hopes up.'

Maggie wasn't the only one getting her hopes up. Alastair swallowed hard as they pulled into the driveway of the castle.

'Hurry up!' Maggie urged, clambering over Mikey to get out of the Land Rover before it had stopped.

Alastair killed the engine but left the lights on and everyone got out.

'Maggie!' Hamish hissed. 'Be careful. It could be anyone in there.'

Mikey caught up with her just as she reached the heavy front door.

'It's open,' Maggie whispered.

'I'll go first,' Mikey said.

'Okay but just hurry,' Maggie said, following Mikey as he pushed the door open. Alastair followed with Hamish and Euan behind him.

'Hello?' Maggie called into the enormous entrance hall of the castle. It was pretty grim in there. The walls were flaking plaster and a damp smell filled the air.

'There's a light on in the next room,' Mikey said, spying a sliver of light from under an enormous oak door.

The five of them edged towards it and Alastair was sure that everyone around him would be able to hear his heartbeat as Maggie pushed the door open into a large living room.

There, standing by a gigantic fireplace, surrounded by suitcases, was Connie, her red hair gleaming in the light from half a dozen candles.

'Connie!' Alastair said.

She turned, her eyes wide as she took in the five of them standing there.

'CONNIE!' Maggie yelled, running into the room and flinging herself at her. 'We thought you'd gone!'

Alastair stood watching. She was still there. She was right in front of him.

Maggie turned and looked at him. 'Tell her!' she said. 'Tell her what you were going to say.'

Silence filled the great room as Connie and Alastair looked at one another.

'Alastair!' Maggie urged. 'You said you'd tell her.'

'Connie,' he said, stepping forward, feeling the intensity of Maggie's gaze upon him.

'We love you!' Maggie suddenly blurted. 'We all love you!'

A surprised laugh escaped Connie.

'We drove all the way to the airport,' Maggie told her.

'So did I!' Connie said.

'So you *were* going to leave?' Hamish asked.

'Yes,' Connie said. 'But I couldn't go.' They all stared at her. 'And then I got back to Isla's and she handed me this envelope.'

'The key to the castle!' Hamish said.

'It looks like the place is going to be mine,' Connie said.

'Didn't I say?' Maggie said. 'I told Connie she should buy this place! And I just knew she'd be here tonight.'

'Did you?' Connie said.

'Well, I wasn't sure but I hoped for it – I hoped for it *so* much!' Maggie said, a huge grin plastered on her face.

'So, you're staying?' Mikey asked.

Alastair watched Connie closely for her response and saw her swallow.

'I'm not sure yet,' she said.

It was then that Euan stepped out from the shadows and the room was so quiet you could have heard the wings of a bat beating if one had decided to fly down from the battlements at that precise moment.

'Connie, lass,' he said, 'I wish you'd stay.'

'You do?' Connie said.

'Aye,' Euan said. 'I do. There's so much I want to say to you. So much time we need to make up for.'

Connie gave a little nod. 'I know,' she said. 'I was thinking about it on the way to the airport. I felt awful about the way I ran out on you today. I hope you can forgive me. It was just – well – there was so much to take in.'

Euan nodded. 'I fear I may have surprised you.'

'You did,' Connie said with a little smile.

Euan moved forward a fraction and extended his right hand. Connie bit her lip and moved to meet him halfway. Alastair watched as their hands met in an awkward handshake and then something wonderful happened: Euan wrapped his arms around Connie and hugged her.

Hamish gasped and Maggie gave a small cry, her eyes glistening with tears.

When they parted and Euan took a step back, it was clear that Connie also had tears in her eyes and, automatically, Alastair reached inside his jacket pocket and retrieved a neatly folded tissue, stepping forward and handing it to her.

'Here,' he said.

She took it from him and dabbed her eyes. 'I've done nothing but cause chaos since I got here,' Connie said.

'Oh, I don't know,' Alastair said. 'There's been some laughter too, hasn't there?'

She looked up at him, her hazel eyes huge with emotion and he felt a strange tugging that meant he couldn't move.

'Connie,' he said, 'don't go.'

At first, she didn't reply but then, slowly, she spoke. 'Well, I haven't made my mind up yet,' she said. 'I mean, I couldn't go tonight. I knew that was wrong.'

'I mean ever. Don't go *ever*,' Alastair said.

Again, there was silence as Alastair and the others stared

at the beautiful woman before them who suddenly didn't look like a movie star at all but very much like a friend whom they didn't want to lose.

'Maggie's right,' Alastair said at last.

Connie looked puzzled. 'What do you mean?'

Alastair swallowed and took a deep breath. 'We all love you,' he said.

Connie didn't reply and a cold chill passed over Alastair. Was it too late? Had he messed up good and proper this time? Perhaps nothing would make a difference now. Unless . . .

'*I* love you,' he said. 'I think I fell in love with you the very first time I saw you at the loch – when Bounce jumped all over you, remember?'

Connie nodded and her pale face flooded with colour and a smile like a beautiful rainbow danced across it.

'And I can't say how sorry I am for not telling you the truth about Sara,' he said. 'It was stupid of me and I should have told you when she arrived but I was too scared of what you'd think. But I can promise you that nothing happened because I was in love with you. *Am* in love with you,' he said. 'And Sara knows that. I told her before she left today.'

Connie took a deep breath and then spoke. 'And I should have given you a chance to explain. I shouldn't have run away like I did. I have this habit of running away, don't I?'

Alastair smiled. 'But you came back. You came back to your home.'

'And I want to stay,' she said. 'I want to stay so much!'

Suddenly, Alastair caught her up in a tight embrace, spinning her around in his arms until they were both dizzy. Not wanting to be left out, Maggie leapt forward and

Hamish too and, so as not to miss out, Euan and Mikey joined in, making a rugby scrum of laughter and tears in the middle of the castle.

'We love you, Connie!' Maggie shouted above the chaos. 'We *all* love you!'

Chapter Forty-Three

A few weeks later . . .

'I must be mad,' Connie said as she picked up a small boulder that looked as if it should be halfway up a mountain rather than in a room that purported to be a kitchen. 'What do I know about restoring a castle?'

'About as much as I do about writing a novel,' Alastair said.

Connie looked at him and smiled. 'Your novel is going to be great,' she said. 'You just have to remember to write in chapters rather than scenes.'

'Isn't writing a novel a bit of a lonely business?' Isla asked from the other side of the room where she was attacking a wall covered in cobwebs with the help of Kirsty and Catriona. 'Won't you get bored working on your own all day?'

'If I get lonely or bored, you'll find me in The Bird,' Alastair said.

'You could write it in the pub,' Sandy said, 'then we could all help you.'

Alastair grimaced. 'If that happened, I'd end up writing something that was part musical, part western.'

'Aye,' Sandy said, 'Mrs Wallace would make sure all your characters looked just like her, and Angus would have them all striding about at noon with guns.'

Angus, who'd been chipping away at some old plaster in the corner of the room, looked around. 'I've got a nice collection of western novels if you'd like to read them for some ideas,' he said.

'Thank you, Angus. If I get stuck, I'll know where to come.'

'Write a nice romance,' Maggie said from the large fireplace where she was sweeping with Mikey. 'Everyone loves a romance.'

Mikey winked at her.

'What will you do, Connie?' Hamish asked. He was perched up on a ladder clearing a shelf of dusty glass bottles and Bounce was sitting watching, his once shiny nose now matte with dust.

'Well,' Connie said, retying her ponytail, 'I was thinking of retiring from acting.'

All of a sudden, the old kitchen filled with outraged voices.

'No!'

'You can't retire, lass!'

'You're only a youngster.'

'Oh, don't stop acting, Connie!'

Connie placed her dusty hands on her hips. 'You seem to forget that I've been working since I was six years old. I'm getting a wee bit tired of it,' Connie said and then she gasped. 'I said "wee".'

'You're turning native,' Maggie pointed out proudly.

'I think I might be.'

'You'll be "ayeing" and "oching" all over the place before you know it,' Hamish teased, causing Kirsty to give a cobwebby laugh.

'And there's nothing wrong with that,' Euan said. 'Don't forget, she's as Scottish as any of us here.'

Connie smiled and blushed with happiness. 'Okay,' she said. 'I might not retire completely but I'm going to take a good break and do up this castle. Then I'm going to choose my projects really carefully.'

'You're leaving that horrible agent of yours, aren't you?' Isla asked.

Connie nodded. 'I am,' she said. 'He can inflict *The Pirate's Wife* on some desperate young actress who isn't quite as picky as me.'

'But you'll still do a western one day?' Angus asked.

Connie grinned. 'I'll look out for a script,' she said. 'I promise.'

'What about *Twelfth Night*, Alastair?' Hamish asked. 'Are we still going ahead with it?'

Alastair ran a hand through his dark hair. 'Well, I've been having a chat with Connie and we've decided to swap roles.'

'What do you mean?' Catriona asked.

'My novel's going to take up quite a bit of my time and I've decided to take a smaller role in the play.'

'Who's playing Orsino, then?'

'I am!' Mikey said from the fireplace, causing Maggie to beam with pleasure. 'I know I haven't made many rehearsals but that's going to change.'

'So, you're not directing?' Euan asked Alastair.

Alastair shook his head. 'You're going to have a brand new director.'

'Who?' Isla asked.

'Me,' Connie said.

'Connie! That's brilliant,' Maggie said. 'Then you're definitely staying?'

'I'm staying put until after Christmas,' she said. 'But I'll have to make a trip to LA in the New Year. There's so much to sort out and I'm going to see my mother too.' Connie looked across the room at Euan who smiled at her with pride.

'Does that mean you're not playing Viola?' Sandy asked.

'Well, I've been thinking about that and Alastair and I think I could do both.'

Everyone started talking at once again and Connie grinned at them.

'You're all going to have to help me because I'm new to directing and you all know I'm struggling with Shakespeare.'

'You'll be brilliant!' Hamish said.

'You'll be the best director we've ever had!' Maggie said. 'After Alastair, I mean,' she added.

'Tell them about the village hall,' Alastair said to Connie.

She nodded. 'Oh, yes! Seeing as I'm getting a load of builders and decorators in, I thought it wouldn't be a bad idea for them to do up the village hall too.'

Everyone looked at each other and then an almighty cheer went up.

Connie laughed. 'If I'm going to be spending any amount of time in that place, it's *got* to have proper heating!' she said. 'And there's another thing I was going to get your opinion on.'

'What's that?' Alastair asked.

'If I can get planning permission for the great hall or salon, I was thinking about having a cinema here in the castle.'

A stunned silence greeted Connie's announcement.

'A cinema?' Kirsty said at last. 'Here in Lochnabrae?'

Connie nodded. 'With a popcorn machine and those nice red velvety seats and everything.'

Kirsty's eyes doubled in size and suddenly she was leaping about and everyone was joining in, laughing, cheering and whoop-whooping.

'Civilisation comes to Lochnabrae,' Angus said once everyone had calmed down. 'Just one thing, Connie. You will be—'

'Showing westerns?' Connie said. 'Bet on it!' And she held a very dusty hand out to shake Angus's even dustier one.

It was a sunny spring day with a sky the colour of forget-me-nots and, after a morning of clearing as much dust and debris as they could, everyone collapsed on a grassy bank outside for a picnic made up by Connie, Maggie and Isla earlier that morning.

Maggie sat with Mikey, the two of them looking like a pair of lovebirds, Hamish was sitting with Kirsty, picking cobwebs out of her hair, and Bounce was rolling on his back in a patch of cool grass that smelt of rabbits. And Connie? She was sitting with Alastair.

'I've been thinking,' Connie said. 'It'll make things much easier if I actually live in the castle.'

Alastair almost choked on his sandwich. 'You're joking!' he said. 'You can't live here until it's properly restored. The place is lethal.'

Connie looked up at the soaring turrets and sighed. 'I suppose,' she said.

'You stay at Isla's until things are safe here,' Alastair said. 'Unless—'

'Unless what?' Connie said.

'Unless you move in with me.'

Connie looked shocked for a moment. 'But your place is tiny.'

'Aye, well, I'll admit there's not much room but I did manage to fit a double bed in it,' he said with a smile. 'Just in case a beautiful Hollywood actress came my way, you understand.'

'But aren't they a rare breed up here?' Connie asked.

'Oh, I don't know,' Alastair said, leaning forward and kissing her. 'You've just got to know where to look.'

VICTORIA'S TOP TEN ESCAPES

Scotland
I fell in love with Scotland the first time I visited it as a child with my family and I've been back many times since then. The Highlands and islands are particularly beautiful with deep blue lochs and fabulous white beaches. Skye and Mull are favourite destinations and the little village of Plockton helped inspire Lochnabrae.

Suffolk
Like Connie Gordon, I recently ran away – swapping the London suburbs for rural Suffolk. My husband and I now have views across fields of horses at the front of our cottage and apple and cherry orchards at the back. Suffolk boasts some beautiful rolling countryside, fabulous medieval buildings and a gorgeous coastline.

Dorset
I've set several novels in Dorset now and visit as often as I can. I adore Lyme Regis, and the Marshwood Vale is a favourite place to walk with its bluebell woods, hedgerows full of cow parsley and red campion and its views stretching to the sea.

The Yorkshire Dales
I spent six years in the Dales and even got married in a medieval castle in Wensleydale. I never tire of its landscape with its craggy limestone pavements and beautiful waterfalls.

Venice
I think Venice is the most beautiful city in the world. I love the architecture and the rich colours of the buildings and all the reflections. It's also wonderfully easy to get lost in the backstreets

of Venice. Just dare to venture off the beaten track a little and you'll find a magical mask shop or a forgotten canal.

My garden
Nothing beats sitting in the garden on a warm summer's day, surrounded by roses and watching our hens. Last year, we rescued some ex-battery hens and it's an absolute delight to watch them pecking around the garden and taking dust baths. It's so easy to forget everything else when you're in a beautiful garden.

The coast
We're so lucky in the UK because you're never far from a fabulous beach. My favourite coastlines include Pembrokeshire, Dorset, Chichester Harbour, and the north Norfolk coast. With the sea breeze in your hair and sand between your toes, the coast is one of the best places to run away to.

A stately home
I adore old buildings – anything from crumbling medieval castles to elegant Georgian manor houses. Favourites include Snowshill Manor in Gloucestershire, Trerice in Cornwall, Blickling Hall in Norfolk and Haddon Hall in Derbyshire. They're perfect places in which to escape the twenty-first century.

Our front room by the fire with a good film
We've just moved to a nineteenth-century cottage and have a real fire and I love losing myself in a good film with the fire roaring beside me.

The bath
I love taking long, warm baths with a good book! It's the ultimate in escape and is a little luxury that everyone should enjoy.

Also available from Avon

The Perfect Hero
Victoria Connelly

They only exist in the movies – don't they?

Die-hard romantic Kay Ashton runs a B&B in the seaside town
of Lyme Regis and is dumbstruck when the cast and crew of a
new production of *Persuasion* descend. Kay can't believe her luck
– especially when she realises that heart throb actor Oli Wade
Owen will be sleeping under her very own roof!

Meanwhile, co-star Gemma Reilly is worried that her acting isn't
up to scratch, despite landing a plum role. She finds a sympathetic
ear in shy producer Adam Craig who is as baffled by the film
world as she is. Kay thinks the two are meant for each other and
can't resist a spot of matchmaking.

When Oli turns his trademark charm on Kay, it seems that she
has found her real-life hero. But do heroes really exist?

Featuring a cast of characters that could have stepped out of a
Jane Austen novel, this is the perfect read for fans of **Katie Fforde**
and **Alexandra Potter**.